Early praise for The Quarryman's Girl:

The Quarryman's Girl will especially engage the children of immigrants, and those of us from blue-collar backgrounds. Author Melanie Forde loves her characters and depicts them living the lives that working class folk live. The details are rich and true to life. Forde's novel hums with the kind of stories our parents and grandparents told. Her novel is our story.
—*Danusha Goska, author of God Through Binoculars*

Praise for Decanted Truths:

"With its pitch-perfect evocation of people and places from a bygone era and interesting premise, the novel is a must read for fans of historical fiction … A stunning book that expertly explores the difference between mistakes and sins." —*The Prairies Book Review*

"The author did a wonderful job with character development … *Decanted Truths* is perfect for anyone who wants to get invested in a novel full of secrets … A wonderful book to … get sucked into." —*The Book Adventures of Emily, book blogger*

"This is a great read … if you like historical stories … The slight paranormal gifts that you see with the family … really make the story even more connected."
—*Jessica Bronder, JBronder Book Reviews*

"Amazing study of two Irish families as they assimilate into America … The author creates a literary novel of intelligence … It is a unique gift, an unusual examination of people."
—*Virginia Williams, Rosepoint Publishing*

Praise for Reinventing Hillwilla:

"The well-paced, well-plotted story creates that bond with characters struggling through discordance with others, loneliness, catastrophic illness, coming of age, long-distance romance and the struggles of survival in harsh, bitter winter conditions … The author has an intelligent, articulate writing style that pops with little glimmers of Irish humor…"
—*Virginia Williams, Rosepoint Publishing*

"A moving exploration of relationships, family dynamics and notions of home … Forde draws carefully sketched, rich characters and weaves a convincing reality from their intricate emotions." —*The Prairies Book Review*

"This story wraps up the series beautifully … with a powerful message about living your life, whether the first half or second … This is one series that should be on everyone's shelves."
—*Jessica Bronder, JBronder Book Reviews*

Praise for On the Hillwilla Road:

"A great story and follow up to *Hillwilla*! I couldn't wait to read *On the Hillwilla Road*. Beatrice is still considered an outsider and is trying to find common ground without offending the locals. Clara is trying to find her way and is still so confused. But she is a great kid and you can't help but encourage her. I really like how Beatrice and Tanner are getting closer; I just wanted to slap both of them at times for being so dense and difficult."
—*Jessica Bronder, JBronder Book Reviews*

"This appealing story … is replete with vivid descriptive passages … The drama is related from many views, creating a rich tapestry incorporating setting, events and characters … *On the Hillwill Road* is a refreshing and thought-provoking book."
—*My Merri Way, book blogger*

Praise for Hillwilla:

"Melanie Forde has given us a 21st-century Back-to-the-Land novel with a troubled protagonist, but also with a preternaturally responsible English setter, an assurance that the ending will be a happy one."
—*Sue Hubbell, A Country Year*

"A great, heartwarming story! I loved the scenes; I could feel myself right there in the pages. You can't help getting sucked into the story and keep reading into the late hours wanting to know what is going to happen next. This is a stand alone book but I could see other adventures for [Beatrice] in the future. I can't wait to read what Melanie Forde comes up with next."
—*Jessica Bronder, JBronder Book Reviews*

"Forde's writing is insightful, funny, and thought-provoking from start to finish. [Her] poetic delivery of life's spit, sprinkled with the virtues of tolerance, empathy, and humor ... delighted me and gave me pause to reflect. I am not talking sappy, just good writing; writing that connects the reader with the human spirit."
—*Charlie Hackbarth, author, Tales of the Trail*

"*Hillwilla* beautifully shows that animals are amazingly human in their love for those they value."
—*Ronald Hart, syndicated libertarian humorist*

"I had a blast in 'Seneca County,' West-by-God Virginia. These characters read as real."
—*Dear Author, book blogger*

"A beautifully written book with a no-nonsense protagonist ... The story is so well crafted, and Melanie has taken a lot of care in introducing and then building up each and every one of her characters."
—*The Bookworm Mummy, book blogger*

The Quarryman's Girl

The Quarryman's Girl

A Novel

Melanie Forde

Mountain Lake Press
Mountain Lake Park, Maryland

Also by Melanie Forde
   Hillwilla
   On the Hillwilla Road
   Reinventing Hillwilla
   Decanted Truths

<u>Author's Note</u>
This is a work of fiction. Although the novel draws inspiration from the author's
family history, none of the characters—apart from some historical figures, whose
incidental mention is intended merely to establish authenticity of setting—represents
any real person, living or dead.

The Quarryman's Girl
A Novel

ISBN: 978-1-959307-00-6

Published in the United States of America
by Mountain Lake Press

Cover design by Jutta Medina
Cover photo by the author
Author's photo by Picket Fence Photography

Printed in the United States of America

CONTENTS

CONTENTS

To the women who stare back from the mirror,
the women who vibrate my vocal chords,
the women who trigger laughter, tears, sanity, insanity:
my sisters, my blood.

Tell me of Your Secrets, Mary Rose

Tell me of your secrets, Mary Rose.

Could you really turn
Rum-cherries into wine?
Rags into quilts?
Leftovers into pie?

Did you really know of poultices,
Foul-smelling and brown,
That sucked evil out of wounds
And regenerated skin without a scar?
Were you really born blue and still,
To be brought back to life
With a plunge through December ice
From savvy Huron midwife hands?

I, too, have quick fingers,
Have uncovered the secrets
Of yeast and fermentation,
Even of warp and woof.

I, too, have studied herbs.
But still the magic eludes me
That danced in your veins,
That shimmered in your December moonlight.

We share both blood and birth month.
Isn't that enough to share secrets
With the lonely little girl
Shivering under Orion's belt,

Hopping from one foot to the other,
From one decade to the next,
Waiting for a shooting star,
Waiting for magic secrets,

Mary Rose?

ONE

Salvage Work

After wiping his hands with a rag, Vince Dowd clasped them behind his back and without saying a word walked slowly around the odd-looking vehicle in his driveway. His companion shifted from good foot to bad foot and back again multiple times.

"Thanks for squeezing me in after you finished work," Nate Kagan said, for the third time. "I don't imagine you have many free Saturday afternoons, huh? So what do you think?" He pointed at the green 1925 MG.

Vince finally broke his silence: "How much you pay for this thing?"

The young man groaned, "You're gonna tell me too much, right?"

"Naw, it's not that I think you got a dud. Probably won't cost all that much to fix her up. But it'll take time. For a seventeen-year-old car, the engine doesn't look too bad. That folding roof probably needs to be replaced, though, but I dunno about finding the parts. Your old man would know better than me. Do you really wanna steer a right-hand drive car around in Boston traffic? And you'll freeze your ass off in winter, even if do we get that roof water-tight. Still, I gotta admit it has style."

Nate beamed. "I like the bullnose radiator a lot better than the flat-nose models, don't you?"

"Mm-hmm." Vince bent forward to thumb grease off the side mirror. "You're not gonna fit much in a two-seater."

"Yeah, but those running boards are so wide you could strap a suitcase on 'em."

"Uh-huh. Might not break any speed records, but it'll do fifty without cracking a sweat."

"So, you'd be willing to work on it?" Nate cleared his throat. "What would you charge for the labor if I helped out?"

Seeing the young man's nervousness, Vince smiled. "Tell you what. You pay for the parts, and if you're willing to give me a hand with some chores above and beyond this Cowley Bullnose, we'll call it even."

"Sure! What can I help you with?"

Vince beckoned his guest toward the front stoop. With some difficulty, Nate arranged his heavily shod left foot on one of the lower concrete steps.

"I've got another kind of salvage mission in mind," Vince continued. "My mother's got lots of stuff needs fixing, more than I can find the time for. I imagine that's only gonna get worse. She's a pretty good fixer-upper in her own right, but she doesn't have much focus these days. And she's too proud to hire a handyman or plumber herself, even if she has the money. But I figure she wouldn't be insulted if you showed up. You think you could drop by, say, once a week? Tackle some chores for a couple of hours?"

Nate frowned. Seeing the disappointment on Vince's face, he flicked a wrist and added, "Oh, I'm more than willing. I like your mother. And it's not that I can't find the time. But it kinda depends on how complicated the handyman jobs are. I'm good with the basics, but a skilled carpenter I'm not. And if electrical repairs involve more than changing a fuse, I could blow up both me and Madame Rose."

Vince chuckled. "'Madame Rose.' She got a big kick out of you calling her that. She got a bigger kick out of seeing you perched on the seat of that horse cart old Sol used to drag around town. Whatever happened to that sorry nag?"

"Zayde shot him. Tsuris was getting awfully lame. Hurt all the time. And it was harder and harder to find hay and grain around here. Not many farmers left. It was the right thing to do. But I bawled my eyes

12

out."

Vince nodded. "I liked Tsuris. Ma did, too. She used to feed him carrots. More and more, I miss the old times, before the world went to hell in a handbag. Jesus! I sound like I'm ninety-seven instead of thirty-seven. Anyway, the jobs I had in mind for you to tackle at Ma's are pretty basic. Some painting, caulking. Stuff like that. I can handle the carpentry and electrical repairs."

"Hey, I'm only twenty and I miss the good ol' days, too! What's going on in Europe is downright terrifying. And this war isn't gonna be over anytime soon."

"I think you're right. And you and me might just be in the midst of it before it's over."

Nate shook his head ruefully. "Not me. I tried to enlist the week after Pearl Harbor. Dad had a fit when he found out. But…" he added, patting his left ankle, "they don't want a clubfooted soldier. I thought I could clerk in some Army logistics office to free up the guys capable of marching through the mud and snow. But nope. I guess things can't be all that bad if the Army wouldn't take a willing volunteer, however clumsy."

"Too bad the surgery didn't work. I guess modern medicine can't fix everything."

"The surger-*ies* didn't work. Maybe if they'd operated sooner, when I was a baby." He shrugged. "Doesn't get in the way all that much. When the Japs bombed Pearl Harbor, Dad decided my failed operations were proof of divine intervention. I was being saved from military service. I was being saved for law school. Ugh!"

"That still the plan?"

"Yup. Better than med school, I guess. I puke at the sight of blood."

Vince laughed, slapped the younger man's shoulder, and rose stiffly. "I need a beer. You want one?"

Nate bobbed his head up and down.

"Be right back. Meanwhile, you start making a list of the parts we'll need for that English hot rod of yours. After we cool off, maybe we can swing by your old man's junkyard. He still stays open all day Saturday, right?"

Nodding, Nate retrieved the pen and small notebook he always carried in one pocket or another. He flipped through page after page until he found a blank one. All those inked scribbles. All those observations, insights, longings. All those triggers for poems and short stories and novels that would never get published. Not now, now that he was one year away from law school. Nate Kagan didn't want to be a lawyer or a doctor or, God forbid, an undertaker like his Uncle Milton. Nate Kagan wanted to be a writer.

Oblivious to the number of minutes that had passed, the young man neglected to jot down his list of parts. Still absorbed by his earlier scribbles, he jumped when the screen door squeaked behind him. A barefoot Netty Dowd, seven years young, inched the door open and gingerly sat down beside him, her eyes glued to the glass of beer held in both of her hands. "Don't spill, don't spill, don't spill," she scolded herself.

"Hi, kiddo," Nate said, relieving her of the sweating glass.

"Daddy lets me slurp off the foam," she said, solemnly holding his gaze.

"Then you can slurp off your dad's glass." Nate grinned.

Unperturbed by the refusal, the child sat down, resting her chin on one knee and poking at a stain on the cement stoop. "My nana's got a new dog."

"Yeah? What kind?"

"Mostly Newfy-land."

"Newfoundland? That's a big dog. I remember Madame Rose always had big dogs."

"You know my nana?"

"Sure do. I used to ride shotgun with my grandfather when we'd make our rounds. Mrs. Dowd was one of our stops."

"Ride shotgun?"

"I sat beside him while he drove."

"Did you have a shotgun to protect you and your grandfather?"

Nate chuckled. "Don't be so literal. It's just an expression."

"You made rounds? Is that like making pie?"

He sucked in his breath sharply. "It just means we had a regular route we'd drive, with regular stops to do business with regular customers. Your nana was one."

"What did you sell her?"

"She sold to us. We collected old newspapers and rags. We'd pay her a few coins and then sell what we collected to a place that would turn the old stuff into new paper. They'd give us a few more coins."

"Your grandfather is the Ragman?" Netty asked with wonder. "I thought he was like a character in one of my storybooks. Daddy used to say that back in the old days, Rumpelstiltskin turned straw into gold and the Ragman turned newspapers into coins. Back in the old days, the Ragman would come right to the house. But now Daddy takes the papers away himself. Sometimes I help him tie them up with twine. And he gives me a whole dime. Does that money come from your grandfather?"

Nate shook his head. "He doesn't do that work anymore. So your father is dealing with someone else. Someone else is getting the old stuff to the mills to become new stuff."

Netty theatrically swept an arm over her head. "Poof! My magic wand will turn icky old newspapers into Cinderella's gown."

"Think you could wave your wand over that green car in the driveway and make it like new?"

Netty scuttled up to the top step and imperiously unfurled an arm toward the driveway.

"Beep, beep!" On the other side of the screen door, Vince interrupted her spell-casting. Netty hopped down three stairs to make way for her father and redirected her attention to the driveway, her eyes boring into the green MG.

After settling onto the bottom step, Vince tapped his daughter's bare foot and raised his glass above his head. He asked, "Did you introduce yourself, Netty?"

The child leaned forward, sucked the foam from her father's beer, wiped her mouth with the back of her hand, and stifled a burp. "Oh! I'm Netty."

Nate extended his right hand toward her. She eyed it with confusion before realizing she was supposed to shake it.

"I'm Nate," he said.

"Is his grandfather really the Ragman?" The girl turned toward her father.

"Well, these days Sol Kagan and his son own a junkyard. You've heard me talk about Sol's Salvage, right?"

"Do you work in the junkyard, too?" Netty's head snapped back toward her guest.

"Only in the summer. I go to school. College. Boston University."

"I'm gonna go to college," she proclaimed. "So I can be a famous author."

"Hope you have better luck than I'm having," Nate said glumly.

"If you plan on going to college, Netty, you better get the kind of grades that Nate here gets. So you can win a scholarship, just like he did. But I thought you wanted to be Miss America?"

"Oh, Daddy! That was when I was little."

"Silly me. And you know what else? Nate is headed for law school after he graduates from college. That means he'll be a lawyer."

"Are those the people who make laws and marry brides and grooms?"

Vince paused for a sip. "I guess some lawyers do that. Others *un*-marry brides and grooms. Some lawyers defend people accused of crimes. Others help people write wills and set up businesses and..."

"And shuffle paper and butcher the English language," Nate interrupted.

"I don't get it," Vince said. "If you hate the idea of law school so much, why would you apply?"

"Because lawyers, as my parents regularly remind me, make good money."

"Ah, money. The old bugaboo. Sounds like my old man talking about the police force. I disappointed him by not wearing the blue like my brothers."

"Regrets?"

The older man shook his head. "The salary and pension would sure be nice. But I just wasn't cut out for police work."

"My daddy's a mechanic. The best mechanic in West Quincy," Netty interjected.

"Well, that's why I'm here. If anyone can whip that MG into shape, it's your father." Nate paused, casting a worried glance at Netty then at Vince. "Of course, being a cop could come in handy these days. Can't cops claim an exemption from the draft?"

Vince abruptly upended his glass onto the browning patch of lawn beside the steps and stretched upright. "Go inside and see if your mother needs help in the kitchen, Netty. Nate and I need to head to the junkyard to scrounge some parts for his car. Tell your mother I'll be back before dinner. C'mon Nate, time's a-wastin'. We might not be able to do anything about this sorry world, but let's see if we can't do something about that old heap of yours."

TWO

Cossacks, Wolves, and Family Truths

The visit to Sol's Salvage was productive. Vince learned of several options for roof replacements, options that turned up more frequently than he had imagined. Sol's manager promised to keep an eye out. Because no junkyard visit was ever complete without a personal inspection of the rusting heaps, Vince took a cursory tour and spotted two parts needed for other repair jobs. Delighted not only with those finds but also with the expeditious manner of discovery, he suggested a detour to his mother's house, since he had more than an hour to kill before dinner. He wanted to observe her reaction to Nate, whom she had not seen in years. He wanted to make sure she would be comfortable with the new handyman.

He needn't have worried. Despite the spectacles, gangly frame, and limp, the college boy could turn on the charm. He opened with *"comment allez-vous*, Madame Rose?" and parted with *"à bientôt!"* Vince half expected Nate to kiss his mother's hand.

Vince was also relieved that his mother took no detours to Crazy Town during the admittedly brief visit. She actually seemed to remember Nate, even though he had grown six inches since he had last accompanied the Ragman to the Dowd homestead.

As the two men settled into Vince's car, Nate commented, "Your mom hasn't changed much. Still as active as ever. What was she baking? The kitchen smelled great!"

"Yeah, cooking is one area where she hasn't slowed down any."

Then he bit his lip, in a silent prayer that his mother would remember to turn off the oven.

"I take it she *has* slowed down in other ways, huh?"

"What? Oh. Well, she *is* almost seventy, and not a one of those seven decades has exactly been easy."

"And?"

"And what?" Vince countered testily.

Nate shrugged. "It just seems like you're worried for some reason. For some reason I didn't see."

"She looked completely normal to you?"

The younger man fanned his hands. "Hey, I've got a great-aunt who talks to her dead cat. I mean whole conversations. And she's ten or so years younger. By comparison, Mrs. Dowd looks like a walking advertisement for mental health."

"How'd you know I was worried about her mental health, not her arthritis or her ticker?"

"Because your mother hiked up and down those stairs like she was training for the next Olympics. Jeez, Vince, maybe you should be the one applying to law school!"

"Sorry. It's just … it's just that if I say it out loud, it might make it true."

Nate waited, eyes fixed on the passenger side of the dashboard.

"I guess we all get forgetful after a certain age," Vince continued. "We might get someone's name wrong. But sometimes Ma gets the year wrong, maybe the whole decade."

"You're afraid she's got senile dementia?"

"Is that what you call it? That sounds a lot scarier than simple-minded."

Nate smiled sheepishly. "Sorry, I guess I was showing off the miserable year I spent in pre-med. It's just a fancy way of describing the skewed mental faculties that trouble some old people."

"So what causes it? Why do some old people get 'skewed' and others don't?"

"You're asking the wrong person. My great-aunt has hardening of the arteries, so her brain doesn't always get enough blood. But there may be a lot of reasons why some people go off track with age."

"Does the problem ever get better? Or does the person just keep getting worse until they can no longer figure out how to eat and talk and walk?"

Nate shook his head slowly. "Dunno. Has your mother seen a doctor?"

"Hah! Ma wouldn't see a doctor if she broke her leg. Why waste money on modern medicine when she has a million home remedies she inherited from some crazy old Indian woman up in Quebec. You know the damnedest thing? A lot of those salves and teas work."

"She got any for senile dementia?"

Vince sighed as he downshifted for a red light. "I don't suppose so. The Indians probably just parked the feeble-minded on an ice floe and shoved it out to sea."

"Isn't that the Eskimos?"

"Eskimos, Abenakis, Iroquois—what's the difference? They all had to survive in a rough, bitterly cold climate. That makes for cold-blooded practicality."

"My family knows from cold-blooded and practical. Snow is a constant in my *zayde's* stories about his childhood in Russia. To hear him tell it, they were always running through the snow from something. Cossacks. Wolves. Like some tale from the Brothers Grimm."

"Wolves, huh?" Vince turned to his passenger and smiled. "Ma has a couple of wolf stories, too. As a kid, I lapped 'em up like maple syrup. My favorite was about how her father's parents started their married life. Up there in Quebec, the wedding celebration can go on for days, usually in some relative's house, where the whole clan descends. Since this was a rural area, the distance the guests had to travel could be considerable. So anyway, the party's over, the food and booze are all gone, and the newlyweds head for their new home. In the dark. And just like your grandfather's stories, there's a ton of snow on the ground. So my great-grandparents are traveling by sleigh..."

"Sleigh? Gee, that sounds so exotic! I don't ever recall any mention of a sleigh in my grandfather's tales. The only horses I remember in his stories were the ones the Cossacks rode, whipping them in hot pursuit of fleeing villagers."

"Jesus! That *does* sound like a fairy tale gone bad."

"Doesn't it? I'd never admit this to my family, but I enjoyed the drama. Good grist for some of the early stories I wrote as a kid." Nate tapped the notebook in his shirt pocket. "But go on. We were in the middle of a sleigh ride over snow. Are we in open country?"

Vince shook his head. "The route they were traveling was flanked by heavy woods. A bit of moonlight cast spooky shadows from the evergreens. But the young couple was too content to be scared. They were well fed, well oiled, and snuggled down in blankets to keep warm. Some of the partygoers had rigged the sleigh with bells and paper flowers, so it was making a happy racket. My great-grandparents got a kick out of listening to the bells, the horse's muffled hoofbeats, and the whoosh of ice chunks shooting off the sleigh's runners. With all that noise, it was hard to hear anything else."

"There was something else to hear, I gather?"

Vince nodded. "My great-grandmother, Clara, thought she heard a high pitched yelp off in the distance. She mentioned it, and her husband slowed down. He didn't hear anything. But the horse started whickering, twitching its nostrils. My great-grandfather—Magloire Quentin, how's that for a name?—jiggled the reins and the horse got going, faster than before. They went on for a while, when the bride tugged on the groom's elbow. She heard it again. Surely he did, too? So ol' Magloire stopped and cocked an ear. Yup. There it was, a mournful howl from the woods in back of them. By this time, the poor horse was downright dancing in place. They started off again. Real fast this time. Clara rearranged the blanket so she could turn around in her seat. With a gasp, she spotted something: a shadow crouching at the edge of the woods."

"Oh, cripe!"

"Yup," Vince nodded. "One by one, a whole wolfpack—damn near a dozen of 'em—slinked out from the trees and began loping over the tracks made by the sleigh. Heads lower than their bony shoulders, tails at a forty-five degree angle with their hind legs, all padding noiselessly behind the sleigh." Vince paused at an intersection before making a left turn.

"Well, don't stop now! What happened?"

"The wolves ate my great-grandparents, and I was never born." Vince grinned evilly at his passenger.

"Aw c'mon!"

"Okay. Supposedly, the wolves got close enough that the

newlyweds could hear the panting. Then dawn emerged, and the pack broke off the chase. That's the trouble with family stories that get passed on by word of mouth. They either go nowhere or they get altered to the point of ridiculousness. I seem to remember one version that had the wolves eating a little neighbor girl, whose bloodied remains were found in the snow. Ma never explained how the wolfpack had time to do that while stalking the sleigh."

"I know what you mean. My *zayde's* stories change from telling to telling. Wouldn't it be swell to track down those stories and root out the truth?"

"You really think there is such a thing as truth in family history?"

The young man abruptly tucked his chin to his chest. "Wow, that's cynical!"

Vince's fingertips danced over the steering wheel. "It's just that family is complicated. Every event gets viewed in a different way by each family member. And when the event gets told and retold to the kids and grandkids by various relatives, the story changes every time. Shit, I can think of things that happened just a few weeks ago that my brother Hank and I would describe with completely opposite words. As close as we were growing up, we're different people and won't always see the world with the same eyes. No matter what the facts of the matter are."

"Okay, but what about tracking down the facts?"

"Lotsa luck if what you're tracking goes back a generation or more."

"But isn't that exactly what historians do?"

Vince shrugged. "Didn't Churchill say that history is written by the victors? It still depends who's doing the telling. Just look at our Civil War. I used to work with a guy from Virginia who grew up calling the Civil War the 'war of northern aggression.'"

"Oh, swell," Nate groaned, rubbing his head. "For senior year, I'm supposed to work on an honors thesis exploring some aspect of family history against the backdrop of world events, against supposed historical facts. Now you tell me there's no such thing. I wonder how that's gonna go over with my professor."

"Aw hell, Nate, what do I know? I never finished high school. I just like to read a lot. And lately I love reading about Churchill. What a bulldog that fella is!"

Nate groaned again. "This stupid thesis has already gotten me in

Dutch with my mother. See, I was gonna write about the Jewish communities in what used to be White Russia. She didn't like me telling outsiders how poor my grandparents' generation was, how oppressed. As if writing about that stuff would make us less American. She always worries what other people think. And even if I can somehow calm her down, I'm having a hard time getting Zayde to focus and tell the unembellished truth. His stories wander all over the place. They're long on entertainment but short on facts. I'm still not sure which village he grew up in. A couple have similar names, depending on the spelling, which gets tricky going from the Cyrillic alphabet to English. And it's not like I can trot off to Russia to do my own research, like you could drive up to Canada. Have you ever done that?"

"Done what?" Vince asked, pulling alongside the curb outside the Kagan home.

"Have you ever actually seen where your mother grew up?"

"I've visited the area but haven't been to her childhood home, which now belongs to someone else. Her folks were just tenant farmers and never owned the place. But I have stayed in a really old farmhouse some cousins inherited. It goes back to the late seventeenth century. Been in the family all that time."

"Wow! Nearly three centuries of history so close at hand. I didn't think that was possible in the New World, unless your ancestors came over on the Mayflower. You don't suppose...?"

"Don't suppose what?" Vince asked as he turned off the engine.

"Well, like I said, I have this thesis for honors history. Since I keep running into trouble sorting through my grandfather's background—while dealing with my mother's social angst—maybe I should write about a different bunch of relatives, like Madame Rose's folks?"

"But they're not your family, not even from the same corner of the world."

"So what? Shakespeare wasn't Italian, but he did a nifty job writing about the Montagues and Capulets."

"They weren't real families, were they?"

Nate chuckled. "All right, you got me. I'm more of a writer than a historian, which means I can spot a good tale. Sounds like your mother has some good ones to tell. Stories that won't get me into trouble with *my* mother. Stories I can work into the thesis requirement while exercising my creative writing muscles. It may be the last chance I get to do that."

"You're going to law school, not prison, Nate."

"Yeah, yeah. Look, I'll be at your mother's place doing odd jobs anyway. I can get her talking, which she'll probably like. Meanwhile, I can keep my eye on her for you, which *you'll* probably like. I bet that's the main reason you tapped me for this handyman job, anyway." He winked as he pushed on the door lever.

Vince laughed. "You always were a smart kid. Okay, sure, write about the Quebeckers if you want. No skin off my nose."

He shook his head in fond admiration as he watched the tall youth clump up the brick steps to the front door.

THREE

Mood Indigo

Rose Dowd stood naked in the dry tub, pondering her options. After just an hour of weeding her vegetable patch, she was exhausted and sticky. How nice it would be to have a shower, like a modern householder. Shrugging, she filled the adjacent sink with warm water, dunked her facecloth inside, scraped it over the bar of soap, and squeezed it over her neck and shoulders to run off the sweat and the soil particles. She screwed up her lips at the unappetizing grayish bubbles circling the tub drain. After repeated squeezings, her skin was no longer sticky, and the water by her toes ran clear. But she hardly felt refreshed.

Rubbing a worn towel over herself, she accomplished little drying. The briskness of her movements only raised new beads of moisture over chest and back. Giving up, she pulled her slip over her head and groaned in disgust as it clung to her body. She balled up the damp towel, ran it across the over-sink mirror—and gasped.

"Who you looking at, old woman?" she challenged the mirror. She stepped back to review a gravity-challenged female torso. Rose shook her head at the wattles beneath her chin, the pleats between her breasts, the liver spots peppering her arms. She shook her head.

"See what this climate does to you, Rose? Makes you old and saggy. So much wetness in the air, all the time. Even the woodwork sweats."

A snicker sounded to the left. "You look just fine to me, my little cabbage," said Francis Xavier Dowd, sitting on the closed toilet seat, elbows on wide-spread knees, rope-veined hands dangling fretfully, for lack of any useful task to accomplish.

Rose plucked her hairbrush from the side and cocked it at the apparition of her late husband. "I hate when you call me that. *Mon petit chou!* Pah!"

"And didn't you call all the gossoons just that when they were wee ones? Where'd you think, I learned it, old woman?"

"I look green and round to you, eh?'

"You look nicely rounded, darlin'."

"I look old and saggy and wrinkled. It's this heat, I tell you."

"Ah, here we go again. Time to go back to that frozen wasteland you call home."

Rose shot defiance at the ghost image. It intensified as she scrutinized his attire: collarless work shirt, sleeves rolled up to elbows, suspenders keeping those brown trousers from sliding down his skinny Irish ass. And a slouch cap! "And what you doing wearing that cap indoors, you?"

Francis whipped off his hat, and placed it over his heart in mock contrition. "Don't lay into me now. Like you used to with those hooligans we call our sons."

Rose couldn't help chuckling. In the endless effort to teach her rowdy boys some manners, how often had she snatched hats from heads when her teenagers dawdled too long before finding the hallway hat rack? She clicked her tongue as she recalled one incident when all five rowdies—sons plus husband—had ganged up on her and actually sat down for supper with their caps on. Rose had circled the table and, one by one, removed the sweat-stained assortment of offending headwear. She thrashed each removed cap on each miscreant's shoulder and then, instead of depositing them on the hat rack, marched outside and dumped them in the large mud puddle formed by an overflowing gutter, the gutter son Hank was supposed to have cleaned.

"Aye, you showed us," commented Francis, reading her thoughts. "So, back to your other complaint," he added. "The Massachusetts weather. So it's off to Quebec, is it? To get properly refrigerated?"

Rose closed her eyes, the better to conjure the gentle summer air of her childhood, where the humidity rarely became oppressive, not even in late July when the high temperature generally stayed below eighty. She was about to tell Francis how cool the summer nights always were and how gentle the breezes wafting in from the St. Lawrence. But when she reopened her eyes, Francis was gone. Again. He never stayed long. Just long enough to bring a bemused smile to her lips or an annoyed frown to her brow.

Rose frowned now as she regarded her reflection yet again. "That's Quebec, yeah? Cool breezes, clean air. Not hot and dirty like here." Then she pursed her lips. "No, Rose, you remember things too pretty, you. Not so clean air in winter up there."

She suddenly recalled the thickness of wood smoke from October through April, with each farmstead spewing ash and sparks skyward as if seeking divine response against the brutal Labrador Current. But at least the furnaces and fireplaces were more widely spaced than in the Boston area, with far fewer industrial smokestacks adding their effluvia to the cold, heavy air.

Then again, she realized that the Quentin family might have benefited from more industries in Quebec. Maybe her father would have been able to generate enough income to keep all those bellies full. Almost any factory job would have proven more productive than the over-worked soil of their farm, one of all-too-many long, narrow, cheek-by-jowl strips of valley stretching north and south along the river. Maybe René Quentin could have kept his little tribe in Quebec. And maybe his eldest daughter wouldn't look so old.

"*Tu me gosses!*" (You're getting on my last nerve!) Rose chided the crone inside the mirror, the crone that was spoiling before her very eyes, like meat left out of the icebox. Clearly, the perverse Massachusetts summers were robbing her prematurely of firm muscles, smooth skin, clear eyes. She wasn't really old, just too warm. The remedy, as Francis had intuited, was to visit Quebec every summer.

Rose chuckled at the memory of expounding that theory to Francis for the first time, some thirty years earlier. Tongue firmly planted in cheek, she had told him he could take care of the house, the dog, the garden, and the boys while she headed north. He would get his reward when she returned radiantly cleansed of age. The first time she

26

announced this plan, her husband abandoned his usual Corkonian bluster, and his pale blue eyes radiated alarm. It was clear that Francis would miss not merely all the work Rose accomplished; he would miss *her*. She had not lost her power over him. In their forty-odd years of marriage, Francis won most of the battles, but Rose won the wars.

Ten summers later, Rose would return to Quebec, courtesy of her youngest son. Among her children, Vincent had the liveliest interest in the French Canadian side of the family. He had become an accomplished motorist and could fix most of the common complaints afflicting an automobile. So why not drive north for a weekend? Gas was not rationed back then and was ridiculously cheap. Vincent was already working at a shoe factory but not full time. So he had Saturdays free. Sometimes Friday afternoons. A four-hundred-mile trip did not daunt a seventeen-year-old male. He drove through Friday night, while his mother napped off and on. They stayed with cousins overnight Saturday then headed for home early Sunday afternoon.

They repeated the excursion once more, a few years later, with two of Vincent's friends sharing the driving. The young men didn't seem to mind a middle-aged woman in their midst, especially since she had stuffed multiple sandwiches, summer sausages, homemade bread, and other baked goods into a picnic basket. But she bowed out of further trips after the young men entered serious relationships with the opposite sex. Knowing Vincent would prefer his intended, Nora, in the passenger seat, Rose cited the aches and pains of rheumatism as incompatible with bouncing over rough roads. She was touched that he had asked her to join in the northbound trek, even if he hadn't really meant it. Eventually he stopped asking.

"*Ma fois!* (Well, really!) It's all Vincent's fault!" she laughed into the mirror. Chiding one jowl, squeezed between thumb and forefinger, she added, "You there! A few more summer trips to Quebec and poof! You gone."

Rose finished dressing. Before heading for the kitchen, she checked briefly to see if Francis had returned, but he had, as usual, left no trace. Also as usual, she felt disgruntled by the cavalier way he could pop up then fade from the scene so quickly. She frowned again then realized something else was putting her in a bad mood, something she couldn't quite pin down. Noting the beads of moisture that had indeed blossomed on the kitchen door, she wondered if she was merely revisiting her annoyance with Massachusetts weather. No, this was something more troubling. Suddenly, she retrieved a fragment of a memory: It had something to do with Vincent, of all people. As she struggled unsuccessfully to bring to mind the cause of her discomfort, she experienced something close to panic as her heartbeat stumbled then sped up. Was the missing memory that bad? Surely, her dutiful youngest son could never be the cause of such a dramatic reaction.

Placing a steadying palm over her heart, she recalled feeling this same panic several times in the recent past; when she mislaid her keys, for example. Why? Because she was losing her mind, that's why. Every memory that fell into the sewer was proof of that. As that sewer filled up, the rotting recollections would broadcast their stink to the entire world. Everyone would soon know that Rose Dowd was feeble-minded.

She took a deep breath and concentrated on shoving the panic deep down into her gut. Within a few minutes, her mood lightened as she focused on preparing dinner. She had not lost her skill with cooking, at least. She enjoyed feeling competent in the kitchen. She began to whistle cheerfully, even though hers was not a cheerful tune. It was "Mood Indigo." Rose readily remembered not only the music but the title. She even remembered the name of the performing artist, Duke Ellington. She remembered Vincent had given her an Ellington record a few years back. She didn't know whether it was for a birthday or for Christmas, but that didn't matter. If her brain could retrieve such moments, surely she was not so far gone after all.

Her whistling stopped abruptly, not because she forgot the tune. She stopped because she remembered the reason for her pique at her youngest son. He was foisting a babysitter on her! As if she were a dimwitted toddler. As if she was … feeble-minded.

Rose could still recognize manipulation when she saw it. And she saw it during that recent visit by Vincent and Nate Kagan. The Ragman's grandson was supposed to serve as Vincent's eyes and ears to count how many times she mislaid keys, or forgot to turn off the gas range, or left the front door open at night, or mistook her new dog Jolie for her old dog Jolly. Her eyes welled with resentment.

If Vincent could play games, so could she. She would suffer this nonsense of recounting her history for the young Jew's project. If that got Vincent off her back, it would be worth the assault on her pride.

Besides, spinning stories of Quebec could be pleasant. She had no trouble remembering the *distant* past.

It would be even more fun if she doctored her past. Why not tell the college boy she hadn't grown up in Quebec after all, but in Paris? Tell him she had lived within spitting distance of the Seine, not the St. Lawrence. Her father had not been a farmer, but a … what? How about a pirate? Yes! And she used to sharpen his knives before he left for work, the work of raiding boats that plied the Seine. She giggled at the silliness of it.

But no, no, that would only get her into more trouble with her son. Surely Nate would query Vincent about the discrepancies in family history. Still, the idea of pulling the wool over both men's eyes had appeal. Rose chuckled, adding a generous pinch of cayenne to the stew pot.

The smile faded abruptly as another fallen memory began reeking from the sewer. Rose conjured another intrusion into her life, another threat to her freedom, her independence.

"Izzy! A visit from Izzy!" she cried, dropping the wooden spoon into the stew and staring at the messy droplets dancing on the stovetop enamel.

You, ma soeur! You play spy, too? You think you gonna put one over on your older sister, eh? You gonna sit under my roof and count how many times I forget someone's name?

Rose squinted at the wall above the stove. She wasn't seeing the stained ceramic tiles. She was conjuring an image of Izzy, spectacles halfway down her prominent nose and aimed at a scrolled list on her lap. With an old-fashioned inkwell pen in hand, Isabelle Quentin was adding to the long list of mental lapses committed by Rose.

Then, in this kitchen-tile vision, Isabelle summoned a uniformed man wearing jackboots and a peaked cap. Standing, she straightened her angular shoulders and thrust the list into the Nazi's hands. He scanned the paper, allowed a whisper of a smile to pull at his mouth, and said, "We have ways of dealing with people like this." He saluted Isabelle, who nodded. Then both disappeared from the wall in front of Rose.

"*Saccajé chien!* (Holy crap!) That fella with Izzy, he sure looks like Peter Lorre, eh? What are you thinking, old woman? How come you remember some dumb old movie, but you forget to feed Jolly this morning?"

29

Shaking her head, Rose resumed stirring. She chided herself not only for conjuring the ridiculous vision, but also for being so loath to see her younger sister, someone who had been her closest friend in the whole world, someone who had been her only support during some very lean years.

How many years since you and Izzy close, eh? You remember why you not close anymore? Sure you do. Simple-minded or no, you don't forget that your little sister damn near ruins your life.

Rose's stirring hand froze. Her face sagged. For ten minutes, she stood, silent and unmoving, over the steaming stewpot, as she recalled the falling out. Shaking her shoulders back into life, she reminded herself, "But you get over it. You survive."

Nevertheless, Rose sensed a new threat from her sister, the threat of insight.

Izzy knows all your tricks, old woman. No being invisible around that one.

FOUR

Cutting through the Weeds

Despite her earlier fantasies, Rose decided to have nothing to do with the Ragman's grandson. The new handyman could fix what he liked, but she would keep her distance. She would tell him no stories at all, true or fantastical.

That plan crumbled the very first afternoon he showed up to do some chores. She was in the parlor, where she was doing little else but pointedly avoiding Nate, who was installing new screening on the porch. An ominous crash sounded from that direction. Telling herself it was in her self-interest to investigate, Rose dashed to the porch.

Nate was semi-recumbent, extricating his corrective left shoe from the lower rung of the stepladder, now on its side. When he saw Rose, standing with folded arms, he offered a sheepish grin and explained, "Didn't fall very far. Nothing's hurt except my pride."

Shaking her head disapprovingly, Rose offered the young man a surprisingly strong hand to lever himself upright then waggled an index finger. "Maybe you stay off ladders with that crippled foot, yeah? You no good to me if you break your leg."

"Nah, it takes more than a tumble. My *zayde* says we're from sturdy peasant stock. Takes a lot to break us."

His pluck was undermined by a limp, more pronounced than usual, as he righted the stepladder.

Thrusting her right hand toward the wicker settee, Rose commanded, "You sit. I get some ice."

When she returned, Nate was probing his naked, deformed foot with his fingertips. Sitting down beside him, she swatted his examining hand away, held his lower leg with her left hand, and deftly moved his foot a few degrees with her right.

"Ow!"

"The Ragman's right. No break. But lotta swelling unless we stop it quick." She shoved a wicker hassock toward Nate and deposited the wounded foot on it then squashed an ice-bag over the ankle.

"I guess with four sons you've done your share of mending sprains and bruises, huh?"

"Sprains and bruises. Diphtheria and the Spanish flu. Mumps and measles when the boys are little. Broken hearts and hangovers when they get older."

"Lots of broken hearts?" Nate asked inquisitively.

"Lots more hangovers," Rose said, grunting slightly as she settled onto the seat beside the young man.

Recalling his mother's righteous gossip about the alcohol-fueled misadventures of this or that Irish neighbor, Nate was unsure how to react. Of course, Rose's "boys" were only half-Irish, so perhaps the frequency of hangovers in her family was not worrisome. He had little experience with the phenomenon himself. The only hangovers he had ever witnessed involved fellow students who would periodically show up, several shades paler than usual, for a Monday morning class. No one in his family ever drank much. And his small circle of friends consisted of serious students not given to partying. He corrected himself: not *invited* to parties. What's more, he had no clue about the Quebecois relationship with alcohol. French Canadians weren't in abundant supply in Quincy nor in Boston. But for the sake of academic accuracy, this was a subject he should bring up with Madame Rose—discreetly.

Rose scrutinized her guest's face and, for the first time since his arrival, smiled. It was an ironic smile but an improvement over her

32

previously inexplicable stern expression. "You go somewhere inside your head, *mon cher?*"

"Yeah. Sorry. It's what we writers do. So, what's your hangover cure?"

"Not getting a snoot on. Works every time."

"No, seriously. I'm not sure I've ever qualified as drunk, but I may need a hangover cure some day and would like to be prepared. So what have you got? And where'd you learn it? Is this the kind of knowledge mothers pass down to daughters in Quebec?"

Yikes! Really discreet, Kagan!

Rose slapped her knees. "Lotta people get snoots on during the holidays. And we have lotta holidays in Quebec. My papa, he says the good food and drink are rewards for all them church days. Not just Christmas and Easter. No, sir! We have *La Chandeleur* on Groundhog's Day. We have St. Jean Baptiste Day. We have All Saints' Day and the very next day *Le Jour des Morts*. Lots more. I forget."

"Wait a minute. You had to go to church on Groundhog's Day? Why? Were you praying for a quick end to winter?"

"Pah! In Quebec? In February? Old Man Flint only just getting started with his chokehold on the weather. No, in English, you say Candlemas, because that day we get the candles blessed."

Nate extracted his ubiquitous notepad and began scribbling furiously, much to Rose's amusement. Holding up a staying palm, he sputtered, "Wait! Old Man Flint? Blessing candles? Why did candles need to be blessed? So they wouldn't die out when you most needed them?"

Rose shrugged. "I forget. Something about the light Christ brings into the world. But any winter day is good for a celebration. Take your mind off the cold and the dark. And how much food is in the pantry."

"Gee. You were hungry?"

"Sure, some winters the pantry, it gets pretty low."

Nate scratched his head with his pen. "But don't these celebrations involve food, as well as drink?"

"Yeah, sure. But we all share our food. So for one day, at least, we have plenty to eat. Also we have lotta hunters, trappers, fishermen in the family. If they get lucky, we have a big spread. My papa's family especially. They're *voyageurs*, long time ago. You know what a *voyageur* is?"

33

"The guys in the fur trade? I mean, the ones who actually trapped the beavers or minks or whatever?"

Rose nodded. "*Coureurs de bois*. How you say? Yeah. Runners of the woods. Vincent, he finds fancier words. Some story he reads calls them 'knights of the forest,' except they ride canoes instead of horses. Paddle them when they can. Carry them when they can't. You know how you tell a *voyageur* from a farmer or shopkeeper? By his big chest and shoulders and his short, skinny little legs. That's how my papa looks. Except the fur trade is almost all gone by the time he's born. So he farms instead of paddles. You know how else you tell a *voyageur*? From the liquor on his breath and the song on his lips."

"Ooh, that's good!" Nate whispered then paused to shake out his exhausted scribbling hand. "So these were the fellas that got drunk at your religious celebrations and needed a hangover cure?"

Rose slapped her thigh. "Pah! The *coureurs de bois* know how to hold their liquor, them! No hangovers. But I remember my Uncle Jacques. He looks a little green around the gills one Christmas Eve *reveillon*. That's the big meal we all eat after Midnight Mass. My mama spends days cooking. Her and her cousins. Me, too. I peel a ton of potatoes. She says Uncle Jacques has to eat what she puts down in front of him. Hangover or no. So she fixes him up with a cure."

"Which was...?"

"Hmm, I think raw egg yolks. Peppercorns. Yeah, yeah, yeah, I remember now. And canned tomatoes. And instead of vinegar, she adds brandy. Lotta brandy."

"Hair of the dog that bit him?"

"It works, yeah?" Rose's smile suddenly disappeared, and she began twisting her hands in her lap. "That's the last *reveillon* up home."

"How old were you when you moved away?"

Still caught in some memory of her last Christmas Eve celebration in Quebec, Rose didn't answer. "My Great Uncle Edward is there, too. My mama's uncle. My papa hates him. I think because he keeps shop. Has money. Has what they call fine airs. Pretty manners. Clean fingernails. Maybe Papa feels small beside him. But Izzy knows different."

"Izzy?"

"My little sister. Isabelle. Born two years after me. Christmas morning she tells me she thinks Mama and Uncle Edward, they gonna get

34

married. Mama gonna leave Papa. So Papa makes us leave Quebec."

"Huh? How could this Edward guy marry your mother? He was her uncle, for Pete's sake!"

Rose waved her hand in front of her face, as if she were dismissing an annoying gnat. "Izzy's dream. She and Papa never close. But Edward? She and Edward tight as ticks. Much better to have Edward as a father. So Izzy dreams up this idea. She figures if Edward and Mama get married, she gets a better papa and suddenly we get money and nice things and eat good. She's only nine, maybe eight, when she comes up with this idea. What does she know how the world works, eh?"

"Unlike you, huh?"

Rose shrugged. "I know what Papa says back then. He says the farm, it's going bust. We have no money, little food. We need a new start."

"And Izzy was too young to realize how tough things were?"

"Oh, she knows. Not much gets past that one. Even though she needs glasses since very young, those eyes of hers cut through the weeds. They see the invisible and the visible." Abruptly, Rose pivoted her rump on the bench to peer intently at Nate. "What am I gonna do, *mon cher*? If Izzy comes here for a stay? She'll see everything!"

Nate regarded his hostess sympathetically. He suspected why Rose was suddenly anxious. This was a resourceful, can-do woman for whom mental decline would be especially tough. It wasn't surprising that she would want to hide it. Although he himself had not seen any egregious memory lapses yet, someone living under the same roof with her for more than a day or so might zero in on Rose's dementia, if that was indeed what she had. And if the younger sister was as sharp as described, Rose would be hard-pressed to keep her secret. He recalled stories about aged Eskimos abandoned to ice floes after they lost their physical or mental powers. Nate shuddered briefly, realizing that Rose's bleak childhood in frozen Quebec might not have been all that different from life in some godforsaken outpost in, say, Greenland. Rose didn't want to float out to the lonely sea on a chunk of ice.

Anxious to smooth over the awkward pause, Nate asked, "Have you got any examples of how sharp Isabelle can be? Something from your childhood in Quebec, maybe?"

Rose closed her eyes, as if sorting through old memories. When she reopened them, they no longer radiated fear. "Yeah, I tell you something. How Izzy knows stuff about Mama and Papa, bedroom stuff. A little kid like that."

Nate gulped, but figured the writer in him could overcome whatever embarrassment the imminent tale might involve. "So, what did little Izzy figure out?"

FIVE

Chilly Memories

Seeing the young man's discomfort, Rose managed a chuckle. Even though the twentieth century was almost half over and young people often acted as if they had invented sex, she realized that folks not born on a farm were often uncomfortable about natural processes.

Nate eyed her quizzically but said nothing, waiting for his storyteller to settle into her tale.

Pointing at his left foot, she began, "You gonna want to take that ice bag off your ankle before I'm through. Might be plenty hot this summer day. But we gonna go way back to a place that's always cool. Especially in winter. Especially in the woods."

"What's the year?" Nate asked, still holding his ubiquitous pen and notebook at the ready.

Rose waved dismissively and frowned. He instantly regretted interrupting her flow. Mentally, he vowed to let the story unfold however it would, for however long it took.

"You know them long skirts girls wear years ago? Long, but they don't go below the ankles. A good thing, because they get plenty wet with so much snow on the ground. But they're wool, so they keep us warm anyhow, even when the wool, it gets soaked with snow. But them long skirts can make it hard to move. Especially when you carrying stuff. Stuff you don't wanna drop."

Rose closed her eyes and nodded for emphasis. "Precious stuff. It's late March and not so bad outside. Temperature is way up there. Maybe just freezing. Izzy and me, we carry cast-iron pots outside. They're small, but heavy. And steaming."

"What's inside?" Nate asked impatiently.

"Shh, I get to that."

I tell Izzy, "Look around for a stump or flat rock, eh? If we set them pots on the snow, they gonna maybe freeze."

"I know what to do. I'm not a baby," she says. She's already pouting, her.

I point to a boulder. It's almost flat on top.

"No, silly, look at the snow around it. Too many footprints. Not clean enough."

I look around for a good spot. I get impatient. My stomach, she rumbles. That smell coming from the pots ... well, it's something.

"Saccajé chien!" cries Izzy.

She yells so loud, I get startled. And since when does she cuss? Izzy who's so proper, her. So the pot sloshes. I spill a little. A small dribble of maple. Like liquid gold, yeah? Then I see Izzy's mitten pointing to a fat stump near some old fence.

How can she see it? Her, with her nose always in books. Her, who never sees the birds circling right above. But there it is, for sure. Some funny eyes on her, that one.

I trudge toward her. Carefully, so I don't spill no more. When I catch up, I say, "Mama gonna take a switch to your bum, she hears you cuss like that."

"Who's gonna tell her, eh?" Izzy scrunches up her squinty eyes.

Funny how that little one could look so fierce. She's maybe eight years old. And scrawny. It tickles my funny bone seeing that tough little four-eyed girl. I forget being mad cause she makes me spill some syrup. I laugh. I bop my fist on the blue woolen scarf on her head.

We set our pots on Izzy's stump. We walk around looking for the right spot in the snow.

"Hey, Izzy, over there! Nice and clean snow there. Not even signs of little nuthatch feet."

I guess I'm showing off a little. I love to spot tracks and know who's making them. I learn so much from Mère Agathe. So much about the outside world I want to share. But I don't know why I bother with my little sister. She don't know a nuthatch from a gull, her. If she don't read it in some fancy book, something from Montreal or Boston, it don't matter. She calls Mère Agathe "ignorant" and "crazy old Indian"—not to her face—because Mère Agathe, she don't know how to read.

Funny thing is, our recipe for maple taffy? It don't come from no book. I get it from Mère Agathe. Of course, lotta white folks know how to make maple taffy. Grandparents and parents pass the recipe on to the kids. They probably think them *voyageurs* invent it. But I know better. I know it comes from the Hurons and Abenakis and Micmacs, maybe even the Iroquois. From years and years ago. Centuries. And that makes maple taffy extra special to me.

It always bothers me how I don't look nothing like Papa. Look at these light blue eyes. And before I get gray, my hair is light brown. Before I get all these damn liver spots, my skin, it's real fair. And I have Mama's upturned nose.

Izzy's the one got Papa's Indian blood. Them high cheekbones, olive skin, long pointy nose. Okay, maybe she don't look Abenaki. But she sure don't look like her people come from Brittany and Normandy, like Mama's folks way back. I think maybe she looks Italian or from way south in France, where they grow olives and hardly ever get snow. You know, you see Izzy and Mére Agathe together, you think they're nana and granddaughter. But she don't want to look like Mère Agathe. Maybe that's why she laughs at what I learn. Huh, I guess we're never satisfied with what we are.

So anyway, Izzy and me find the right spot. Now we gotta spill out the syrup just right. I worry if my little sister can manage. "You sure your pot's not too heavy for you?"

She shoots me one mean glare. Then she marches off to get her pot. She tilts it just so, drizzling that hot maple syrup on the snow. Then she inches forward, still dribbling. Whaddya know? She draws this thin, real straight, gold-brown line on the white snow. Real pretty! Real neat.

So I figure she knows what she's doing, her. I can pay attention to my own pot. I show off a bit. Hold that pot with just one hand and make a big arc. Oh, how pretty them maple swirls and loops are! Just like painting a picture on the snow. My pot is bigger than Izzy's. But I empty it *tout de suite*.

"Pah! You make a mess!" Izzy scolds me. "Your taffy sticks. Will not taste the same. Some will have more maple than others. Mine will be nice and even."

I shrug and start swizzling clean wooden sticks into my maple swirls. I wait a bit, till the cold air sets the taffy. Then I pick up the lollipops. Mine are way bigger than Izzy's. But hers, they're neater. That's *tiguidou*, okay. We're both happy with our work. Izzy, she chomps into her maple lollipop, closes her eyes, and coos. And damned if she don't polish it off just like that. That's not easy with something so sticky. And there she is bending down to scoop up another one. Despite the sticky chewing, she polishes off her first stick just like that and scoops up another.

"Hey! We save some for Domithilde and Exilda, yeah?"

"Exilda doesn't have enough teeth to eat this!"

"She can suck on it, though."

So then I dig into my pocket where I put a long piece of yarn. I loop them taffy sticks together to make them easier to carry back to the house. We gonna save some for the littlest ones. Izzy gets grumpy. She'd rather gobble them all up. But she picks up the rest of hers to take back for the others.

I get why she's grumpy, her. For years it's just the two of us. For years, Mama says she's too … how you say? Frail, that's it. She's too frail to have more babies. And then what do you know? Suddenly Mama's pregnant. And she's not so frail. Gets bigger and bigger, puffy all over. Goes all nine months. And out comes chubby, healthy Domithilde. And you know what? Even before our baby sister is weaned, Mama's belly swells up again. Nine months later, here come's Exilda, yelling like some lumberjack. I think maybe it's a miracle that Mama's so healthy. I'm glad. But then come all the chores. Suddenly Izzy and me are taking care of these babies and Mama, she don't have much time for us.

I want to ask Mère Agathe. She's a *sage-femme*. She delivers all us kids. What's the English word? Midwife. If anyone knows what Mama's woman trouble is and why it suddenly goes poof, it's her. But then I worry. Mama and Papa, they pretty private, like most folks in Quebec. You don't talk about family stuff with outsiders. Not even neighbors living close by. Our neighbors the same way. The whole time we live up there, I can't remember one time when a neighbor comes over our house. I can't remember being inside a neighbor's house. Our only visitors? They family. Aunts and uncles and cousins. Lots of cousins. I sometimes wish Mère Agathe is my *grandmère*. She feels like my *grandmère*, but she's not. I even think maybe I ask my aunts what's wrong with Mama. But I don't feel close to them. So I don't ask nobody. And I stuff that worry about Mama deep down inside. It's good Mama can make babies again, but what if that trouble comes back, with the next pregnancy? What happens to Mama then? What happens to us?

But the worry, it don't go away, not even after Exilda shows up. So as Izzy and me carry our maple sticks back to Exilda and Domithilde, I decide to talk about what's going on with Mama. I don't figure my little sister gonna know much, but I feel like I'm gonna choke on the worry if I don't let it out a bit.

Izzy, she turns to me and squeezes them squinty eyes of hers even more and shakes her head. Like I'm too dumb to be her sister. "Silly!" she says. "Mama was never sick. She and Papa were mad. They didn't like each other. And then they made up."

"How come you know this?"

She kinda shrugs. I remember exactly what she says. Every word. "For a long time, Mama and Papa didn't talk. Papa, he never kissed Mama, not even on Christmas Day, when everyone else got two kisses on the cheek. And they never made noises in bed. They still don't talk much. But now they make noises at night."

Imagine that! All these years later, I still wonder. Sure, Izzy grows up on the farm, just like me. She sees the pigs go at it. But she never pays much attention, not even when she sees them sweet little piglets all tucked together sucking on the big sow. So I guess she knows where babies come from. But she never has much interest in any of that. She sure don't have much interest in boys. So how does she figure out what's going on with Mama and Papa, eh? But she watches everything, interested or no. And stores it up inside, cause one day all that information might come in handy. That brain of hers, it's always working. She picks up signals coming from Mama and Papa like she's listening to some radio show. And me, I never pick up on any of that. I never notice the quiet between Mama and Papa. And later, I never hear noises from their bed, neither.

That Izzy, she don't miss a trick. She's sharp, her ... and scary.

Two-thirds of the way through Rose's story, Nate ran out of space in his little notebook. He thought of interrupting her, asking her for some note paper. Truth be told, he wanted to interrupt her many times. He felt frustrated, both in Rose's parlor and now, in the privacy of his small bedroom as he reviewed his chaotic scribbling. Maybe the idea of using the Quentin family for his history thesis on immigrants would entail more challenges than he could master, not least of all because his subject was so old, so easily diverted, and possibly suffering from dementia. He also recognized his own youthful impatience as an impediment to drawing her out effectively. Nor did it help that storyteller and biographer were the products of two very different cultures, making it even harder for him to follow her meandering, singsong narration.

Early on, his right knee had started twitching as he wondered what on earth two little girls playing in the Quebec snow had to do with Rose's apparent worries about her younger sister's powers of observation. Hours later, he realized if he had tried to guide her onto a more linear path, she might never have reached her destination. And he would have missed insights into the sisters' complicated relationship, as well as some Quebec color. But he was left with a jumble of words that would challenge his organizational powers. And each useful insight he had gleaned about this immigrant family opened up a slew of unknowns, questions needing answers. So is this what writing was all about, constantly wrestling with chaos? Maybe becoming a lawyer, dealing with a limited set of variables, wasn't such a bad plan after all.

SIX

Testy Conversations

Vince slammed the phone onto its black cradle. "What a busybody!" His sister-in-law Gert was never more annoying than when in gossip mode.

"Who was that?" Nora asked, entering the living room with a full laundry basket.

"Gert. Now that Hank's running for city council, she's turned into a *grande dame*. The *grande dame* can't afford embarrassing relatives, I guess. Gert's embarrassed because some cop with a hair across his ass stopped Ma. She and that new mutt she acquired were hoofing their way to Swingle's Quarry to pick blueberries. I guess the cop was afraid she'd get run over."

"What's embarrassing about that?" Nora challenged.

Vince grinned, awash in affection for his wife. She was more judgmental than most and was easily embarrassed herself. But she had a soft spot for her mother-in-law. For all of Nora's impatience with the hoi polloi of West Quincy, she never once flinched at Rose's singsong accent, grammatical errors, or occasionally unkempt appearance. She actually valued the older woman's resourcefulness, practical skills, and general outlook on life. Perhaps because of the chilly distance separating Nora from her own mother, she appreciated her mother-in-law's knack for nurturing.

Nora's defiant expression faded. Balancing the laundry basket on the sofa back, she said, "Wait. Why was Rose walking? Why wasn't she driving? That's kind of a long way."

"Dunno." Vince shrugged. "Maybe it's a good thing. I wonder about her driving these days."

"Don't be silly! You taught her to drive ages ago. You said she was a natural. I've seen it, too. Rose is a good driver. For heaven's sake, even Francis would let her take the wheel when they went anywhere together."

Vince snorted. "Pa was proud, but he wasn't stupid. He knew he was a godawful driver. He figured if he planned on getting places in one piece, it was better riding shotgun and letting Ma take over." He paused. "But these days, I dunno what's going on in Ma's head. Maybe she forgot to gas up the car? Or maybe she used up her gas ration for the week? Nah, she never comes close. Maybe she forgot how the new ration stamps work?"

"Things are that bad?"

"I dunno. Sometimes she seems fine. But she keeps calling Netty 'Maryellen.'" Seeing Nora's eyes frost over, Vince instantly regretted the slip of the tongue. The birth certificate for Nora's and Vince's only child read "Antoinette Marie Dowd." Unfortunately, the girl just wasn't an Antoinette, despite Nora's insistence on preserving the high-society tone of that birth name. Unfortunately, everyone but Nora called the scrawny little towhead "Netty"—unless her mother was within earshot.

Nora clicked her tongue. "What does that prove? No one in your family ever got a name right on the first try. Look at you! You can't even call your own daughter by her proper name."

Vince nodded contritely. "True, but I'm still worried. So worried, I've got another set of eyes on the problem. You know that college kid whose car I'm fixing?"

"The kid with the clubfoot? He's gonna spy on your mother? Vincent Dowd, what on earth are you thinking? Sharing family business with an outsider? A Jew? And he's barely out of knee pants himself.

How can he possibly assess your mother's state of mind?"

Vince raised his palms defensively. "Nate's a good kid. Smart as all get out. But more than that, he's a real softy. A sensitive type. Wants to be a writer. And he already knows Ma, from way back. He's the Ragman's grandson, remember? The little boy who used to call her Madame Rose? She always got a big kick out of that." He waited to see if his wife's expression softened.

Nora folded her arms over her chest defensively. At the same time, she nodded thoughtfully. "I remember that little boy. He was kinda cute. And amazingly well-spoken."

"Even more so now. I invited him over to Ma's the other day and watched how he acted toward her. Kind, respectful. He genuinely likes her."

"Maybe so, but what about her? Isn't she gonna feel resentful if she thinks you have someone spying on her?"

"Gimme some credit, Nora. I wasn't that heavy-handed. I told Ma Nate's gonna be doing some of the handyman chores around her place, stuff I don't have time to do. I told her that will be his way of paying me for the labor of fixing up his MG. And all of that's true. God knows, I don't have the time to do everything that needs doing in that old house. And I've long since given up on my brothers lending a hand."

"Hah, your brothers! How often do they even *visit* her, let alone help out? Honestly, I just don't understand how you ended up the family caretaker. I thought the youngest member of the family was supposed to be the spoiled one."

Vince grinned. "Yup, that's me, the pampered baby."

Nora grimaced. "Really, Vince, can't you get your brothers to help your mother out more? It's not like any of them live far away."

"Aw, they mean well. They're just busy with their jobs and families."

"And you don't have a job and family? 'Jobs,' plural?"

Vince shrugged.

"Look, maybe I can help out a bit myself," Nora said. "I'll damn well make a more reliable spy than that Nate kid. I was planning on going over to your mother's tomorrow anyway. She found a box of old toys in the attic and thought Antoinette might like some of them. Why don't I use that visit to snoop around? Find out the story behind her walking all that distance. And have a little talk about road safety."

44

"Yeah?" Vince couldn't conceal his surprise. "Well, okay. Just don't overdo the lecture." He nearly edited out that last comment but wanted to spare his mother exposure to Nora's overbearing inclinations, however well-intended.

Nora's irises dulled from blue to gray. She swung the laundry basket onto her left hip and marched toward the bedroom. The door slammed behind her.

Vince cursed himself for curdling a sweet moment with his wife. Then he cursed himself for answering the phone in the first place. Something happened to communication when facilitated by modern technology. Without being able to see facial expressions and body language, partners in conversation became desensitized. Even he, raised to be polite, had fired a few shots at his sister-in-law. And she had certainly gotten on his last nerve. Then there was the accursed problem of the woman at the center of that testy conversation, the woman who had raised him to be polite, the woman who was probably losing her mind. He did not look forward to the reports from Nate or Nora. He did not look forward to the difficult—face-to-face—conversation he must have, sooner rather than later, with Rose Dowd.

SEVEN

Choices

"Sit, sit! You walk all this way to see me on a hot day? You rest while I put the coffee on."

Rose shooed her guest toward a chair by the kitchen table, while she bustled about the old stove, retro-engineered to work with either wood or natural gas.

Nora folded her hands on the table, cleared her throat, and began. "Heard you had a little run-in with a cop the other day."

"Eh?"

"Gert said someone who works with Hank spotted you near Swingle's Quarry and wanted to know why you were walking along the road. You had this one with you?" Nora angled her head sideways to indicate the big black dog sitting alertly by her hip.

"Ah, *saccajé chien!* I almost forget. He scares poor Jolie to death, his big cop car stopping us like that? I ask him if I'm speeding."

Nora chuckled. "Did he have the good grace to laugh?"

Rose whooshed a hand past her face. "Pah! No one has a sense of

46

humor no more. He tells me I'm … what is it? Endangering the traffic. How about that, eh? Like maybe I dent one of them big Fords with my basket."

Smiling, Nora rose to take the full cup from her hostess. "Thank you. Now sit and drink yours, will you?" She motioned toward the opposite seat.

Rose complied. "I should make ice coffee, a day like today," she said, dipping into a skirt pocket, retrieving a giant handkerchief, and mopping her face with it.

"Well, even though that cop sounds like he was a little prig…"

"Prig? That means stick up his butt, yeah?"

"Exactly. Even though he had a stick up his butt, the cop was kinda right about it being dangerous. For you. You know the way people drive these days. Someone coming around a curve could have clipped you. Or your new dog here."

Rose's face crumpled as she looked at the Newfoundland mix. "Ah, I don't think about Jolie. I feel awful if anything happens to her." Rubbing right thumb and index finger together, she motioned toward the shaggy beast, who sidled up to her mistress. "You a good girl, yeah? You protect me on the road. But I don't protect you so good, eh?" Turning back to Nora, she smiled and said, "Next time, we take the car."

"Why didn't you drive the car the other day? Maybe you didn't have enough gas?"

"No, I lose the keys."

"Don't you have an extra set?"

Rose frowned, as if the idea of an extra set of car keys was completely alien. "It's *tiguidou*. Everything okay. I find them. Just this morning."

"Well, it happens," Nora said, sipping her coffee. "We can all get forgetful sometimes. Where'd you find them?"

"Silliest damn thing, right here." She cocked her head backward.

"On the kitchen counter?"

"No, right beside."

The only thing beside that particular counter was the icebox.

"Ohh," Nora groaned.

"Why so sad? Cold keys work just as good as warm keys. Here, I get us come crackers and cheese, go with the coffee."

As Rose rummaged about the icebox and cabinets for a long time,

Nora frowned, desperate to come up with a rational reason why her mother-in-law might have put car keys in the icebox. Her frown deepened when her hostess returned, depositing the "treat" on the table. The block of cheddar bloomed with blue mold. The "crackers" were a beaten-up package of Oreo cookies. "Umm, no, I'm not really hungry. The heat, you know? It makes me not want to look at food ever again."

Rose nodded. She made no move to sample the goods herself.

Nora offered up a silent prayer of gratitude, sighed, then steered the conversation to the ostensible reason for the visit. Once it was addressed, she could flee.

"Do you need me to bring the toy box down from the attic?" She asked.

"Toy box? Ah, no. In the living room. *Allons-y!* (Let's go!) We take a look, yeah? You choose what you want."

As Nora levered herself upright, she whispered, "Wow," marveling at the older woman's energetic gait.

Rose looked over her shoulder quizzically then waggled an index finger. "No toys for you, little one. These for Netty."

Nora bent over the toy box, her nostrils absorbing the smell of must and unfulfilled dreams. So many of the battered treasures inside were reminders of loss: dolls and stuffed animals loved and abandoned by Maryellen—the only daughter—taken by pneumonia before her thirteenth birthday. Nora swayed with sudden lightheadedness, as two fat tears splashed bright circles of color onto the dust-dulled toys. She slumped to her knees on the living room carpet.

With surprising agility, Rose dropped to the floor beside her. Readjusting her skirt, she tucked her ankles sideways and patted her daughter-in-law's thigh. Then she pulled the box closer and plopped several items into Nora's lap. "No need to be sad, you. Toys, they cheer you up."

Nora scrutinized a ratty teddy bear and a doll missing one eye. These pathetic artifacts triggered a mirthless laugh.

"See?" challenged Rose. "What I say? I get you to laugh." She plucked the toys from Nora's lap, shook her head, and tossed them onto the carpet. "You see something a lot sadder than you? Can't help but cheer you up."

Nora turned her head to scan the other woman's face, which suggested irony, not simplemindedness.

"Okay, now you tell me. Why so sad?" Rose prodded.

"Oh, I guess these old toys got me thinking about the passage of time, about all the things we lose with the years."

"What? You a young woman, you."

Nora shook her head as she retrieved a wooden yo-yo, its varnish only slightly discolored. She unwound a few inches of string and wrapped it around her finger, searching for frays. "Antoinette might enjoy this," she murmured.

"Sure, and her father can show her some tricks. He's good with it."

"This belonged to Vince?"

"Vincent, Hank, Dave … I forget."

"Not Maryellen?"

Rose shook her head. "What about *this* for Maryellen?" she asked, retrieving a floppy-eared stuffed dog, with the fake fur abraded from decades of use. It looked like it had comforted all five Dowd children.

"I think … Antoinette," Nora said, emphasizing her daughter's correct name, "has been spoiled by your Newfoundlands. First Jolly, now this mix, Jolie. She won't settle for anything less than a real dog."

"Yeah, okay," Rose said, tossing the limp plaything aside. "And what about you? You don't wanna settle, yeah?"

"What do you mean?"

Rose shrugged. "Sometimes we get sad cause we want something. But can't have it. So what can't you have?"

"No, I'm being silly." Nora fished into the box and discarded a popgun and set of jacks. "It's not like I don't have enough on my hands with Antoinette, especially with all her health problems. If there's a bug going around, that child will catch it. Who knows what other problems another child might bring?"

"Ah," Rose nodded. "The gossoons, like my Francis says, bring lotta trouble. But they bring lotta fun, too. Nothing like the smell of a new baby, eh?"

Nora's posture crumpled even further. She squeezed the bridge of her nose to short-circuit the new tears threatening to erupt.

Her mother-in-law, now scooping into the carton's contents to expose the bottom-most toys, appeared oblivious to the younger woman's distress. Or perhaps she was giving her a chance to collect herself.

Nora explained, "It's just … you know I had a miscarriage two years ago, right?" She waited for an acknowledgment, but Rose was focused on the pathetic playthings. "I was pretty beat up. Took a long time for my 'friend' to return. I thought maybe I was going into the change early. But then things got back on track. Until a few months ago."

Still retrieving and discarding various toys, Rose nodded. "You get pregnant, yeah?"

Nora sighed. "I get pregnant. At least I think so. I was more than a month late. And except for that year after the miscarriage, I'm ridiculously regular. But there were no other changes, and I didn't want to look like a complete fool, rushing to Dr. Kelley with so little evidence and me feeling fine. But then, just last week, I started bleeding. A lot. With bad cramps. Do you think I was pregnant and had an early miscarriage?"

"Maybe so. Maybe no. As you get older, the monthly blood no longer comes so regular. How you feeling now? No more bleeding?"

Nora shook her head. "No more bleeding. I felt weak for a while, but I'm okay now. Just sad. And guilty."

For the first time since this saga began, Rose looked her in the eye. "*Ma cocotte!* (sweetie!) Why guilty?" From her skirt pocket, she pulled out her gigantic sweaty handkerchief and dropped it into Nora's lap.

Nora paused before taking the offering then pressed it under her nostrils to address her sniffles. She angled her head to one side, hitched up her shoulders, inhaled sharply, and opened her mouth. But no words came out.

"You think maybe you do something bad to the baby?"

Nora choked off the sob rising in her throat. Nodding, she croaked, "I kept smoking. And some of those hot days, I had a beer or two. I know some doctors say pregnant women should give up cigarettes and alcohol. But I just can't relax without my Pall Malls. And relaxing was harder than usual once I thought I might be pregnant. My brain just kept spinning with plans and worries. You know?"

"So now you think you're some murderer?"

Nora's eyes bulged at the question. "Is that what *you* think I am?"

"I think you're a lady who maybe gets pregnant, maybe not. Maybe cigarettes and a glass of beer not so good. But little ones come into the world all the time from mothers who starve, mothers who work too much, mothers who get beaten up by their men. If God wants to make a baby, He's not gonna be stopped so easy. I ever tell you how *I* come into the world?"

Nora shrugged. She had heard the story many times.

"I tell you then. My mama, she has no trouble carrying me. All nine months, healthy. We have a good harvest. We have enough food, good food. Okay, I'm a winter baby but even Old Man Flint, he's in a good mood that year. My nana, she brings the Abenaki *sage-femme* in time, what you call a midwife. She feels my mama's belly. Everything *tiguidou*. Head where it should be. Feet where they should be. Except when I pop out, I don't look so good. Blue. Sure, babies look like grub worms till they fill their lungs. Then they look like red devils." She paused to chuckle. "Your Vincent? Red face. Big nose. Big fists pumping the air. And howling? *Sainte Anne*, what lungs on that one! And he…"

Rose stopped abruptly, swiveling her head. "Where the coffee cups go?"

Nora tensed her shoulders, exhaled, and said. "We left them back in the kitchen. But continue your story. You weren't a red-faced infant like Vince?"

"Ah, I tell you this before? No, I'm blue in the face, me. The *sage-femme*, she whacks my bottom real good. I don't cry. She whacks me again. Harder. Still nothing. So you know what she does? She cuts the cord, scoops me up in her arms, all sticky-wet, and runs outside. She runs all the way to the horse trough. Not too cold that day, but cold. Thin ice on water in the trough. And what do you think she does? Bam! She drops me right through the ice and into the water. Then she scoops me up again. I cough and spit and let out one big cry. So loud they could hear across the river. My face gets plenty red then."

"It's a wonder you didn't freeze to death."

"Yeah, Mama worries I catch pneumonia. That's why she tells Papa to hitch up the sleigh. Very next day, I take my first sleigh ride. Sure did. On Christmas Day. Snowing. But off we go to St. Patrice's to get me baptized. In case I catch pneumonia, I don't go to limbo."

"*Did* you catch pneumonia?"

"Nah, I'm tough, me. Even as *petit bébé*. Like I say, when God wants someone to come into this world, He gonna make it happen. Blue face or no. Snow or no."

Nora shrugged skeptically.

"But you know what? Sometimes I think it's not God. Maybe it's me. Maybe I just want to get born so bad, I gonna get born in spite of everything."

Nora snorted. "That's downright sacrilegious, Rose! But I like the idea. Maybe we all have more say about life than the priests would have us believe."

"You got that right. You know what else I think? We all choose our time to die. Maryellen, she's strong when she catches pneumonia. Not even a bad case. But she dies real quick. Maybe she's just ready to go. Vincent, he's only eight and still kinda puny when he gets the diphtheria. The whole house is closed up. Quarantine. His older brother gets real sick and can't eat, can't get out of bed for a week. But Vincent? Three days later, sickness all gone. He's not ready to leave. Too many things to do. Quarries to swim in. Blueberries to pick. Cars to fix. Nora to marry. Netty to snuggle."

Nora pressed the side of her head into her mother-in-law's shoulder. "Don't you choose to die anytime soon, okay? I don't know how you do it, but you always make me feel better."

EIGHT

Quarry-Berries

Elbows splayed on the flour-dusted kitchen table, chin on stacked fists, Netty whined, "I don't get to do anything. Everyone's already seen Nana's new dog. Everyone but me. And everyone but me gets to pick quarry-berries. Summer's nearly over, and the berries are almost all gone. It's not fay-uh!"

"You get to make blueberry pie, filled with all the berries I picked at the quarry the other day," Vince argued cheerfully. "That's fun, isn't it?"

"I guess," she responded, spinning the empty Py-O-My box on the tabletop.

"And if you feel up to it, later," her father added, "we'll bring one of our pies over to Ma's. And you can finally see her new dog."

"Promise?" the girl asked, brightening.

"I promise, as long as you feel okay. You weren't feeling so great this morning, remember? And it's pretty hot out. Don't want you getting all sweaty and light-headed. So we'll see, okay?"

"You always say that," she grumbled. "So how come it's okay if I get hot and sweaty inside, with the oven on?"

"My daughter, the lawyer. But hey, if you don't like the hot kitchen, you can always go grab a comic book and read it on the porch, where it's cool. Or maybe take a nap. I can make the pies myself."

"Nooo! I wanna help make the pies."

Vince smirked. "Not too hot?"

"I'm fine," Netty said with annoyance, realizing she'd been out-foxed. "And I'll be fine for visiting Nana and Jolie, too."

"Promise?"

"We'll see," Netty said, with an even wider smirk than her father's.

Turning his attention to the bowl he was stirring, Vince said, "Okay, this Py-O-My mix is starting to look like dough. Rip off a big piece of wax paper and lay it down over there, so we can start rolling it out."

Netty's exuberant tug at the wax paper dislodged a nearby table knife, which somersaulted onto the linoleum floor, where it bounced twice and twanged raucously.

"If you make a mess in there, you better clean it up! You hear me?" The throaty female voice scolded from the living room.

Vince and Netty clenched their teeth, tightened their neck muscles, and inhaled sharply before Vince called out, with excess cheer, "Will do, Nora!"

Turning to his tiny accomplice, he touched an index finger to his lip, then to his ear. She stifled a giggle and cocked her right ear at the kitchen doorway. After a minute, girl and man could just make out the fat slap of a Bicycle playing card on a table. The solitaire game had apparently resumed in the living room. Vince grinned, dramatically brushing his forehead with the back of his wrist. The seven-year-old co-conspirator beamed up at him.

"So, lemme divide the dough into quarters and get started." Vince spun each quarter in his palms and arrayed the balls in a row on the table. "Grab a pinch of flour, will ya? Now sprinkle it over the paper. Good. I can start rolling. Gotta do it from the center out, like this."

"Netty stood on tiptoe for a better view. "Let *meee*, Daddy!"

He handed her the rolling pin. Her first pass barely had any impact. Her second pass made a ridge in the center, before squeezing a thin band of dough into an awkward finger shape. "No, like this," Vince explained, gently moving in back of the little girl and placing his palms over her knuckles on the handles.

The process took twenty minutes, but the end result was a reasonable approximation of a circle. The second, third, and fourth circles were done in just a few minutes each, after Netty, interest waning, ceded the rolling pin to her father. But she insisted on being the one to fill the shells with the plump, sugared blueberries, which she had long ago dubbed quarry-berries, with a nod to their origin: the partially wooded areas around the city's abandoned granite quarries. Once she emptied the berry bowl, she delicately poked at each blue pile to even out the depth.

As her father began to move the top pastry circles into place, she wailed, "Not yet! Cinnamon!"

"Oh, that's right. I forgot. I still don't think cinnamon goes with blueberries, but okay. Sprinkle a spoonful on top."

After adding her favorite ingredient, Netty sat down abruptly and hugged her knobby knees to her chest. Vince noticed the purple stains under her cornflower eyes and the razor edge to her shins.

"Why didn't you let me go with you when you picked these berries?"

"Don't you remember? You were feeling crummy. And it's a long hike from where I can park the car."

"Nana Rose can hike it okay. If she can, so can I. She's old. I'm young."

"Just because Ma insists on hiking up to the quarry to pick her own blueberries doesn't mean she should." Vince shook his head.

"She told me she goes swimming there, too."

"She used to. But not these days."

"Annie Donahue called me a liar. She said girls aren't allowed in the quarries. Only boys. And the boys don't wear swim trunks. Are there really naked boys in the quarries?" Netty pursed her lips in disapproval.

Vince laughed, anticipating the flood of indignant questions about the male swimmers. He finally diverted his daughter by mentioning the poison ivy that thrived in that habitat. It triggered a discussion of one neighborhood girl's particularly gruesome rash.

Undeterred, Netty returned to the original subject. "Why doesn't Nana go swimming there anymore?"

"She's old and achy, and that water is freezing. And I think she misses having Jolly as a swimming buddy."

"I miss Jolly, too."

"We all do, Netty. He was one great Newfoundland."

"Vince tucked both pies in the oven and began cleaning up the mess on the kitchen table and in the sink. Netty slid off her chair and sidled up to him. Pressing her head into his left hip, she said softly, "But not as much as I'd miss you. You aren't gonna go away like Annie's father, are you? He went away to fight Jamps."

"Japs, Netty," he corrected, with a chuckle, while at the same time thinking that Jamps might be an easier enemy. He imagined plump little men wearing strawberry-colored uniforms. Handing his daughter a towel and pointing to the just-washed flatware, he added, "I don't know what's gonna happen, kiddo. Can't make any promises. Your mum thinks if I land that job at Fore River, I'll get an exemption. That means I can stay put. The country needs shipyard workers almost as much as it needs soldiers. Also, I'm kinda old, and they're calling up the younger fellas first."

Vince did not mention the other factor that might sway the local draft board: Netty. Everyone knew the child was in perpetual ill health. Her young life was already scarred by several hospital stays, with no conclusive diagnosis for her challenged immune system. He was already working two jobs to keep up with the doctor bills. He had no idea how Nora and Netty would cope if he was inducted. He supposed he could send them all his pay. He didn't imagine any great need for money in the fetid jungles of the Pacific.

But sometimes Nora's and Netty's hardships paled in his thinking. Sitting out the war, as the expression went, didn't seem right. He didn't care about the slitted glares shot at him by grocery clerks or fellow congregants at St. Mary's—always women, resentful that their husbands or sons had been ripped away while this robust male before them was shirking his duty. Vince had a tough hide. It did not wither under their basilisk eyes. But he knew the war needed to be fought. He had reached that conclusion long before his own country entered the arena just seven months earlier. For several years now, his priority after returning home from his first job—before catching supper and then putting in the hours to fix whatever cars awaited him on the cobblestones right outside the front door—was to suck the evening Globe dry of details about the catastrophe that Europe and East Asia had become.

"Daddy?" Netty tugged on his baggy pants leg and looked up at him through an errant blonde strand, which she blew off her nose. "I'm

56

ready to dry the mixing bowl."

"No, I better do that. It's too heavy for you."

"I'm not a baby!" she objected, thrusting her right hand upward.

"All right, but be careful. Mixing bowls don't grow on trees, you know."

The little girl clucked peevishly, "You always say that. The only things that grow on trees are leaves, Daddy."

"I stand corrected. Wait! That goes in the cabinet up there. Let me put it away."

"I'll do it," Netty said primly.

She deposited the big bowl on the table then thrust a hip at one of the heavy wooden chairs. After repeated shoves, she bulldozed it into position beneath the target cabinet. Bowl in hand, she climbed onto the seat and, on tiptoes, nudged the crockery into position. Panting, she brushed away a few long strands glued to her sweaty face and sat down on the wooden chair.

"I can dry the rest," Vince said. "Just keep me company."

A chill skittered up his spine when Netty offered no protest. She resumed her knee-hugging posture on the chair and idly prodded her naked toes.

Looking up suddenly, she asked, "Can we walk to Nana's? It's so pretty out, and we haven't taken a walk together in a long time."

"You sure you won't poop out on me? Then I'd have to carry you *and* your nana's pie."

With a forefinger, Netty solemnly crossed her chest. "Swear to God."

He shook his head but suspected the pleading would continue—unless fatigue kicked in before the pies were cooked and cooled. What Netty lacked in physical stamina was balanced by mental persistence. And so, after weighing the risks of exhausting his daughter or his gas ration before the end of the week, Vince succumbed to the little girl's wheedling.

They would clear just two cobblestone streets before Netty was on his shoulders, sharp heels thumping against his lower ribs.

NINE

Fixing Things

Netty's energy revived at the sight of the shaggy beast sprawled on the peeling paint barely covering Rose Dowd's porch. "Lemme down, Daddy," she protested, drumming her fingertips on Vince's cap.

"Easy, kiddo," he replied, grabbing her waist, hoisting her over his head, and setting her down. Her sneakers barely kissed the grass before she hurtled herself at the dog. "Wait! Don't charge the poor thing. You don't know how she'll react."

Vince needn't have worried, because Jolie calmly shifted to a more upright position, all the better to receive a neck-clasping hug from the little girl. The giant, probably taller than her predecessor and appearing to be a mixture of Newfoundland and Great Dane, unfurled a fat pink tongue and slurped Netty's left forearm.

"Yuck!" Netty squealed, unclasping Jolie's neck. As she knelt to wipe off the profuse saliva, she lost her balance and keeled over on top of her new friend. Jolie merely swiveled her massive head to bathe Netty's entire side. "Daddy, help!" the girl yowled, giggling at the same time, as she tried to right herself.

Laughing, Vince climbed the porch stairs, set the pie box on the railing, and extended a hand to pull his daughter out of the furry embrace.

The screen door groaned open. "Ah, I think I hear company," said Rose. "You see my Jolly comes back home, Netty?"

Netty and her father exchanged confused glances.

"Uh, Ma, this is the dog you just got from the pound. And it's a girl, not a boy like old Jolly."

"Yeah, yeah, sure. A pretty girl. That's why I call her Jolie."

Vince couldn't decide whether his mother understood that the beast before them was not the loyal Newfoundland whom he had put down just two months earlier because of horrific arthritis. Perhaps she was making a joke, playing on the similar appearance of the two dogs. Or perhaps she thought this pound mutt really was Jolly. Or maybe she considered the new dog the reincarnation of her beloved, long-time companion. The last two choices were worrisome. But he tried to cheer himself by admiring the mental agility implicit in her choice of name for the newcomer.

He could conjure no cheer, however, over the sorry state of the dog's coat, which had acquired new mats since his last visit. Maybe he should wield a scissors and remove those knots, which must make the summer heat even harder to bear. And maybe he should take pruning shears to the wisteria bearing down on the porch roof. No, that last task was one Nate could handle. Nor was much expertise necessary to scrape the peeling paint and apply a new coat to the porch. Certainly, the young man could handle that task, as well.

"Brought you a blueberry pie, Ma," Vince said, retrieving the gift. "I guess I picked more berries than I realized."

"I helped make the pie," Netty boasted, as she finally turned her attention away from the dog.

"And I bet it tastes extra good, with that special touch only Maryellen can give."

Netty frowned and poked an index finger into her chest. "I'm Netty, Nana!"

"Sure you are." Rose cupped the child's chin. "Except when your mama's around, yes? Then you're Antoinette." She winked conspiratorially.

Netty grinned broadly. It was no secret that the seven-year-old was uncomfortable with the name on her birth certificate. It seemed to come with such high expectations. Her mother often lectured her that some-one with the grand name of Antoinette would be sure to get a good education, marry well, live in a fine house, and be a fixture in society. Netty didn't understand what all of that entailed, but she worried about falling short of those high goals. She was stressing enough as it was since hearing she would need to master multiplication and division when she began third grade in a few short weeks.

Entering the kitchen, Vince noted that the screen door refused to close properly. One hinge was about to fall off, with all three screws nearly popped. "I'll trade you a screwdriver for the pie," he called after his mother, who was motioning for her guests to sit at the kitchen table.

Rose headed for one kitchen drawer, Jolie padding loyally behind her. Vince sucked in his breath when she retrieved a table knife and regarded it quizzically before rummaging through another drawer. It took four tries before she located the "junk" drawer where the Dowds had stored basic household tools for some forty years.

"You want a slot head or a Phillips?"

"Phillips," Vince replied, relieved. His mother had always been a resourceful woman. She had grown up working on a farm, had raised four boys, and managed the lion's share of household chores in her Quincy homestead. It would be painful—perhaps more so for Vince than for Rose herself—if she was to lose that identity thanks to whatever was going on inside her brain.

"Phillips," he repeated with excess cheer. Rising to take the correct tool from his mother's hand, he added, "I'll just tighten up that hinge before the screen door falls off."

"Oh, yeah? I don't see the loose hinge. Okay then. You do that." Then turning to Netty, she commented, "Always a good boy, him. And you always a good girl, too, Maryellen."

"Nana! I'm Netty." Exasperated, the little girl pointed both index fingers at her chest.

"What I say?"

"You called me Maryellen. Again."

"Pah, silly me. You look like her, you know. Both of you with blonde hair."

"But she's dead, Nana."

"Not in here, little one," Rose said patting her heart.

Sadness melted Netty's exasperation. "I'm sorry, Nana. You can call me Maryellen if you want."

"Nah, you got a good name, you. So we'll just call you Jolie. Jolie for a pretty girl."

"Naaaaa-na!" wailed Netty, but stopped abruptly when she noted the smirk on her grandmother's face, and the winking right eye.

Returning to the kitchen, Vince reported, "Well, I tightened the hinge a bit, but I'll have to replace the frame. It's rotten and won't hold the screws much longer."

"I maybe have some wood you can use. In your father's tool shed."

"I'll check later." He sighed, knowing that the tool shed, which was disorderly enough when his father was alive, would be a chaotic wreck, offering up more problems than solutions even if it probably did contain some useful pieces for framing. He sighed that the hinge remedy could not be knocked off in a few minutes. He sighed because the task would require carpentry skills beyond Nate. He sighed that his brothers never seemed to be around the old homestead to notice all the chores that needed to be done. And he sighed because he had overheard his mother mistake her granddaughter for his long-dead sister, Maryellen.

"Sit, Vincent. I get us some lemonade."

He sat and tried to figure out when he could find the time to fix the screen door. That calculation, though tedious, was less onerous than the next task he assigned himself. It was high time he talked with his mother about all these memory lapses. Maybe they could jointly work out a strategy for improving her mental nimbleness. Perhaps he could encourage her to post notes around the house: like, "shut off the stove" or "lock the door before going to bed." He shook his head sadly. Was he supposed to pin a note to his daughter's shirt, a note reading "Netty"? He exhaled heavily.

Was it really all that ominous that his mother had called Netty "Maryellen"? Twice, within one half hour? Maybe it was just a harmless slip of the tongue, after all, and did not mean Ma actually thought she was talking to the daughter who had died three decades earlier. Nora had a point when she commented about the Dowd family's predilection for fumbling names. Truth be told, he himself often called Dave "Eddie" and Eddie "Hank." As the youngest of four boys, Vince considered himself lucky if he was called the annoyingly childish nickname "Vinnie." That was preferable to being the Dowd boy too insignificant to be remembered at all. He was not a policeman like his brothers. He was not a World War One veteran like the oldest Dowd boy, Dave. He was not a candidate for city council like Hank. He was not the owner of a new home in Braintree like Eddie. He was just Vince/Vincent/Vinnie, who never finished high school and had trouble paying the doctor bills and keeping enough coal in the cellar bin. The only noteworthy achievements in his thirty-seven years were marrying Nora, a Bostonian of "good stock," and fathering Netty, who for all her health problems and scruffy demeanor radiated light and intelligence and sweetness.

Briefly, all of Vince's responsibilities evaporated when his mother placed a hefty slab of pie before him, along with a tall, cool glass of homemade lemonade. He recognized the chipped plate from his childhood and also the bent fork. He closed his eyes to conjure a vision of all eight Dowds gathered around this same kitchen table: his mother and father, his bachelor Uncle Dinny, his three brothers, and his older sister Maryellen, even though she had died when Vince was just four. And sometimes Tante Isabelle wedged into a spot at the table when she had a holiday from her job as nanny to a prosperous Back Bay household. Although infamous for her stern demeanor toward her professional charges, Izzy was off-duty when visiting her sister. She couldn't care less if her nephews acted rowdy. She would drift off in a blue-gray cloud of cigarette smoke. A decade would pass before Vince saw another woman smoke. Like his aunt, he now drifted off, too, at the very same table. How animated the conversation had been back then — punctuated by burps and laughs and flying hands. Vince snorted, recalling how his father Francis (always "Francis," never "Frank") would chide Rose and Izzy for waving their hands around. It was a sign of their foreignness, the elder Dowd had claimed, even as his own hands stretched left and right to emphasize a point or flew into the air to signal exasperation.

Members of the Yankee class didn't talk with their hands, which was why Vince always felt he was missing key linguistic cues when conversing with them. Maybe when you had a comfortable stash, you didn't worry so much about being properly understood. With enough money, you could afford to sit on your hands and conserve your energy. Although he remained wary of the rising influence of Italian immigrants competing for scarce jobs, Vince felt comfortable with their manual eloquence.

And hadn't Nora's dramatic hand gestures settled Vince's nerves during their first date fifteen years earlier? Set up by mutual friends, the couple had stared awkwardly at one another initially, each wondering what they could possibly have in common. She was the lace-curtain daughter of a Boston postal clerk; he was the rough-handed son of a Quincy quarryman. But when their companions began discussing Greta Garbo's performance in *Flesh and the Devil,* Nora's hands fluttered into life. They expressed enthusiasm, nervousness, elegance, and sensuality in a way her words could not. She was not a cold princess after all. There was something warm and vulnerable beneath that haughty exterior. Vince resolved to nurture it.

Mottled fingers suddenly waggled before his unfocused eyes. "Vincent!" Rose teased. "You gather the wool again, no?"

"What? Oh, sorry. I guess I *was* wool-gathering. Remembering so many meals at this table. Sometimes it seems like a century ago. Other times like just yesterday."

She shrugged. "Time's a funny thing. I don't always remember so good what happens yesterday. But the lessons from Mère Agathe? They come back like that." She snapped her fingers.

"Was Mary Ag ... Aga ... was she your teacher?" Netty said while cramming a large piece of pie into her mouth.

"Not like you think. She never goes to school. But, oh, what that woman knows! She knows how to deliver babies, how to heal burns, where to pick wild mushrooms in the woods — the good kind."

Netty gaped. Flakes of pie crust perched on her lower lip fluttered down onto the table. "You ate stuff from the woods? Didn't it taste gunky? What if it was poison?"

Rose pointed to the remaining pie. "You think blueberries taste gunky? You think blueberries are poison? They come from the woods."

Netty cocked her head to the side and bit her lower lip, chewing on her grandmother's input. "I ate an elm leaf once. It tasted awful."

"Netty! What were you doing eating an elm leaf?" Vince gasped.

"Annie dared me. It was fuzzy. It tasted fuzzy, too."

Her father rolled his eyes in his mother's direction. "As if she doesn't have tummy troubles enough."

Rose flicked her wrist dismissively. "We eat a peck of dirt before we die, eh? Every one of us."

"Nana?" Netty tapped her grandmother's elbow. "Can you teach me what that Mary lady taught you?"

63

"Sure, why not?" Then seeing Vince cringe, she added. "Maybe we start inside, though? I teach you to make root beer, yeah?"

"Daddy makes that sometimes. Mummy gets mad when one of the bottles explodes."

"Ah, Vincent never measures. Too much yeast maybe? Your father and me, we make so many brews together, years ago. Root beer, wine from our elderberries and rum cherries, tea and beer from our hops."

"I seem to remember getting a squash on from that first batch of rum-cherry wine. I was what, ten?"

Rose laughed. "Your eyes always bigger than your head."

"You know, Ma, this old house was a good place for growing kids."

"Yeah? I always wish you boys have more room to run around. More room like me and Izzy on the farm outside Lévis City. Before everything changes."

"Once a farm girl, always a farm girl. If you could go back to the old homestead, you think you'd still want to live there?"

"*Comme ci, comme ça*. My sisters, they all scatter to the wind. Not so much fun without them. But like you say, Vincent, that farm's a good place to grow up."

An ominous gurgle interrupted the adult ruminations. Eyes wide with panic, Netty clapped a palm over her mouth and bolted for the bathroom.

Vince rose abruptly, tripping over the dog. By the time he righted himself, loud retching echoed down the hallway.

"*Saccajé chien!* Is that Maryellen?"

Vince lacked the energy to substitute the correct name. He merely nodded and trudged toward the bathroom.

"You go check," Rose said. "I fix up some tea. Cure her tummy good and quick. No need for Nora to worry about the upchuck."

Vince sighed at the mess on the bathroom floor and at the tears streaming down his daughter's face. He smoothed her blonde hair and asked, "You think you're through?"

She nodded unconvincingly. "I'm sorry, Daddy."

"It's okay. You stay here near the toilet, just in case, while I mop up around you."

He wrung out the sponge at the bathroom sink and listened to the chokes and sniffles coming from the distraught child. Fixed on the haggard face staring from the mirror, Vince thought of his mother's words

64

and hoped she could indeed fix up Netty. Just like she had fixed up so many problems in his youth. For an instant, he forgot all the evidence of his mother's senility. For an instant, he imagined he was ten again. With no perpetually sick daughter. With no fretful wife. With no late mortgage payment. With no Jamps to fight.

After driving her son and granddaughter home, Rose cleaned up the kitchen and poured herself a cup of the spearmint tea she had served Netty. Shaking her head, she complained, "I tell Nora to put some slippery elm in Netty's oatmeal. Every day. Fix up that tummy good. But Nora, she gets all big-eyed. She don't wanna give her kid sawdust, she says. So she takes Netty to this doctor and he gives her stuff that makes even more trouble for the tummy. Too bad. I bet Mère Agathe, she knows what to do."

"Pah!"

Rose whipped around and saw her old mentor examining the half-pie on the counter.

"The *petite fille?*" began Mère Agathe. "Her trouble? It's not the tummy. It's not the lungs. It's here." She poked her heavily veined temple with a bony finger. "That mother, she makes the little one sick, with all the worries, all the hopes, all the fears. That mother tells the girl she's sick. Poof, the girl, she's sick."

"Ah, Nora. She tries hard, her. She loves that little girl. She ... wait, you know Nora?

"If *you* know Nora, little one, *I* know Nora. That's how it works, no?"

Rose nodded thoughtfully. After a pause, she asked, "Mère Agathe, what's wrong with me?"

Mère Agathe wrapped her shawl more tightly around her shoulders. "You gotta figure that out. You gotta fix yourself up. Lotta people need you. That little girl, she gonna need you."

And just like that, as if someone had turned off an electric bulb, the ancient Métis woman's light was extinguished.

TEN

Bridging Time

Nate wished he were in the Hearse, instead of the Rattletrap. His mother, who didn't know how to drive, had a habit of assigning names for each vehicle used by the Kagan family and Sol's Salvage. The names always stuck. As a two-seater pickup, the Rattletrap had poor air circulation, which is why Nate's shirt was already glued to his shoulder blades on this muggy day, already stifling even though the hour was not yet ten o'clock, and even though he had been on the road just ten minutes.

The Hearse was a Chevrolet saloon car with ample room inside, four doors, and good circulation with all the windows rolled down. Nate assumed it had acquired its pejorative nickname not because it was big and black. His mother named it for what it wasn't: the 1935 Cadillac sedan in which her sister-in-law was shepherded around town.

No, Nate corrected himself. The car he really wanted to be driving right now was his green MG. With the top down, he'd have all the fresh air he needed. But he had no idea when that sleek sports car would finally move off the packed-dirt strip that passed for Vince Dowd's driveway. Vince kept discovering new problems, all too often necessitating hard-to-find parts. Mrs. Kagan, of course, had taken one look at that low-slung speedster and dubbed it the Deathtrap.

Nate chuckled at his automotive preferences: the Deathtrap and the Hearse.

His smile faded as he focused anew at the task at hand. He had tedious work to do at Madame Rose's: scraping the peeling paint off her porch floor. After that, he faced even more hours sanding. He wouldn't finish for days, perhaps weeks, if he couldn't work around his duties at Sol's Salvage. He just hoped that his hands wouldn't ache so much that he couldn't wield a pen or work a typewriter. At least the tedium factor would probably be alleviated by one of Rose's freshly baked treats. Maybe brownies or toll house cookies. Or pie. Ooh, he could really go for a slice of blueberry pie. And he could cool off with some freshly made lemonade.

He hoped she'd join him on the porch and spin more of her stories about Quebec. He wouldn't be able to take notes if his hands were occupied by a scraper. But he had already learned that he was hard-pressed to keep up with the notetaking, anyway, partly because he lacked any shorthand skills, and partly because the old woman rambled down this side path and that. Given the way his *zayde* spun stories, Nate believed Rose's meandering monologues were fairly typical of old people and not necessarily signs of cognitive problems. He suspected that after a certain age, the brain was so filled with interconnected memories that there was no linear way of sorting them out. Besides, some of the side paths were interesting.

Nate frowned at the realization that what *he* found most interesting was probably not what would best serve his honors thesis. Rose kept drifting back to Quebec and intimate family details irrelevant to a history paper on how immigrants adjusted to their new life in the United States. Nate had happily abetted those drifts. As he turned onto her street, he vowed that this time he would make a concerted effort to focus the old lady. He wanted to hear about her family's early experiences after moving to Quincy. What difficulties had the Quentins encountered mastering English? Did they suffer prejudice from neighbors? Had René Quentin found a job easily? Was he paid the same wage as his non-Quebecois co-workers? Were immigrant quarrymen paid the same as men born in this country? Were the Quentins accepted in their local church, then dominated by Irish-Americans? Was Rose's marriage to Francis Dowd, an Irish immigrant, considered scandalous? What cultural problems did the newlyweds have to overcome? Yes, from now on, Nate would approach his first-person research scientifically. Not like he was writing a novel.

Thirty minutes passed before Nate was set up to hear Rose's stories. First came idle chit-chat about the steamy weather, then came the task of laying out his tools, including broom and trash can for the debris. Then came the predicted baked goodies. Alas, they were raisin-oatmeal cookies, not pie. Rose kept returning to the kitchen to retrieve forgotten napkins, plates, and glasses of lemonade before she settled into the wicker chair on the porch.

Nate sat on the floor and began scraping with his right hand, while his left hand fed his mouth the occasional bite of cookie. Once he had the rhythm down, he asked, "So, what was the hardest thing for you to adjust to when you moved here to Quincy?"

"The weather. Too hot."

"Sure is today, anyway. Are summers that much hotter here than in Quebec?"

Rose nodded. "And winters are dirtier."

"Dirtier? How so?"

"Old Man Flint still visits plenty. But not so much snow here. In Quebec there's plenty. Covers up all the dirt. Here? Pah! So many cars and, when I'm first here, so many horses. Ugly gray piles of slush everywhere. Horse *merde,* too. And it smells, yeah?"

"I've heard you use that expression before: Old Man Flint. Is that the same as saying, 'Old Man Winter'?"

"I don't know this Old Man Winter. Flint is Indian. Kinda like Cain in The Holy Gospels."

"Huh?"

"That's what we call the Bible."

"An Indian Cain and Abel. This sounds interesting."

"You betcha. I never hear about this Flint and Sapling until I'm eight years old. The nuns, they never tell us nothing. They never tell us the Indian story of how the world gets born." Rose shook her head disapprovingly and took a sip of lemonade.

"Wait! Sapling? Creation story? What does this have to do with Old Man Winter … I mean, Old Man Flint?"

Rose chuckled and waggled her fingers at Nate. "You so impatient, you! I explain everything. I tell you the story just like Mére Agathe tells me. When I'm eight. When we go to see the ice bridge and…"

Nate raised his scraper in frustration. "Wait! Mère Agathe? That's the old Indian woman who brought you into the world? And what's this about an ice bridge?" He groaned in anticipation of how difficult it would be to remember all these details."

Rose tapped an index finger against her lips. "Shh, I tell it all. You listen. I talk, yeah?"

Nate sighed and nodded.

Our farm, it's in Lévis City. Not much of a city. Mostly just long skinny plots stretching south from the river. We're on the other side of the St. Lawrence from Quebec City. We don't get to Quebec much. Never enough time. Never enough money to buy stuff there.

But there's one thing I really want to see there. The ice bridge. Papa, he never has time to take me. But Mère Agathe, she takes me. She's half-Indian, not full blood. She's what they call Métis. I'm not much more than eight years old. So it's probably January. January 1890. Yup, Mère Agathe and me, we walk right over the river. On ice.

I squeal like our pigs when I see that ice bridge. So many people are crossing and just looking at what Mother Nature makes. Mother Nature and folks on both sides of the river. When it gets cold enough, the river, she freezes on top. Big chunks of ice. People in Quebec City and people in Lèvis City, they push them blocks together in one line. Bit by bit, they build a bridge of ice. Plenty thick. Plenty deep. Plenty strong. Strong enough to hold horses and sleighs and people.

I get mad because I can't see much ice with all them horses and sleighs and people in the way. I'm little, you know? So I slip my hand out of Mère Agathe's hand and run ahead. Oh, how she laughs. And then I get impatient waiting for her to catch up. I turn around and stomp my foot on the ice. I yell at her, "*Vite! Vite!* Quick! Quick" She don't hear what I say, but she sees big clouds come out of my mouth with each word.

She laughs again. "You puff like a choo-choo train."

"It's really true?" I ask as she gets close. "We really can walk across the river, all the way to Quebec City?"

Mère Agathe nods and smiles. But her smile, it don't last long. We hear this big groan. It's what they call ice heave. Downriver. I don't know what it means. But Mère Agathe knows. She knows that St. Lawrence, it's not dead. Water roars and bubbles beneath all that ice. No siree, that river's not dead. But we gonna be dead if we slide off that bridge.

The old woman pats her chest. "We need to turn back, little one. It's too far for me. And too cold. Old Man Flint, he tells me 'another day.'"

Well, this is the first time I hear that name. I don't want to turn back yet. But I wanna hear about this Flint fella. So I let her pull me back toward where we come from. I figure I can get her talking. "Who's Old Man Flint?" I ask.

"I never tell you this story?"

"You never tell me this story."

"Flint helped make the world. So the Iroquois say."

Now this surprises me. Why does she tell an Iroquois story? Where I grow up, no one ever has anything good to say about the Iroquois. Not white folks. Not Métis. Not Indians. So I ask, "I hear your people are Abenaki."

Mère Agathe spits. "Pah! Abenaki, Iroquois. All the same in the beginning,"

"Don't they hate each other?"

She's getting impatient. I can tell because she clicks her tongue. "That's another story. You want to hear about Old Man Flint or no?"

I do, but I'm mad she acts so cross. So I just shrug.

"Back before there were people like you and me," she says, tapping her knuckles against my chest, then her own, "there was Sky World. The people who lived there never suffered, but they never lived much, either. Although no one ever died in Sky World, no one was ever born."

"Then how they get there?" I'm a smart aleck already.

"They're just there. Always. From the beginning. But then something changed. One woman, she got pregnant. Her husband didn't like that so much. He didn't like Sky Woman changing, wanting to nest, worrying about the future. He didn't like his wife cooing to her belly."

"Jealous, huh?"

Mère Agathe nods. "So one day, he got so mad he ripped up the biggest damn tree in Sky World. When he did that he made a big hole. He was afraid of what he saw through that hole."

Now I'm getting interested and wonder what he sees.

"Sky Man saw another whole world below," she explains. "Our world. Except it was all roiling water. All ocean. No land. But Sky Woman, when she saw the hole, she got curious. She walked right up to it, knelt down, and peered at the waters far, far below. And what do you think her husband did?"

I shake my head.

That old Métis lady's a good storyteller, her. She makes a strong push with her palms. Out from her chest. Really fierce. "He pushed his wife through the hole! That's what he did."

I suck in air. Surprised. Shocked. I can't believe anyone would do that to a pregnant woman.

She nods. Real slow. Real serious. "You bet he did. But birds, flying between Sky World and our world, they saw her fall. So they took wing, just like that." She tries to snap her fingers, but they're hard to snap with woolen gloves on. "And they broke her fall, until Sky Woman could land safely on the back of a giant turtle."

Now this don't make much sense to me. Biggest turtle I ever see, one of them really old snappers, couldn't hold a falling pregnant lady. "The turtle don't get crushed?" I ask.

"This was a very, very big turtle. Larger than all Quebec. But a turtle shell isn't such a good place to live. So the other creatures, they dived down to the bottom of the sea and brought up mud. They covered the turtle's back with mud. The mud grew and grew, until it became all of Canada and all of America. So now Sky Woman had a place where she could live."

This makes me frown. "But what does she have to eat? What does she have to drink?" I ask.

"Well, remember, this was Sky Woman, from a magical place. She was smart enough to figure out how to live her new life. But first she needed to have her babies."

This is the first I hear of "babies." So I ask, "More than one?"

"*Oui.* Twin boys. Sky Woman knew there were two when they were still in her belly. And even before they were ready to come out, she named them Sapling and Flint."

Funny sounding names, no? Which is what I tell her.

"Maybe to you," she says, "but they fit the boys. Sapling was soft and gentle and kind. He would create animals to feed the new people of earth and to pull their plows. He would create plants for eating and plants for healing sickness. He would create rivers for fishing, drinking, and traveling.

"But that Flint was very different." She turns up her collar suddenly, like she gets a bad chill. "Flint was hard like granite, him. He created dangerous animals—animals that would kill and eat people. Flint created jagged cliffs." She points to the mountains, snow-covered, way off in the distance. The Appalachians.

"And then Flint created winter," she says, her voice all low. She shivers.

I shiver, too. I'm eight years old, yeah? I hear all sorts of scary stories by then. *Ma fois,* I tell scary stories to six-year old Izzy. Even to the little sisters. But there's something about the way Mère Agathe tells a story. Makes you sit up and listen. With big eyes.

"Couldn't their mother stop Flint from being so mean?" I ask.

"No. She died in childbirth. She delivered Sapling first, with no problem. But Flint was in such a rush to get born, he ripped himself out of his mother's left armpit!" She makes a claw with her hand and swooshes it down from her left shoulder to left hip.

I shudder. But then I think about it and screw up my face. "Wait!" I say. "How do Flint and Sapling manage without their mother?"

"Remember, they were magical. Right from birth, they could take care of themselves. Right from birth, they set about shaping the earth."

"They sound like Cain and Abel in the Holy Gospels. But Flint doesn't kill Sapling? They live together even though they're so different?" I'm a curious kid, me.

"The world needs both of them. It isn't all flowers and sunshine, you know. The flowers won't grow without rain. Stormy winds send seed pods to new places to put down roots. Fires burn out plants and animals, but clear spots where new things can grow. And the rocks of the mountains and the water of the rivers, they need each other, too."

This confuses me.

Mère Agathe puts her hands on my shoulders and turns me toward the frozen river. "You think the St. Lawrence would exist without those rocks over there sending rain water down their slopes? Over there, the Laurentian foothills." Then she spins me in the opposite direction, toward the Appalachians. "Or those rocks over there?"

I'm getting dizzy, me. But what she says makes some sense. Except I can't figure out how the mountains need the river. So I ask her to explain.

"There wouldn't be any life on those rocks without water, now would there? The river mist turns into clouds that rain on the mountains. And over time, all those raindrops wear down those ancient hills, so they're not too hard to climb, not too hard to mine the iron and granite and gold inside."

With her fingers, she drums the stocking cap on my head. Over and over, just like years and years of raindrops. "Ow!" I yelp.

"Like I say. Even your head, hard as rock, would get all soft and mushy if it spent enough time out in the rain. Think what would happen when the water froze inside your ears and eyes and nose. Why, your skull would crack open like a melon." She makes like she's gonna chop my head open like a melon.

Even though it's a good story, I'm not sure I believe all this. I guess I my face shows what I'm thinking, because she asks, "What? You don't like my tale?"

"I think maybe you make up the scary parts."

"Maybe so, maybe no. But stories, especially ones with scary parts, help us make sense of this life. You'll find out. One day, you'll make up your own story. Maybe you'll decide it's more true than anything those big eyes can see right in front of you."

She gets me thinking. As we trudge through the snow, back to Lévis City, I sneak looks at her now and then, from the corner of my eye. I wonder about her story. Not the one she tells about Sky World, Flint, and Sapling. I wonder about her *own* story. I look at her, all wrinkled and old, but tough and hard, too. She's just like Flint, I think. I care about Mère Agathe, but she's scary like a witch sometimes. I don't want to be like her, I think. I want to be like Sapling.

Except then I realize this old lady, she's not born old. Years ago, she's young, soft, and willowy. Just like Sapling. If it can happen to her, it can happen to me. How awful to be hard and flinty!

But then I remember something Papa says. He's just back from a long, long

72

trip. Down the Saguenay River. He doesn't talk much about the water. He talks about the granite cliffs towering over the river. Hard and rugged, you know? He can't stop talking about them cliffs. Using big, fancy words. He calls them "*puissant, majestueux, magnifique.*" Powerful, majestic, magnificent. I think how wonderful to be described that way.

As we get near the farm, I ask Mère Agathe, "Which one of those two brothers do you like best? Which one should I try to be like?"

"Why ask me?" she says. "That's your story to tell. And who knows? Maybe you'll have many different stories before you're done." She raps on my head with her fist. I think she's showing affection, but you never know with her. Then she says, "You have a long life ahead, little one, much longer than you can imagine."

ELEVEN

Taking Stock

Nate stared at the bent, hole-filled strip of metal in his grease-stained hand. "What in God's name are you?" he groaned. Once again he flipped through the grimy pages of the auto repair manual his father had long ago liberated from a local trade school. He desperately wanted to avoid bothering his grandfather yet again to identify one of the parts he was supposed to inventory. Did other junkyards take comprehensive inventories of their stock? He was wrestling with chaos, because most of the stock lay in rusting heaps scattered throughout the acre that was Sol's Salvage yard. His father insisted this task was essential, to keep the "tax man off my back." Nate suspected it was busy work for a clubfooted college boy who lacked the physicality or expertise to strip down the cars that entered the yard. Nate felt like he wasn't contributing much to the family business, the business that fed all of them, clothed them, and sheltered them. Truth be told, he didn't seem to be making much of a contribution anywhere, at a time when the world badly needed young men like him to roll up their sleeves and set right everything that had gone so terribly wrong.

Still staring dejectedly at the mystery part, he limped into the junk-yard office. He didn't raise his head until he reached the service counter, on the other side of which stood Vince Dowd, eyebrows raised in amusement.

"What's got you so grumpy?" Vince asked.

Nate thrust the mystery part across the counter.

"What'd this poor gasket ever do to you?"

"It's a gasket? Looks more some giant bottle opener. What kind of gasket?"

Vince took the part from the younger man. "Looks like it's for an exhaust manifold. Probably for an old Ford pickup. But I could be wrong. I don't work on many trucks."

"Close enough," said Nate, making a note on his clipboard. "You're a lifesafer. I really don't know what I'm doing. Or how one's supposed to take inventory in a junkyard in the first place."

"Junkyards take inventory?"

"What do I know?" Nate splayed out both palms. "I'm just the hired help. Can I ring that up for you?" he added, pointing to the clunky universal joint sitting on the counter.

"Yup. By the way, I've got a line on an ornamental radiator cap for your MG, if you want to spend the money. Or you can stick with an ordinary, cheap cap to replace the cracked original."

"Let's go with the cheap version."

"You're the boss." Vince handed over the cash for his purchase. "How's the porch job going at Ma's? If you need another hand at sanding, I can probably put in a couple of hours next Sunday afternoon. If you're free then, that is."

"Sure. Madame Rose was really chatty last week. Had some interesting stories. Did you know the St. Lawrence freezes in winter, enough for people to cross it?"

"No kidding? I've never been up there in winter. Brrr, autumn is bad enough." As he slid his change into his pants pocket, Vince asked, as casually as he could manage, "So, how did Ma seem to you last week?"

"She sure has no memory problems when it comes to the old days. The only thing I noticed was the number of times she traipsed back to the kitchen. She made some goodies for us to eat and kept forgetting to bring stuff out from the kitchen. Napkins, plates, things like that. Not sure that's any sign of a failing mind, though."

75

"I suppose not. Hell, when I'm doing any job, I never seem to assemble all the tools I need without multiple trips. How was her mood?"

"She seemed chipper, like she enjoys our time together, having an eager audience for her stories. Wasn't always that way. That first day I showed up, she was cool, distant."

"That doesn't sound like Ma. You have any idea what was going on."

"Maybe she resented me intruding into her space? Maybe she figured out you're keeping tabs on her through me?"

Vince scratched his head. "Well, if that's the case, she can't be all that feeble-minded."

"You've got a point. But there was something else going on, too. I don't think it had to do with me. Something about her sister. Izzy? She acted like she was afraid of her."

"Afraid? There's been some tension between the two of them for years. Izzy and she were real close for most of my childhood. They got together often. Izzy came over our house whenever she could get time away from her job. Most holidays, Izzy was at the table. But then the time between visits got longer and longer. I remember being curious but never thought to ask what was up. And Ma never said. They weren't completely on the outs, would be polite to each other at the odd family gathering. But Ma acted kinda like you said: cold, distant. But certainly not afraid. Izzy's her little sister, for Pete's sake!"

Nate shrugged. "I got the impression Izzy was coming for a visit soon. And your mother's dreading it."

"Huh. That's news to me. I don't know why Ma would be afraid of a visit. And I don't know why Izzy suddenly *wants* to visit. It's probably been a couple of years since she put in an appearance at the old house."

"Hey, what do I know? I'm just piecing impressions together, with no real facts to back them up. For all I know, Madame Rose was feeling weighed down by something else entirely. One look at the newspaper these days would weigh anyone down."

"You can say that again."

The conversation flagged uncomfortably, but Vince made no move to haul his purchase back to his car. He just stood at the counter, head down, right hand idly tapping the universal joint. "Got some news today," he said at last, eyes focused on the counter.

Nate inadvertently shivered. Even though the older man's

76

expression was unreadable, his easy-going demeanor had suddenly changed dramatically. Nate leaned forward slightly. And waited.

"Yeah. My brother Hank has a buddy on the draft board, and ... "

"Aw, gee, Vince."

Vince nodded and finally looked up. "Hank found out I'm classified One-A. Looks like they're starting to take the old farts like me now. Hank's pal said I'll probably get called up before summer is out, before Netty enters the third grade."

"Aw, gee. How do you...? I mean, what about...?" Nate stammered in a clumsy effort to craft an appropriate response.

Vince finished the younger man's first question. "How do I feel about it? I honestly don't know. If it were just me, I'd be okay with it. Shit, I'd seriously consider enlisting, in hope of getting into an outfit where I could fix stuff. Jeeps, tanks, whatever. I'd be good at that. But what the hell, anyone can fire a gun, and I figure I'm strong enough to go toe to toe with some other poor slob wearing the wrong uniform."

"But it *isn't* just you," Nate said softly.

Vince shook his head slowly. "Nope. Of course, plenty of guys with wives and a whole passel of kids are going off to war. And somehow the families make do. But Nora ... I just don't know how I'm gonna tell her,"

"I wish I could go in your place, Vince."

Vince smiled. "You're a good kid, Nate. But someday you may be glad that foot of yours kept you out of this craziness." Grinning, he added, "Besides, I know how much you're looking forward to law school. You wouldn't want to miss out on that, now would you?"

Nate snorted. "Very funny."

TWELVE

A Blue Summer Day

It was a good summer day. Sunny, but not hot or muggy. Not like the summer weather in Quebec, but Rose wasn't sweating much, not even after weeding her victory garden. Calling her green beans, tomatoes, and cucumbers a victory garden made her feel patriotic, American, even though the three rectangles would have been sprouting vegetables whether or not her adopted country was at war. The tomatoes were only starting to come in, but the green beans were abundant, so she thought she'd share them with her daughter-in-law. Because it was a good day, Rose knew where her car keys were and decided to use up a bit of her gas ration to visit for a spell. But first, she would call Nora. Although some people enjoyed unexpected guests, Nora was uncomfortable with any kind of surprise. So Rose waited until her party line was free and dialed the number. Because it was a good day, Rose remembered more than the "Granite 2" prefix. She didn't need her phone directory.

"*Allô*, Nora! You could use some green beans? I got lots to spare."

"Oh. Rose? Green beans? I guess so."

"It's okay I come over now?"

"You want to come to the house?"

"I figure I go there instead of you come here, since you need to save gas. Me, it don't matter so much, yeah?"

"All right. I guess. So you'll be coming in, what, a half hour or so?"

"Maybe sooner, *ma cocotte*."

Rose was not overly sensitive about the lukewarm reception she often received from the younger generation. She realized that an old woman with little money, zero social standing, and a tendency (even on her good days) to tell stories she had spun many times before could prove tedious, but Nora was generally receptive, probably because she enjoyed a bit of mothering, something in short supply from her own standoffish parent. Ah, but that's the Irish, Rose would remind herself before judging Louisa Gavin.

It never occurred to her that Nora might not want to see her, so the younger woman's reaction to the phone call was somewhat perplexing. Prone to mood swings, Nora often sounded tense or anxious over the phone. But this disconnectedness was new.

When Rose arrived at the tiny brown clapboard house, she could hear music even before she shut off the engine. She didn't know the tune, but she knew the singer. It was that colored woman who always sounded so sad. Sad and a little drunk. That Billie Somebody. Billie really had the blues today.

Rose grabbed her basket of beans and called out "Allô!" as she hiked up the concrete steps. No response. She rapped on the screen door. Only Billie responded, with a peal of sorrow. The door was unlocked, so Rose stepped inside. The shades were all drawn, and despite the lovely weather the windows were shut. The little lamp on the living room radiator cover was turned on, but its 40-watt bulb barely penetrated the gloom, colored gray from cigarette smoke. Rose followed the haze, which thickened in the kitchen. There as well, the shades were drawn against the afternoon sun. Sitting at the small oak table was Nora, her back to the living room entrance, her eyes focused on the ice box. The table was cluttered with magazines, newspapers, dirty dishes, trivets, dish towels, an overflowing ashtray, a half-empty packet of Pall Malls, and a Diamond matchbox with scratched-up friction strips.

Nora didn't seem to hear her guest enter, perhaps because that Billie's wailing reached a crescendo at that moment. Rose pulled up a chair. Still no response from her hostess. For lack of any room on the

79

tabletop, Rose settled the basket of beans on her lap and waited.

Finally, Nora turned, a small smile on her face, and removed the long cigarette bobbling between her slightly parted lips. "I think beans taste best with butter, don't you?"

"Butter's good. Salt, too."

"Mm." Nora took a puff from the long cigarette then crushed it into the ashtray and immediately extracted a replacement. She pulled out a Lucifer, struck it, and stared at it a few seconds before lighting up. "I've never cared for margarine. Tastes funny. Butter's best. But it's so hard to get these days. The war. Always the war."

"Where's Net ... Antoinette?" Rose asked abruptly.

"Outside."

"I don't see her when I come in. She playing in some kid's yard?"

"I guess so."

Knowing that Netty's frequent illnesses complicated her ties with other neighborhood girls, Rose stood up, nearly overturning her basket to peer out the kitchen window, facing into the backyard. She exhaled relief when she saw the little blonde head bent over an assortment of dolls and stuffed animals, with whom Netty was having an animated, if one-sided conversation.

"Okay I lower the phonograph? That sad lady singer makes it hard for me to hear you."

Receiving no response, Rose returned to the living room and turned the record player's volume knob counterclockwise. When she re-entered the kitchen, tears were rolling down Nora's face.

"*Ma petite!* What makes you so sad?"

Rose fished into her skirt pocket and pulled out a large handkerchief, with which she blotted her daughter-in-law's face. Nora didn't react at first then registered surprise. She raised a hand to her cheek to investigate. "I'm crying?"

"You're crying. You know why?" Rose stopped blotting and peered into the younger woman's eyes.

Nora laughed mirthlessly. "Life," she said. "It's just ridiculous sometimes."

"How so?"

"Do you know about Vince?"

"What about Vincent?"

"He's One-A."

80

"Is that bad?"

Nora nodded grimly. "It means the draft board has classified him at the top of the list. Even at his age. He could be called up for military service any day. He could be half a world away in a few months. He could be dead in a few months!"

Rose shook her head. She had never focused on what immediate effect the newly launched war against Hitler and Hirohito might have for her nearest and dearest. She'd already seen one son troop off to France in the Great War. Mercifully, the armistice was signed just a few weeks later. It was hard to fathom that the same generation would be asked to fight yet again, no matter how just the cause.

"No, Vincent is strong. He's gonna be all right." Vincent was indeed strong and resourceful. But Rose wasn't sure those attributes would be enough. Her childhood on the farm had exposed her to many lessons about the randomness of fate. The best-tended crops sometimes failed. The most robust pigs sometimes died.

"But *I* won't be all right," Nora continued. "How will I keep a roof over my head?" she waved her hand toward the cracked plaster in the ceiling. "We're barely paying the mortgage now. And how could I possibly take care of this place without Vince? And who will be around to take care of me? Of Antoinette and me?"

Nora seemed to shrink into her chair, to childish proportions. Rose clasped the softly weeping woman's shoulder. The grip was half-hearted, just as Rose's grip on her current reality grew suddenly weak. She was transported to her own grief, decades earlier when she was half Nora's current age, when she, too, worried how she would keep a roof over her head and food in her belly.

"I have Izzy, at least," she said abruptly.

Nora looked up from her handkerchief. "What?"

"Izzy and me, we figure it out. You will, too." The old woman's voice suddenly sounded not just distant, but hard, flinty.

THIRTEEN

War Talk

Netty Dowd morosely eyed her mother bustling about the kitchen. Netty's job was to pare the apples Nora planned to put in a pie. Nora rarely cooked anything from scratch, but today was an exception. "Don't sit under the apple tree, with anyone else but me," she sang, at the top of her voice. She pirouetted and poked an index finger into her daughter's shoulder three times, to punctuate the song's next line, "No, no, no!" Netty jerked away from the intruding finger.

"Why so gloomy, Gus?" she teased her daughter. "I thought wienie roasts were your most favorite thing in the whole world."

"Summer's over and I didn't get to do half the things I wanted to do. And now that school's starting, there won't be time to go swimming or pick berries or finally see the quarries."

"I thought you were looking forward to third grade," Nora asked as she stopped rolling out dough and turned her attention to a package of Armour hot dogs.

"I was," Netty said, twisting the stem off one McIntosh. "But I just found out Annie Donahue is moving. She and her mother are gonna go live with her grandmother in Weymouth. Annie's my only friend. I don't think any of the other kids like me."

"Why wouldn't they like you, Antoinette? Here, let me have the paring knife a minute, will ya? I can't break through this stupid cellophane with my fingernails."

When Netty complied, Nora plunged the knife into the package with gusto. "Ah, finally," she said, shredding the torn wrapper.

A dozen frankfurters tumbled onto the kitchen's worn linoleum. Netty braced for a litany of curses. Instead, her mother bubbled forth with high-pitched giggles.

"Oh, look at all the fallen soldiers!" Nora laughed, stooping to retrieve the hot dogs.

Netty gasped. "You're gonna eat 'em? You told me never, ever eat anything that's been on the floor."

"It'll be our little secret," Nora said, bouncing the tip of one frankfurter on her daughter's head.

Once again, Netty flinched. Oblivious to the reaction, Nora dashed to the icebox, her hands struggling to hang on to the retrieved wieners. Abruptly dumping them onto the adjacent drainboard, she jerked open the icebox door and peered inside. "I hope we have enough piccalilli," she murmured. "You can't have a wienie roast without mustard and piccalilli, now can you?" Pulling out the jar she sought, she waggled it toward Netty and asked, "Think this will be enough for the gang?"

Netty shrugged. "How many are coming?"

Nora giggled again. "You know, I'm not really sure. Oh well, it doesn't matter. We've got plenty of beer. At least I think we do. Well, Vince can always go out and get more."

"On Labor Day?" Netty asked. Even at her tender age, she had accompanied her father on enough excursions to package stores to know they were never open on holidays. More than a few times, her father had grumbled about the "stupid blue laws," which were apparently as vexing as stupid in-laws, like Uncle Hank's wife Gert.

Her mother didn't respond. She had resumed rolling out the pie dough, with flour flying into a sunbeam.

"Do you remember your Great-Aunt Izzy? Nana Rose just told me she's visiting for a couple of days. Rose never even invited her. She just announced she wanted to visit. For the first time in quite a while. Isn't that strange? So your nana will be bringing your great-aunt to our

83

Labor Day wienie roast." Nora clicked her tongue disapprovingly.

As Netty squinched her eyes in an effort to associate a face with the name, her mother continued. "She'll probably put the kibosh on the whole party. Old sourpuss. She's been threatening to visit your Nana Rose all summer and finally made good on the threat. I can't very well invite Rose without inviting her houseguest, now can I?"

"Is Izzy the one with the glasses?"

"Glasses and a nose that could cut steak."

"Huh? How can a nose...?"

"Take my word for it. Izzy's nose is a lethal weapon."

"And she's Nana's sister?"

Nora nodded.

"They don't look anything like each other."

"Nope. And they don't act anything like each other, either."

"Was someone casting aspersions about the size of my nose?" chuckled Vince, as he opened the door connecting kitchen and cellar.

"Not *your* nose, your aunt's."

"Same difference. I got my noble schnoz from Izzy."

"It looks fine on a man. It's hideous on a woman's face."

"Yeah, yeah. Wanna give me a hand here, Net ... Antoinette?" Vince groaned as he nearly dropped one of the brown bottles in his arms.

Netty jumped to the rescue. In her effort to retrieve two of the bottles, she nearly dropped them herself. "Oops. You said the root beer wouldn't be ready for another day, Daddy."

"That was before this spell of hot weather. Even down cellar it's pretty close. So that will make the yeast work faster. We'll see if two days of curing are enough."

After finding a space for her bottles on the crowded kitchen table, Netty clapped her hands and said, "Let's open one now and see."

Her father shook his head as he scanned the inside of the icebox for a place to nestle his bottles.

"Please, Daddy? Just one?"

"In a bit. It won't taste very good warm."

"Don't you dare open a warm bottle of root beer in this kitchen," warned Nora. "It might explode and make a mess. I'm having enough trouble getting this pie dough right. I don't need it drenched with sweet fizzy stuff."

"Want me to give you a hand?" Vince asked. "It looks like you got a couple of projects going at once there."

"I can handle things just fine, thank you very much."

Vince and Netty exchanged concerned looks, as they gauged whether Nora's words presaged an eruption of anger or hurt feelings. But she quickly added, "Besides I feel like I can handle just about anything now that I know you'll be sticking around home for the duration of this stupid war. Now shoo! Leave me room to work here. Go get the fire started, Vince. Antoinette, throw the paper plates, napkins, and hot dog rolls in that paper bag and take them outside. Take the big bag of marshmallows, too."

Once outside, Netty distributed her cargo on the picnic table, while her father tossed an armful of kindling into the outdoor stone-and-concrete fireplace he had built years earlier. "Seems like we should wait till the company arrives," he grumbled. "If your mother is still rolling out pie dough, it must be a while before anyone is due to show up."

"Mummy said they'll be coming any minute," Netty corrected himself-importantly.

Vince shrugged and peeled off a double page of the Sunday Globe to roll into a torch. He paused briefly to scan the headlines. "Nice to have some good news from the war for a change. Looks like the Japs may be wishing they hadn't taken on Uncle Sam." Turning to Netty, he added, "We've got a lot to celebrate this Labor Day, kiddo."

"Is that why Mummy's so happy?"

Vince just smiled.

"Because you're not gonna go away and fight Jamps?"

"Because I'm not gonna go away and fight Jamps."

War talk dominated most of the conversations that afternoon and evening. In his backyard, Vince and his brothers dissected all the details they had read in the papers about the previous month's invasion of Guadalcanal. Over and over again, they reminded one another that the United States was finally on the offensive in the Pacific, that the Allies had just denied Japan the ability to threaten Australia and its vital support and resupply function. Emperor Hirohito, they predicted, was about to pay a heavy price for Pearl Harbor. Repeatedly, the men speculated whether the one-two punch of the Guadalcanal campaign and earlier events in Midway would bring the Pacific war to an early conclusion. Vince reminded his brothers that those two victories had not come without major losses. Joining the conversation, Nate Kagan brought up one of the worst developments of recent weeks, the battle of Savo Island. He asked the men if they knew anyone who had worked on or served on the *USS Quincy*, one of four heavy cruisers lost in that naval defeat. While Vince shook his head, Hank ranted about the annoying way radio reports were mangling the name of the ill-starred cruiser.

"If I hear that New York announcer say 'Quin-SEE' one more time, I'm gonna unload my service revolver into the radio. Chrissake, the boat was named for the city that built it."

Quincy residents—who sported a large chip on their shoulder from living in the shadow of more cultured, more affluent, more respected Boston, just across the Neponset River —had long griped about the perennial mispronunciation of their hometown's name. "Everyone knows it's 'Quin-ZEE,' not 'Quin-SEE,'" Dave complained.

"It gets my goat even more because that poor tub was made right here, right in Fore River," added Hank. "Right where our baby brother starts work in another week." He slapped Vince on the back.

"You got the okay from the shipyard?" Nate asked, turning to Vince.

"Yup. I start a week from today."

"And he's already been switched from One-A to Two-B," added Dave.

"That's the draft deferment for war industry workers?"

Vince nodded.

"So when do *you* sign up, kid?" Hank asked Nate.

"I tried. They won't take me, because of…" The young man pointed toward the ground.

Hank snorted derisively and was about to press the issue when Vince tugged on the college student's elbow and said, "Gotta haul more beers from the cellar. Gimme a hand, Nate."

As they hiked up the slope to the house, Vince said, "Don't let my brothers get on your nerves. It's not like any of them will be heading off to the recruitment office, the old farts. Even if they weren't beyond draft age, you can bet they'd lay claim to the deferment as cops. And if they didn't, their wives would make their lives a living hell."

"I bet Mrs. Dowd's relieved you got the shipyard job. And the deferment."

"That she is, Nate. That she is."

Even before the two men entered the kitchen, they could hear raucous laughter from Mrs. Dowd and her partners in conversation; daughter Netty, sister-in-law Gert, and Mrs. Riley from across the cobblestone street.

"I know! That man is so embarrassing!" Nora was exclaiming, contorting her face into an exaggerated, winking leer.

"You look just like him!" Mrs. Riley laughed.

"Imagine," Nora continued. "Not having to put up with Jimmy the Ice Man and his dirty jokes! And actually being able to keep a tub of ice cream for more than a day."

"Yay! More ice cream for me!" shouted Netty.

"What's happening with Jimmy the Ice Man?" Vince asked.

"Nora's giving him the heave-ho once you guys get a real refrigerator. With all the new bucks you'll be raking in from Fore River," Gert explained. "Glad to hear you're finally getting yourself a decent job, Vinnie."

Vince rolled his eyes and beckoned Nate to follow him down the cellar stairs. When they returned, each carrying a bucket filled with ice and beer bottles, the laughter had ebbed.

"We're in the kitchen!" Nora shouted, while squinting her eyes, pursing her lips disapprovingly, and dramatically arcing an index finger from bridge to tip of nose. Her cohorts suppressed giggles as a pie-carrying Netty skipped in from the living room, with Rose Dowd and her sister following a few steps behind.

"Sorry we're late. Damn pies take longer to cook than I figure," said Rose, scooting some empty beer bottles and dirty dishes aside to clear space for the pies she and Netty carried.

"Damn pies always take longer to cook when the oven's not on," clarified Izzy, pursing her lips disapprovingly.

"No matter. We're still serving up hot dogs and haven't started on dessert yet," said Nora, smiling at her mother-in-law. The smiled faded slightly as she turned to her other guest. "Good to see you, Izzy. It's probably been a whole year, right?"

"Two years and three months," Izzy corrected.

Gert giggled again. "Hi, Rose," she said in a girlish tone as she waggled her fingers in greeting. "Aunt Izzy," she added, one lugubrious pitch lower.

"Gert? Hank's wife, eh? Put on a few pounds, I see."

As his sister-in-law's face reddened, Vince balanced his bucket on the top of a chair and offered, "Hey, you girls look like you could use a drink. Help yourselves." He aimed his chin at the beer.

Rose pulled out a bottle. Izzy pushed her glasses into the bridge of her nose, sniffed, and raised an eyebrow. "You have a real drink, *mon cher?*"

Vince laughed, angling his head toward the window. "Whiskey and gin are on the picnic table. In the back yard. Once we dump our loads, we'll play bartender. Follow me, ladies."

Izzy, Mrs. Riley, and Netty followed the two men. Rose hung back.

"So how's it going with your houseguest?" Nora asked, grinning wickedly.

"Eh, *comme ci, comme ça.* We catch up some. Tell old stories. Maybe we don't kill each other."

"So how long's she staying?"

"Not sure."

"Doesn't she have to get back to her job?"

Rose shrugged and took a slow pull on her beer.

"Please tell me she still has her job."

The older woman shrugged again.

"If she loses her job, she won't have any place to live. Oh no!" Nora thudded a palm across her chest. "Is that the reason for this long-anticipated visit? She's wants to talk you into letting her live with you? Oh Rose!"

"She don't say. But that family she takes care of? Something wrong there."

Gert interjected, "I thought the little rug rats she took care of would be about ready to march off to war themselves."

"Oh, she's been raising the next generation for a while now," Nora explained.

"You don't know none of this?" Rose asked.

"What do you mean?"

"I thought maybe you and Vince set up this whole visit. So Izzy keeps an eye on me. Then I have two babysitters."

"You mean Nate? That's just to help with all the stuff needs fixing around the old homestead. Besides, it seems like you and he are getting along pretty good."

"He's a good boy, him. The Ragman's grandson." Rose nudged an elbow into Gert's side. "You know about the Ragman? Him and that old beat-up horse, years ago, they come by our house—what?—every month. I give the poor horse carrots. I give the little crippled boy sweets. He's such a good…"

"Did you hear Roosevelt's address?" Gert interrupted, turning to her hostess. "Not one word about the war," she added disapprovingly. "All that talk about economics, cutting inflation. Boring."

"Well, it was a Labor Day speech, after all," Nora said.

"He better not be thinking about cutting Hank's wages is all I can say. Things are tough enough as it is."

"Could be a lot tougher," Rose murmured. "Like in France, other places. Nate, he has some folks still in the old country. No one hears from them. Maybe that Stalin puts them in prison. Maybe that Hitler, he kills them. One of the boys Izzy raises? He's in some hospital way over on the other side of the world, with all them palm trees. Wounded in his first battle. May never walk again. So many young boys like that. So many not coming home. Ever."

Nora slumped into one of the kitchen chairs, a dull expression on her face.

"Ah, me and my mouth," Rose said, patting the younger woman's thin shoulders. "I make *ma cocotte* sad. But for no reason, eh? Your Vincent, he's safe. He has the deferment, no?"

FOURTEEN

Just Like Old Times

Even though it was the second week of September, the temperature was well into the eighties, and the humidity was worthy of late July. Nevertheless, Rose was in her garden. Tired of weeding, she focused on the less taxing job of tying off the unwieldy tomatoes vines. She couldn't resist harvesting nearly a dozen, even if the prospect of canning them was unappetizing in this heat.

"Hey, Izzy!" she called toward the porch, "You could maybe eat a salad for supper? Got lotta tomatoes and one cucumber still. Or maybe an omelet with tomatoes and onions inside, yeah?"

Silence. Rose straightened her back and shaded her eyes to get a better view of the porch, backlit in the late afternoon sun. From this distance she couldn't see her sister's face but could make out the thin woman's panted legs folded tailor-style in the wide Adirondack chair. "I get my legs twisted like that, I never get out of that chair," Rose muttered.

Cradling the tomato-filled basket over her left hip, she trudged toward the house. When she reached the top step, she noticed a book butterflied on the floor. "Hey, Izzy, you drop your..." Rose called then slapped a palm over her mouth. Her sister's head lolled against the chair back. The mouth was open, revealing a few gaps where lower teeth should be, plus an assortment of silver fillings. A speckle of spit whitened one corners of the lower lip. Rose craned her head toward the chair to listen for sounds of life.

You never know at this age. Ah, breathing.

Rose settled onto the top step, her back against the railing, and eyed her younger sister. She took in the blue bulges at the ankles, the accordion pleats on the forearms, the wattles even on that skinny neck, the thick glasses whitening the closed eyelids.

When you get so old, ma soeur?

You should talk, old woman. You look in the mirror lately, eh? Izzy still got dark hair on her head. You're all gray or white, you.

Reaching for the dropped book, Rose examined the title. "How Green Was My Valley," she whispered.

A cough interrupted her attempt to decipher the flyleaf synopsis.

"You need longer arms, sister," croaked Izzy, pushing her glasses against the bridge of her nose.

"I wake you, eh? Sorry."

"I was just resting my eyes."

"Pah, and I was just jumping jacks."

"That makes utterly no sense," Izzy chided.

Rose shrugged.

Even when she sleeps, she don't miss a trick, that Izzy. She watches everything you do, old woman. She hears everything you say. And she tells you everything you do wrong. Everything your loved ones do wrong. Just like old times.

Clearing her throat, Izzy continued, "You should read the book. It will recall our charming childhood. Just like Lévis City, the hero's hometown is a wasteland. Everyone he knew is gone. Dead or moved away. The town is a shell of its former self. Just like the soil on our old farm."

"Why you want to read a book like that?"

"Why wouldn't you? It's useful to reflect on the past, if only to learn lessons, avoid future mistakes."

"Not so much future left, yeah?"

"Maybe not, but I'll be damned if I give up the ghost now." As if to underscore her message, Izzy abruptly unfolded her legs, leaned forward with surprising agility, and snatched the book from her sister's hands. Within seconds she refolded her legs, positioned the book about six inches from her face, and appeared lost in its message, as if she were all alone on the porch.

Offended by the abrupt termination of their conversation, Rose looked around for more rewarding companionship. Jolie obliged by rounding the corner of the house just then, a mouse tail dangling rakishly from her pendulous flews.

"Ack, Jolly! Mouse guts not a good snack. Give you worms."

Rose clamped her left hand over the dog's snout, then pointed it downward as she tugged gently on the thin rodent tail with her other hand. Jolie turned mournful eyes upward, sighed, and released her squeaking trophy. Rose walked to the edge of the yard and tossed the mouse into the brush. When Jolie braced for pursuit, her mistress raised an index finger to her nose and scowled. The massive mutt slumped, dejected, into a down-stay. Rose laughed. "You a good boy, you."

"You'll confuse that beast if you keep telling her she's a boy," Izzy called over the top of her book. "You never should have given her a name so close to your old dog's."

"Yeah, I do something else wrong," Rose grumbled as she and her furry companion approached the porch.

"What is this *penchant* you have for black pets?" Izzy continued, pronouncing the word the French way. "There was that ridiculous crow you trained back on the farm. 'Noir,' wasn't it? Could you have been less original?"

Ignoring the jibe, Rose smiled at ancient memories. "She was smart, that one."

"I always wondered how you knew it was a she." Izzy laid her book face down on her crossed ankles.

Rose shrugged. "The way she acts. I just know she's a girl raven. A raven, not a crow. Don't you remember? That Noir, she's special. A real talker, her."

"Oh, that's right. Ravens make all those odd sounds."

Rose savored the victory of successfully correcting her know-it-all

92

sister.

"You really did a pretty decent job training her," Izzy added.

Rose's smile broadened. "I get help from Mère Agathe. Not much she don't know about animals."

"That old woman scared the wits out of me. I never could understand why you liked being around her."

"Not so hard to understand. She pays attention to me. Who else does that?"

Izzy nodded slowly. "Mama was always so frazzled. Either that or too sad. And Papa? He never liked anyone, did he?"

Rose stroked Jolie's massive head thoughtfully. "I always think he likes you best. Because you look like him."

"Didn't make him any more inclined to take me with him when they pulled up stakes all over again to move back to Canada."

"No," Rose replied shaking her head sadly. "And you even younger than me. Just fifteen, no?"

"You know very well how old I was. But what's the point of hashing things over. Water under the bridge."

"You the one bring up that water, eh?" Rose chided.

"Well, I shouldn't have. What's done is done. What's the point?"

"So much for—how you say?—reflecting on the past. You ever wonder how things go if we move to Manitoba with everybody else?"

"You and I would probably be dead from working our fingers to the bone. And you would never have met that oaf Francis and had your brood. And I…" Izzy stopped abruptly.

Rose angled her head quizzically. "You would be some kind of teacher anyway, eh? Nanny or something. You like telling people all the stuff you learn in books."

"I was a governess, not a nanny."

"Was?"

Izzy hitched up her shoulders, paused, and explained, "I didn't lie, you know. I really am taking a vacation. The Winthrops owe me two weeks. That's why I'm here, with you. Well, that's part of the reason. The other is…" Izzy rubbed her hands together fretfully.

Rose just waited, petting Jolie's soft head.

"The other reason," she continued, "is that I need time to collect my thoughts before I go back. When I go back, you see … when I go

93

back, I'll have to start clearing my things out of the brownstone. Now that the youngest Winthrop is off to college, my services are no longer required, it seems."

"What about the little ones, the grandchildren? They still need you, yeah?"

"They *do* need me, given that flibbertigibbet mother of theirs. *Sac-cajé chien!*"

Her eyes wide, Rose erupted in laughter and slapped her thigh. "That word!" she choked.

"Flibbertigibbet?" Izzy asked, arching one brow in offense. "It means a person who…"

"Not *that* word," Rose said, "the French one. You hate when I say it. I never think I hear it from your lips. Not since you and me little ones."

"Well, sometimes that hideous linguistic corruption has its place," Izzy groused.

"So what you gonna do?"

"The flibbertigibbet is going on vacation later this month and needs me to 'babysit.' That's the word she used, like I'm some schoolgirl who looks after some poor abandoned child in the late afternoon. That's what they think of me, after all these years? A baby sitter?"

"So what happens when the mother, the flibber one, when she comes back home?"

"I'm out. For good."

Izzy's eyes held her sister's face hard, in search of a reaction. The stare was so fierce Rose needed to avert her eyes. She focused on the bump she felt in Jolie's left ear. "Ah, nasty tick, *ma cocotte*," she whispered, probing the thick fur with an index finger.

As Rose struggled to get a grip on the bloodsucker, her sister raised both palms in exasperation. "Did you hear me?" Izzy demanded.

Rose nodded, reaching for the kitchen shears sticking out of the basket of tomatoes. With sure hands, she scissored the extracted tick in half. Only then did she return her glance to her sister. "So you're not here to spy on me?"

"Spy on you? Why on earth would I? What could you possibly be up to that would merit spying? Unless you've offered your services to Herr Hitler, perhaps? Maybe he needs someone to remove ticks from that German shepherd dog of his."

Rose knew there was an insult buried somewhere in that response but didn't have the energy to analyze it. "Vincent," she replied. "Worries about me. Thinks maybe my mind goes off the tracks."

"When has it ever been *on* the tracks?"

"So, how come you call me to say you want to stay here for your vacation, almost right after Vincent brings the Ragman's boy to snoop around? You never visit me no more, except for weddings or funerals. So I figure must be some other reason than vacation."

"Well, it's not like I would be sure of a welcome, is it?"

Rose sighed. "You telling me all this time you want to visit?"

Izzy waved a dismissive palm, and Rose returned her focus to Jolie, now pawing at her lap.

"Am I supposed to know who this ragman's boy is? Is that another one of your colorful West Quincy characters? Ah, you mean the crippled Jew! The boy who showed up for hot dogs on Labor Day, He's Vincent's spy? You sure he's up to the job?"

"Maybe not. He's too nice, him. So then maybe I think you get the job."

"Because I'm *not* nice, you mean."

"You always think smart is better than nice, no? And you smart, for sure."

"And you, *ma soeur*, are showing a newfound flair for diplomacy."

Rose placed both palms on her lap, straightened her back, eyed her sister, and asked, "So, no spying. You just need someplace to live, yeah? Nowhere to go once the flibber woman comes back?"

Izzy's posture crumpled. "I'm not looking for charity. I just needed some time to think where I'd go. I have some money saved. It's not like I have no options. I could probably get into one of those new apartments run by the Boston Housing Authority. I'm old enough. But they're just so…"

Rose stroked Jolie's paw, bent over the dog's massive head, and planted a kiss between the eye wells. Still looking at the dog, she said softly, "You move in here."

"Really? You'd let me live here? You'd be all right with that? We're very different, you know. And a lot has happened between us."

Rose shrugged. "All those years ago? We're different then, too.

Back when we're young. But we don't do so bad, eh? Maybe we live like in the old days, just the two of us again." Rose stood, rubbed her lower back, and headed for the kitchen. "I get dinner ready."

"Rose?" Izzy called as her sister was halfway inside.

"Yeah?"

"Thank you."

Rose nodded.

As the screen door closed, Izzy flicked at the single tear having the audacity to approach her cheek. "Like the old days," she murmured.

FIFTEEN

Patterns

"**D**addeee! We're gonna be late!" Netty wailed from the car.

Standing on his mother's porch, a gallon of paint in each hand, Vince swiveled his head toward the driveway and yelled, "Hold your horses! I'm coming." Turning back toward his mother, he placed the cans on the porch floor and said, "This should be enough paint. And I put a bag full of brushes on that chair." He pointed at the Adirondack to the right of the door. Nate should be here any minute. You've got a good painting day. Nice and dry. Not too warm."

Rose flicked her wrists in a shooing motion. "Go! Go! You and Netty have fun at that movie. What's it called again?"

"*Bambi*. She's been dying to see it. Don't know how she's gonna be if anything happens to those big-eyed deer."

"Netty's a big softy. Just like her Daddy. Go! Go!"

Raising his hand in a casual salute, Vince skipped down the stairs toward the car.

A smile on her face, Rose watched him start the car and back out down the driveway.

"He *is* a softy," growled a male voice.

Rose folded her hands over her chest and glared at her late husband, slouched against the porch railing. "You say that like it's bad."

"Oh, Vincent's a good, strong lad. Would have made a good quarryman. But he's just too soft for his own good."

"How you mean?"

"Well, you've got four sons. How come Vincent is always the one fetching and carrying for you? You think he's any less busy than Hank, Dave, or Eddy?"

"No. He's easy to ask. The other boys, they always have excuses. Good excuses. They say they want to help if only this and that don't get in the way. So after a while, I don't ask no more."

"Exactly!" The apparition smirked. "Hank, Dave, and Eddie are artful dodgers, they are. Smart lads. They've got the Irish knack for charming their way out of trouble, and all without rubbing anyone the wrong way. I raised 'em good and proper. But Vincent, he's you all over again. Can't say no to anyone. And just like you, he'll probably work himself to death. Hank, Dave, and Eddie will be spending the city's pension money for decades after they retire. Not Vincent. Not that he'll ever have a pension anyway."

A hot flash surged up Rose's spine. "If I'm the one gonna work myself to death, how come I'm breathing in this nice fresh air, eh? You the one who's dead, no? Where you get that damn lung trouble anyway? From working all them years at the quarry."

"Hmmph. At least I know how to say no, unlike you and our youngest son. Who is it, darlin', who just said yes to that spiteful Izzy? You're still mad at her and never got an apology. And here you are, giving that woman the keys to the kingdom."

"*Tu me gosses* (You're annoying me), Francis! *Tu me gosses!*" Red-faced with anger, Rose pivoted smartly, ripped open the screen door, and slammed it behind her.

A heartbeat after the door stopped vibrating, she heard a light tap on a horn. Turning back to the porch, she saw the Sol Salvage sign on the side of the beaten up truck in the driveway. Her eyes darted to the corner where her husband's ghost had been holding forth. "You stay gone a while, you!" she warned in a hoarse, low voice. "How I gonna explain you to the Ragman's grandson? And when you come back, you better be nice to me!"

Rose smoothed down her skirt, fashioned her lips into a smile, and waved at Nate.

"Hey, Madame Rose," he said, waving back. As he reached the bottommost porch step, he stopped. "You okay? You sure you're up to this paint job we're gonna tackle?"

She flicked her right hand in exasperation. "Ah, I just have a fight with my Francis. I mean, I just remember this fight I have with my husband. He really gets my ... how you say, sheep? He gets my sheep, him."

Nate raised his eyebrows in confusion, then cracked a big grin. "Oh. Goat! He gets your goat!"

She slapped her forehead with the fingertips of her right hand. "Ah, silly me! Goat. Yeah, that's it, goat not sheep."

Nate chuckled. "When you stop and think about it, goat makes no more sense than sheep. Wonder where that expression came from anyway?"

Thirty minutes later, the two were parked on their butts on opposite ends of the porch, each working from their own gallon of gray paint, applying their own chosen brushstroke pattern on the floor and periodically scooting toward the other, toward the escape route that was the stairs. It was a convivial arrangement, even if the initial distance inhibited conversation. Nate was just as glad, because it gave him time to process what had apparently happened earlier—Rose angrily conversing with her dead husband. He didn't know whether this was another sign of dementia, something he should report to Vince. Or perhaps it was just a comforting ritual elderly widows and widowers indulged. But how comforting could it be to relive or invent a *spat* with a spouse?

As the painters moved within reasonable range of conversation, Nate mused, "My parents have their share of arguments. I guess all married couples do, huh?"

"You betcha!"

"More often than not, the things they fight about aren't earthshaking. How to spend money. Which side of the family to spend Thanksgiving with. But occasionally their values diverge. Mom is really interested in social status. Dad? He'd rather be comfortably dressed than wear a suit and tie. Heck, he'd drive the family to temple in that grease-smeared truck. Mom, she…"

"What's temple?"

"Synagogue. Our church."

"Ah, sure. You go regular?"

"Not as regular as my mother would like. That's one area where I'm more like Dad, and my *zayde*. That's my grandfather, Sol. The fella you know as the Ragman."

"I like the Ragman. You say hello for me, yeah?"

"Sure."

"And I like the Ragman's grandson." For the first time, Rose looked up from her painting job. She winked. "You think you're like your father then?"

"Funny, I never really thought about it. Nate smiled in return. "When kids are little, they're probably closer to their mother, don't you think? Especially sons. Especially Jewish sons."

Rose closed her eyes briefly, as if in deep thought. She shook her head. "Around here, I see lotta Irish mothers and Italian mothers like this with their sons." She raised her free left hand and crossed the first two fingers. "Just like your people. I think maybe it's about hard times, not that the mothers love sons more than daughters."

"I don't follow."

"You live a hard life, you hope your son will keep you from what my Francis always called the poorhouse. So you push him to finish school, get a good job, make good money. You don't think about that so much with daughters. You don't figure they have much chance at finding good jobs. You hope they find a man who takes care of them."

Nate nodded. "Well, that describes my mother perfectly. With my father, it's more about making sure I have enough money to take care of myself when he's gone. With my mother, being assured of filial support is only part of it. The other part is bragging rights."

Rose chuckled. "Your mama, she wants to brag to her friends about you, yeah? We all do that, *mon cher.*"

"Did you? Do you?"

"Sure, I brag about my sons the cops. But I brag about my Vincent, too. He's special, him."

"Is he your favorite, then?"

"Don't you know mamas, we don't have no favorite kids?" She winked again.

"I gather that's what mothers are supposed to tell their children. All that stuff about everyone being loved equally. I can't imagine that's true. But what do I know? I have no siblings."

"Okay, I tell you true." She cocked a dripping paintbrush in his direction. "But don't you tell no one. I have two favorites: my first born, Maryellen; and my last born, Vincent."

"Do you know why?"

Rose shrugged. "Francis, he tells me it's because those two are like me. He's wrong. They're so much better than me. Smarter, for sure. Kinder."

The rhythm of Nate's brushstrokes slowed as he digested her words. "Were your other sons more like their father?"

She stilled her brush in mid-stroke. "Maybe so. Hank, at least. You know he runs for that city council job? Gonna be a politician, just like my Francis."

"Sounds like a pattern to me."

"I guess. And my Eddie, he's got what them Irish call the gift of gab. That tongue of his can be sharp sometimes, too. Just like Francis."

"Sarcastic, huh?"

"Yeah, that's what you call it." Rose shook her head slowly. "Lotta sarcastic words."

Realizing that the conversation had veered far away from his planned agenda, to explore the preceding argument with Francis's ghost, Nate commented, "That probably caused a few marital spats."

"You betcha. That Francis, he can make me so mad, him! Really gets my *sheep*." She emphasized the last word to make it clear her malapropism was intentional this time.

Nate struggled to craft a follow-up question that would dig more deeply into the old woman's marital relationship, without appearing too intrusive.

"But my Francis," Rose continued, "he has lotta pretty words, too." She sighed.

"A real silver tongue, huh?"

101

She nodded vigorously. "And pretty to look at, too."

"How'd you meet? How old were you?" Nate figured if he couldn't explore sources of marital tension, at least he could answer his questions about how a couple from two different cultures managed to get together. That topic would at least have some relevance for a history paper researching the process of blending cultures.

"A wedding. Right here in West Quincy. At St. Mary's. Me, I'm twenty. Francis a couple years older."

"You went to the same church?"

"Yeah, but I never see him until that wedding. Big party after the couple gets married. I spot Francis right away, as soon as he comes in the door. Hard to miss, him. Got the broad shoulders of a *voyageur*, but real tall, too. I like what I see."

"Love at first sight?"

"Love? I just remember thinking, this fella, he gonna make healthy babies. Healthy grandbabies and great-grandbabies, too."

Nate gaped. "I doubt many women would have that thought when they first meet their future husband."

Rose shrugged. "Maybe more than you think. Women gotta be practical. And I grow up on a farm."

"Looks like you were right. You and your husbands certainly produced a bunch of strapping sons, from what I've seen. Were you also right about all the grandchildren? I only know about Netty? Does she have a bunch of cousins?"

She put the paintbrush on the lid of the can so she could count on her fingers. "There's Netty and … yeah, yeah, Rosemary and Jane. Two others. Dave's kids. All grown up now. Rosemary, she moves way out west somewhere after she gets married. Ohio? And Jane, when she's still a girl, goes to live with her. Bad blood between Jane and Dave's wife."

"Do you ever see them?"

"Not for a long time. Rosemary sends Christmas cards."

"Your other sons don't have children?"

Rose shook her head. "Gert, she can't make babies. You know what she says? She says none of the women in her family ever able to get pregnant. Nora and me, we chuckle about that. Nora wonders how Gert gets born."

102

"Isn't there another son? I don't remember their names."

Rose resumed the finger count. "Dave? No. Hank? Ah, you mean Eddie. No, no kids. Ah, *saccajé chien*! I forget. I forget my only grandson!" She rapped her head with the knuckles of her left hand. "Eddie and his wife, they have a baby boy. Something wrong in the baby's head. So sad. They put him in a hospital place. He dies there. Eddie's wife, she don't want to talk about it. She don't want to have no more kids. Maybe that's why I forget? How can I forget? What is the *bébé's* name? Jimmy, maybe? Joe? Johnny?"

Nate shifted weight from one hip to the other, only partly to relieve the discomfort of his painting posture. He regretted bringing up the subject of grandchildren, because it had apparently triggered another mental lapse in Rose. Worse than that was witnessing her struggle with that lapse. As he applied more paint to the floor, he was aware of her mumbling additional names in an unsuccessful effort to identify her dead grandson.

Desperate to stop the litany, Nate changed the subject. "So how long after that wedding at St. Mary's before you and Francis had your own wedding?"

"Hmm? Let me think. Two years. Maybe more?"

"That's a long courtship, isn't it? Especially back then, when women got married awfully young. Are long courtships typical in Quebec? Or is it an Irish custom?"

Rose clicked her tongue and began brushing at a rapid pace, perpendicular to her earlier pattern. "It's Izzy. She don't like Francis. She thinks he's some gangster. She thinks he's not good enough. She thinks she's gonna be all alone if I get married." She sighed then looked earnestly at her co-worker. "I never leave her alone! Never. Not after all we go through together." Rose looked down and slapped the paintbrush on the floor, with gray splatters landing on her skirt. "But Izzy, she don't want to live with Francis and me. So we wait until we're sure Izzy's gonna be okay."

"That was kind of you," he replied, aware he had stepped into an emotional minefield. Unsure how to proceed, he chose, yet again, to change the subject. "Where is your sister anyway? Vince said she was visiting you for a week or so?"

"She goes to her church in Boston. She don't like St. Mary's. Not fancy enough. Too many immigrants, she says. She's gonna have to get used to St. Mary's pretty soon, though."

"Why is that?"

"She's moving in with me."

"Really?"

Rose nodded. "Your people, they pray, right?"

"Sure."

"Maybe you could say a little prayer for me. Pray Izzy and me don't kill each other."

SIXTEEN

An Epidemic of Shell Shock

Vince didn't like driving in Boston. He didn't like much of anything about Boston. His travels "in town" usually extended only a few miles beyond the Neponset River to visit Nora's parents in Dorchester. But today's adventure led him to another, far more impressive — and impressively noxious — river, the Charles, near Boston's northern extreme. Somehow, he managed to find a parking place only a block away from the Winthrop brownstone where his Aunt Izzy had lived for decades. Somehow, he managed to extricate her worldly belongings from that congested chokepoint and was now reasonably confident of relocating them safely to his mother's house. His confidence rose only after his truck tires hummed to the grooved concrete in the Neponset River Bridge, transporting him back to North Quincy.

"Did you just bless yourself?" Nate Kagan asked, riding shotgun. "That's what you call it, right? When you draw a cross on your chest?"

Vince nodded. "I hate Boston."

Nate raised his eyebrows. "You got something against nice architecture, museums, theaters, universities?"

"I got something against all those people crowded together, all that traffic, and that stink! Can you imagine paying a bundle for some fancy Back Bay house so you can smell the sewage flowing down the Charles?"

Nate shrugged, leaning to his right to scrutinize the side-view mirror. "I think we lost your aunt."

"They passed us a while back. Just as well. If they arrive ahead of us, Ma might have a chance to calm Izzy down before all the upheaval of unloading her stuff."

"She didn't look too happy."

"No surprise. This is a huge change for her. And that Winthrop woman made her feel even sadder."

"She sure acted like she couldn't wait to clear the hired help out of her place. Like we were gonna muddy up the marble foi-yay."

"That what you call the front hall? So that really was marble, huh?"

Nate nodded. "At least the son seemed okay. Forbes? Seemed like he was actually fond of your aunt and might miss her."

"I've seen him a couple of times before, and he always acted decent. I'm grateful he was willing to drive her to Ma's. We would have had trouble fitting three people in this truck. By the way, be sure to thank your old man for letting us borrow it."

"You've kept this old pickup running for over a decade. Least he could do. Hey, I was hoping I could interview Miss Isabelle about her childhood in Quebec. I haven't gotten all that far with my family history project and need to turn the initial outline in to my adviser soon. But maybe today isn't the right time?"

"Play it by ear. Speaking of which, I'm surprised Ma hasn't talked your ear off so much that you could fill an encyclopedia with her memories."

"She certainly has some colorful stories. Useful ones, too. But she's not so good about pinning down dates and places. Maybe her sister could help out there."

Vince sighed. "You think Ma's mind is slipping even more?"

"Madame Rose certainly has her good days, when she's sharp as a tack. But other times, she's ... befuddled. Sometimes a lot. She kinda reminds me of a crank engine in winter. It sputters a bit at first, but once you get all the cylinders firing, it hums along pretty good. Maybe mental stimulation gets her cylinders going."

"You think Izzy living with her could help?"

Nate bobbled his head from side to side. "Maybe. But for all I know there's some pill that could make her sharp again. What about having a neurologist look her over?"

Vince frowned at his passenger.

"A brain doctor," Nate explained.

"Yeah, I know what a neurologist is. What I don't know is how we'd pay for one. Besides, you've gotten to know my mother some. Whaddya think the odds are that she'd see a doctor, unless she had one leg falling off? Besides, she's pretty crafty about covering up her forgetfulness."

The conversation inside the truck faltered. The younger man suddenly fretted that he had overstepped. The middle-aged man was a prisoner of his thoughts.

Although Vince hated to see summer end, hated to lose the sizzle of sunshine on his overworked muscles, hated to lose the long days that allowed him to fit in so many chores, he was not immune to October foliage, a hard act to beat in Massachusetts. Even in urban areas, you could count on eruptions of gold, retina-searing crimsons, and a whole spectrum devoted to orange. But not even the sugar maple standing vigil beside one of Quincy's last, gracious stone houses dating from an earlier century could brighten his mood today. More than once in earlier Octobers, that maple had enticed him to go out of his way on his morning commute, just so he could parse the colors in the frosty, low-angle light. Several years ago, Vince, a lifelong fan of classical music, decided that calling those leaves yellow or orange or brick red was like describing Vivaldi's "Autumn" as a catchy tune. But today, the stately maple, in peak color, barely registered. His mind was too focused on his mother's dimming light to appreciate the tree's incandescence. When his eye finally took in the foliage, the leaves merely reminded him how ephemeral their glory was. How short life was. How powerless he was to restore his mother's mental vigor, to protect his daughter from the debilitation of new illnesses, to calm the waters buffeting his wife between paralyzing lethargy and frantic energy. He could no more fix those problems than he could keep the horrors of Nazi-occupied Europe, Japanese-controlled China, or Stalin-subjugated Ukraine from subverting his own community's once unshakable confidence in the future.

Vince didn't even hear Nate's question about the new shipyard job. Or the subsequent query about planned construction on Willard Street.

Nate gave up. The final two miles passed in silence.

Rose stood in the doorway of the room that would be her sister's. She wore a sad smile as she regarded the quilt on the bed. Turning her head to the left, she said, "You a good girl, Maryellen, for letting me give your aunt that quilt."

The little girl with straggly hair and an even stragglier stuffed animal clutched to her chest smiled and shrugged. And disappeared.

Maryellen's disappearance coincided with noise on the porch. Izzy and her former charge Forbes Winthrop had arrived. Rose hurried downstairs. She paused at the landing to wave cheerfully at Izzy, listlessly depositing her coat on the coatrack by the porch door. Izzy didn't return the wave. Probably didn't see the wave. Looking at her deflated sister, Rose conjured newspaper photos of veterans of the Great War.

Shell-shocked. They use that word for all them poor boys who come home after the war, with minds that hurt. Well, Izzy, your mind must hurt.

She hoped some of the pain might go away once Izzy saw her well-ordered room, a vase of still-vibrant goldenrod sprays on the bedside table. And the quilt on the bed. It was the one Rose had made years ago for Maryellen. Unused for decades, it was pristine if somewhat musty from sitting in storage in a big cedar chest. For years after her daughter's death, Rose hadn't been able to look at it. The quilt was supposed to celebrate Maryellen's passage into young adulthood. Tired of lollipop and bunny themes, the adolescent craved furnishings that reflected her changing status. Rose happily complied by crafting a double-sided quilt with a leaf theme. One side featured the warm colors of autumn leaves, interspersed with white snowflake squares; the other side alternated between the pale greens of spring and the bolder greens of summer. It was a work of art, according to the few people who saw it. Maryellen was not among them.

The quilt was supposed to be a gift for her thirteenth birthday, but pneumonia claimed her ten days shy of that landmark. So Rose tucked the work of art away. She couldn't bear to see this reminder of promise unfulfilled. Thinking of the quilt, she would berate herself for waiting to give it to her only daughter. Why wait for some stupid birthday? Why not present it as pure serendipity, at a time when Maryellen would not be expecting anything? Imagine how happily surprised the girl would have been!

Rose knew why she had waited. French Canadians were notorious for their frugality. If she had bestowed the quilt when it was finished, two months before the thirteenth birthday, then she would have needed to come up with another gift for the actual birthday. Never mind that she would have put a smile on her daughter's face. Practicality prevailed, and Maryellen had one less smile in her short life.

So in addition to symbolizing loss, the quilt also symbolized guilt. Rose couldn't exculpate herself for all the years when her French Canadian frugality had been absolutely essential. The years when she and Izzy had struggled to keep food in their bellies created a pattern that was hard to break.

Rose's increasing forgetfulness did not extend to the quilt. She knew exactly where it was and why it was hidden from view. But repurposing it for Izzy, she thought, might cleanse the quilt of its negative symbolism. At the same time, Rose recognized the irony of this waste-not, want-not choice. Here she was, being frugal yet again.

Alas, the autumn leaves and snowflakes artfully covering the bed did not bring a smile to Izzy's shell-shocked face. Her mood was not helped by the rapid departure of her driver. Forbes Winthrop left immediately after dumping the two suitcases on the floor of Izzy's bedroom. The lanky young man did pause at the front door to blow a kiss at "Tante Isabelle" and offer a hearty, "You take care, now!" along with an equally hearty smile, reflecting the long-toothed but perfectly straight dentition of his Brahmin genes.

Izzy never saw the blown kiss. Abandoning the ramrod posture she had demanded of her young charges, she allowed her shoulders to slump and her head to bow. Looking at the kitchen's worn linoleum, she nodded dully in response to Forbes's breezy farewell.

Nods and shrugs were the only answers Izzy could muster for questions about where her possessions should go. Rose found herself wishing for a grammatical correction from her younger sister. She would have welcomed an eye roll about the antiquated bathroom fixtures or a gasp of disgust over Jolie's hot-breathed exuberance.

The heavy mood was unleavened by the arrival of Vince and Nate. Izzy appeared utterly disinterested in the placement of her cherished mahogany secretary, her bureau, rocking chair, or leather-bound collection of Shakespeare's tragedies and histories. Eventually, the two men stopped inquiring and made their own choices about where furniture items and the heaviest boxes should go. With Rose's agreement, they aligned the smaller cartons on the living room floor for later sorting.

"Well, that's the last of it," Vince announced, after a final check of the Kagan truck. "Now, don't you two girls overdo it. Anything heavy needs moving, I'm only a phone call away, okay? Gonna be swell having you nearby, Izzy. Makes me think of the good old days, with all of us gathered around this kitchen table," he stroked one of the scarred kitchen chairs fondly.

Rose patted her son's shoulder. "We gonna be just fine. You a good boy, you." Angling her head to get a better view of Nate, standing awkwardly behind Vince, she added with a wink, "You, too, Ragman's grandson."

Nate doffed his slouch cap and grinned. "*Avec plaisir,* Madame Rose."

"See ya! Ma, Izzy? Don't get into any trouble now."

Izzy lifted a limp hand in thanks or farewell. When the men were gone, she looked around the kitchen and repeated, "Like old times." And shuddered.

SEVENTEEN

It's All Relative

Struggling against nausea, Nate tried mouth-breathing to lessen the impact of the cigarette smoke filling the bus, along with the chicken-soup emanations of sweaty bodies and the stench of wet wool.

When mouth-breathing didn't work, Nate decided to distract himself from the unpleasant realities of public transport by enumerating all the factors causing his foul mood. First was the meeting with his thesis adviser. Professor Leibowitz had been downright surly. The young man now wished he had never provided an example of the interviews he was conducting with Rose. He made the mistake of selecting the anecdote about Flint and Sapling and the frozen St. Lawrence. The professorial reaction was shouting: "For Christ's sake! What does some old lady's childhood memories from nineteenth century Quebec have to do with the immigrant experience in twentieth century America? Get focused, Kagan! You've got a lot of writing to do in the second semester, and you'll never finish if you're bogged down in irrelevant research this far into the first semester."

Maybe the professor was right, but the dressing down felt more like vengeance. The adviser was miffed that the head of the history department had overridden his objections to the thesis topic. Leibowitz didn't consider anyone from Canada a real immigrant and thought Rose was utterly "inconsequential" because her family had never been targeted by pogroms or lynchings or burning crosses. None of the Quentins had even been arrested, for pity's sake! No worthy dissidents in that lot, not in the "old country" nor in the new. Just a bunch of boring "French Canucks" eager to toe the line and fit in. Most of them were "so dumb they supported the wrong political party!" Nate had no idea what side of the political aisle got Rose's vote. Probably not the one the good professor would have chosen for her. It never occurred to the young man to ask. He was far more interested in the insights into her culture and especially into her family dynamic, past and present. Nevertheless, he resolved—yet again—that future sessions with Rose would focus on her experiences *after* coming to the United States.

The second reason for Nate's malaise was the reason why he was on this wretched city bus in the first place–he lacked his own mode of transportation. The green MG was probably growing roots into the packed soil of Vince's driveway. It was no closer to cruising down Furnace Brook Parkway than it was a month ago. He second-guessed himself for assigning the makeover to Vince. Maybe he should have begged his parents for the money to take the old car into some shop blessed with multiple mechanics and a healthy parts department. Surely such a garage would have finished the job by now! Admittedly, Nate enjoyed the newfound camaraderie with Vince. He would never have found friendship in some anonymous garage, where the mechanics would invariably sneer at a college kid unused to working with his hands.

Nate's physical limitations had always gotten in the way of friendship with contemporaries. Yes, he had halfway convivial relations with certain classmates, of the studious, unpopular variety. But the liveliest conversations with them focused on the last exam, the idiosyncrasies of various professors, or, when they were really feeling their oats, the odds of ever bedding a girl as attractive as Teaching Assistant Weintraub.

Nate also sighed over one concomitant of his friendship with Vince–he had acquired a second family in the Dowds, with some of the same obligations imposed by one's blood relatives. At least the Dowds would see nothing shameful in chucking law school to pursue a writing career. He actually felt accepted, just the way he was, by Rose and Vince. But he didn't like scrutinizing Rose's cognitive abilities on Vince's behalf. And he didn't like that he was starting to worry about Rose's future, even Vince's future.

His foul mood also traced back to his own family dynamic, as his parents endlessly hovered over the law-school application process. Would he earn high enough grades on the entrance exams for his target institutions? Had he gotten sufficiently glowing recommendations from his college teachers? Had he written suitably inspiring essays? Did he wear the proper clothing for his interviews? And by the way, did he have time to work at the junkyard next Saturday? And on your way home from classes today, could you pick up some cold cuts in Quincy Square?

He snapped out of his reverie of misery quickly enough to pull the cord for the next stop. Even though city buses could generally be relied on to pull up to every single stop on Hancock Street, Nate needed time to extricate his foot from the beneath his seat and get reasonably balanced to walk down the center aisle.

As he clumped onto the sidewalk, the light rain shower turned into a bitterly cold downpour. "Oh yeah, there's the weather, too," he mumbled to himself, coming up with yet another reason justifying his bad mood.

After getting the items his mother requested from the delicatessen counter of the five-and-ten-cent store, Nate approached the exit and shuddered. It was now sleeting and home was nearly a mile away. Because of his limp, a mile was a challenging walk on the nicest day. Today it would be an exercise in gloom. The only protection he had was a cap and an insubstantial jacket. He decided to wait inside the store's main entrance to see if the weather improved.

A few other shoppers had the same idea. As Nate watched their collective breath steam up the door and windows, he noticed a vaguely familiar car pull up outside. The driver beeped and waved vigorously. Wiping his foggy eyeglasses in an unsuccessful effort to identify the individual, he glanced around to see if any of his fellow shoppers would claim the vehicle. When no one made a move, he jerked up his jacket's meager collar and stepped outside. The driver leaned over and, with some effort, rolled down the passenger window. "You need a ride?" shouted Rose Dowd.

Nate sprinted toward the Ford. "Thanks, Madame Rose!"

"I see you in the store and call out, but you don't hear me. Already looking wet and cold, you. So I think maybe you don't have no car. You going home?"

Nate nodded and shivered.

"Wish this car had one of them new heaters, but it's better than outside. Your folks live near the hospital, yeah?"

"Yes, you'll take that right up there."

Rose smoothly rounded the corner. "I don't come to the square so much, but I gotta cheer up Izzy. Real sad, her. I figure I get bright material and make new curtains for her bedroom." She cocked a thumb in the direction of the shopping bag on the back seat.

"That's nice of you."

"Hey, if I cheer her up, my life, it gets easier."

Nate laughed then pointed at the two-story clapboard house that was the Kagan residence. He desperately wanted to make a speedy exit, dump the cold cuts in the refrigerator, and seek out the solitude of his tiny bedroom. But he owed his chauffeur.

"Can I offer you some coffee?" he asked. "Oh wait, I don't think Mom was able to find any. But we've got tea. It might be rationed, too, but it's easier to find. How about a hot cup of tea to warm you up before you head back home?"

"Tea's good," Rose said, pulling close to the curb.

He sighed, as she turned off the engine and swiftly exited the Ford. After catching up with her, he escorted her to his front door and ushered her into the kitchen. He stifled a groan when he heard his mother come halfway downstairs. Hurrying back to the front hallway, he saw her frozen on the steps, swathed in her chenille bathrobe.

"Oh, good, you're not a burglar," Mrs. Kagan said, patting her chest. "Did you pick up the liverwurst and roast beef?"

"Yup. Just about to put the stuff in the refrigerator."

"Did you ask them to slice the roast beef paper-thin?

"You can practically see through it, Mom."

"Don't get fresh! I've got one of my headaches. It's this awful weather. Maybe a nap will make me feel better."

"Hope it works." Nate waved at his mother's retreating back and exhaled relief that she had not seen Rose. His mother would have had one of her "balloon ascensions" if a stranger had caught her in her ratty bathrobe. In the middle of the afternoon.

Back in the kitchen, he was surprised to hear the kettle heating up on the gas range. Two mugs, two spoons, and a bottle of milk were on the table, in addition to the omnipresent sugar jar. Rose, still in her coat, was opening and closing cabinet doors.

"You don't mind me getting a head start, no? But I don't find the tea."

"I'll get it. You sit. You're the guest."

She complied, after draping her coat over the chair back. "Nasty cold for this early in November. And I see a black woolly bear the other day. Gonna be a hard winter."

"Swell," Nate said grimly, as he dropped Lipton tea bags into the mugs and brought them to the stove, where the kettle was whining.

When he returned with both cups, he noticed Rose staring at the sugar bowl.

"You got enough sugar for tea?" she asked. When he nodded, she giggled as she shoveled two heaping teaspoons into her cup. "Mm, nice and hot and sweet. Takes the chill out of my bones. This is some November, eh?"

"Awfully cold," he agreed listlessly.

"I don't think I see a November this cold since way back, when Izzy and me worry so hard how we gonna get through the next few months without freezing to death."

"Was this back in Quebec? I imagine November is a pretty cold month up there."

"Not Quebec. Right here in Quincy. Early days, when Izzy and me are on our own. I'm almost eighteen. She's fifteen."

Even though Nate didn't feel like being social, much less focusing on the research for his history thesis, he recognized opportunity when he saw it. Finally, Rose was poised to talk about the early days as an immigrant. "I thought you were younger when you first came to Quincy."

Rose waved a hand. "Pah, we come to Quincy six, seven years earlier. No, this is after the rest of the family leaves us behind. My Papa, he gonna buy a big farm in Manitoba. Can't afford to take Izzy and me. We're the oldest."

"Wait a minute! Your parents abandoned the two of you? At such a young age?" Knowing when Rose was born, he counted on his fingers, "So the cold November you're recalling would have been in 1890? Wow, two teenage girls left on their own way back then.

"But back up a bit, please. How did this come about? I didn't realize there had been two migrations: one from Quebec to Quincy; the other from Quincy to, where did you say, Manitoba? Wow, that's a long way off, isn't it?"

"So far away, I never see my parents again."

"Wow! Just, wow!" Nate assumed a more erect posture and tapped his fingernails on the table with anticipation. "So the first migration didn't take, huh? What was wrong with Quincy?"

Rose shrugged. "Papa, he has *voyageur* blood, you know? Hard to stay in one place. Hard to live without wide open spaces."

"But why would he have left Quebec for Quincy in the first place?"

Rose leaned far back in her chair. "I tell you the story. The way I see it. Maybe Izzy sees it different. Maybe Papa, too. But I tell you *my* story, yeah?"

Nate nodded his encouragement. Rose took a deep breath and began...

Up in Quebec, the land, it breaks Papa's heart, I think. That soil gets worked too hard. Not just our land, but all them farm plots on the St. Lawrence. Same crops year after year. They take too much from the earth, without giving back. So all that time he spends, planting seeds in the ground, tending to them little green lives. And what do they do? They die on him! Not enough to pay the landlord, sell stuff, feed ourselves or our pigs. So the pigs, they get sick. Too many of them die. We get poorer and poorer. Hungrier and hungrier. And Papa, he gets tireder and tireder, him.

Then he hears about this place in Massachusetts with lotta quarry jobs. Papa, he knows something about quarries. We got them up in Quebec, too. Friends of Papa work the granite in them quarries. Need lotta muscles back then, before all them big machines that drill into the rock. Well, Papa's plenty strong, him. He knows he can do the work. And you know what? I think he likes the idea of beating up the earth. He don't need to be gentle with granite. Not like with little seedlings. He don't have to pray that there's granite in the ground, like he prays for the little seedling taking root. Nope. The granite, it's already there. And it's plenty tough. My papa, he brags that granite is tougher than the hardest steel.

Being a quarryman isn't as good as being a *voyageur* like Papa's grandfather and great-grandfather. But it's rugged work for a rugged man. A proud man. That's why he don't wanna follow all them Quebecois farmers who leave the tired old farm to work the mills in New England. Why does he wanna turn out cloth when he can rip out big rocks? But it's not just that. He don't like what he hears about them mill towns. Lowell and Nashua and places like that. All them places are like little Quebecs, where people keep speaking French and send their kids to Catholic schools run by Quebecois priests and nuns. Where people buy all their stuff from a company store. My Papa, he has enough of that back home, where he's supposed to bow and scrape to priests and nuns and landlords and shopkeepers and bankers. He don't wanna live like that no more, where everybody knows your business. Even if it means he's gotta learn another language. That we gotta learn another language.

So when I'm eleven, we come to Quincy and its granite quarries. No one speaks French here. But not everything changes. We still don't own the house we live in. Papa still has a boss he works for. But he don't have as many worries. Will the seedlings grow? Will he be able to harvest them before the rain beats them back into the ground or frost kills them? He don't have to worry about how much money to set aside—in a good year—to make the soil a little better or to buy new gear to replace all the broken-down stuff. He don't have to tip his hat to the banker with smooth hands and clean fingernails. He don't need to beg for more loans or more time to pay money back.

Now, we don't know this, Izzy and me. Not even Mama. But once we're here in Quincy, Papa starts putting money away, every week. We don't know this because Papa always complains he don't have no money after he pays the rent and buys kerosene and firewood and food. So when we outgrow our skirts and undies, we make do. My little sisters wear lotta clothes that are already beaten up by me. I don't got no big sister whose clothes I can wear. So I get some really old stuff from Mama. And lotta times I lengthen sleeves and hems with scrap material. Maybe from skirts with burn holes because someone stands too close to the fire. Maybe from worn sheets.

You gotta understand. My papa, he's not like that Mister Scrooge. He isn't mean about saving money. He just sees money different. Money isn't for fun stuff. Isn't even for emergency. Nope. I think for him, money is freedom. That little stash he builds up every week? That gives him room to jump when he wants to, when he's ready.

And whaddya know? He saves up enough money to make a really, really big leap. All the way to Manitoba. To grow wheat. He knows something about that, because most years he grows some wheat on our farm in Quebec. This land in Manitoba, it's perfect for wheat. Lotta land there. Big farms, not those narrow little strips in Quebec. He finds out about Manitoba wheat farms from a second cousin, another fella who comes from Lévis City.

Mama finally figures out what's going on. See, my papa don't have much school. He can read some but can't write. So he goes to Mama and asks her to write letters to this Cousin Herbert, who lives in Maine and travels plenty for logging jobs. Cousin Herbert finds out about this Manitoba place from other fellas in logging camps. So with Mama's help, Papa writes Herbert to ask about farmland that might be up for sale there. Cousin Herbert writes back about this old, sick farmer who needs to leave his wheat farm. It's in a place called McCreary. He gotta sell real quick.

Mama, she's more interested in other stuff. She asks Cousin Herbert about what this McCreary place is like. She don't like hearing it's two thousand miles away. But she feels better when she finds out it has lotta French-speaking folks from Quebec. Maybe she can make friends there. She never has no friends here in Quincy. Of course, she's pretty busy popping out babies. In the seven years they live here, she has five more.

What Cousin Herbert writes about McCreary also makes Papa sure that place is for him. It's kinda like the Old West in all them cowboy movies. Wild. Not many people a fella has to bow and scrape to. He really likes that Mc-Creary has lotta Indians. Working right next to white folks, going to the same church, shopping at the same stores. My Papa, he's always so proud of his Abenaki blood. He looks like a Red Man, although that's mostly because of all the sun he soaks up, working outdoors all the time. Anyway, Papa figures he'll fit into McCreary just fine and dandy.

So Mama and Papa tell all us kids about this McCreary. My two little brothers get all excited. They gonna have some big adventure, them. My little sisters, the ones old enough to be in school, they get grumpy. Don't wanna leave their friends in Quincy. Izzy and me, we wonder how we gonna finish high school. But then Papa tells me, no problem. We can keep going to Quincy High School, 'cause we're not going to this Wild West place. He can't afford to take us. Can only feed so many mouths. Can only pay for so many train tickets. Izzy and me, we're adults now. I'm already taking on some odd jobs, he says. So Izzy and me can get jobs.

Izzy pipes up: "How we gonna work jobs and go to school?" I wonder where we gonna live and how we gonna pay for it.

Mama says she and Papa gonna pay an extra month's rent on our house, after they leave. She hears about this rooming house where we can stay starting in December. They don't have no extra rooms until then. Mama says Mrs. Halloran, she's the lady runs the rooming house, will let us work off our room and board if Izzy and me clean all them rooms in that big house. And if we take care of the littlest Halloran kids.

So Mama and Papa and all the kids leave in late October. They pay the rent for November. Only thing is, Mama and Papa don't know how cold that November gonna be. Just like this November. One week later, we run out of wood for the stove. I tell you, I look hard at them apple trees in that yard. The trees, they don't belong to us. So we gonna get in trouble if we chop them down. But I look around for an ax anyway. *Sainte Anne!* You get cold enough, you do a lot to get warm. You get hungry enough, you do a lot to eat. But I don't find nothing. That last ax must be on its way to Manitoba.

That's when we stop doing business with the Ragman. The fella before your grandfather. When we look around for axes, we see all them Boston Globes, tied up with twine and waiting for the Ragman. Izzy and me, we ask ourselves what we need more. The coins we get from selling them stacks of newspaper? Or the heat we get from burning them? Well, newspaper, it burns pretty fast. Between them Boston Globes and the small tree branches lying around, we keep the kitchen stove going, enough to boil water and cook food.

We spend lotta time in that kitchen. We wash up there, with cold water from the sink. Izzy does her homework there. Only problem is, Mama, with all her planning, don't think about the gas bill. So the gas gets cut off and we're in the dark. There's a hurricane lantern in the basement. Full of kerosene. So we try to keep that going. And we find a bunch of beeswax candles. Most nights, there's Izzy, sitting at the kitchen table, wearing her coat, reading some damn book, with a candle beside it. No wonder she wears them big, thick glasses today! *Ma fois!*

Izzy says she's gonna stay in school. She wants one of them diplomas bad. See, she's so smart, she's already two grades ahead. The latest skip is from tenth to eleventh grade. So here she is, a senior, just like me. She can get her diploma the same time I get mine, the next spring.

But I figure, what's a diploma gonna get me? More firewood? Besides, how am I gonna earn enough money to keep us going if I spend all day in class? I never like school the way Izzy does. I get bored. Better to pick up more pay than pick up some algebra book. So even before Mama and Papa leave, I start looking for jobs cleaning houses. I find out the people in West Quincy clean their own houses. They don't got no money to pay housekeepers. Then I hear about East Milton. Not too far to walk and people got enough money to pay other people to beat their rugs and dust their furniture and clean their windows. They pay even better money to get their clothes mended and buttons sewed on. After a few months, I pick up sewing jobs, too. Pretty good money, you betcha.

But what I like best about East Milton is the heat. Most of them houses where I work got coal furnaces, with radiators in every room. Them weeks when Izzy and me freeze every night at our old house, I'm an icicle when I show up for my cleaning job. But by the time I scrub the first floor, I'm sweating like our pigs. Gotta take off my sweater.

Same way with Izzy. She's not scrubbing floors or beating rugs, but them classrooms got radiators. And when the weather's not too bad, she works up a sweat walking all that way to school.

But, *Sainte Anne*, the weather's awful cold most days. Them weeks in that cold house, the nights are bad. Izzy and me can have any room we want, with just us in that old house. But to stay warm we sleep in the same small bed. We cover it with an old bedspread Mama leaves behind. We put our coats on top of that. Not too bad. Sometimes we even wake up sweating. But you know what's tough? If we gotta go. There's the outhouse in the backyard. There's the frozen bedpan in the bedroom. Brrr!

Nate sat mesmerized by Rose's story, And by the nonchalance with which she told it. Many questions occurred to him, but he didn't want to interrupt her flow. It was almost dark by the time she left. After he waved at her from the front door and re-entered his warm, tight house, tended by parents who loved him, however much they might hover and annoy, he scowled at his earlier list of miseries. "You dumb, dumb jerk," he said in a low, sad voice. Apparently, even misery was relative.

EIGHTEEN

Resurrection

After peeling the blanket from her head, Izzy looked around the sunlit bedroom to orient herself. After dreaming of the cold realities of half a century earlier—the very same experiences Rose had related to Nate a few days ago—her sleepy brain wasn't entirely sure of the year or precise locale. She took a deep breath to steady herself. "*Saccajé chien!*" she grumbled upon seeing the equally deep exhalation hang in the air.

With more energy than she had marshaled for weeks, Izzy hastily changed into woolen slacks and sweater then felt the bedroom radiator. Its tepid temperature triggered a groan. After a brief stop in the frigid bathroom, she marched downstairs to the kitchen, where Jolie pressed a cold, wet nose into her hand. After letting the dog outside, Izzy turned on every gas jet on the range and set the oven to three-fifty. She propped the oven door open with a wooden spoon and briefly rubbed her palms over the opening.

The next stop was the basement to look for any signs of life inside the coal furnace. Through the slits in the cast-iron door, she spotted a pale ember or two. The adjacent coal bin, she noted, was nearly empty.

"Rose!" she bellowed.

The shout was loud enough to startle the dog outside. Jolie's barking carried up to the second floor, where his mistress had only just begun to stir.

Rose, too, had difficulty fixing the time and place. She had likewise experienced dreams of the old days, after the parental exodus to Manitoba. Extracting a forearm from beneath the covers, she wondered at all the freckles. Hers was a complexion that tanned, not freckled. Her continued study of the alien forearm revealed hundreds of tiny accordion pleats. This was the arm of a wrinkled old woman with liver spots. She wasn't seventeen. She was nearly seventy. Then why was it so cold? This must be the house she had shared with Francis for forty-odd years, a house that was well-tended, well-insulated against the weather, and well-heated, even when Old Man Flint was doing his worst.

And who was that shouting? It sounded like Izzy. But Rose hadn't lived with her younger sister since they were in their early twenties. Maybe she was wrong about the time and place.

"Rose!" came the second shout, more of an angry scream.

Despite her disorientation, Rose recalled that Izzy's anger should not be ignored.

She followed the third scream to the basement, where an elderly version of her younger sister stood with left hand on hip while right arm unfurled dramatically in the direction of the furnace.

"You let the fire go out? In this weather?"

"Ah, I let the fire get too low," Rose murmured, more to herself. "I fix," she added, reaching for the nearby shovel.

"How?" Izzy challenged, pointing to the few pieces of anthracite in the bin. "Is the coal truck just late? Or did you forget to schedule a delivery?"

"I don't know," Rose said shakily.

"You don't know? *Mon Dieu*! Where are your household records?"

Rose's posture crumpled. She opened her mouth, but no words came out.

In a calmer tone, Izzy said, "Let's go upstairs and look for old coal bills. I bet you keep them in the kitchen, eh?"

Rose nodded, and the two women climbed the stairs. After fruitlessly searching two kitchen drawers, Rose found a likely stash of papers in the third. She spread them on the kitchen table. Her sister pored over them.

"The electric bill. Gas," Izzy murmured. "You don't pay by check? Ah well, thank goodness they're all stamped 'paid' at least."

"I pay the bills with cash. At Dunphy's drug store. First of every month. Always on time."

"But you don't have monthly coal bills, do you? Do you remember when you last paid for a delivery? Do you remember which coal service you use?"

Rose shook her head sorrowfully. Then, abruptly, she shouted, "Granite Coal and Oil!"

"All right, if I know what to look for, this might go faster." Izzy flipped through more papers. "Aha! Here it is. Looks like you paid for a load in the spring. Nothing since then?"

Rose shrugged.

Looking at her watch, Izzy decided, "They should be open by now. You phone Granite Coal and Oil and order up an immediate delivery. Let's go into the living room."

Wielding the old bill in one hand and beckoning her sister with the other, Izzy strode out of the kitchen. She pointed Rose toward the seat near the phone and thrust the receiver into her hand. "Dial 'Granite two,' that's four-seven-two," she began.

Rose petulantly snatched the bill, dialed the number, and cleared her throat. Covering the mouthpiece, she back-waved at her sister. "You go make coffee. I fix."

"Yeah, you'll fix," Izzy grumbled. But she headed to the kitchen anyway.

When she returned with two cups of coffee, she found a dejected Rose, hand resting on the cradled phone.

"Well?"

"They need a week to schedule deliveries."

Give me the phone," Izzy said, shooing Rose out of the chair.

Describing herself as "Mrs. Dowd's secretary," Izzy berated the "young man" for failing to follow through on Mrs. Dowd's call to schedule a coal delivery for Halloween week. She reminded the "young man" how many years the Dowds had been "clients" of Granite Coal

123

and Oil. She threatened to switch their business to a rival company. She threatened to call the mayor's office and the Better Business Bureau if the coal truck didn't show up at the "Dowd residence" before the close of business that very day.

"Tomorrow afternoon? I'm not happy, but that will do, I suppose. Our man will open the chute before he leaves for the day." Then Izzy hung up, a satisfied smirk on her lips.

"But I don't call them for Halloween," Rose objected.

"The little twit doesn't know that." Izzy sipped her coffee. "Is there a chute you need to open?"

Rose nodded. "I do that right now. Before I forget, yeah?" Before she left the living room, she added, "You're back, huh?"

"What?"

"You're so sad these past few weeks. But now you feel better, no?"

"I believe I'm merely cold," Izzy snapped.

When she was alone in the living room, she added, "Hmmph, I guess I *am* back."

NINETEEN

Warming Things Up

Rarely was Rose Dowd idle. Never did she take an intentional nap. But as the sun rose to its highest point in the November sky, she excused herself, pleading the need to have a "lie-down" for an hour or so. Her sister's reaction was a frown. Rose assumed it signified disapproval but perhaps some concern as well.

Lying fully clothed atop the worn comforter on her bed, Rose replayed the events of the morning. Her shoes tapped together at the recollection of each embarrassing revelation–the frigid temperature inside the house, the dying embers in the furnace, the nearly empty coal bin, her inability to recall her last contact with Granite Coal and Oil, her initial failure even to resurrect the name of the company that had fueled her furnace for nearly twenty years. She shuddered imagining how she must have looked as Izzy grilled her.

Ayouille! *(Ouch!) You look like Vincent looks when he shoots out the shed window after his brothers teach him how to plink tin cans. Ha, ha, he looks like he gonna pee his pants, he's so scared.*

Don't laugh, old woman! The way you are now? You gonna pee your

125

own pants soon enough. First the mind. Then the bladder, eh?

What's worse, you look like the foolish child in front of Izzy, of all people. She bawls you out like she's some scary teacher. And she's your YOUNGER sister. You the one supposed to be in charge, no? This is your house, eh? But you don't take care of it so good. Izzy's right to be so cross.

Why don't you call for coal way back in late summer? Just like you always do? You think maybe the coal bin gonna fill itself? Or maybe Old Man Flint, he don't visit this year? Pah! Winter always comes. Hard times always come. And once upon a time, you the kinda lady ready for all that. Ready to keep a roof over your head, over little Izzy's head. Ready for the whooping cough and the Spanish flu and the broken bones. Ready for the tree that falls on the roof. Ready to find out about Francis. Ready to drive him to the hospital when he can't breathe. Ready to bury him, to bury Maryellen, because that's what gotta be done.

But now? You ready for anything else? You ready for your future, old woman?

The force with which Rose rapped her shoes together sent a spike of pain through both bunions. She moaned.

One second later, a huge black muzzle lay over her throat. Jolie had apparently followed her upstairs and, after keeping vigil on the bedroom floor, realized the time had come to intervene. Rose stroked the dog's massive head and withers, and allowed a single tear to roll down one cheek. Jolie raised her head to snuffle the salty skin. Then she unfurled her long tongue to rinse the sorrow away.

Rose angled her head away and chuckled. "Ah, you a good boy, Jolly."

The dog eased back a few inches to scrutinize her human quizzically.

"Ah, *saccajé chien*! You a good *girl*! You a good Jolie."

Rose's mournful sigh was muffled by the dog's head, now draped over her chest. Her fingers weaved into the fur at Jolie's nape and gave it a few gentle tugs. "Why you don't tell me to get more coal, eh? You let me look like a useless old fool in front of Izzy."

Jolie groaned happily and relaxed even more of her weight onto the recumbent human. Then she jolted back at a marked change in that human's breathing.

"*Sainte Anne*! I forget something else, Jolie! I forget Netty!"

After struggling to ease the gigantic dog away from the bed, Rose stood and sprinted for the stairs, with Jolie clumping behind her.

"Izzy? You still here?" she called from the foot of the stairs.

"Where else would I be?" Izzy laid the book she was reading face down on the kitchen table. "This is the only room that's inhabitable." She aimed her cigarette at the hissing burners on the stovetop.

"I forget Nora. She needs me to take care of Netty after school. But we have no fire in the furnace until tomorrow. This old house is too cold for a little one."

"This old house is too cold for a polar bear."

"You come with me to the living room, yeah? We see if we can get the fireplace going. Plenty of wood out by the shed."

"I thought the fireplace was out of commission. The chimney wasn't safe or something."

"No, *la cheminée*, she's fine. But the damper..."

"Are you *sure* the chimney's all right?" Izzy interrupted. "Last thing we need is a fire. On top of everything else."

"Chimney's just fine. But that old rusty damper gets stuck. Last winter, I wanna make fire for Christmas Eve when I hang the stockings I always hang for *les enfants*, even though they big, strong men. But the damper, it won't budge. Maybe me and you make it open, yeah?"

"Very well," Izzy said, stubbing out her cigarette.

After Rose removed the fire screen, she and her sister spent several minutes studying the right-angled iron lever protruding from the hearth opening. Rose explained that the lever needed to be cranked counter-clockwise to open the damper. Izzy argued that it needed to be pulled downward. They tried jiggling it, pulling it, turning it. When some soot fell, Rose dashed to the kitchen to retrieve a flashlight. But shooting its beam inside the chimney showed the damper was still firmly closed. After another visit to the kitchen, Rose returned with a long screwdriver, which she inserted into the iron rod's right angle. While Izzy held the business end of the screwdriver against the rod, Rose pushed down on the handle. With no success.

"Why don't you phone the crippled Jew boy? He's been pestering us for stories about Quebec. We can swap a few stories for his help."

Rose frowned. "His name is Nate. And he's a nice boy, him."

"Yes. And he's also young, male, lame, and Jewish. So he's a crippled Jew boy."

"*Mon Dieu*! And you a sixty-seven-year-old Quebecoise who never marries. How you like it if someone calls you an old maid Canuck, eh?"

"Oh, just phone him, for heaven's sake! I'll call him whatever you like if he can get the fireplace going."

Opening the door for Nate, Rose pointed at the wooden tool caddy he hefted by his right hip. "You come all prepared, I see."

He grinned. "Yeah, I almost look like I know what I'm doing."

Enveloped in the haze from her cigarette, Izzy groaned from the kitchen, "That's encouraging."

"Hello, Isabelle!"

"Why don't you call her Izzy, like everyone else?"

"Because Isabelle is a lovely name for a lovely lady. It just sounds right. Just like Madame Rose is right for you."

Another groan sounded from the kitchen, as Rose pointed the way toward the living room.

"Your timing couldn't have been better," Nate said, as he settled onto the hearth apron. "Wednesdays I only have morning classes. Just got home five minutes before you called. I was thinking of stopping by your place anyway. Vince is worried about that bathroom light that keeps shorting out when things get too steamy in there. Asked if I could install a new fixture. I'm pretty sure I can do that without electrocuting all of us."

"How much I owe you for that?"

"Don't worry about it. Vince will settle with me later. Meanwhile, I'm hoping I can pester you two ladies for more research for my thesis. But first things first," he added, shining a flashlight inside the chimney. "Lemme figure out how this damper rod works."

After moving the andiron, Nate lay halfway inside the hearth and peered upward into the flashlight beam while working the damper lever with his right hand. "Ugh," he exclaimed as soot fell onto his face. "Yup, cranking this thing counterclockwise is what we do. I'm getting some movement, but only a bit."

"What I tell you, Izzy?" Rose called toward the living room doorway, where her sister now stood watching the proceedings.

"Can you hand me the oil can, Madame Rose? The damper hinge looks rusty. Maybe a few squirts will limber it up."

Minutes passed, with more cranking, a few sharp thrusts up inside the chimney with a small crowbar and more than a few coughs from Nate. When he scooted out of the hearth, his glasses were nearly opaque with ash. "Okay, it's opening up a lot more. Let's see what happens if I give it some gas."

He stood by the fireplace opening and slammed down on the lever with both hands. The damper voiced a ragged protest, shooting a large gray cloud onto the hearth. When the dust cleared, Nate jolted backward and yodeled, "Jesus!"

Revulsion twisting his soot-stained face, he pointed at the long-dead raccoon now lying on the hearth.

"Ah, poor little fella. You try and get warm, yeah? Bad idea." Rose reached for the fireplace tools and swept the matted, desiccated remains onto the small ash shovel. "I take you outside."

Looking at Izzy, the still shaken Nate commented, "It's a wonder the thing wasn't stinking up the place. I guess the closed damper kept the smell out. Yuck. Well, I better get back inside there and work the damper a few more times to get rid of the rust and other crud."

Nate followed through, the damper's squeaking gradually decreasing in volume.

"Jesus!" he repeated as a little avalanche of ash, dirt, and wood clinkers—but no additional mammals—fell onto the hearth.

Izzy, now standing just a few feet away, commented, "You certainly have a cavalier way of invoking a God that's not your own."

"What?" Nate asked, turning his grubby face toward the older woman.

"You're a Jew. Why don't you invoke, I don't know, Yahweh or King David? Why take the name of our lord in vain?"

Nate stifled the urge to respond, "Oh for Christ's sake." But he couldn't stop himself from commenting, "If memory serves, Jesus was one of my people." Wiping his dirty glasses with his handkerchief, he leveled his myopic blue eyes at Izzy.

She glared back. Nate was the first to tire of the staring contest. He turned his back on his companion, picked up the oil can, and aimed another few drops at the damper hinge. Then he resumed his cranking, mostly without any squeaks. As he brushed the hearth debris to one

129

side with a whisk broom, another mini-avalanche descended through the open damper. Coughing and sputtering, Nate retrieved his handkerchief to mop his face. Looking at the mess he wiped off, he exclaimed, "King David!"

The room was silent for half a minute. Then Izzy erupted in a throaty laugh. Still bent over the hearth, Nate peered up at her through his smeared glasses. And grinned. Izzy smirked back.

"What's so funny?" Rose asked as she returned with the empty ash shovel.

"We were discussing Bible history," Izzy replied in a deadpan tone, as she stubbed out her cigarette.

"That's funny?"

"If you have the right perspective. Like Nathan here."

TWENTY

Fireside Tales

As Rose welcomed Netty into the kitchen and bade farewell to Nora, rushing out the door to make her medical appointment, Izzy dragged an easy chair close to the now-crackling fire in the living room.

"It's drawing good now," Nate said from his perch on the raised brick apron. "You got time for a few questions about Quebec?"

Izzy shrugged. "It's not like I remember much. I was only nine when we left."

"Is that why you have no accent? I don't get it. You're only two years younger than your sister, right? And no offense intended, but no one would ever think she was born here."

"Well, even before we moved, I was determined to learn English well. I was lucky to have a wonderful tutor in my Great Uncle Edward."

Nate suppressed a flinch, as he recalled Rose's anecdote hinting at the possibility of an unhealthy relationship between her mother and her great-uncle. In his psychology courses, he had learned pedophiles were typically repeat offenders. Was Izzy one of Edward's victims, he wondered.

"Tell me about this great-uncle."

"My father hated him. Edward was only five years older than my mother. They grew up together, like brother and sister. They were devoted to each other. Papa saw their closeness as a threat, I guess."

"Was he right?"

"For a while, I thought—wrongly—that he might be. Or maybe I just fantasized about Uncle Edward marrying my mother and becoming my father. He already was so much like a father to me. Certainly a mentor. Yes, I know, that's the ridiculous kind of fantasy lonely little girls dream up. With the benefit of hindsight, I realize the kindnesses that passed between Mama and Edward were nothing more than that. As for Papa, he was predisposed to think the worst of Edward, because my great-uncle symbolized everything Mama left behind when she got married. He was gentle, educated, refined, just like her former life, before her father had a heart attack and left her mother with a mountain of debt. Papa knew she took one hard step down when she married him. And she wasn't shy of reminding him of that fact."

"Why'd she marry him then? It doesn't sound like he had money to bail her out of trouble."

"You're asking the wrong person," Izzy replied, coughing. "Young love apparently does insane things to people. Especially women. My mother was smitten. At least in the beginning."

"How did your parents meet, then, if they were from different social circles?"

"They're distant cousins, actually. So they occasionally bumped into one another over the years. And after grandfather's heart attack, Mama and her mother moved in with an aunt who lived in the same parish as Papa's family."

"So they got to know each other from going to the same church?"

"Yes, just like Rose and her Francis, who met at a wedding at St. Mary's just down the road. They found out they were in the same parish. So they arranged to go to the same Mass on Sundays. He'd walk her home. And one thing, as they say, led to another."

"Huh. I wondered about that. What with the different cultures and all. French Canadian and Irish. But both of them were immigrants, right?"

"God, yes. You'd never mistake Francis for a native-born American."

132

Nate smirked at her hauteur. "But I *would* mistake you for one. So part of that is because of this Edward guy?"

"Yes. This Edward guy graduated from McGill. He saw that I was smart and dying of boredom at the dreadful church school we attended. So he gave me all sorts of books to read. Mostly in English. He'd just dump them on me and tell me to make notes of any questions I had, and we'd talk about them later."

"What kind of books?"

"Everything. But fiction was my favorite. I probably learned more history from reading Shakespeare than I ever learned in history classes. And not just up there at that awful church school, but right here in Quincy, too."

"You're talking my language," Nate said lugubriously. "I'd love to be a novelist. Not a lawyer."

"Are you any good at writing?"

"I like to think so."

"Then for God's sake, don't sit there and whine about lost opportunities. Do something about it!"

Nate shifted uneasily on the hearth apron. He didn't know whether to be offended or encouraged. Stalling for time to parse his feelings, he took several moments to reposition his bad foot into a more comfortable position then riffled through his small notebook.

Before he could think of a comment or even a new, unrelated question, Netty burst into the living room with Jolie following at a saunter. "Nana's bringing cookies. She just baked them. Jolie stole one. What a bad girl you are," the child added with mock anger, wagging an index finger. Jolie leaned forward and slurped the accusatory digit. Netty giggled.

"You'll get worms from that beast," Izzy warned.

Netty regarded her finger gravely then wiped it on her skirt, while Jolie ambled toward Izzy's chair and laid a massive paw on the old woman's forearm.

"Wretched beast!" Izzy chided, removing the paw. "Sit!"

Jolie sat instantly, wide eyes fixed on Izzy. The woman frowned, fingering a clump of fur sticking at an odd angle from the dog's ear. "You have mats, and you smell."

"You're petting her," Netty teased.

"Nonsense. I'm removing a mat," Izzy insisted.

Netty and Nate exchanged grins.

"Did you have a dog growing up, Isabelle?" Nate asked.

"On the farm in Quebec, sure. Not here in Quincy, though."

"You must have missed having a dog after you moved south."

"There wasn't much I missed about the farm."

Entering the room with a plate of oatmeal-raisin cookies, Rose interjected, "Not Izzy. She's born in the country, but she's a city girl, her—through and through."

Rising to help Rose move a small table into place for the treats, Nate asked, "So what did *you* miss about the farm, Madame Rose?"

As she settled into a chair, Rose sighed. "Ah, many things. The snow. The woods. The St. Lawrence. Mère Agathe. My pet raven."

"You don't get enough snow in Massachusetts?" Nate asked.

"You had a pet raven?" Netty squealed.

"Pah, that miserable bird!" Izzy exclaimed. "A born thief. Imagine a cat burglar who poops all over your house."

Netty made a moue of disgust. Rose laughed. Nate scribbled in his notebook.

"Why you want to write about us?" Rose asked, watching the young man's deft fingers moving across a lined page.

"I told you. It's for my history thesis."

"But why not write about that fella Hitler or Napoléon or people who matter. Why us?"

"Because ordinary people *do* matter to history. What's going on in Europe these days isn't so much about the number of armored divisions the Germans have or how many anti-aircraft batteries the English have. It's about Polish villagers watching tanks thunder past their windows. It's about Londoners surfacing from underground shelters to find their homes bombed to smithereens. The human misery caused by this war may be the main reason we got into it."

"What about Pearl Harbor?" Izzy fairly shouted. "That wasn't about sad individual stories. It was about strategy, unimpeded access to resources in the Pacific. Besides, do we really want to send young men to die on foreign battlefields because we're moved by sad stories?"

"All right, I exaggerated," Nate groused. "But I hope the day never comes when individual human experiences have no place in world history."

Rose shrugged. "I don't learn much in school. But I learn more than

134

that Hitler fella. I remember all them lessons them nuns teach, about the Hebrews getting kicked out of this place and that. Getting killed. Getting thrown in the lion den. Getting made slaves. Lots of bad times. Just like now. Lots of death. I don't remember them winning wars, but somehow they don't die off. Why not? Maybe because they have real good storytellers. Their story goes on year after year. So they go on, too."

Nate and Izzy exchanged slack-jawed expressions of wonder.

"Hey, Izzy, maybe we tell this boy our story and we live forever? So what you wanna know, Nate?"

Grabbing for a cookie, Netty said, "I wanna hear about the poopy raven!"

TWENTY-ONE

Merde

Nate sat hunched over the small mahjong table that served as his desk. He buzzed his lips as he reread his write-up of the previous day's chat at Rose's house. He had not compiled a historical account, certainly not anything that would pass muster with the critical Professor Leibowitz, much less move his thesis any closer to the finish line. For one thing, he had cleaned up Rose's sometimes halting and confusing language, all in the interest of improving readability. It may have been wise to avoid reproducing such pronunciation quirks as sounding the "th" digraph as a "d." Endless reproductions of "the" as "dee," or "they" as "dey," would have alienated the reader. At the same time, some of his editing may have deleted valuable cultural references. Worse, he hadn't been able to resist filling in some of the gaps in Rose's story, again for readability. Sighing, Nate gripped the typed pages with both hands, in preparation for ripping them into extinction. But he couldn't do it. What he had written might not make a decent chapter in his thesis, but maybe it would be a decent chapter in a future novel.

"Oh, sure," he groaned. "People are gonna rush to bookstores to read an old lady's reminiscences about the pet raven she had as a kid."

Nate prepared to rip pages once again. Once again he froze, realizing that he knew of one reader who would like just such a story. Himself. Hadn't he been fascinated to listen to Rose? He wasn't old. He wasn't particularly an animal lover. He certainly wasn't of French Canadian heritage. Yet he had proven a rapt audience. Surely, his interest couldn't be all that unusual. Surely, someone else would find the tale appealing.

He laid the typed pages back on the table and scrutinized them once again, this time with an eye to story, not history.

So, I find this injured raven on the snowy ground, yeah?" the old woman explained, flashing all five fingers of her left hand while displaying four of her right. "I'm nine years old. What do I know from ravens?

Nate's pen crossed out the "from" and substituted "about," as he realized his effort to resurrect an elderly immigrant's speech pattern had channeled his White Russian and Jewish grandmother. Shaking his head in disgust, he scanned ahead to the paragraph where he had stopped trying to reproduce Rose's diction and had begun writing about her in the third person, reproducing the nine-year-old perplexed by her discovery.

The little girl rushed the injured bird to her mentor, the wizened "sage-femme" who had brought her into this world. There was little that Mère Agathe did not know about animals. She would know how to help.

Nate twisted his lips as he wondered if that was indeed how the episode played out. He couldn't remember Rose's exact words and now doubted she would have jogged through the frigid winter weather with the traumatized bird in hand. It wasn't as if she could hail a taxi to Mère Agathe's house—assuming the old Indian woman actually lived in a house. He jotted "FIX!!" in the margin then scanned ahead a few more paragraphs.

A week later, after finishing her morning chores, Rose dashed to the storage shed shelf where she had placed the raven's wooden crate, filled with a jumble of clean rags for warmth. The raven was gone! What had happened? The little girl lifted the crate for closer inspection and spotted the blood-spattered rag that had wrapped the bird's injured left leg. "Oh no!" she cried, scanning the frozen dirt floor in search of the raven.

A questioning rasp shifted her attention to the opposite corner of the shed. There stood Noir, as Rose had christened the bird, despite a tiny fluff of white shoulder feathers interrupting the midnight black. Noir was halfheartedly pumping its wings as if intent on taking flight. Rose did not know whether the foot wound would prevent flight. Her wise-woman friend had said that crows seemed to need both feet, as well as both wings, to lift off from the ground. She had assumed the same would be true of ravens, much larger birds. Because ravens had been relatively uncommon in Quebec when Mère Agathe was growing up, she had no first-hand experience with them. Rose squinted at Noir's injured leg. From this distance, she could not see the wound, but the left leg appeared fatter than the right.

Noir stared straight at the girl, angling its head this way and that, to regard this human first with one eye then with the other. It rasped, "Groh?"

The noise sounded similar to utterances the bird had made after accepting the food Rose would bring. She decided it was asking for dinner. She moved a step toward the raven. Noir clumsily hopped backward. Rose stopped and reached into her coat pocket to produce two eggs. Noir eyed them greedily. Now when Rose moved forward, the bird did not retreat.

Nate laughed. At the pace he was writing, his history thesis would be a thousand pages long. "Yeah, sure, so I need a complete rewrite. But still, I can see Rose. I can see her bird. I think maybe what I wrote is good. I gotta save it. For something."

He flipped a few pages ahead to the point where Noir had healed but decided she (Rose was convinced the raven was female) had a good thing at the Quentin farm and would stick around. He laughed when he recalled some of the testy amplifications Izzy had inserted into Rose's narrative.

"You should have seen how ridiculous the two of them looked!" Izzy had exclaimed. "There's Rose, just barely managing to keep her left forearm steady with the stupid bird perched there. And the raven is making these weird noises and staring at her."

"Like a baby, she coo," Rose had explained then made a strangled gurgling noise.

"If the baby was Satan's spawn," Izzy had added.

138

Nate scanned his version of the exchange.

The little girl pointed an index finger at Noir. The enormous raven croaked softly and opened and shut its beak a few times before nibbling at the finger. Figuring that the bird was hungry, Rose marveled that the nibble did not hurt. She had seen the force with which Noir would often grab at her offerings left on the barn floor; chunks of sausage, ripped-off pieces of bread, hard-boiled eggs. Certainly, the bird could hurt her if she wanted to. But the nibbling seemed to communicate affection. And over time, this practice developed into an even more astonishing exchange. Noir would hold the entire finger in its beak, as if it were a pacifier. Indeed, the bird did seem quite tranquil in this mode, which sometimes lasted a full five minutes.

Fascinated, Nate wondered if Rose was right about the "cooing." Or was Izzy's characterization more on point? He set aside the typed pages and rummaged through his notes in search of other characterizations of Noir's "speech."

He saw "Geck!" scrawled at the head of one page. Beside it was the notation, "alarm cry?" Another scribble read, "Kwork," Nate's written approximation of the noise Rose had made in her own effort to approximate one of Noir's common utterances, another apparent sign of distress. ("She says 'kwork' if she sees someone she don't know," Rose had explained, "Maybe a crow. Maybe a strange man.") Nate had no idea whether Rose's observations had any scientific merit. She had been just a child, after all. She could have been anthropomorphizing, as so many pet owners do—a practice that annoyed his mother no end. Somehow that had contributed to her decision to ban all pets from the Kagan household. She was not about to have her only son reduced to a moron, gibbering over some mutt instead of focusing on his legal studies.

Having little experience with domesticated dogs and cats, to say nothing of wild animals, Nate was out of his element. But he was charmed by Rose's recollections and marveled that a poorly educated child could undertake such empirical research. Rose must have been a bright little girl. That somehow made her apparent descent into senility all the sadder. From his own family experience, Nate knew that elderly people suffering from dementia were often able to recall decades-old events with remarkable clarity. But something inside him resisted that explanation for Rose's detailed recollections. Or perhaps he simply didn't want to believe that this endearing old lady faced such a grim future as losing her marbles. What did he know? He had switched from pre-med to pre-law early in his college career—not because of poor grades. Nate just didn't like the black-and-white objectivity required of a physician. He had hoped there would be more grey in the legal profession. His parents had worried when he jumped ship at the end of sophomore year but decided lawyering was almost as good as doctoring. They would still have ample bragging rights to friends and extended family members, and the comfort of knowing their son would earn a comfortable income. There would be precious little to brag about, however, if their son tried to make a living from what his mother classified as "scribbling."

Nate shook his head roughly, to dispel his doubts about his chosen profession and to refocus his attention on the write-up.

"Now I tell you how Noir saves Izzy here," the old woman said. *"You ask her. She knows."*

Isabelle nodded, uncharacteristically supportive.

Nate recalled his surprise that the cantankerous Izzy would confirm anything positive about her older sister's pet raven. "Oh damn!" he shouted, hunching over the typewritten pages. "I went back to reporting the actual conversation." He scrawled "FIX" beside the paragraph introducing this anecdote. He held his pen over the offending paragraphs, but didn't succeed in drawing the intended "X" through them because he became engrossed in the words.

The two elderly sisters peered at each other, neither one saying a word. Rose nodded encouragement. Finally Isabelle began, after folding her hands in her lap. "I was, what, seven, eight?" she asked, looking for confirmation from Rose.

"A scrawny little bébé with glasses," Rose nodded. "With glasses even back then."

"I had been reading. I think it was Louisa May Alcott's Little Men. *Nowhere near as good as* Little Women. *But it was the last book in the stack Uncle Edward had brought me from Montreal. It was Louisa May Alcott, after all. And I was seven or eight. So I got lost in the novel. It was summer, and I had settled on a knoll overlooking the little pond Papa had dug for the horse. We didn't have pigs at the time. Thank goodness."*

Rose drummed her fingertips on the kitchen table. "Get to the good part. Get to the loup!"

Isabelle splayed her hands in exasperation. "Well now you've gone and spoiled it. Who's telling the story, eh?"

Rose tucked her head and said, "You."

"And will you let me tell it?"

Rose nodded, without making eye contact.

"As I was saying, I was lying on that little knoll and was completely lost in the book. It was afternoon and I had finished my chores, so I had free time. We had little ones to look after, but they must have been napping."

"No. It's just Domithilde napping," Rose interrupted. "Exilda still in Mama's belly."

Isabelle glowered at her sister, sighed heavily, and continued. "The point is, I had time to myself and put it to good use. Oh, how many hours I could spend reading. Even as a youngster. Children today? They just don't understand what they're missing. They'd rather go to cinemas than pick up a good book."

(The drumming resumed on Rose's side of the table.)

"I was so at peace. The temperature was delightful. And wouldn't you know it? I fell asleep. The book was splayed open on my chest. But then I heard this horrible noise…"

"Geck! Geck! Geck" Rose shrieked.

Isabelle cocked an index finger at her sister. "Yes. Precisely that noise. And every bit as dreadful sounding."

"It was Noir!" Rose interrupted.

Isabelle squeezed her eyes shut briefly. "Yes, Rose. It was Noir. That bird was circling right above me. Making that awful noise. But as awful as it was, it wasn't as terrifying as the next noise I heard."

Rose panted loudly, lolling her tongue and squinting her eyes.

"The noise I heard was panting. The panting of a wolf. And there it was, perhaps one hundred feet from me, peering around the corner of a run-in shed. Well, I sat bolt upright. And I slammed that book closed. The noise must have startled the wolf, because it took a step back. I got up slowly, figuring sudden movement might trigger a charge. I didn't know what to do but figured I should not act afraid. So I yelled, 'Ha loup!' My shouts made Noir shout out more gecks from overhead. And then Rose came…"

"I'm putting out the wash, me. Have a big metal pan. The kind you

use to grain pigs. The metal's so thin, not very heavy. Holds lots of wash from the line. Good thing it's empty. I start banging it with my hand. Wham, wham, wham, I go on the bottom of the pan. Geck, geck, geck, Noir goes in the sky. 'Ha loup!' goes Izzy on the grass. And that poor she-wolf, she just looks scared. She moves her head around looking for a way out. She looks up at Noir. At me. At Izzy. Then she looks toward the woods, way off. And she takes off. Saccajé chien, *how she runs! Us three, we make a pretty good team, eh, Izzy?"*

Isabelle chuckled. "Good enough to scare a wolf."

"Damn right. Good enough to scare a wolf."

Nate's grin spread across his face. It was a good story told by the two old ladies, as written by him. No, it wasn't up to the suspenseful standards of that English movie director Alfred Hitchcock. But all those old lady detours made the story richer. He didn't know why. But he knew he was right. His writer's gut told him so.

The reluctant pre-law student in him now wondered if, in the interest of full disclosure, he should add a codicil.

As he was leaving the Dowd home late that afternoon, Rose escorted him to the door. "You know that part about the wolf?" she whispered. "All *merde*."

"I don't understand. It's not true?"

"Well, there's a wolf all right. But Noir, she's not Izzy's hero."

"I don't understand.'

"So, I know my bird, yeah? She never likes Izzy. And, well, she's a raven. Big, tough, eats dead animals. Not gonna be afraid of any wolf. Wolves can't fly. So, I wonder to myself, what makes Noir all excited, with that geck, geck, geck." Rose winked at Nate.

"And?"

"And I go visit Mère Agathe. I tell her the story. She laughs. She says she's no expert on ravens, but she knows her crows, yeah? And crows do this thing when they see hunters—men with guns, wolves, bobcats—go for the kill. They get all excited, fly around. You know why?"

"Why?"

"They looking forward to dinner." Rose grinned evilly.

"You mean, Noir was excited because she figured if the wolf got Izzy, the bird could scavenge the leftovers?"

Rose nodded.

"So Noir wasn't a hero, alerting Izzy to danger?"

"Noir's a raven! She's no Rin Tin Tin."

"Why didn't you tell Izzy what the old Indian woman told you?"

Rose shrugged. "Izzy likes her story. She likes the idea of someone watching out for her. That doesn't happen much. Why take that away from her?"

"You're a good sister, Rose."

"Nah, not always. Just ask Izzy."

TWENTY-TWO

Holiday Tempest

Years had passed since Rose hosted a holiday gathering for the extended family. Hank always invited her to join him, Gert, and Gert's unmarried sister for Thanksgiving and Christmas dinner. But this year November came and went without the usual call from Hank. By mid-December, the older woman figured no Christmas invitation was imminent, either. She tried to shrug it off but feared the entire family was gossiping about her mental lapses. Perhaps they thought her befuddlement would cause some horrible scene at the holiday table, some tempest of embarrassment. Then again, she mused, the absence of holiday invitations might have nothing to do with her. Maybe, Rose thought with a soupçon of guilty relief, the problem lay with Izzy.

For almost two decades, until this year, Izzy had spent most Thanksgivings and Christmases with her adopted Back Bay family because she could be relied upon to keep the youngsters in line at the table. When the Winthrops went out of town for the holidays, to take the waters at The Homestead or cross the pond to visit some well-connected

English relative, Izzy claimed to enjoy the peace and quiet of an empty brownstone. Once or twice, she managed to shed her French Canadian frugality and treated herself to Christmas Eve dinner at the Copley Plaza, a hotel as famed for its elegant holiday decorations as for its Old World service and appointments.

There was no seat for Izzy at the Back Bay table this year. So the extended family probably assumed that inviting Rose meant inviting her younger sister and boarder. That was one guest too many for most of the Dowd wives, familiar with Izzy's sharp tongue and judgmental streak. Nora might have been an exception, if only because of her fondness for Rose. But she, Vince, and Netty usually spent Thanksgiving and Christmas in Dorchester with the Gavins. Nora was little inclined, as she put it, "to stick my hand up a turkey's arse," and left that task to her mother, whose holiday celebrations featured sumptuous food, beautiful decorations, and a reasonably cordial ambience, if somewhat lacking in the maternal cosseting Nora craved.

This December, however, Mrs. Gavin complained of palpitations. A medical visit confirmed her worst fears. She told her only daughter she would not be hosting Christmas dinner. Her physician had ordered her to abstain from any heavy labor, fattening food, or the emotional stress that often accompanies holiday preparations. Nora shared that sad news with Rose during one mid-December phone conversation. Rose responded predictably. The youngest branch of the Dowd family would spend Christmas with her. And Izzy.

"So how are you and Izzy doing, Ma?" Vince asked, stuffing the icebox with bottles of Narragansett ale.

His mother shrugged. "Eh, *comme ci, comme ça*," answered Rose, stirring the stock into the flour and turkey drippings in the roasting pan. Wiping her brow with her free forearm, she added, "It's hot in here. You open that window, yeah?"

Returning from the open window, Vince said, "Jeez, I hope you haven't been overdoing it. Hope Izzy helped some."

"I shoo her out of my kitchen the tenth time she tells me I'm cooking something wrong, even paring the potatoes wrong."

"Hoo boy! Is this gonna work out, Ma?"

Rose shifted her attention from the gravy to her youngest son. "Izzy, she's *ma soeur*. Family." She wagged an index finger at Vince before turning back to the stove.

"You're a good sister."

"Izzy don't think so, I bet."

"What happened between you two, anyway? All those years ago?"

"Maybe you ask her someday, yeah?"

"Hey, I'm one of the few people who like Izzy. But she still scares the crap outta me half the time. I'm not walking into that minefield."

Rose pointed toward a cabinet. "I gotta keep stirring. You go pour the cider, eh? Use the pretty glasses over there."

As Vince opened the designated cabinet, he gasped at the sight of his mother's reading glasses, stashed between two glass goblets.

"What's wrong?" his mother asked.

"Nothing." Pocketing the eyeglasses, he covered with, "I'm amazed so many of these old goblets survived all us kids."

"Your Great Uncle Edward. He sends Francis and me eighteen of them glasses. For a wedding present. Crystal. You remember them?"

"I remember. I also remember us boys breaking more than a few when you'd bring them out for the holidays. I think I felt worse than you did."

Rose grabbed the towel resting on her left shoulder and flipped it at Vince. "Go. Pour. Enough time for memories later, yeah?"

After pulling a large brass tray from a lower cabinet, Vince carefully placed the crystal ware on it along with the jug of cider and headed for the living room. He had earlier moved the kitchen table there, on Izzy's orders, so the family could dine "without reeking of turkey grease."

He was surprised to see Izzy and Netty sitting close together on the sofa, engaged in some game. He sighed when he saw his wife sitting alone in a wing chair far removed from the other guests, her back to the Christmas tree.

After pouring the cider and lighting the candles Nora had contributed, he walked toward the wing chair, tray tucked under his left armpit. "Get you anything, Nora? Another beer?"

Nora swirled a half-empty Narragansett bottle. "How about some of that whiskey you brought for Aunt Izzy?"

"You sure? I thought you weren't supposed to drink much since Dr. Kelley put you on those pills."

Nora closed her eyes. When she opened them, she fixed her husband with frozen fury. "I want a whiskey, Vince. Or is that too much to ask? Too challenging? See, what you do is, you get a measuring cup, a third of a cup. I'm sure your mother can show you where that is. Then you pour the whiskey into the third cup. Then you pour it into the glass. Then you get two ice cubes. Then you put them in the glass. Carefully, though, so you don't splash out any of the whiskey. You think you can do that for me, Vince?"

Vince rolled his eyes.

"I said, do you think you can do that?"

Vince bit his lower lip and returned to the kitchen.

"What's got your knickers in a twist, missy?" called Izzy from the other end of the living room.

"You don't need to stick your big nose in my business, Izzy," said Nora, slightly slurring each "S."

"You don't need to act the slattern in the presence of your daughter."

"What?"

"I said, behave! You're embarrassing yourself. Your parents would be so disappointed."

Nora slumped in her chair. She swirled her beer bottle once again. A tear rolled down one cheek. "They would be disappointed, wouldn't they? Look at me! Look where I am. Look who I'm with."

"Nora Gavin Dowd, you get up off your ungrateful derriere. Your mother-in-law is slaving in the kitchen while you do nothing but whine. You get in there and help Rose. Now."

Izzy never raised her voice. Never dropped the cat's cradle she was preparing for Netty. The little girl gawped at her great-aunt. Her eyes widened as she watched her mother trudge wearily into the kitchen.

"Now, where were we?" Izzy asked Netty. "Spread your fingers. A little higher," she instructed as she carefully transferred the intricate yarn structure to the girl's hands.

Nora spoke few words during Christmas dinner, and only periodically did her fork connect firmly enough with any food morsels to bring them to her mouth. Rose, sitting beside her, occasionally patted Nora's thigh and pointed toward one serving dish after the other. Unsuccessful, Rose winked and nodded, "I know your game. You just waiting for dessert, yeah? You hear about my famous minced pie. Okay, we fatten you up later then. Just skin and bones, you."

Izzy pointedly ignored her nephew's wife but engaged the others in fairly animated conversation. After debriefing Netty about the girl's favorite school subjects, she commented, "How refreshing. A child who likes to read. I understand you started reading before you were four. Vincent probably got you started with one of those dreadful pieces of doggerel he's always reciting."

"Remember him reading that story about that Sam McGee? He got some memory, him," Rose patted the thigh on her other side.

"Only because the poem sounded creepy," Vince said with a laugh. "Cremation and all that. And plenty of adventure sledding through the frozen wilderness. What boy wouldn't love that? Besides, poems are easy for kids to remember. Especially with all that interior rhyme Robert Service worked into his stanzas."

"You like them sled dogs in the poem, I bet. Vincent always loves dogs. Right, Jolly?" The massive canine, lying in back of Rose's chair, thumped her tail appreciatively.

"Daddy tried to get me a library card for my seventh birthday. But I was too young, and the lady at the Thomas Crane Public Liberry wouldn't let me."

"Library," Izzy corrected.

"Libe-rare-ee." Netty nodded. "But he got me the book I wanted anyway. On his card. *Little Women*."

"*Little Women*? You know, that's always been one of my favorites, too. But it can be challenging for someone your age. You must be quite ahead of your classmates."

"Well, I didn't finish. And Daddy had to read me some of the hard parts," Netty mumbled into her plate, while kicking her heels guiltily against the chair legs.

"How far have you gotten?"

"Jo just burned off Meg's hair. Right before they're supposed to go to a party. It smelled bad, the burning. She did it with a curling iron, like Mummy has." Fingering a lock of blonde hair, the child added, "I hope that never happens to me. That would be just awful."

"Why would you ever need to use a curling iron, with that lovely, wavy hair?" Izzy added. "You must get that from your father, even if

148

his is dark. Vincent always had a fine head of hair."

"He gets that from Papa," interjected Rose. "You remember that black thatch on Papa's head, Izzy? And it grows fast, too."

"Perhaps. I doubt Netty gets her hair from the maternal side of the family," Izzy commented, then filling the stunned silence with another question. "So which of the March girls is your favorite character?"

"Jo. She does fun stuff."

"And your least favorite?"

"Beth. She's always sick. She doesn't get to have much fun.

"No, it's not much fun to be sick, is it kiddo?" Vincent asked. "But you're probably like your Uncle Hank, not like Beth. Hank was always sick as a kid. Remember, Ma? But look at him now. Big and strong. He just grew out of being sickly."

"So will Beth grow out of it, too, Daddy?"

Nora suddenly looked up from her plate and said, "Beth dies, Antoinette. She dies young. Just like Daddy's older sister Maryellen. Just like so many children are dying in Europe these days."

"Fortunately, we're in America, not Europe," snapped Izzy. "We live in a country that grows so much food we send half of it overseas. We have the best medical care and the best lifestyle. Why do you think your grandmother and I moved here from Canada? Right, Rose?"

Rose, eyes still locked on her daughter-in-law, took a heartbeat to respond, with more heartiness than warranted. "Sure, how you think we get to be so old? America makes us strong. Plenty to eat. Like here. Look at this table! How about some more turkey, little one?"

Rose nudged the turkey platter toward her granddaughter. But Netty shook her head slowly.

"So, how do you like shipyard work, Vincent?" Izzy soldiered on.

"I really like it. It's different every day. I'm still working on engines, mostly. Lots of different vehicles used at a shipyard. But sometimes I get dragooned into other work. First month I was at Fore River, I got to help drop some sheet metal from a derrick hanging over the *Bunker Hill*."

"Hanging over that tall tower in Boston?" asked Netty.

"No, this Bunker Hill is a ship, Ne … Antoinette. The statue and the ship are named for Bunker Hill, the battle fought way back in the seventeen hundreds.

"You were on a big boat?"

149

"One of the biggest. It's an aircraft carrier."

"You're not gonna sail away on that boat, are you Daddy?"

"No, silly, I'm just helping to build it. Me and about a million other fellas."

"A million? Really?

"Maybe not that many, honey." Turning to Izzy, he added, "But I heard that nearly thirty thousand guys are working at the yard now. Thirty thousand! And you wouldn't believe how fast they're churning stuff out. They just launched the *Bunker Hill* earlier this month. And turned out another giant carrier back in June, the new *Lexington*. Two aircraft carriers in half a year! And God knows how many other warships. That's almost unbelievable. What a country to be able to gin up that fast!"

"And isn't it nice that you get to be part of that history, Vincent," Izzy said. "You never could get enough of reading history, as I recall."

"I loved all those Civil War books you gave me when I was a kid, Izzy."

"The Winthrops were going to throw them away. Can you imagine? Throwing something so valuable away."

"Like that Hitler fella," Rose added.

"Throwing books into the flames. Erasing history, literature, science, with one toss of a match." Izzy shook her head.

"Throwing *people* into the flames," said Nora. "The world is crumbling all around us and here we sit, like nothing's wrong. Pretending like everything is gonna be all right. Pretending like we're gonna live forever and never die. But we're all gonna die, aren't we? My mother's heart is already dying. It only just started, but already she can barely breathe. She's going to die horribly isn't she?" Tears suddenly streaked Nora's face. She made no effort to restrain them, to blot her dripping nose, to stanch the flow of words.

Rose patted Nora's shoulder, but the sobbing younger woman jerked away.

Izzy placed both palms on the tablecloth. "That's enough of that, Nora. Think of your…"

"Think of what? Santa Claus? He's as fake as this strong country you're all clucking about. You don't think we can't get bombed just like London? Don't you realize what's happening? Death is happening! Everyone here at this table is dying bit by bit! As soon as we're born, we start to die. And you, Izzy and Rose, you're older than my mother. How can you sit here stuffing your faces with turkey and mashed potatoes, knowing that you'll be dead in a year or two? What's the point? Why are we here to begin with?"

Nora dropped her hands and pounded her right fist on the table. The jolt sent a spoon flying into the air. It landed on Jolie, who lurched upright, bumping into Rose's chair and nearly tipping her over. Rose grabbed the table edge to steady herself, while Nora slumped forward, elbows on table, face buried in her hands. Her shoulders heaved while her sobs alternated with growls of anguish.

Vince rose robotically, walked to the opposite side of the table, where his daughter sat. He scooped Netty, frozen in her seat, into his arms and carried her into the kitchen.

Rose stood and placed both hands on Nora's upper arms. Tightening her grip when she felt resistance, Rose lifted the younger woman from her seat. "We gonna mop you up, eh? Then you have a lie-down and you feel better. A little rest and everything, it looks better." She eased Nora toward the stairs leading to the bedrooms.

Jolie trailed cautiously behind her mistress, leaving Izzy alone, back ramrod straight, arms braced against the table edge. She reached for the half-full whiskey glass beside her plate and took a big gulp. "Ohh, Vincent! What have you gotten yourself into?" she murmured before draining the glass. "Isn't love just grand?"

TWENTY-THREE

Doux et Sauvage

The rattle of pots and pans and dishware was louder than need be as the two sisters cleaned up the mess in the Rail Street kitchen. They themselves were remarkably empty of words. Rose, predictably, was the first to break the verbal silence.

"Ça a pas d'allure!" ("It makes no sense at all!"), she said, more to herself than Izzy. "Nora, she usually don't drink much. Is that why she gets so crazy? Sure, I see her sad before. But not like this. So sad and so angry."

"Hmmph. I suspect something more than alcohol is scrambling her brain," Izzy mused. "Vincent said something about medicine, pills that don't mix with alcohol. Then again, the few times I've seen Nora, she's always struck me as high-strung."

"High-strung?"

"Like Papa's fiddle strings. You wind the tuning key too tight and the string snaps. Maybe Nora has snapped." Izzy drilled the side of her head with an index finger.

"I remember when Vincent first brings Nora home. He tells me how 'sensitive' this Irish girl is. Sometimes she cries just like that!" Rose snapped two sudsy fingers. "A sad movie. When she marries Vincent at the altar. When I make her a special quilt for a wedding gift. Nora cries. Not just a few tears. The faucet wide open. Off one minute. On the next—just like that." She snapped again.

Wiping a speckle of soapy water from her glasses, Izzy mused, "Vincent always liked taking care of things, didn't he? Stray dogs. Children bullied by other children. You. I imagine the idea of taking care of a sensitive wife had appeal, or used to."

Bracing both wrists against the stacked drainboard, Rose stopped herself from complaining about being lumped in with stray dogs.

Oblivious to her sister's reaction, Izzy continued. "There are worse reasons to fall in love, I suppose. Someone or something that makes you feel useful, needed, can be very attractive indeed. I just hope Vincent hasn't taken on more than he can handle." Exhaling abruptly, she said, "Enough of this nonsense! It's been a long day and the kitchen's reasonably tidy. I have a good novel to look forward to. So I'm off to bed." Turning toward her sister, who remained braced rigidly against the sink, Izzy added, "Unless you need something. Are you all right?"

Lowering shoulders into a more relaxed position, Rose replied, "Everything *tiguidou*. You go."

"Fine. But first I need something for this parched throat." Izzy grabbed one of the draining glasses and hovered her other hand over the cold water tap. "No, not this awful tasting well water of yours. Do we have any cider left?"

Rose rolled her eyes and waved a hand toward the icebox.

Hours later, the glow from Izzy's bedside lamp died, leaving the upstairs in gloom. The blackout curtains shut out the pale light from the shaded street lamp four doors down. Rose tried sighing the darkness away. She considered lighting her own bedside lamp, but decided her electric bill would benefit from the gloom. She would face the darkness as she had faced so many things. And blessed sleep would eventually overcome her worries for Vincent, for Nora, for little Netty, for herself. She folded her hands over her solar plexus, stared at the black ceiling, and waited.

Her wait was eventually rewarded, not with sleep but with musings about her own love life. She was exploring random byways of memory more and more since her sessions with Nate, even when Nate was not there to turn her progression of words into ink blots. Izzy's comments after the guests had left headed her down yet another path as she lay, sleepless, in bed. Who was the caretaker in her own marriage? Rose smiled, realizing those tasks were fairly evenly divided. Izzy was right that it was good to be needed, to feel useful. It was also good to feel loved and cared for. Not that Francis would ever strike anyone as sentimental or nurturing. But she knew that a vibrant sapling thrived beneath that flinty exterior.

She spotted it the first time she met him, at the reception following the wedding uniting one of Mrs. Halloran's daughters with a quarry worker. Watching him pull off his slouch cap and crush it in his rough hands as he entered the church hall, she wondered if he would fit through the doorway. His shoulders were so broad. *Ma fois!* Just like a *voyageur!* She felt a pang of homesickness, as conflicting images of her homeland suddenly surfaced. The St. Lawrence groaning beneath its ice pack. The sweet smell of spring grass. The stern limestone cliffs. The radiance of the candles sputtering on the rough-hewn *reveillon* table. The darkness of the boreal forest dwarfing rural Quebec's pockets of civilization. A decade after being uprooted, Rose still missed the *doux et sauvage* landscape, sweet and wild, that had shaped her.

Standing in that reception hall, Rose squeezed her eyelids and tightened her neck muscles, to dam the unbidden images about to flood her brain. Why were these memories seizing her at that particular moment, at a joyful wedding celebration held at a latitude where Old Man Flint had far less power to break the human spirit? When she reopened her eyes, she knew the answer rested with the new arrival striding across the hall. He had probably never laid eyes on Quebec. Yet the *doux et sauvage* character of her northern homeland described him, as well.

Unlike a *voyageur*, the Irishman stood well over six feet. Rose liked the idea of straining her neck to hold a man's eyes. It was not the French Canadian way to be so direct, but it was Rose's way. Besides, she was now twenty, an age that presaged terminal spinsterhood back in Quebec for a still single woman. If she wanted a husband and children, it was high time to take action. So she stared, challenging the new arrival to lock eyes with her. When he did, she couldn't stifle a tiny gasp of surprise at the paleness of those blue eyes. It was a color that could be described as frosty or effervescent. As he approached, his eyes were cool, inquiring, and intelligent. When she smiled at him, his eyes smiled back, sparkling with light and warmth.

All these years later, she couldn't remember how the conversation began, but she recalled that there were few uncomfortable moments. In her culture, women nudged the conversation along with little help from male counterparts. In the Irish culture, the gift of gab was equally distributed between the sexes.

Early on in that first conversation, Francis Xavier Dowd told Rose he was a quarryman. He seemed neither proud nor ashamed of his job. Rose's broad smile apparently puzzled him, because he said something about being happy to have a job that provided regular income, but he hoped one day to find work more suited to his aspirations. "I'd like to find my way into politics, don't you know."

Still digesting the quarryman comment, Rose exclaimed, "My Papa, too. Another quarry worker. René Quentin. Maybe you know him?"

"And which quarry would it be where he works?"

Rose waved a hand dismissively. "Pah, he's gone. Back in Canada three years now. Back to farming. Not in Quebec. Way out in Manitoba, where the wheat grows good."

"Will he send for the rest of the family once he gets the farm going?"

"Mama's with him from the start, with all my sisters and two baby brothers. All except Izzy, two years younger than me."

Genuine concern flickered in Francis's pale blue eyes. "But you and your sister would have been just slips of lasses. Surely you have someone to look after you? An aunt? A grandparent?"

Rose shook her head.

"How have you managed? It's sorrowful enough when men can't find decent work, especially us immigrants. It sounds impossible for two young women to manage all by themselves, with no family to stand by them."

"*Pantoute*! (Not at all!) Everything's fine. Izzy, she teaches the little ones how to read. Me, I find good jobs. From Hough's Neck to East Milton, people know the quarryman's daughter can clean and sew like, how you say, like the dickens. Izzy and me help at the rooming house where we live, too. I clean. She helps with Mrs. Halloran's new *bébé*."

"Halloran's boardinghouse, is it?" When Rose nodded, Francis continued, "And what would you be thinking if I paid a call on you there? You and your sister. We could all go out for ice cream some Sunday afternoon, so?"

One week later, Izzy would have none of that idea. She told Rose to march down to the boardinghouse parlor and wait for her new beau there. Weeks would pass before Izzy finally met Francis. By that time, she was determined to find him unworthy.

Izzy set about thoroughly researching this Francis Xavier Dowd. Gossip was a major form of entertainment in the eighteen-nineties, and there was no shortage of juicy grapes sprouting on the West Quincy vine. Izzy quickly learned that this Dowd person had emigrated just two years earlier, straight from County Cork, which seemed to be where more than half of the local Irish rabble hailed from. They all had an odd speech cadence, with lots or rising intonations and hard R's. All of them talked too much, using ten words when two would do. Drank too much. Laughed too much. Having been in America for nearly a decade now, Izzy considered recent arrivals far below her on the social ladder. It didn't help that Francis was a quarryman.

"But Papa's a quarryman!" Rose protested when Izzy presented her with the disappointing details of the would-be suitor's life.

"*Saccajé* chien! And how did that ever help us? He liked working the quarries so much he ran off to Manitoba the first chance he got!"

"But that quarry job gives him the money. He has enough to pay rent, buy food, and still save. Save enough to pay for the move."

"My point exactly," replied Izzy, as if the quarries had somehow triggered her and Rose's abandonment.

Rose raised both palms to the ceiling and turned away.

"He's some kind of ruffian, too," Izzy called after her sister before Rose could turn the doorknob and exit their room. "He's a Fenian, they say. Killed a constable back in Ireland."

"What's a Fenian?" Rose asked.

"Some kind of … what's the word? Anarchist. They hate law and order. They hate the British. They kill the educated ruling class. People like Uncle Edward. If the Fenians take over in Ireland, the country will be even more thuggish than it is today."

Rose rolled her eyes. She had come to know many Irish people in

West Quincy and knew they could be as kind and intelligent or as nasty and stupid as members of any other race. Nor did she particularly think that a country run by the likes of Uncle Edward would be all that superior. But there *was* the matter of murder.

"Francis, he kills someone?"

"Well, they don't know for sure. But he had to get out of Ireland fast or be arrested, they say. He was so mad to leave, he deserted his sick mother. Left his whole family."

"Pah, not his whole family. His brother Dinny comes with him. Francis tells me:

"*Mon Dieu*, the brother!" Izzy retorted. "Dennis has something wrong with him, people say. Big lout of a man, and he can barely put two words together. Not good for anything, except drinking probably."

"Francis says Dinny, he don't drink at all. A teetotaler. I guess he drinks only tea, yeah? And Dinny is good enough to get work here, even before Francis. As a fireman at Swingle's quarry."

"Now there's a fine recommendation," Izzy harrumphed.

Even at age twenty, Rose had an inkling why Izzy seemed so opposed to Francis. Admittedly, the younger Quentin girl was not favorably inclined toward many men, unless they were of the refined, vaguely effeminate nature of Uncle Edward. But the antipathy toward Francis was rooted in fear. At the time Francis came into their lives, neither sister had recovered from the trauma of abandonment. After fending for themselves for slightly over two years, they had reached a *modus vivendi*, were even able to put away the occasional dollar. But Rose, ever practical, wondered how long they could keep the wolf from their door. Marrying a good wage-earner could improve the odds, for both sisters. What if one of them fell ill and couldn't work? Even a short layoff could have catastrophic financial consequences. Truth be told, it never occurred to Rose that sickness could befall *her*. She figured she could work her way through almost anything. But Izzy was another matter. She'd always suffered from respiratory congestion. The consumption claimed far sturdier specimens than the rail-thin Izzy. One of their fellow rooming-house boarders, a rosy-cheeked, pleasingly plump Irish immigrant, had caught the dreaded disease just six months before Rose met Francis. Fortunately, the girl was taken in by a cousin in Springfield. Unfortunately, the latest news from western Massachusetts was grim. The girl was not expected to last through the winter.

157

Practicality was certainly part of the reason for Rose's attraction to Francis. Only two years older than she, he was in his prime. The hard work of drilling into granite had only toughened him, further developing the already impressive musculature that apparently ran in the Dowd family (from what Rose could see of Dennis, an even beefier specimen). He partook sparingly or not at all of those habits that could shorten a working life. Rose guessed he would be able to work all the way through his forties. He would be an excellent provider. He would probably give her robust babies, too.

Sharing equal import with practicality was lust. Even now, all those decades later, Rose experienced a tingle just thinking of Francis. Even now, after witnessing his muscle mass shrink in his final decade, as silicosis ravaged his lungs, she sighed just thinking of those broad shoulders, those pale blue eyes, and the surprisingly gentle caress of those huge hands. Lying in bed all these years later, Rose imagined herself curling into that large frame. How often had she taken refuge there. How often had she taken pleasure there, even when she was no longer of childbearing age, even when Francis's best days were behind him and libido ranked far lower than his interest in a good night's sleep. She had always been able to transport him from slumber into sex.

Without thinking, the long-widowed Rose reached for his side of the bed and exhaled her disappointment at finding it empty and cold. She snorted at her longing, at her distorted sense of time. She slid a hand down her belly and between her legs, just to see if desire could still trigger the appropriate physical response. Sure enough, she felt that lovely, slippery moisture. She snorted again. "Your mind, she may not work so good. But you not dead yet, old woman."

Her mind was not so weak, however, that it failed to do Rose's bidding: to focus on something other than the desire that could not be fulfilled. Not the way she wanted. So she focused on Francis's shortcomings. He was set in his ways. Opinionated. Wary of anyone not born in Cork or descended of Corkonians. Ulstermen, for example, were lesser beings, to say nothing of French Canadians. Francis had a quick temper and a long memory of past offenses. The yelling didn't bother her as much as the stony silences. There were times when she could no longer summon the energy to cajole him out of his gloom.

Rose felt a stab of guilt. Yes, he was not the easiest husband to live with. But she had certainly been right about him being a good provider. He worked hard and long, and never spent his wages frivolously. He was happy to leave the household budget to her. She was also right that he would give her robust babies. Four of her five children reached adulthood, an enviable statistic for the late-nineteenth, early twentieth centuries. Most of her neighbors had lost more than one of their children to diphtheria or pneumonia or scarlet fever or the measles. She might have wished Francis were a more engaged father, but she was just as happy raising the children by her own well-tuned instincts. Hadn't she seen many fathers undo all the hard work their wives had put into child-rearing? So many fathers of that era would swing between bone-chilling rage when their offspring misbehaved and intrusive affection when the children accomplished something boast-worthy. Rose, on the other hand, was a consistent disciplinarian, affectionate and steady and willing to give her sons and daughter the space they needed to test their wings. In the process, she often had fun with them. She doubted Francis ever had fun with his children. No, he was not the perfect father, either. Yet she knew that having him father her children was something she would do all over again if she could be transported back in time.

Izzy, on the other hand, would probably rewrite history. For Rose, Francis kept the wolf from the door. For Izzy, Francis *was* the wolf. It didn't matter how often Rose, before heading off to meet her suitor, assured her younger sister that she would always have a place in her home; Izzy dreaded yet another abandonment. Rose would abandon her to chase some foolish romance, just as her parents had abandoned her to chase some foolish dream of raising wheat in some godforsaken corner of Canada.

Francis was the wedge between the two eldest Quentin sisters. The rift widened with the decades and did not narrow after his death. Not yet, at least. Rose wasn't all that sure she wanted a closer relationship with her testy younger sister. At this time of life, however, another ally would be welcome–if Izzy was actually capable of dropping her defenses enough to be an ally to anyone. Rose would settle for peaceful coexistence, without the sniping and lecturing.

159

TWENTY-FOUR

Driving & Life Lessons

"You ready?" Vince asked his aunt.

"As much as I'll ever be," Izzy replied. "If this godforsaken outpost of Quincy had decent public transportation, I wouldn't be bothering you with this."

"How about you unwrap your fingers from the steering wheel? Your knuckles are already white and you haven't even cranked the engine."

"But what if this contraption lurches forward and I need to steer us away from disaster?" Izzy's face was five shades paler than usual.

Vince pointed to the emergency brake. "You see that? The brake is on, so we're not going anywhere until you take it off. And we're sitting in this huge, flat parking lot, after business hours on a weekend, so there's not a whole helluva lot for you to hit even if the car should get a mind of its own. Now take a deep breath and…"

"What do you mean, 'get a mind of its own'?"

"Just a figure of speech, Izzy. Besides, I'm right here and I can grab the emergency brake anytime. So relax. Lady as smart as you? You're gonna be a natural. Okay, so press down hard on the clutch with your left foot and keep it there. Put your right foot on the brake then turn the key in the ignition. To the right."

Izzy exhaled a series of sputters as the engine roared into life.

"See? Piece of cake. Now keep both feet exactly where they are and put the gear shift into first, just like I showed you."

"It won't budge," Izzy said.

"Pump the clutch a few times. Try it again. Good. You got it in gear. Now move your right foot to the accelerator and while you gradually raise your left foot off the clutch, slowly press your right foot on the accelerator."

"You expect me to do all that at once?" Izzy asked, incredulous.

"Yup."

After ten failed efforts, Izzy rested her forehead on the steering wheel. Vincent patted her right knee. "This time you'll get it. I can feel it," Vince said.

Turning to him, she met his smile with an arched eyebrow. His smile never wavered, so she sucked in a deep breath and tried again. This time the car lurched forward as Vince disengaged the emergency brake. "What'd I tell ya? Okay, keep giving it a little gas, not too much now, and put it into second. Left foot back on the clutch, shift, then..."

"Why can't I just keep it in first? I don't need to go fast."

"It's better for the engine, Izzy. Hear how loud the engine is? It won't be so noisy once you're in second."

This time, it took only three times to switch from first gear to second. "See, you're already driving!" Vince said triumphantly.

"But where am I going?" she said, both hands glued to the steering wheel.

"Let's just circle around to the left for a while. After that, we'll do a figure-eight so you can practice circling to the right. To get a feel for the wheel."

"Will I have to shift again?"

"Nah, we're doing about fifteen miles an hour, so we're copacetic. We'll save third gear and reverse for the second lesson."

"If I don't kill both of us first."

"You know how many people I've taught to drive? I'm still here. And I haven't killed one of them, either. Not yet, anyway." He winked.

"Thanks," Izzy groused.

"Remember, I taught your sister how to drive. If she can do it, you can do it. Helluva good driver, too, Ma is."

Izzy pried her left hand off the steering wheel to push her glasses higher on her nose. Then she bit her lower lip. The picture of fierce concentration, she gave the engine a bit more gas as the car arced smoothly to the left.

"Wanna try third gear on that access road?" Vince asked.

Izzy nodded tightly. With a minimum of instruction, she succeeded on the first try. With surprising smoothness, she eased the Ford onto the deserted access road leading from the now vacant factory parking lot.

"There we go! Just keep the speed at about twenty, twenty-five." He pointed at the speedometer.

"I don't want to take my eyes off the road!"

"It'll take just a second every now and then to check the dash. And when we get into traffic, you'll be regularly checking your rear view mirror, too."

"Swell."

Fifteen minutes later, after a brief kerfuffle over putting the car into reverse and then working up the gears again, the Ford was back in the parking lot, where Izzy wanted to focus on her steering, After two or three loops, some of the tension eased out of her spine.

"So, Ma really ended up in Braintree instead of East Milton, when she was driving you to your dentist appointment?"

Izzy nodded.

"That sure doesn't sound good. Did she realize what she'd done?"

"She made some excuse, but … wait, what's that noise?"

"Give it a little more gas. The engine's just lugging 'cause the speed's too low. What was the excuse?"

"Excuse? Oh, *saccajé chien*! Now it's roaring. What happened?"

"Your knee knocked the gear shift into neutral. Just put it into…"

Vincent's head jolted forward as Izzy put both feet on the brake and the engine shuddered into a stall.

"How does anyone talk and drive at the same time?" Izzy complained. "I've had enough." She yanked the key from the ignition and thrust it at Vince, as he jerked up the emergency brake.

"Not bad for a first lesson," he said, grinning while palming the key.

"Don't patronize me. I was awful."

"Don't be silly, you instinctively did the right thing when you felt overwhelmed."

"What are you talking about?"

"You remembered the most important pedal: the brake pedal. Same time next Sunday?"

He hopped out, walked around the car and opened the driver's door. Izzy swatted his hand away as he tried to help her out. But she smiled weakly. "Next Sunday then."

They switched seats and Vince restarted the engine. "So, Ma claimed she thought the dentist was in Braintree instead of East Milton? You think that's why you ended up in the wrong place?"

"No. That was just an excuse. She didn't seem to know east from west, south from north. She was just plain lost, Vincent. Lost in an area she's known for decades."

"Crap."

"Don't be crude, Vincent. You've got to do something about her."

"Like what? Put her in some looney bin? And where would that leave *you*?"

Vince instantly regretted that last shot, but it had the desired effect of shutting down his aunt's nagging. After five minutes of silence, he said, "Look, I'm sorry, Izzy, but I've got a lot going on right now and not doing all that swell with it."

Izzy nodded slowly. "Nora, you mean."

"Nora, I mean."

"That medication she's on isn't helping?"

"Not that I can see," Vincent said with a shrug. "Sometimes it makes her loopy, and she falls asleep in the middle of the day. Damn near burned the house down the other day when she fell asleep at the kitchen table with a cigarette in her mouth. Other times she's a bundle of energy, with or without the pills. Last week, I woke up to thuds and a bunch of clanking. It was two in the morning and there she was mopping the kitchen floor. I don't think I've ever seen her mop the floor before. But there she was hefting this big metal pail around, sloshing suds all over the linoleum."

"What did she say when you walked in?"

"She told me she'd spilled some applesauce when she was making dinner and didn't have time to clean it properly. After dinner she forgot all about it. But when she was lying in bed, she remembered and worried the spill would get all tacky. Since she couldn't sleep anyway, she figured she might as well clean things up. She laughed it off and kept right on mopping."

"Well, she certainly seemed highly strung at Christmas. That's not good for Netty to see."

"You're not telling me anything I don't already know."

"Can't you sit her down and tell her to pull herself together?"

"Do you tell someone with tuberculosis to pull herself together?"

"You're saying she has an illness?"

"Oh, Izzy, what do I know? But I don't think a stiff upper lip lecture will solve anything."

The conversation fizzled out, with both occupants suddenly fixated on the windshield wipers Vincent had just startled into action. The rubber blades rhythmically tidying the chaos of sleet were soothing.

"It's a pity, though," Izzy said suddenly.

"What?"

"A stiff upper lip is underrated. Look what it's done for the English. It got them through the Blitz, after all. But ... no, it isn't always enough, is it?" She patted Vince's right knee. "But, God knows, hard work and sheer grit should be rewarded."

"Huh?"

"What did I get for all the years with the Winthrops? When do you get *your* reward, Vincent? Is there no such thing as justice in this world anymore?"

"Not much justice when half the world is in the grip of Hitler and Hirohito."

The conversation faded once again, and the only sounds were the steady beat of the windshield wipers and the clacking of ice pellets on the roof.

As Vincent eased the Ford into his mother's driveway, Izzy slapped the dashboard and said, "I need a drink. You do, too, Vincent. Up in my room is a fifth of Jameson's. I bought it for your birthday next month. But I think you could use it sooner than later. It won't solve anything, but we'll feel better for a while."

"Best idea I've heard in days. Eat, drink, and be merry, Izzy, for tomorrow we may die."

TWENTY-FIVE

Mid-Winter Visitations

It had been a good day. Vince didn't even mind the snow. With temperatures in the low twenties, the snow was feather-light. He wasn't worried about widowmakers crashing into the roof, because the snow wasn't sticking much to the trees. Neither was there any wind. Although eight inches had already accumulated, with perhaps four more coming before the storm petered out, "dry snow" posed far fewer problems for shoveling and commuting.

The frigid air would pose problems for his shipyard tasks, however. All those engines he maintained would be difficult to start. But he actually looked forward to the challenges. He felt part of something bigger, worthier than himself. Fore River was acquiring the reputation as the world's most productive shipyard. As one of more than thirty-thousand reasons why, he no longer felt guilty about his draft deferment. He was truly contributing to the war effort, as warships of every size, shape, and purpose moved into the deep waters of Hingham Bay at a hectic pace.

Would his father be proud of him? Francis Dowd had been so

disappointed at his youngest son's refusal to join the police force, a fast-track ticket to respectability and financial security for the Irish, even in the days of "No Irish Need Apply." Would Francis appreciate the historical continuity of shipyard work? Vince certainly did. The son and grandson of quarrymen, he savored the realization that Quincy's quarry industry had paved the way for shipbuilding, perhaps just as much as the deep-water channels on the city's twenty-seven-mile-long shoreline. Thanks to all those granite quarries, the commercial transportation infrastructure and skilled labor force were already in place when the country needed a shipbuilding dynamo.

Lying in bed in the snow-muffled silence of night, Vince almost convinced himself that his father's opinion didn't matter. Vince knew he was precisely where he should be. That would have to be enough.

He didn't even mind being alone in bed. He had headed for bed earlier than usual, in anticipation of an emergency call summoning him to the yard to wrestle with engines stalled by the cold. But nine-thirty was far too early for the Sandman to work his magic on Nora. Vince had left her playing solitaire on the dining room table. She had accepted his peck on the cheek and wished him good night. She seemed perfectly normal. Vince was tempted to view her Christmas meltdown as one of those aberrations suffered by sensitive people, especially during the holidays. Since then, there had been no slumps of despondency. And her one spell of frenzied activity had some logic behind it.

Vince's next thought, of Netty, was less cheerful. His daughter had picked up some new bug, causing collywobbles for both gut and upper respiratory system. By past standards, however, this latest illness seemed relatively mild. When he had checked her bedroom en route to his own, Netty was sleeping peacefully, with the therapeutic steamer making more noise than the little girl's congested breathing.

Vince's mind drifted to some pleasant interactions at work that day. He had joined several fellows warming themselves around an oil drum, repurposed as a fireplace. Half of them were drinking from coffee thermoses laced with whiskey. Technically, alcohol was banned, but supervisors recognized its warming powers in a season when hawsers dripped icicles, and the east wind peppered exposed skin with frozen salt. History lover that he was, Vince particularly enjoyed that day's discussion around the glowing oil drum. Who was "Kilroy?" By now,

American newspaper readers were familiar with photographs of the ubiquitous graffiti marking the passage of G.I.s through the Pacific and North Africa: a bald forehead, two bulging eyes, and one large nose overhanging a wall, with the notation, "Kilroy was here." Half of the oil-drum debaters insisted Kilroy was one of their own, a welding inspector whose chalk marks certified the soundness of ship rivets. The other half insisted the graffiti had begun with some P.F.C. named Kilroy. Vince had no opinion but enjoyed the good-natured ferocity with which the two sides presented their arguments.

The smile evoked by that memory widened as Vince remembered that tomorrow marked his thirty-eighth birthday. It didn't matter that no celebration was likely. Nora could be counted on to wish him well, perhaps with an embarrassed confession that she had never gotten around to purchasing a gift. Annual exchanges of birthday gifts had faded since Netty's arrival. Birthdays were for children, the parents reminded each other. But Vince was still young enough at heart to feel both special and hopeful as he launched a new natal year. Perhaps that upbeat feeling traced back to the birthday celebrations of childhood, for him and his brothers. His mother would always bake a cake, uniquely decorated to reflect the birthday boy's interests. He was free to eat the whole cake if he wanted, instead of sharing. She would often invite the boys' friends to join in the festivities and never blanched when the hooligans roughhoused in the living room or crashed into shrubbery in pursuit of an errant football. She would often invite Aunt Izzy to the celebration, which meant an extra gift—in Vincent's case, a much appreciated book.

His smile faded as he contemplated his mother's current problems. Like Nora, she had seemed "normal" in recent weeks, for the most part, anyway. How long would that last? Shaking his head, he willed himself to stop pursuing that path, lest he never find sleep. Instead, he focused on the cozy susurrations from the radiator and the delicious contrast between the warmth inside the bedcovers and the slight chill on his face. He could feel his body melting into the mattress and knew he would soon be swept away into his own unique and endlessly interesting dream world.

The first dreams that came were fleeting images. There he was, skipping on a scaffold forty feet above Fore River. There he was, cheek on fist, elbow on desk, as his second-grade teacher droned on. There he was, in some ridiculous costume, as he clumsily partnered Nora in a ballroom festooned with candelabras. There he was, sitting hip-to-hip with a large wolf sharing a view of the ice-bound St. Lawrence.

And there Nora was again, standing on top of the bed in her own ridiculous costume. A plastic cone served as a hat. Streamers dangled from both wrists. A party horn wobbled between her lips. She stood there motionless, watching him, then jolted into life, jumping up and down, flailing the streamers at him, and blowing the party horn's paper coil in and out. Amused by the phantasm, Vince marveled at its vividness. He could actually feel the mattress bounce with every barefooted jump. He could all-too-clearly hear the party horn and the noise-maker Nora began twirling with her right hand.

"Wake up, wake up, wake up," shouted the apparition. "It's midnight, the start of your birthday. We don't want to let one minute of it pass before wishing you happy birthday. Isn't that right, Antoinette? She gestured toward the dark corner behind the cracked door. The wan glow from the hall light barely penetrated the shadows, but Vince could make out a small silhouette, arms apparently clutched to chest. "C'mon, c'mon!" coaxed the apparition.

The little figure unsteadily emerged from the shadows. It halfheartedly waggled a streamer toward the bed and whispered, "Happy birthday, Daddy."

Vince sat upright, so quickly his head spun. He lit the bedside lamp, which triggered giggles from Nora and some more jumps on the mattress. Netty's face telegraphed confusion.

"I bet you thought we'd forget," exclaimed Nora, still bouncing. "But we didn't, did we, Antoinette? No siree, Bob! We didn't, did we?"

"No siree, Bob," repeated Netty solemnly.

Propped up against his bed pillows, Nate Kagan gingerly raised the shade. His room was so small that the only place for the bed was smack up against the wall containing the room's solitary window. The siting was unfortunate in winter, with the late January chill penetrating both the storm window and interior window. With his thumbnail, Nate scraped away the ice glaze to get a better view of the snow scene below. He sighed. Walking was difficult enough for him without slippery conditions. Nevertheless, the poet in him savored the snow's talent for muffling dissonant traffic noise and temporarily making the dirty world disappear.

He worried briefly at the brightness of the scene, as the snow magnified the dim yellow from the downcast street lamp, making his comfortable suburban neighborhood vulnerable to German bombers. No, he reminded himself, the Nazi war machine had neither aircraft carriers nor bombers capable of reaching America's shores.

He chided himself for reading newspaper accounts of the war close to bedtime. The news was so depressing. The Nazi conquest of Western and Central Europe was complete. So far, the physical damage inflicted by British and American bombing raids on *Das Vaterland* was minimal. Soothing normalcy still prevailed for the majority of Germans, in sharp contrast to their counterparts in London or Warsaw. Vince tried to take comfort from the stalled Nazi advance on Stalingrad but shuddered at the human toll for the starving residents of that besieged city.

He jumped when he heard a crash downstairs. "Sorry," yelled his *zayde*, "I bump into the *verkakte* chair in the dark."

How many other Jews of his age had jumped this very night at nocturnal crashes, as well-polished jackboots kicked in house doors? But he reminded himself this was America. It couldn't happen here. Except...

How many German Jews had thought the very same thing a decade earlier? Pogroms happened in uncivilized Eastern Europe, they told themselves, not in civilized Germany, where Jews were well-represented within the professions, academe, the business elite, the arts.

Even in White Russia, his family's ancestral homeland, Jews had enjoyed comfortable lives in cities like Minsk. They accounted for close to ten percent of the country's population in the nineteen-twenties. Yiddish numbered among the official languages. Then came the Great Purge of the nineteen-thirties, with Jews figuring prominently among the victims. Then came the Hitler–Stalin pact, with Moscow promising to purge the Soviet Union of Jewish "domination." When that pact fell apart and the Nazi tank turrets slued east, Stalin started deporting untold numbers of Byelorussian Jews to Siberia. The Central Committee didn't want unreliable elements undermining the defense of the western borders. Then came the German occupation and systemic extermination of the Byelorussian Jews.

Although Nate's grandparents had emigrated decades earlier and produced American-born offspring, secure in their U.S. liberties, other relatives had rejected the wisdom of emigration. For years, Zayde received scolding letters from the relatives who had stayed behind. Surely, he would come to his senses and return to the bosom of his family, taking with him all those dollars he had earned in America? Despite his annoyance, he maintained contact and occasionally sent home gift packages filled with hard-to-get items. Before double-wrapping each package, he would stash several twenty-dollar bills among the more boring items, like socks and underwear, in hope of eluding detection by Soviet officials, almost as starved as the Byelorussian Kagans for what hard currency could procure.

The familial scolding stopped shortly after the new decade began. Zayde heard not one word from the Old Country until last week, with the arrival of a yellowed and tattered letter written more than a year earlier by a Gentile neighbor of Zayde's niece. It had moved through a network of friends and relatives in various European cities before finally arriving in Quincy. The neighbor reported that Zayde's niece, along with her entire family, had disappeared during the German advance on White Russia. Armed thugs had burst into their home in the middle of the night and taken the family away. The identity of those thugs was unclear. Some claimed the intruders were Soviet commissars. Some blamed advance units of Nazi *Einsatztruppen*. Also unclear was which identity presaged the worse fate.

After receiving the letter, Nate's father placed a dusty shoebox on the dining room table. It contained family photographs. The Kagans suddenly wanted to view the likeness of the missing relatives, as if that act could somehow keep them in this world.

Squinting at the inked inscription on the back of one photograph, Nate's father asked, "This is Kuzina Gittel, right?" He had never met that branch of the family.

"Could her face stop a clock?" Zayde asked, grimacing.

"Umm, well, she's not very attractive."

"Then that's your cousin."

"Lemme see, Dad," interrupted Nate. "Yikes!" he added when

seeing the photograph.

"Stop that, this instant!" scolded Nate's mother. "Who knows what's happened to that poor woman! How can you talk about her like that? God keep her from harm!"

The Kagan men assumed properly contrite expressions as they examined more photographs of Kuzina Gittel. Unable to discern a family resemblance in the sharp features and arched brows, Nate felt oddly relieved. If that perpetually scowling face had looked like his father or grandfather, then her tragedy would feel more personal.

Before the Kagans dispersed, Zayde commented, "One thing I remember about Gittel. As a *maideleh*, she was crazy for dogs. Dogs were crazy for her, too."

And suddenly, Gittel's tragedy became personal for Nate.

In the week that followed, the dog-loving Gittel would often surface, unbidden, in his thoughts. He could make her disappear when he was occupied with schoolwork and chores. Not so easy as he lay in bed, waiting for sleep to overtake him on a still and snowy night.

Staring at the ceiling as he now lay in bed, Nate conjured Gittel's scowling face. He wondered about the reason for the disagreeable expression. Was her life marked by hardship? Or did she just need eyeglasses? She had found a mate and mothered two children, so she must have had her appealing moments. Did she smile at her children? Did she smile at her dog?

The Gittel image Nate had projected onto the ceiling took on a life of its own. She began slowly wagging a finger at him, as a doleful-eyed spaniel suddenly appeared at her side. It wagged its tail at the same slow tempo as Gittel's accusatory finger. Her mouth was making exaggerated movements, trying to communicate something to her American cousin. In frustration, she stomped her foot, clad in a shoe almost as ugly as Nate's own corrective footwear.

He winced and shook his head abruptly, in hope of shaking Gittel off the ceiling. But when he reopened his eyes, there she was, still scolding him. He turned on the light to extinguish this apparition. As Gittel faded, Nate heard her say, "Witness!"

"Sure, as if Cousin Gittel knows a single word of English!"

But Nate sensed her message was significant, no less so because he knew it was generated by his own psyche. He pondered the meaning.

Perhaps he was supposed to stand witness to Gittel's fate? To history?

"So what am I doing writing about the history of some dotty old French Canadian lady? Am I supposed to run off to Europe and become a war correspondent? What do I know from journalism?"

But the seed of an idea had burrowed into his grey matter. Just maybe, his research into Quentin family history would limber up the intellectual muscles needed for more compelling historical reporting. And more. Perhaps he could become a Jewish Hemingway, with war reporting as the grist for the next Great American Novel.

"Mom would kill me," he whispered, while thinking, just maybe, *Dad would be proud.*

The front walk was shoveled. A hurricane lamp and half a dozen unlit candles were positioned around the house in case the electricity failed. Two five-gallon jugs of water stood on the kitchen counter in case a power outage killed the electric well pump. Just the right amount of coal was in the furnace to ensure a steady fire, not too hot to overload the pipes with steam and not too weak to burn out until well after sunrise.

"Not so bad for a seventy-year-old, eh?" Rose thought as she lay staring at the steady downward onslaught of snowflakes outside her bedroom window. They made her entire corner of West Quincy disappear. She saw no neighboring houses, no parked cars, no sidewalks. She could have been back on her isolated Quebec farm. Safe and secure in the knowledge that Papa would keep them all warm and fed and safe, whatever the weather might bring—back when Rose believed René Quentin could actually do all that and always would.

This fantasy of childhood contentment, combined with fatigue from all the physical exertion, quickly dispatched Rose out of the war-plagued twentieth century, out of her Quincy bedroom, out of an aged body wrestling with dysfunction. She was back in Quebec. Not at the farm, but in a forest clearing, in mid-winter. Although the snow was hip deep, Rose recognized the clearing. Mère Agathe had taken her there many times, in spring, summer, and fall, to gather herbs to heal and mushrooms and roots to eat. It was a magical place.

Turning full circle at the center of the clearing, Rose could see nothing but hemlock, tamarack, and jack pine. If she lay on her back, the tops of all those giant conifers would converge in one perfect point. Staring at the dark green wall encircling her, she felt so small. Not because she was a child. Because she was a mere human. A mere human, all alone in the northern wilderness. Her sense of awe gradually faded, to be replaced by washes of panic. Her heart began skipping beats. A pulse throbbed inside her upper abdomen. Nausea restricted her throat. Her breathing became shallow.

"Maybe I don't survive! What can I do?"

Her peripheral vision picked up a quiver in the drooping, snow-encrusted hemlock branches to her right. The quiver grew to a tremble, then a convulsion, as a figure emerged from the green wall.

"*Jésus, Marie, Joseph!*" Rose exclaimed. She relaxed a little—but only a little—when she recognized Mère Agathe, swathed in a woolen blanket whiter than the snow.

A bony index finger emerged from the blanket and wagged at Rose. "Hard times coming, little one. And you not ready, eh? High time you get ready, no?"

"What? How?"

The Métis savant swirled that accusatory finger away from Rose and toward her own head. "Your head, it don't work so well. You gotta get well. Well! You hear? Quick!"

Heart racing, Rose said, "I don't know how."

"You know someone. She knows how. She knows you well. Very well."

"What?"

"You remember Sapling and Flint? Gotta be like both to survive, to help each other survive. Hard and soft. *Doux et sauvage.*"

"I don't understand."

"Not much time. You get well first, little one. Well!"

The old one melted back into the boreal wilderness, leaving Rose trembling, cold, and terrified. She began to shiver convulsively. She willed herself to get moving, get the blood flowing. She forced her legs to push through the snow, one step at a time. She had no idea where she was going, until she suddenly found herself at a window … her open bedroom window in Quincy, with snowflakes floating over the inner sill. Rose slammed the window shut and rubbed her thinly clad upper arms.

"*Saccajé chien!* What foolish dream you dream, old woman! And now you walk in your sleep, too? *J'suis tanné* (I'm fed up)!" she concluded with disgust as she tromped back to bed.

Convinced this phantasm was the result of an overtired brain or that extra serving of pot roast, Rose burrowed under the covers. Gradually, her heart resumed normal rhythm. Feeling a pleasant numbing of arms and legs, she welcomed the first outriders of slumber and hoped they would bring no further dreams. As the numbness spread from limbs to brain, she heard an old woman's whisper, "Fix yourself, little one. Do it quick! Before it's too late."

TWENTY-SIX

Story Time

"I'll tell you a story about Jack-a-Nory, and now my story's begun. I'll tell you another about his brother, and now my story is done."

"Noo, Tante Izzy!" Netty wailed. "That's what Daddy always says. I wanted a real story. No fay-uh!" She kicked at the bed covers.

"Who do you think taught your father that rhyme, missy? Now take a nap. Or maybe you'd rather march right over to Gridley Bryant Grade School and tell your teacher you're not sick after all?"

"Why can't I just go home?"

"Because your mother isn't feeling well herself and can't take care of you. You'll go home with your father tonight, after dinner. Besides, you don't have any dog at home, now do you?" Izzy beckoned to the black boulder doubling as a door stop. Tenting an eyebrow, Jolie rose and trotted to the bed, feathery tail making slow loops. "She can keep you company, but she's not allowed on the bed. You hear?"

Netty nodded, sucking on her lower lip as she combed the furry head with her fingers.

"In two hours you can come downstairs. There's the clock on the

175

table. You wait until the little hand is on five. Not one minute before!"

After closing the door to her own bedroom, Izzy peered through the half-open door of her sister's room. She saw Rose's open mouth and closed eyes and heard the stertorous but even breaths. "Christ, it's like the Spanish flu over again."

Halfway down the stairs, she hissed at a loud knock on the front door and hastened her descent. She flung the door open as Nate Kagan's knuckles were about to meet wood for the second time. "Keep it down, boy!" Izzy whispered. "I've got two invalids on my hands, and I'd just as soon they stay asleep."

"Sorry. I knew Netty had caught that bug making the rounds. Is Madame Rose down with it, too?" He made a show of wiping his feet on the front mat before entering.

"Yes. She caught it caring for the little one. So now I'm pulling double duty as nursemaid. Lucky me."

"Hope you don't catch the bug, too."

"I never get sick," Izzy snapped. "See if you think it will fit in that corner." She pointed to the far corner of the kitchen. "That's really the only place with enough room."

Nate extracted a measuring tape from his pocket and clumped toward the designated spot. "How'd you convince Madame Rose to get a water cooler?"

"I told her I'd pay for it myself. Told her I would not drink one more drop of that vile tap water. Fortunately for me, your father located one on the cheap."

Winding the tape back into its metal container, Nate nodded. "Yup. Should fit. But regular deliveries of the water jugs will cost you. In the long run, wouldn't it be less expensive to get hooked up to the public water system?"

"Rose claims that would cost a fortune. What a penny-pinching Quebecker considers a fortune, of course, may not be what any sane person considers expensive. I'll have to look into it, see if I can afford it myself. For now, this is my solution."

"Okay, let me get my gear."

With the help of a hand truck, Nate huffed and clumped and wrestled the Victorian-era water cooler into position. Then he and the hand truck returned with a glass jug of water. Given the young man's balance problems, installing it took far more effort.

Izzy folded her arms over her chest and squinted at her purchase. "You sure I won't catch typhoid from that thing?"

"Nah, we flushed it out with a bleach solution and then regular tap water. There really isn't much to get infected in the first place."

"What do I owe you?"

"You already paid for it."

"I mean, for the installation."

"How about some more stories? And any family documents you might be able to show me. Stuff like birth certificates, naturalization papers. Those details will probably never make it into my thesis, but it's amazing what insights you can get from sterile official documents. I've already checked old census records for birthdates and entry dates on all of you."

"It would have been polite to seek our permission first," Izzy huffed.

"It's all a matter of public record, Isabelle. You can go down to City Hall and look up my family, too. They totally loused up the spelling of a few names, but the basic dope is solid."

"So, you know how old I am?"

Nate stifled the laughter welling up in his throat but didn't abort the grin spreading across his lips. "I know what the papers say. And I know what I see before my eyes, a gracious lady in her prime."

"Pah, you should be Irish, you. Or a politician. These days, that's all too often one and the same. Wipe that silly grin off your face! I haven't decided to forgive you, young man. But I owe you for the water installation. Now go into the parlor while I see what I can find."

After twenty minutes, Izzy returned with a small strongbox and plopped into a worn wingchair. The abruptness of her descent dislodged some yellowed documents perched atop the strongbox. Nate retrieved them from the floor.

"What you have in your hand are papers I found in the kitchen tool drawer, of all places. I was looking for a screwdriver to lever up the old latch on this box. Why Rose would choose that location to store legal papers is beyond me." She whirled an index finger above one ear.

Nate pushed his glasses into the bridge of his nose as he scrutinized the documents. "Looks like some papers from the quarry. Boy, that old-fashioned writing is hard to read. This one says your father was a quarryman. But this one describes the job as quarry engineer. Oh wait, that's for Rose's husband. What's the difference?"

177

Rose shrugged. "I think a quarry engineer had a higher skill level. Francis operated a pneumatic drill for a while. I think Papa just hammered wedges into the granite."

"This is interesting. Looks like an old health exam to get hired. Lists your father's height as five-feet-six. Wow, you're probably taller than that. He was a short fellow, wasn't he? But he was no lightweight at one-sixty-five. Hmmph, not much of an exam."

"It wasn't in the bosses' interest to find any ailments. They needed all the workers they could get. The men would get sick soon enough after getting the job. Losing fingers, limbs, or getting silicosis, like Francis."

"Silicosis?"

"They breathe in so much granite dust that the lungs get clogged. Eventually, the lungs fail, fill with fluid, and the patient drowns, gasping for air."

"Sounds like a miserable way to die."

Izzy raised her eyebrows. "Is there a good way/"

"What about your father? Did he end up with health problems from quarry work?"

"Papa was strong, that one. I remember one time a winch failed and sent a huge chunk of granite his way. It nearly sheared off his calves as it slid down the hill. Not one bone broken. But he was horribly bruised and could barely walk. He missed work one whole day. We couldn't afford it. So the next day, he went into work, regardless. He hobbled down the road with Rose supporting him—and catching catcalls as the pair of them entered the yard. The boss shut the men up, telling them to leave her alone, 'Leave the quarryman's girl be, boys!' She was so proud. As if being a quarryman's daughter were like being some kind of duchess."

"Maybe she just felt good that someone stood up for her. Sounds like neither one of you had that happen very often."

Izzy sighed. "Good heavens, this is getting maudlin. Are we nearing the end of the questions?"

Nate raised an index finger. "One more, about this residency permit for your father. On the line where he's supposed to sign, there's just an X. He couldn't read or write?"

"He could read some. But couldn't write one word to save his soul."

"What about your mother?"

178

"She had only a parish school education. But she was fairly well-read, thanks to Uncle Edward. His love of books rubbed off on her. Not that it helped her any." Izzy shook her head. "Way, way back, I remember her occasionally reading some book to Rose and me. Books she got from Uncle Edward. But with every pregnancy, there was less time for reading."

Nate nodded absentmindedly while opening the strongbox. "Okay to look in here?"

"I brought it so you could see my baptismal certificate. There. In front."

"Wow, look at the ornate penmanship! And the ink blobs. Not all that easy to read, but let's see if I can translate. 'We, the undersigned priest...' What's that, the royal we?"

"It may refer to the godparents. A formal baptism is a joint undertaking, with the godparents promising to stand by the child and renouncing Satan on the child's behalf."

"Really? That sounds so medieval."

"Maybe, but the world would be a lot better off if Herr Hitler's godparents had taken their vows more seriously."

Nate shrugged and continued reading. "'We, the undersigned priest, baptized Marie Isabelle, born one week ago...' How come you go by your middle name, not by Marie?"

"Isabelle is my real name. I guess you'd call Marie my religious name, a way of invoking protection from the Mother of God. Just about every baby girl baptized in Quebec is Marie Something. And every boy is Joseph Something."

"So the name on your sister's baptismal certificate would read Marie Rose?"

"In her case, Marie Rose de Lima. I guess our mother figured she needed even more saintly intercession."

"I don't understand.

"Rose de Lima was a saint."

"So what happens if you actually want your daughter to be called Marie or your son Joseph? Are they baptized 'Marie Marie' and 'Joseph Joseph'?"

Izzy squeezed her forehead. "You are picking nits, boy. Surely none of this is relevant to your schoolwork."

Chastised, Nate continued. "It says the godparents were 'not able to sign.' Does that mean what I think it means?"

Izzy nodded. "That they were illiterate? Probably. There was a lot of that going around back then."

"Yeah, I guess that was true of any country in the nineteenth century."

"Don't be ridiculous. I've never met a single person born in America who couldn't read and write. No matter how poor they started out."

"I'll bet you'd find plenty in Mississippi or Georgia."

"Have you never read some of the Civil War books containing letters soldiers wrote back home? Amazingly articulate. Northerners and Southerners alike. This country is a beacon of enlightenment, compared with where I came from."

"You sure don't miss Quebec like your sister does."

"I do not miss Quebec one bit. As for Rose, well, she has this inexplicable nostalgia for our life as tenant farmers. Maybe that's why she kept her accent. I could probably speak like a proper Bostonian by the time I was twelve. I remember mimicking this one teacher, right next door at the Gridley Bryant School. Miss Adams. My word, what refined diction!"

"Why was that so important to you?"

"In my experience, if you look and speak like a ruffian, you get treated like a ruffian."

"But French Canadian doesn't mean 'ruffian.'"

"'French Canuck' does. Americans regard French Canucks as ignorant, brandy-soaked backwoods louts. If you aspire to nothing more than becoming a logger or a quarryman or wife of same, then being a French Canuck is just dandy. I wanted a better job, with more security, more respectability. So I was determined to speak like an educated Bostonian."

"But Rose had more modest goals?"

Izzy snorted. "That's one way of putting it. Especially after she became smitten with that Francis. Besides, it was easier for her. She has a way with people, which made it easier to find work. And then there's the way she looks. Fair, with gentle features. Just like our mother."

"And you don't look like your mother?"

Izzy sighed, "I do not. I look like my father. Sharp features and an olive complexion. And you know what that means!"

"No, what does it mean?"

"Indian blood. My father's grandmother was Abenaki. Or Huron. Or Micmac. I never could keep all those tribes straight."

"I thought the French settlers got along well with the Indians, that having Indian blood didn't cause problems. Not like having Negro blood here."

"Having such dark skin and angular features certainly limited Papa's marital prospects. He was positively ancient, mid-twenties, before he married. He was lucky to find my mother, a fair beauty. Her family's disastrous economic circumstances made her willing to marry down."

"Ouch!"

Izzy raised both palms in exasperation. "It's the way of the world. Her financial plight made it impossible to make a more genteel match. My father's appearance made it impossible for him to find a respectable job. Which is one reason why he ended up in some windswept rural outpost in Manitoba. He probably felt more comfortable there than in Quincy. Less judged."

Nate squinted one eye skeptically.

"As a Jew, you certainly understand what I'm saying, Nathan."

After a pause, he replied, "Sure, there's prejudice. But what's the point of burying yourself in the Old Country, like your father did. Just to fit in? Where would I be if my grandfather hadn't left White Russia?"

"We have more in common, you and I, than anyone might suspect, no?"

Nate considered that assertion. He was certainly glad to be an American, but unlike Izzy he didn't feel shame or bitterness about his heritage. He struggled for a response that wouldn't give offense.

He was saved by the bell. Netty toddled downstairs with a ringing alarm clock in both hands. Seeing the glower on her great-aunt's face, she quickly depressed the alarm button and explained, "It just went off and woke me up. Otherwise, I would have stayed in bed like you said. Besides, I need a drink of water for my sore throat." For emphasis, she snuffled and hacked.

Izzy snatched the alarm clock and harrumphed, "I certainly didn't set the alarm for four o'clock. I wonder who might have done that?"

Netty stared up beatifically. "Maybe an elf?"

"An elf indeed." Izzy couldn't completely suppress a smile. "Very well, go get a glass of water. We'll have some quiet time downstairs, reading. If you won't sleep, you can do something useful. How about

181

returning to *Little Women*? The older girls were just about to press a call on the Laurence boy next door. You can read the chapter aloud to Nate and me."

Netty was halfway into the kitchen, when Izzy remembered the water cooler. "Wait, Netty! We have a new contraption for getting water." She started to rise but her sweater caught on the chair.

Nate waved her down, saying, "I'll show the kid how to use the contraption."

Following Nate's twenty-second tutorial, Netty filled her glass and exclaimed, "Ooh, look at the bubbles!"

"You like that, huh?" Opening the cooler's cabinet door, he added, "And look at this. You can stick a chunk of ice in there and get really cold water. How about you pour me a glass, too, so you can see more bubbles."

Netty retrieved another glass and was briefly mesmerized by the glugging cooler, until a frown replaced the wonder on her face. "Don't laugh if I get the words wrong," she said abruptly.

"What? Oh, you mean when you read *Little Women*? Nah, I won't laugh. Cross my heart and hope to die."

"It's too hard for me. But I got tired of all the baby books and wanted something interesting."

"Hey, that's how you learn," Nate said. "Why'd you choose *Little Women*?"

"Because of the four sisters. They have fun together, play together. If I had a sister, I'd always have someone to play with."

"Not sure it always works out that way, kiddo. Your grandmother and great-aunt are sisters, after all, and they seem pretty different."

"Tante Izzy is just like Aunt March in the book. Don't you think?"

Nate snorted appreciatively. "Well, I never read the book, but I actually did see the movie. That was the character played by Edna May Oliver, right? Boy, what a hatchet face that woman has! Scary!"

"Just like Aunt Izzy. You think so, too."

"Don't you go putting words in my mouth! Get in trouble all you want, kid, but don't bring me into it."

Netty solemnly pinched her lips with her fingers, turned her hand clockwise, and threw away the imaginary key. Then she gave Nate an exaggerated wink.

Nate winked back as the conspirators returned to the parlor.

182

TWENTY-SEVEN

Taking the Waters

It wouldn't be like this in Quebec. Damned New England weather! So hot. So humid. I sweat like a pig. Flash after flash of heat. Must be pregnant. I do everything Mère Agathe tells me, years ago, when she explains best times to get pregnant. Count backwards from when my blood should flow. Wait until the moisture down there has just the right feeling. Then I crook my finger at Francis. He's eager, you betcha! But right now, you not so welcome, mon chou *(my cabbage). You make me too hot. Right now, all I want is the cool breeze.*

Rose awoke briefly to hurl the covers off her torso. But she was soon transported back to that first summer after she and Francis had married. The dream perfectly replayed reality, or at least Rose's memory of reality. She recalled dropping like a water-logged seal onto the kitchen chair beside her husband and complaining that it was much too hot to cook his dinner. Far from getting annoyed, he offered a solution.

"It's time you were baptized," he said, folding his Patriot Ledger and slapping it on the table.

"You crazy? Of course, I have baptism."

183

"Not a Quincy baptism, you haven't." He took her hand and pulled her off the chair.

A few minutes later, they were hiking down the road, with Francis stonewalling all her questions about their destination. She soon figured it out, when they detoured into a brushy path leading to an abandoned granite quarry.

"Wait here, lass, while I reconnoiter," Francis said, stashing his young wife in the shade of a giant elm.

He returned with a boy of around fourteen. "Meet Wally. He and his mates just finished their swim. I paid him to be our lookout. He knows if he turns around to have a look, you'll be the last thing his eyes ever see. Ain't that right, Wally?" Francis's smile radiated cheerful menace.

Off Rose hiked with her husband, traipsing through Queen Anne's lace and clumps of chicory, her skirt catching on the occasional blackberry brier. They came to a clearing, surrounded by walls of rock. She made the mistake of looking down and wobbled slightly when she saw the water more than twenty feet below the ledge where they stood.

"Easy, lass," Francis said, as he took her hand. "We'll be wanting to tuck our clothes away. You don't want to look like a drowned wharf rat on our walk back home."

Francis began to strip. Rose hesitated, shocked at her husband's utter lack of embarrassment. She had certainly seen him naked but she couldn't think of a single lovemaking session that took place in full daylight. Completely naked now, Francis stood, hands on hips. Rose took the time to notice the two-toned arms, brown from the sun and white from his bloodlines. She also noticed the challenging grin. She accepted the challenge enough to hazard another look at the water so far below. Her second glance wasn't as frightening as the first. The water was a lovely green. A cool green. Her clothes, sticking to her sweaty armpits, chest, back, and groin were suddenly repugnant. She stripped them off with speed. Unlike her husband, who had taken the time to fold his clothes and lay them carefully in a rocky cleft, she just rolled hers into one big ball, which she kicked into a corner with a white foot. She returned Francis's challenging stare.

"So, what we do now, you see, is take a deep breath…"

Before Francis could finish his instructions, Rose made the sign of the cross, took two long strides to the edge, sprang a few feet in the air, and cannonballed downward, laughing and yelling "*Mon Dieu! Mon*

Dieu! Mon Dieu!" until the impact extinguished her supplications.

Saccajé chien! *That water, she's cold! I never know water so cold in summer. I think maybe this water, she's the last thing I ever feel. Down, down, down I go. I wonder if I ever come back up.*

But up Rose came, gasping and laughing and spitting out quarry water. Cycling both legs and making a scooping motion with her left hand to stay afloat, she peeled her hair from her face with her right hand and felt the last of her hairpins skitter down her back. Luxuriating in the quarry's icy embrace, she heard a shout and laughed as Francis torpedoed through the water to catch up with her. He grabbed her by the waist, lifted her in the air, and slid her torso down over his own, her long hair enshrouding both of them as they kissed. Rose broke away and knifed twenty yards through the water, with her husband in pursuit. Although a strong swimmer, she struggled to keep her nose clear until she adjusted to the low buoyancy of quarry water. They continued this game of aquatic hide and seek until their lips turned blue from the cold.

"Let's climb up on that ledge," Francis said, pointing to a niche only four or so feet above the water.

"No, too soon. I don't want to feel hot again."

"Just for a while. To rest. Then we'll dive in again."

Francis scrambled up first then reached down to help her. She pulled him back in the water, then backstroked away, daring him to follow. Laughing, he shook his head and swam back to the ledge. "You swim all you like. I'll keep watch, now, in case Wally fails us," he shouted.

In the distance, they both heard Wally shout. "No! No! Don't go there! The quarryman's girl is swimming. And the quarryman will kill you dead if you don't leave her be. I tell ya, he's a big sonofabitch."

Years later, when the hot flashes returned for a different reason, Rose would revisit the frigid quarries. She tried to get Francis to join her. He resisted, saying he was too old for such foolishness. But she cajoled him into at least accompanying her, to stand guard. She wanted another baptism in that rock-lined font, to cleanse herself of sweat and cares and years. She wanted to immerse herself in her youth, back when she was indeed the quarryman's girl.

After Francis died, Rose figured she would never again swim in the deep, cool water. But one withering August day, she trekked off to one of the deepest pits, with her faithful Newfoundland at her side. She wore a ghastly looking bathing suit under her sun dress, so she wouldn't

185

shock anyone with her nakedness. As far as seeing naked boys, well, hadn't she raised four boys of her own? If they didn't mind, why should she? Of course, they *did* mind, until she worked a deal with the oldest teenager. The same one who initially tried to scare her off, until he noticed the nearly two-hundred pound dog flashing his canines. Rose told the leader of the pack she would go away and return Thursdays at five, stay for an hour, and leave. The boys who frequented that quarry were rarely there at that time of day. Rose had little fear that the leader of the swim pack would tell any adults about the crazy old lady with the funny accent, since the pack's mothers had told the boys that quarry swimming was far too dangerous. If they didn't drown they could bet on a maternal belt-thrashing.

Rose returned the following Thursday, just to see if the plan worked. She and Jolly had a lovely swim, but she rarely returned. It just wasn't the same without Francis. Once she persuaded Vincent to join her, both of them wearing beach apparel, but it wasn't the same. She was his mother and couldn't feel young and free in his presence.

She had put the quarries out of her mind, except for picking blueberries in early July. But right now, they were calling to her hot, sweaty body. Why was it so hot? Rose had kicked the covers completely off, but her damp housedress still weighed heavily on her chest, feeling oddly tight. She had no idea whether she'd been dreaming of the past or merely remembering it. She certainly didn't feel rested.

Sitting up in bed, she scraped some random gray hairs straggling over her eyes to scrutinize the alarm clock on the table. It read five-thirty, which utterly confused her since the bedroom was completely dark. She should be seeing some light from the east-facing window and hearing the first few birds on a summer morning. And why would it be this hot so early? She swung her legs over the side of the bed, with some difficulty. She could almost feel her brain sloshing around inside her skull when she rose, but she often felt dizzy on a hot day. She wobbled to the closet and pulled her old bathing suit off a hook, stripped off her nightgown, which looked oddly like a house dress, and changed. She couldn't find any sundresses but was now so hot she didn't care. She would be much cooler walking to the quarry in just her bathing suit. Now all she had to do was walk downstairs and out the door without disturbing anyone. She wasn't sure who was there to disturb.

The boys? That Vincent's an early riser, him. No, wait, Vincent lives

186

with Nora and Maryellen in their own house. Francis? Maybe Francis, he'll come along and swim. Maybe he'll stand guard. Maybe the Rag- man's grandson comes along, too. Wait, why would the Ragman's little boy be here?

Rose shook her head to clear the cobwebs. Her brain only sloshed around more, triggering some nausea and another hellacious hot flash. "The quarry water, it clears my head. I feel better after a nice, cool swim."

She willed her feet to move out the bedroom door and onto the landing. This was a new sensation, thinking through every muscle contraction. The novelty was almost amusing. Grabbing onto the rail, she concentrated on placing her right foot on the first step. She tried to position her left foot on the next step, but that proved too challenging. So it merely joined the right foot. She repeated the pattern, two-stepping down each stair. "See, you figure it out!" she congratulated herself.

Her confidence foundered on the last two stairs. Her feet just would not obey her brain. And then her hands disobeyed the cerebral instruction to keep hanging on to that railing. Then her legs decided they needed to bend. With a dull thud, Rose sprawled on the floor at the foot of the stairs.

Slowly, she struggled into a sitting position, her back against the wall.

"I just take a little rest. Then I swim and cool down and everything be *tiguidou*."

"Everything is not *tiguidou*, Ma," fretted Vince, sitting on the edge of his mother's bed. "I've called Dr. Kelley to look you over."

"What? How you get here? How come I'm back upstairs?" Rose's hands fluttered over the collar of her nightgown. "Where's my bathing suit?"

"Remember, I was gonna pick up Netty to take her back home? I'd only just arrived when you did your swan dive. Nate was on his way out, but he helped me haul you back upstairs. Izzy changed your clothes. And I changed the bed linens. They were soaked. You've got yourself quite a fever, Ma."

"Don't need no doctor. Just need to…"

Izzy, who had suddenly materialized at bedside, aborted the protest by cramming a thermometer under her sister's tongue. Her scowl ensured the thermometer stayed put. Tall Izzy, standing perfectly erect, one hand on hip, the other palpating Rose's wrist pulse, radiated authority.

Feeling a bit intimidated himself, Vince tried to lighten the atmosphere. "Remember how hard it was to keep us kids from squirming when you'd take our temperature, Ma?"

Rose tried to work her tongue around the glass impediment, in an effort to respond.

"Be still, Rose!" Izzy commanded. "There are other places we can stick that thermometer, you know."

Vince winced at his mother's meek nod of compliance. He looked up at his aunt and waited for the all-clear signal.

"Well?" he asked, when Izzy finally extracted the thermometer and squinted at its mysteries.

"Almost one-oh-four," she said.

Vince whistled. "Jesus, no wonder she was talking ragtime."

Izzy placed a palm on her sister's forehead. "We'll get it down. She already feels cooler since I gave her those aspirins."

"Swell. That means her temperature had probably been over one hundred four."

"Fever has its uses, Vincent. It's the body's way of killing germs."

"Unless it kills the patient first."

Izzy glared Vincent into contrite silence.

Rose patted his hand. "No, Vincent. She's right. Mére Agathe always says fever is the grippe's worst enemy. You wrap yourself in blankets and sweat out the grippe. Gotta keep drinking water though or you dry up. Maybe I could get a glass of water, yeah?"

Vince rose and headed for the bathroom, when Izzy shouted, "No! Get it from the new water cooler in the kitchen. Nice, clean water."

Izzy took Vincent's perch on the edge of the mattress and eyed her sister. "So if some makeshift sweat lodge is the remedy, why were you intent on swimming in the quarry? That would be quite the sight in February. What were you thinking? Don't you leave me all over again." Izzy wagged a finger at the patient. "I'm too old for any more adjustments."

188

The lecture was interrupted by the arrival of Vince, holding a glass of water and ushering in Dr. Kelley. "Look who showed up!" Vince said.

"I hear you haven't been feeling well, Rose," Dr. Kelley said, settling his black bag on the bed and pulling out his stethoscope.

"Pah, Vincent worries too much, him. Just got the grippe. I have it before. I get over it."

"All right. Let's have a look." Turning around to Vince and Izzy, the doctor added, "Give Rose some privacy, please."

Vince nodded and walked out the door. Izzy arched a brow and stood her ground. "I think not. You may need assistance."

Ignoring her, Dr. Kelley listened to Rose's breathing and heart rate, thumped his fingertips on her chest, looked inside her mouth, nose, and ears, pulled down a lower eyelid, examined her fingernails, and probed her limbs. "Now follow my finger with your eyes," he instructed. "Good. Have you been out in the sun lately? Or maybe under a sun lamp?"

Rose shook her head.

"No? Can you tell me what month we're in, dear?"

"February?"

"And what day of the week?"

"Umm, maybe Tuesday?"

"And who's the president?"

"That New York fella with the cigarette holder and the glasses and all the money. I vote for him, yeah?"

"And do you remember his name?"

"*Bien sûr* (sure)! Rockefeller. John D."

"Why did you want to go to the quarry, Rose?"

Rose stared at him incredulously. "To swim. Get cool."

"People don't swim outdoors in February, Rose. They'd catch pneumonia."

"What about them L Street Brownies?"

"What? Ah, you mean that crazy Dorchester bunch that takes a swim every New Year's Day." Dr. Kelley chuckled softly. "All right, let's see what your temperature is now."

189

Vincent bolted up from the parlor loveseat when Dr. Kelley and Izzy, hands folded over chest, entered the room. Resting his medical bag on the arm of one chair, Dr. Kelley began, "Well, the lungs are a bit congested, but she doesn't have pneumonia. Just a bad case of that virus making the rounds. Her fever has already come down to one hundred one, so I think the crisis is over. The weakness from the high fever probably caused the fall. At worst, she might have some bruises. Check her temperature every four hours, and call me if it spikes. Make sure she drinks plenty of fluids. And she should be fine in two days.

"As you pointed out, Vincent, your mother is confused. I'm not so sure it's senility, though. I took some samples to check for something else that might be causing, not just the confusion, but some odd coloring here and there. It will take a while to get the results back, so I'll be in touch in a week or so."

"Thank you, Doctor. Appreciate you coming out here so fast. Can I get you anything before you head back in the cold? Some coffee? I think Ma still has some cookies?"

"Nothing, thanks. Mrs. Kelley is holding dinner for me, so I'd best be off."

After seeing the doctor out the door, Vince returned to Izzy, scowling in the parlor. "Whaddya suppose that was all about? Samples? Coloring?"

"I told you we should have called a Jewish doctor! What does an Irish doctor know?"

TWENTY-EIGHT

Tense Relations

"Finally, a perfectly normal temperature," Izzy said, extracting the thermometer from her sister's mouth and briskly shaking down the mercury.

"Good. I get up now. Lotta stuff to do," Rose said thrusting the bedcovers from her torso.

"I'll make you a deal, Rose. If you can walk to the bathroom without falling, I'll let you do whatever you want." Izzy folded her arms over her chest and pointed to the hallway leading to the bathroom.

Grunting, Rose pushed the bedcovers away from her hips then her legs. She eased her legs over the side of the bed. And coughed. Then coughed again. The second cough sent a shard of misery into her forehead. Covering her brow with one hand to still the pain and steady herself, she stood up gingerly. She took one tentative step then crumpled, only just managing to deposit her rear end on the bed instead of the floor.

Izzy maintained her rigid posture. And smirked.

Rose pushed both fists into the bed to raise her torso upward. Halfway toward this goal, her wrists betrayed her. Her derriere thudded back onto the bed. She rubbed her left wrist and looked plaintively at Izzy, whose posture remained unchanged. "Maybe you could help, yeah?"

Izzy snorted. "Not a chance. You've probably sprained your wrist. Maybe you can aim for a broken leg with the next try. So, are we done with the childish experimentation?"

Rose nodded contritely, leaned back onto the propped up pillows, and hugged the skewed blanket to her chest.

"I'll bring you some bouillon. That will help with the congestion."

"Ugh, I hate bouillon. Maybe some hot tea."

"Bouillon is better for you. You'll drink it and like it, missy." Izzy sniffed, pivoted sharply, and left the room.

"Missy?" Rose grumbled, after her sister was gone. "Who's the older sister, eh?" She sighed with frustration that her body was being so uncooperative.

First the mind. Now the arms and legs. What's next?

A low chuckle sounded from the corner of the room. She swung her head sharply left, a movement that triggered a wave of dizziness.

"I told you, darlin'," said Francis, sprawled in the easy chair, with left ankle over right knee. "Bringing that adder under your roof was a bad idea. Why, she's thoroughly enjoying lording it over you."

"Pah, that's just Izzy's way. She takes good care of me. Who else I got to do that?"

"High price, to pay, if you ask me," snorted her late husband with amusement.

"I don't ask you," Rose replied peevishly. "You never like Izzy, you."

"No, I can't say I ever did. But I treated her with respect because I knew what she meant to you. And how was I rewarded? With slander!"

"Slander? That means she tells bad stories, yeah?"

"Damnable lies are what she spread! First, Her Ladyship tells everyone I'm a bloody murderer. Some bloodthirsty Fenian who killed a copper back in Ireland, says she."

"But you do work with them people, no?"

"Oh, Rose, I simply ran a few messages back and forth. Passed

192

along some information here and there. Dinny and me both. But it was enough to catch the interest of some coppers, so we figured we'd best get our arses out of Ireland before we landed in some Brit jail."

Rose had heard the story before and never understood the youthful passion that apparently drove her husband to risk his freedom. It wasn't as if she considered it immoral to break the law, just not very practical. French Canadians, she thought, were far more pragmatic than the Irish. They managed to preserve their culture in an English-dominated country. And you didn't see them tossing bombs at government buildings in far-off Ottawa.

"But I did love that feeling of being part of something bigger than meself," the apparition continued. "Once I came to this grand country, I figured I'd have even more opportunities to experience that feeling again. You married yourself a political animal, my little cabbage. You knew that going into the bargain."

Rose shivered at the annoying endearment. How like Francis to tease her when she was down, as if teasing would somehow jolly her out of her mood. "So you blame Izzy 'cause you don't get to be some political big shot?"

"Indeed I do! Was it not Herself who caused that ruckus at May Driscoll's bar? In she barges. Like Carrie Bloody Nation, without the hatchet. Shouting at poor May! Spouting all sorts of lies about May and me. Right when the boyos in the backroom were eyeing me for a representative's seat. I was this close to jumping from Quincy's City Council to Beacon By-God Hill. I was supposed to be the 'clean' candidate, the upstanding, up-from-bootstraps family man running against a corrupt old rake who had bedded the wives of one-too-many colleagues. And suddenly, thanks to dear Isabelle, I'm just another thick Mick who can't keep his fly buttoned. Fare thee well, Beacon Hill and whatever that might have led to."

"Izzy thinks she protects me. Against that May."

"And did you feel protected, darlin'? Or just humiliated? For no bloody reason! Her meddling damn near drove you and me apart. Which was probably what the jealous old spinster was aiming for in the first place." Francis shook his head wearily.

Rose sighed, deeply enough to trigger a coughing bout. When she recovered, she growled, "And I choose you over Izzy, yeah? But now

193

you're dead, you. Izzy's alive. And needs me. Maybe I need her, too."

"There's no reasoning with you, woman!" Francis harrumphed. And promptly evaporated from the easy chair.

Rose was glad he was gone. She needed a break from his intensity. She knew he'd be back. Death had not ended their spats any more than it had ended their flirtation. Intense relationships never really died, Rose thought. Which was precisely why she and Izzy once again lived under the same roof.

TWENTY-NINE

Dark Thoughts

Vince wished for total darkness, the darkness he recalled from child-hood, when his little corner of Quincy was halfway rural, when Ma kept chickens, before Pa sold one of their two acres to survive one of many financial emergencies. There had always been nearby neigh-bors, but none of them was foolish enough to burn gas lights after nine or ten at night. Electric street lamps would not arrive until Vince was well into his teens. Admittedly, nocturnal trips to the outhouse could be treacherous, but how exhilarating it was to gaze at all those crystalline pinpoints in the sky. Vince never studied astronomy and didn't know the names of even the most basic constellations, but he thrilled at the ancient, diamond-faceted geometry etching the heavens.

He could not recall ever having the classic childhood fear of the dark. When something went bump in the night, he figured darkness was his ally. Familiarity was his navigator both inside and outside the old house. It would give him the advantage over any ogre lying in wait. And if he couldn't see where the ogre was, well, the ogre probably couldn't see him either.

As he matured, Vince appreciated how darkness softened ragged contours and erased the unsightliness of the blighted chestnuts and the junk his father would collect because "it might come in handy." He understood that total darkness fostered deep sleep. Any child of Rose Quentin couldn't help absorbing some of the wisdom handed down from Mère Agathe. Even Rose's least receptive sons agreed that sleep was the single biggest healer for whatever ailed mind or body.

Vince's body might be reasonably hale, but his mind was aggrieved. He was woefully tired of being dutiful. The dutiful son, the dutiful husband, the dutiful father. He was tired of mopping up Netty puke. He was tired of righting the chaos created by his mother's confusion. He was tired of teetering to the arrhythmia of his wife's moods.

Turning his head to the left, Vince felt a renewed longing for utter darkness, instead of the crepuscular gloom radiated by two fifteen-watt nightlights. Nora did not share her husband's regard for darkness, so dim lights glowed wearily in both bedrooms, the hallway, and the bathroom. Vince wished he could not see the barrier demarcating the marital bed. He marveled how Nora's right shoulder, for all its thinness, loomed boulder-like above the mattress. She had always slept on her left side, always facing away from him. In better days, Vince would venture across the mattress's no-man's land to approach the border delineated by his wife's spine. Ever so quietly, ever so gently, he would spoon her. If she didn't move away, he would nuzzle her neck and inhale her unique scent, that combination of shampoo, lotion, and her own lightly acidic, salty essence. Despite the boulder imagery suggested by that imposing shoulder, Nora was not made of stone. How often had she melted into his embrace.

These days, however, Nora didn't melt; she melted down. Like lethal lava.

Vince sighed, loudly enough that Nora stirred. Normally, he would welcome that development as the prelude to intimacy, even if only a cuddle, with Nora nestled by his side, head resting on his left shoulder. But these were not normal times. He held his breath, desperately hoping she would remain asleep. He lacked the energy even to anticipate which Nora would emerge from slumber—the perpetual motion machine, the lethargic and inarticulate slug, or the weeping shrew. His body relaxed somewhat after her even breathing resumed.

It tensed again when he remembered that he needed to contact Dr.

196

Kelley regarding his mother. The good doctor had yet to share the results of those mysterious tests. The very need for medical tests was always alarming, whether the patient was eight-year-old Netty or seventy-year-old Rose. In Netty's case, the tests never provided the answers for her compromised immune system. It was nice to know his daughter didn't have leukemia, a disease about which he had once been blissfully ignorant. But all those needle pokes didn't move Netty any closer to robust health. What was the likelihood that the "samples" taken by Dr. Kelley would lead to the restoration of his mother's mental sharpness?

Vince turned his head to the right and groaned at the alarm clock, perfectly visible in the dim light. Three o'clock. Just two hours before he'd have to rise and prepare for work. He needed those two hours of sleep. The new job was demanding, requiring him to master multiple engine types, many of them new to him. But unlike people, mechanical parts, regardless of how they were fueled into action, followed logical patterns that would reveal themselves with patient observation and resourceful tinkering. Vince was both patient and resourceful.

He felt some of the tension drain from his jaw. He realized the new job made him happy. It afforded so much freedom, as he was constantly on the move, troubleshooting problems all over the enormous yard, with no bosses hanging over his shoulder. He was often surprised to hear the noon whistle. Often he thought the time was closer to ten.

The variety kept boredom at bay. It wasn't merely the diversity of engines demanding his intuitive skills. Several times each week, he was pulled off strictly mechanical duties and recruited to help with other tasks. In wartime, bosses didn't always have the leisure to wait for dues-paying union specialists to arrive to handle certain jobs. Vince particularly enjoyed getting shopped out to assist ironworkers. Something approaching friendship was already developing with one of them, Walter, a Mohawk from upper New York State. Indian ironworkers were highly valued at shipyards and construction sites throughout the country. Even before the war broke out, they had acquired a mystique for their skill at climbing skyscraping heights and balletically navigating thin girders.

"Why should you fellas be any better at climbing and balancing than any other Tom, Dick, or Harry?" Vince once asked Walter.

"You ever notice how the average white guy walks? Like a duck, feet splayed out. Indians walk with feet pointed straight ahead. It's easier to control each footfall, which comes in handy whether you're skipping across a girder or creeping up on a deer. Comes from centuries of hunting in the woods."

Hearing that response, Vince stroked his chin. He had certainly read about the stealth of Indian hunters in Cooper's *Leatherstocking Tales*. Maybe Walter was right.

"But why are you better at climbing?"

"You ever spend much time in the woods?" Walter asked.

"Some."

"Then you know there's lots of shit in the woods. Lots of shit that can eat you. And most of it can outrun you. So when you're getting charged by a bear or a mountain lion, the top of a one-hundred-foot tree looks mighty fucking inviting. Amazing how good you can get at tree climbing when your nose hairs are twitching from bear stink."

"But bears can climb trees."

Walter grinned.

"You're full of shit, Walter, you know that?"

"It's just no fun talking to you, Vince."

Vince recalled another recent conversation, as he and Walter were blowing into their gloves and stamping their feet to fend off the east wind, while they waited for a load of sheet metal to guide onto a crane. Vince broached a delicate subject. "It's funny to think that me and you would have been at each other's throats a few centuries ago."

"Who says we aren't now, white boy?'

"One of my great-grandfathers was full-blooded Micmac. Or maybe Abenaki. I forget. Anyway, his ancestors spent a lot of time fighting the Iroquois and, more often than not, getting butchered by the Iroquois."

"Yeah, but us Mohawks? We're the nice branch of the Iroquois family."

"Bullshit."

Walter chuckled. "Not gonna buy that, huh? Yeah, we had killing down pretty good. Probably would have wiped out all the pussy tribes if we'd had enough time before European settlers moved in."

"Ah, the good old days," Vince teased.

"Hey, we're just waiting to show off our stuff again. My old man was a scout in the Great War. Put a few streaks of paint on his cheeks. Carried a tomahawk on his belt. Made the Krauts shit their pants."

"He ever use that tomahawk?"

198

"Sure, how else you gonna open a can of beans?"

Lying in bed, Vince smiled. It was as if he had two lives now. In one he was weighed down, hemmed in by his responsibilities, all too often without receiving much appreciation for the load he carried. In the other, he was a respected member of a team, valued for his resourcefulness and work ethic. In the other, adventures awaited him, swaying forty feet over the water with brine stinging his eyes.

He grinned at the realization that part of him was reverting to childhood, those summer afternoons when he and his brothers would hare off to the quarries for misadventure. At the age of five, he began pestering Dave to teach him how to swim. One day, his older brother relented, promising a swimming lesson at one of the abandoned quarries. All four Dowd boys hiked down the road, through the shrubbery and vines until reaching a rock wall, which they proceeded to climb. Vince scrambled after them and was delighted when everyone stopped and stripped. The cool breeze felt so good on his naked skin, but the goosebumps grew to uncomfortable proportions as his toes gripped the edge of rock and he looked down, down, down.

"This is how you swim, kid," said Eddie, casually stepping off the ledge, then pinwheeling through the air while screaming, "Help!" When Dave and Hank guffawed, the horrified five-year-old deduced Eddie wasn't about to die. Then Dave jumped, making an even bigger splash.

Paddling around in the deep water, the two divers called up to the younger brothers on the ledge. When the raucous invitations produced no results, Eddie and Dave began squawking like chickens.

"C'mon, Vince, we gotta dive," Hank complained.

"But I don't know how to swim."

"You'll figure it out once you get down there."

"What if I don't?"

Hank shrugged and said, "Then I guess you'll die." He laughed and patted his little brother on the shoulder. Then his hand moved between Vince's shoulder blades and shoved.

Vince's pinwheels made Eddie's look like the fluttering of fairy wings. Unlike Eddie, he was too shocked to scream. After a seemingly endless descent, he ripped through the surface of the water and kept going. Down, down into the dark water. Random shafts of sunlight penetrated the depths and allowed a distorted view of the massive rock walls all around. He was surprised they had so much color. He was surprised he'd opened his eyes under water. He was surprised to be, quite suddenly, free of fear. This sense of weightlessness was so exhilarating, he didn't struggle. His descent eventually stilled and he began to rise, effortlessly. Feeling the need to take a breath sooner or later, he raised his arms as if to climb. He soon learned that such movements accelerated his ascent.

Once at the surface, he took a big gulp of air, then frog-kicked his way back under the water. He heard a commotion above him. "Get the dumb fuck before he drowns!" shouted a distorted voice. Vince kicked away from the voice. He didn't get very far, because something yanked at his hair and pulled him upward. When he surfaced, he stared with wonder at a red-eyed, dripping face, yelling, "Whaddya trying to do, you little shit? Gimme a heart attack?"

All these years later, the memory of that first quarry dive still tickled Vince. He had indeed figured it out. He was soon the Dowd boy climbing to the highest diving perches. One reason was to show off. The other was to prolong that freeing, effortless descent into an unknown universe, far removed from the cares of the day.

So when Walter the Mohawk asked for help checking the rivets on a crane fifty feet above Fore River, Vince complied. Yes, he wanted to prove himself. But he also wanted to resurrect that sensation freeing him from the cares of the day.

In this, his other life, dutiful, responsible Vincent Dowd was free.

THIRTY

Snowbound

"Who is that on the phone?" Rose asked from the stairway.

"Go back upstairs, you're still sick," Izzy ordered.

Rose embedded one fist into her hip and glared. The show of defiance would have been more effective if her other hand didn't have a death grip on the railing to prevent yet another fall.

"It was Nora," Izzy said at last. "Netty needs to be picked up. School is closing early because of all the snow. Brilliant decision. Now all the little ones have to fight their way home in miserable weather. Or wait God knows how long for someone to pick them up."

"*Bien sûr*, I go now."

"You'll do no such thing. I don't care if the school is next door, you're in no shape to walk the distance even in dry conditions. Which is exactly what I told Nora. She can't retrieve the child, she says, because her hill hasn't been plowed. Nora can't do much of anything these days, it seems. I told her I'd walk over and pick up Netty. I also told her we'll keep the child overnight if necessary. By the time Vince gets off work, we'll probably have two feet of snow."

"You know how to get there?"

"Rose! I attended classes there for three whole years. I think I can figure it out. Now go back to bed!" Izzy waved a dismissive hand at her now coughing sister, who complied. She marched toward the coat rack to begin suiting up for the adventure. Jolie plodded after her, sat down, panted toward the door then looked at Izzy, looked at the door. "*Saccajé chien!* Do I look like I need supervision? Fine, come along, just don't knock me over."

Jolie wagged her agreement.

Izzy scratched the massive head. "If there's one thing I cannot abide," she told the dog, "it's a helpless female. I don't know how Vincent manages with that one."

Once buried in heavy coat, gloves, stocking cap, muffler, and tall mud-boots, Izzy slammed her hip into the storm door to confront the Arctic blast outside. When the door was only one-third open, Jolie charged ahead, galloping exultantly through the drifts. A white crust quickly coated the dog's muzzle, but Jolie the Newfoundland-mix was unperturbed, charging forward then romping back to share the experience.

"Fine, you break trail for me. Just don't shake that coat anywhere near ... Arrggh!"

As if on cue, Jolie spun out snow spirals from her dense fur.

Although the school was next door, a long chain-link fence separated the two properties, so Izzy was wheezing when she finally reached her destination, after hiking to the end of her road, onto another short road, then reaching Willard Street, the thoroughfare onto which Gridley Bryant Grammar School fronted. After warning Jolie to remain outside, she opened the school's heavy double-doors and breathed a sigh of relief when she spotted Netty and several other children inside the entranceway. The teachers were still helping their charges prepare for Mother Nature. A few children were half-sprawled on the floor as they wrestled with boots too narrow for wadded pant legs and leggings. Netty must have been one of the first to be properly swathed. What little of her face was visible wore a sweaty glow, and her mittened hand tugged at her scarf. Her eyes widened when she saw Izzy.

"Your mother can't get the car down your road," her great-aunt explained. "So you'll stay with your nana and me until your father can pick you up. Are you ready?"

Netty nodded and traipsed behind her. She squealed when she saw the mound of snow that was Jolie, waiting outside. "Poor Jolie! Are you all cold and wet?"

"Hmmph, I doubt this beast can ever get too cold."

"Ooh! It's an adventure. It's like we're in the North Pole and we have Jolie instead of reindeer. Didn't you and Nana Rose live close to the North Pole?"

"*Too* close. Watch your step. It's slippery where the snow is packed from footsteps."

"This is fun!"

After a few yards of pushing through the drifts, Netty's exuberance faded, and she had to concentrate on every footfall.

"Let's stop a minute to catch our breath," said Izzy, after they reached Willard Street. Not one vehicle was in sight. They spotted just one other pedestrian, on the opposite side of the road. Even from this distance, it was obvious the person was shivering.

Once on the other side, Izzy would have walked past the snow-dusted individual, but Jolie began wagging her tail with gusto and stopped to sniff the stranger's boots.

"Jolie?" said the stranger. "What are you doing out here, girl?" He shifted his heavy book bag so he could pet the dog more easily.

"Nathan?" asked Izzy. "Is that you doing an imitation of a snowman?"

"Isabelle? Netty? What are you doing out in this blizzard?"

"Doing something a lot more intelligent than standing still. School closed early, so I'm taking Netty home with us. Why are *you* here?"

"When I saw how bad the weather was getting, I cut class and took the subway to Ashmont Station, but my usual bus never showed up. So I took the first one that came by and got off here, hoping to catch another bus to take me closer to home. But I've been standing here a while and … nothing."

"You'll catch pneumonia, boy! Come with us. If Vincent can make it to our place once he gets off work, maybe he can drive you home. Otherwise, we can put you up on the sofa."

"Aw, no, I couldn't put you out," Nate protested shakily.

"Contrary to popular opinion, I don't bite. Not much, anyway." She tugged at his heavily padded elbow until he nodded agreement.

When the quartet reached safe-haven, Izzy smelled the aroma of strong tea even before she peeled off her outerwear. "Mon Dieu, Rose! I told you to stay upstairs and rest!" she shouted into the hallway. Peering into the kitchen, she saw her sister sitting at the table, two teapots and three cups in front of her.

Rose shouted back, "I rest here. I rest upstairs. *Comme ci, comme ça.* In the hallway, Izzy stripped off Netty's damp socks then ordered Nate to help her bring all the damp items into the living room to spread around the glowing hearth. Netty dashed into the kitchen while the two adults draped mufflers, knitted caps, socks, and gloves over chairs, which they then moved close to the fireplace. Nodding toward the kitchen, Nate asked in a low voice, "How's she doing?"

"The fever's long gone, and the cough is clearing up, but she's still weak."

"What about...?" Nate touched a finger to his temple. "Vince told me the doctor was running some tests to see about her ... confusion."

"Poisoning. The samples he took contained both lead and arsenic.

"You're kidding me! Arsenic?"

Izzy nodded grimly. "That was what Dr. Kelley suspected. Something about her coloring. He didn't expect to see lead, too. But that could be the cause of her addled spells."

"So what now?"

"They're running tests on samples taken her from her well. I *told* Vincent it was the damn water! The doctor claims even contaminated water wouldn't necessarily taste bad, but I've no doubt that's the source. So your delivery of that cooler was timely."

"Gee, I guess so," Nate said, rearranging the last chair and biting his lower lip thoughtfully. "You know, I just remembered something. My father was complaining about stupid civil servants recently and buttressed his argument with a local scandal from an earlier decade. Some Quincy residents threatened to sue the city for hiring a big pesticide outfit to spray for gypsy moths. The spray made them sick, they claimed. What was the stuff in that spray? I think there was some form of arsenic. I can ask my father. I'll bet he remembers exactly what it was."

"Please do. In any event, getting her off that vile water will be the first step. Come. Let's go into the kitchen." She crooked her arm.

"Is there any treatment?"

"The doctor mentioned some possibilities, which I'm sure Rose will reject, since they might not work anyway. Apparently, it took years of exposure before any damage was done, which is why Rose's visitors shouldn't be in any danger."

"Can Madame Rose get better on her own?"

"Kelley thinks any organ damage will reverse itself. As for the mental damage, no one knows."

Nate raised both hands with fingers crossed as he and Izzy entered the kitchen, now filled with wet dog reek and Netty squeals as the little girl regaled her grandmother with polar adventure tales.

"I made a huge pot of chicken soup last night for the patient, here. We can all have that for lunch. Dinner may be out of a can though," Izzy added, heading toward the cupboard. "Hmm, lots of baked beans."

Netty made a gagging noise and smirked at her grandmother. Smiling, Rose swatted the child's shoulder. "We got plenty eggs from Mrs. Drinan's chickens. I scramble up later. And the A&P, it has the first bacon in weeks."

"Ooh, breakfast for dinner," Netty said.

Muscling the soup pot from icebox to stovetop, Izzy growled, "I'll scramble you, if you don't rest like you're supposed to. Besides, young Master Kagan here might not appreciate the bacon."

Wide-eyed, Netty turned to Nate and asked, "You don't like bacon? I thought everyone liked bacon!"

"I like bacon, but I'm not supposed to have it."

"Hurts your tummy, huh?"

"Something like that. Hey, if you have some onions and bread, I'll play chef tonight and make all of us fried egg and onion sandwiches."

Flipping a thumb in Nate's direction, Rose said, "A good boy, him. You remind me of my Vincent. He likes to cook breakfast, too."

"And don't forget Daddy's quarry-berry pies."

"Who you think teaches him how to bake pies, eh?" Rose was about to chuck Netty's chin, but retracted her hand to stifle a cough.

From the stove, Izzy cocked a ladle at the table. "See? You're still sick and need to rest!"

After lunch, Izzy ordered her sister and grand-niece into the parlor, while she and Nate washed up.

"You're taking excellent care of the patient," he said while drying a bowl. "You'd never know…"

"Never know what?" Izzy snapped.

"Well, I sort of got the impression that you two sisters had a falling out years ago. None of my business, of course, except I wonder if I'm missing some information relevant to my thesis."

"So you're asking from a purely scientific point of view. Idle curiosity plays no role?" Izzy eyed him skeptically over her glasses.

"Your history *does* make me curious, personally and academically. The two of you must have been so close after your parents moved to Manitoba. There you were, pooling your resources. Could you have survived without each other, I wonder?"

"I wondered that, too. Especially when Rose decided to get married." Removing one hand from the soapy water, Izzy etched a line in the steamed-up kitchen window. "Everything suddenly clouded over. My very future." She leaned into the window and cleared a bit more steam.

"You felt abandoned?"

Izzy continued staring at the cloudy pane. "Wouldn't you?"

He nodded thoughtfully. "So how'd you manage?"

"Oh, Rose offered to take me in. All four of us—her, Francis, Francis's halfwit brother Dennis, and me—would have jobs. Her plan was for all of us to contribute our income to afford a decent place." Izzy shook her head vigorously.

"Isn't that what lots of immigrants did? In-laws living together? Parents and adult children living together? All so they could afford somewhere decent."

"Hmmph!"

Nate furrowed his brow. "I suppose living with the in-laws might get in the way if you wanted to find a husband of your own." Izzy's glare made him instantly regret that piece of speculation.

"Why do people assume that marriage solves problems? It creates more than it solves. Just ask Rose. Besides, I wasn't some charity case."

"So what'd you do?"

"I asked anyone and everyone if they knew of a family needing a live-in governess. And I got myself out of that boarding house and into the Winthrops' brownstone even before the last banns of marriage were posted for Rose and Francis."

"Good for you!"

"Good for me, indeed!" Izzy attacked the soup pot in the sink.

As Nate waited to dry the pot, he asked, "So you didn't see much of your sister after you moved to Boston and she got married?"

"Oh, for heaven's sake, she was always inviting me over for this and that. Thanksgiving, Christmas, Easter. And then the children started coming. And then Francis moved them here. When I wasn't tied up with the Winthrops, I was often at this very kitchen table. Not all that willingly, mind you. Dennis was a dolt. Francis was a boor. And Rose was preoccupied. But I did enjoy the children."

"But I thought…" Nate stammered.

"You thought what? That those get-togethers came to an end? Well, you'd be correct."

"Why? If you were around, seeing your nephews grow up, the falling out must have happened, what? Fifteen, twenty years ago? What happened?"

"If you want to know, ask Rose. We all have our stories to tell. That's hers. Not mine." She yanked the plug on the sink, dried her hands, and marched into the living room.

What a loser you are, Kagan, Nate thought, after turning around for the hundredth time on Rose's cramped sofa. The large crucifix dominating the opposite wall made him uneasy, even though it was barely visible in the gloom. And the anodyne effects of his post-prandial toddy had long since worn off. His sins awoke him at two o'clock.

There was the sin of his physical disability. *Three lousy miles to my own bed and it might as well be thirty*. He needed some driver to come to his rescue, but none was available. The side roads had yet to be plowed, keeping all but the most daring at home. That included his father and grandfather. Vince had been called in for another shift at the shipyard, to handle all the problems caused by the foul weather. So there was no rescue from him, either.

There was the sin of being twenty-one and still a virgin. He had hopes for Betty, a classmate who was no looker but had a lively sense of humor and didn't seem to mind his limp. They had been to two movies and dinner. She seemed to have fun every time. But lately she was acting standoffish, probably because she wearied of taking the smelly subway everywhere. Nate's MG was currently buried under the snow in Vince's driveway, where it awaited additional scrounged parts.

There was the sin of general loneliness. Nate had a study buddy, with whom he shared the occasional beer. Nate hung out with Ben—who had acne, thinning hair, a weight problem, and a slight stutter—mainly to be kind. Ben hung out with him because kindness was something rarely experienced from contemporaries. It wasn't much of a friendship. Lying on that narrow sofa, Nate was depressed to conclude that Vince Dowd probably qualified as his closest friend, a middle-aged husband and father with precious little time or energy for the kind of socializing twenty-one year-olds were supposed to crave.

There was the sin of not really craving most of the socializing Nate's more popular classmates enjoyed.

There was the sin of being genuinely interested in the lives of the two old ladies upstairs. What was wrong with him? How many other young men would actually enjoy chatting with dotty Rose or bantering with the acerbic Izzy? Nate hoped he didn't have some oedipal fixation. He suspected his enjoyment of Rose and Izzy traced back to the writer in him. That inner novelist also eavesdropped happily on restaurant conversations, to absorb how strangers from different walks of life spoke. He was fascinated by their different vocabulary choices, even their grammatical errors and speech cadence.

There was the sin of acting like a complete moron earlier today. First, he had been way too pushy with Izzy. Of course, the tension between her and her sister was utterly irrelevant to his history thesis. But it piqued his writer's curiosity. He had made her uncomfortable and angry. And then he overdid the effort to make nice, cooking up his stupid fried egg sandwiches for everyone, talking too much, and generally acting like a dancing bear. Even Rose and Netty stared at him as if antennae were twirling from his temples.

There was the sin of making no progress toward his new goal of skipping out on law school and finding some kind of work reporting on the war. He had made some half-assed inquiries among classmates pursuing degrees in journalism—half-assed because everything hinged on his finding the courage to tell his parents law school was not for him. While making little progress toward launching a journalistic career, he had covered his bases by applying to Harvard and Boston University Law School. He figured Harvard would reject him. Maybe he'd get lucky and B.U. would as well.

"Oy," he moaned at the dark ceiling. At this utterance, something stirred nearby. His nearsighted eyes scanned the living room. Perhaps the dog had sauntered downstairs? He reached behind his head for the side table, where he had folded his glasses. As his hand groped around the table, it bumped into an unfamiliar object, soft and warm and feeling a lot like skin. Whipping around, Nate could just make out a large shape, occupying the chair on the other side of the end table. "What the...?"

"Shh, *mon cher*," the shape whispered. "Go back to sleep. That diphtheria, it's no match for my strong boy." Rose moved her hand from the teacup on the end table to Nate's forehead. "See? Fever almost all gone. My Vincent's a strong one, him. You sleep now and you be *tiguidou* come morning. You betcha."

Nate lay back, unsure whether he should turn on the nearby lamp, unsure whether he *wanted* to see the tableau now playing out in the darkness. He willed his pulse rate to slow. At her dottiest, Rose posed no threat, he reminded himself. His heart was almost back to normal rhythm when a barely audible lullaby wafted from the shadow beside him. Shivering, he strained to make out the French words. He thought he caught the refrain. *Fais do do?* He translated the first word as the imperative for "do" or "make" but had no idea what the singer wanted done or made. As he struggled to recall some French colloquialisms, his focus shattered as the apparent lullaby came to an abrupt halt when Rose began sobbing softly, "Oh, Maryellen, *ma petite!* My poor, lost *bébé!*"

THIRTY-ONE

Home Front Extremes

It was early March. It was New England. So the weather was a study in extremes. Just days after Nate's MG was excavated from snowdrifts, he was sweating in the sun as he pointed at Vince's beaten up, size-twelve boots, protruding from underneath the car. "Good luck finding replacements for those things, now that shoes are being rationed. What happened to them?"

"My partner dropped his end of the sheet metal we were carrying. Sliced right through the leather. Without that steel toe insert, I'd be in sorry shape. Hand me that socket wrench, will ya?"

Nate placed the wrench in the grease-stained palm materializing behind the right front wheel. "Jeez! Glad you're okay. Fore River sure is churning out LSTs lately. I wonder where they'll be carrying all those tanks. Is it part of the Lend-Lease Act or are they for American landings? Seems like we're getting a lot closer to getting troops on the ground in Europe. Finally."

"Dunno," Vince replied as his creeper rolled into the clear. He sat up, pulled a grubby rag from a rear pants pocket, wiped his hands, and hefted himself upright. "You still got beer in your bottle? Don't know about you, but I'm sweating buckets and could use another break."

Nate nodded, and both men relocated to the shaded cement stairs where they had stashed the bottles during their last break.

"Nice to hear some encouraging news from several fronts, even if we have to put up with expanded rationing," the younger man said. "You ever hear of this Eisenhower fella before?"

"Nope. Just what I read in the papers. When I first heard that name, I thought he must be a German general. I hope they know what they're doing, because the guy's never been on a battlefield himself. But he's sure covered a lot of terrain, working with MacArthur in the Philippines before the war, going to England last year to command U.S. troops stationed there, and now the North African landings."

"And here I thought he was a relative of yours and you'd have the inside dope."

"Huh?"

"Eisenhower married a Dowd. Well, I guess she spells it differently."

Vince chuckled, took a drink from his bottle, and shook his head. "I wonder if this Eisenhower is the reason why Rommel is finally on the run in Tunisia. If he can outfox that crafty sonofabitch, that's saying something."

"I doubt the British would give the credit to an American general."

"You're probably right. So, have you gotten any closer to finding some news service to hire you?"

"Maybe. A classmate of mine works part-time at the Globe and knows someone with the Associated Press. Says the AP is building up its overseas bureaus like crazy and needs bodies. So maybe they won't be too picky about hiring a recent college grad with no formal training in journalism."

"You told your parents, yet?"

Nate nearly choked on his last swig.

"I'll take that as a no," Vince teased. "The clock's ticking. They're gonna be a lot more upset if you wait until the night before you hop a plane to London."

"I know," Nate groaned. "But ... families. There are so many minefields to cross when broaching tricky subjects."

"Tell me about it."

"That reminds me. I may have stepped on a mine or two with your aunt the other day."

"You're not the first. What set her off?"

"Like an idiot, I got curious about her relationship with Madame Rose. Isabelle was acting so motherly when Rose got the flu. In that prickly way she has, but still kinda sweet. So I mentioned it was hard to believe there had been a rift between the two of them."

"Christ! And you still have all four limbs?"

"It was really that dumb a question? What happened that was so awful?"

"I don't know the full story. I gather that Izzy's nose got out of joint way back when Ma got married. She felt scared, abandoned, and all alone. But things got worse much later, when I was around twenty. Izzy stopped coming around not long after my Uncle Dennis died. I don't know whether there was any connection. For all I know, it wasn't one big fight, one big misunderstanding. With every family, the little things kinda build up, you know? Stupid stuff like one person leaves dirty towels on the bathroom floor and the other person gets a hair across their ass from constantly picking up the towels."

"You've done your share of towel-dropping, Vince?"

"My answer would be 'no.' Nora may have a different answer." Vince grinned. "So do you think Ma is any better since she's stopped drinking the contaminated well water?"

Nate flashed on the snowbound evening when Rose confused him with Vince and then with her late daughter, but decided against burdening his friend with those details. He covered by taking another swallow of beer. "Can't really say. She certainly has days when she seems quite sharp. But she still has others when she's foggy."

"We just found out the city's gonna hook her up to the public water system soon. She'll have to pay some fee, but it's nothing like they were charging a decade ago. The health department wants to seal the well, too, as a public health hazard."

"A health hazard they helped cause, from that bug spray years ago. Lead arsenate, for chrissake!"

"Yeah, I'm glad your father had such a good memory about the spraying that was done. We passed the info on to Dr. Kelley, and he had himself a little chat with some cronies at the city health department. Maybe that's why the public water hookup will be so cheap."

Nate shrugged. "Who knows the way bureaucracies work. Maybe the city's afraid your mother will sue them. Or maybe it's because of your father? Didn't you say he was a city councilor for a while?"

Vince snorted derisively. "That was almost two decades ago. Once upon a time, my old man thought he might be cut out for politics. So he chatted up this guy and that to make his interest known. He even joined the local temperance union as a way to make connections. Not that it stopped him from breezing by the Brewer's Corner pub every Friday night for a pint of Guinness. And by God, he actually got himself elected. Served two or three terms. Not bad for a penniless Mick laborer who didn't cross the Atlantic until he was in his early twenties."

"Not bad at all. So what happened to his political career? Did he lose the fourth election?"

"Nope. He never ran. I'm not sure why, but had the impression he had grown disillusioned with politics. I remember him grousing about some of the 'eejuts' on the city council and in the mayor's office. Not just the Republicans, but his fellow Democrats, too. He said he had more stimulating conversations with the Italian and Polish stonecutters who could barely speak one word of English."

"Your father's impression of politicians sounds a lot like my perception of lawyers."

"Like I said before, Nate, you better jump off that train quick. Or it's gonna steam on to a place where you don't want to be. If you don't make the leap now, the next time I see you, you'll have an 'esquire' after your name, you'll be wearing a pinstriped suit, sporting a pot belly, and saying things like 'whereas.'"

"God forbid!"

Vince drained the last bubble from his bottle, slapped his knee, and asked, "Well, I think we've farted around long enough, if we're gonna get that car of yours on the road by spring."

"Gee, I just thought. What will I do with the MG if I go off to Europe? You know anyone who might want to buy it?"

"I can ask around. But first things first. Let's get it running reliably. C'mon."

Before the two men could return to the driveway, Netty popped her head out the front door. "Wait, Daddy! Mummy has something for you."

"Wait, wait, wait!" cried Nora excitedly from inside the house.

213

Netty darted to one side, to avoid a doorway collision. She caught her father's eye and grimaced, sucking air between clenched teeth—an apparent attempt to communicate some kind of warning.

Nora was carrying a tray covered with a kitchen towel. "I just had a little baking fit. I've been wanting to try out that oatmeal cookie recipe your mother gave me. I thought you boys could use a sweet treat to make you more productive."

With dramatic flair, she flipped the towel off the tray, knocking one of the cookies onto the concrete steps. Nate retrieved it and eyed it warily, unsure of whether he was supposed to eat it or return it.

"No, no, that's yours, Nate," Nora giggled. "Just wipe off any dirt and pop all that sweetness into your mouth."

Nate stared at the cookie again and wiped it on the relatively clean front of his trousers, which now wore a black stain.

"Well?" Nora asked, beckoning him with her free hand.

Nate chomped into the cookie. A charred oatmeal flake dropped onto his shirt. "Mm," he said, aware of his hostess's intense gaze.

"Yummy, right? Here, Vince, it's your turn." She pushed the tray toward her husband.

Vince eyed the flat, black disks then looked at his hands. "Aw, gee, honey, my hands are grubby. I'll get your tray dirty."

Nora thrust the towel at him. And waited.

He wiped his hands, gingerly picked up one of the cookies, popped the whole thing in his mouth, and made loud crunching noises. After swallowing hard, he nodded and said, "Nice."

"Just like your mother makes, right?"

Vince nodded, but added, "Maybe a just little bit flatter than hers."

Netty and Nate both flinched.

Nora was unperturbed, however. Waving a dismissive hand, she said, "Oh, that's because we didn't have any baking soda. But that doesn't matter much. As your mother always says, 'Every fault's a fashion.'"

Vince could not remember his mother ever using that expression, but nodded agreeably. "How about we take the cookies with us to the driveway, so we can munch as we work? Okay?"

Handing the tray to her husband, Nora exclaimed, "Sure! I've got to go back anyway and start on that meatloaf recipe I clipped from Good Housekeeping. I've just got so much energy today. Shame to let it go to waste."

"But it's not even three o'clock, Nora. Kinda early for dinner isn't it? And we've got another hour or two before we'll be finished."

"Is it that early? Gee, I've been so busy I hadn't even looked at the clock. Well, I can just pop the meatloaf in that new refrigerator of ours until you're ready. That will give me a chance to peel some potatoes and get them boiling. Or whaddya think about boiled onions? No. That won't do. Peeling them always makes my eyes water. That's why I have you do that. I know! I'll leaf through that Fannie Farmer cookbook I've never opened. You know, the one Mother gave me a few years ago. Yes, there's an idea! I may just use up our sugar ration for the next month. But what the heck. Life is short, right? So eat all the cookies you want, boys. I'll come up with something else for an after-dinner treat. Bye, boys! Don't work too hard." She fluttered her fingers at them and scooted back inside.

Netty paused to smirk impishly at her father before following the cook.

The two men walked wordlessly to the driveway. Once at their destination, Vince motioned toward the nearby trash can. Nate grabbed the metal handle and yanked upward. Vince slid the tray's contents inside. "I'd leave 'em out for the neighborhood dogs, but I'm too much of an animal lover. Burnt hockey pucks and cold meatloaf! I can hardly wait to see what dessert will be."

THIRTY-TWO

Knee-Deep In Memories

Ice bag in hand, Rose limped into the kitchen to quell the shrieking teakettle. "Izzy, okay I pour your tea?" she shouted.

Izzy bustled into the room and clucked, "Oh, for heaven's sake, I'll take care of it. I was coming to shut the kettle off. Why did you get up, with your knees hurting?"

"Because the sound hurts my ears." Rose tugged on one earlobe for emphasis. "My ice almost gone. Maybe I go to bed early." She shook the ice bag into the sink to remove the few remaining shards.

"First sensible idea you've had all day. Why you decided to get on your hands and knees to scrub the floor I'll never understand. There is such a thing as a long-handled mop, you know."

"The maid, she must be using it."

"Very witty, *ma soeur*! Don't blame me if you can't walk tomorrow. I told you spending all that time on your knees was a stupid idea."

"Yeah, I'm stupid, me," Rose said, adding a poor attempt at a chuckle. As she opened the hot-water tap to melt that last piece of ice, she added under her breath, "And you always right, ma soeur. Always

216

gotta be right."

"What?"

"Good night. C'mon, Jolie, we go upstairs."

Lying in bed, hands folded over her stomach, Rose sighed then groaned out her frustration with her sister. Jolie raised her head and yodeled softly.

"Go back to sleep, *mon loup*. Everything *tiguidou*," Rose said in a soothing tone, then whispered to herself, "Everything except knees that ache and head that don't work right, and Izzy that acts like Izzy." She sighed again and nestled deeper beneath the covers. She groped for the silver rosary beneath the pillow, made the sign of the cross, and began the Apostle's Creed, with confidence that softly murmuring all those prayers would shut out the cares of the day, shut off her brain, and open the door to sleep.

Rose hiked up her skirt, eased down one stocking and looked at the red glow on her right knee. "Look, Izzy! See what those stairs do?"

"Well, what did you expect? I told you it was a stupid idea to climb those stairs on your knees! What do you know about the Scala Santa anyway? A little heathen like you?"

Rose noticed that her younger sister was very old, much older than she, a young girl with long brown curls bouncing against her pinafore. "I want to see if I could do it. I want to make a devotion to Saint Anne. Your favorite saint, no? The patron saint of spinsters."

"You know perfectly well she's the patron saint of Quebec. Uncle Edward and I are going to see the basilica. You don't need to come with us. You won't appreciate the art anyway."

And just like that, Izzy was gone, and Edward, who had only just materialized, had disappeared, too. Rose limped in the direction they had headed, toward the actual shrine dedicated to Izzy's favorite saint. As she crossed the street, she looked up, up at the church's twin bell towers and felt a vibration coming from them. It tickled her toes, snaked up her legs, then coiled up her spine. A vibration of power. Dumbstruck by the sensation, she didn't notice a familiar figure approaching her.

The old woman rapped her knuckles on Rose's head. "Wake up, little one. Lots to do."

"Mère Agathe? You're here? In a church?"

Agathe pressed a forefinger into her lips. "Shh, the roof, it might fall down on me. A pretty roof, no?"

Rose nodded. It was indeed pretty. And just like that she was inside the basilica. She twirled around several times, her long hair spinning out behind her. The twirling generated an internal kaleidoscope of stained-glass windows.

When she stopped, she was looking straight into the wooden face of St. Anne herself, far, far above her. St. Anne stared back, a kindly stare for a wooden face.

"She likes you," Mère Agathe said and pointed upward, "The grandmother of Jesus." Then the old woman pointed at Rose. "And the grandmother of Netty."

Rose looked down at the liver spots on her bare forearms. She was no longer a young girl. The realization made her sad and made her knees hurt more.

Mère Agathe nudged her side with an elbow. "Look at all these people."

Rose looked left and right at the crowd that had suddenly gathered. They were all staring upward, not into the saint's slightly sad wooden face, not at the child Mary in her arms, but at the crown on her head, a wondrous creation of gold, diamonds, rubies, and pearls.

"Pah," Mère Agathe continued. "All they see is gold and jewels. Very pretty, but look at what the grandmother of God is made of. Do you see, little one?"

Rose squinted, unsure of what she was supposed to see.

"Solid oak. Carved from one giant tree. You think that wood ever gonna break? You gotta be tough like her, little one. Look at her, look hard. She's strong like oak. And she's kind, just like a nana. Gotta be both. Doux et sauvage, *little one."*

Still squinting, Rose tried to absorb whatever lessons the wooden statue might impart. Feeling sad that no wisdom was flooding in, she sighed. She sighed again when she realized her old mentor had disappeared, along with the crowd. Alone in the imposing sanctuary, Rose gazed up one last time at the statue. St. Anne winked a wooden eye.

Rose winced at the dry toast before her. Unable to find butter in the store for more than a week, and unwilling to purchase loathsome margarine, she resolved to eat her morning toast with no adornment. Her resolve failed her, and she pushed the unappetizing breakfast away.

"I know! I make milk toast." As she headed for the icebox to fetch the milk, she remembered she was also out of sugar. "Pah!" she exclaimed, slumping back into her chair, propping her chin on her fists, and staring at the toast. Dimly hearing a voice telling her to be tough, she laughed suddenly. "You gonna let rationing make you sad, old woman? You tougher than that, you." Pointing at the toast, she said, "And you, you gonna be a sandwich for lunch, yeah?"

As she wrapped the piece of toast in a clean towel, Izzy entered, pushing her glasses closer to her nose to examine the kitchen table and counters. "Have you seen my pack of Lucky Strikes? I guess I forgot to bring it upstairs last night. It's my last pack, and I can't find it anywhere."

"You forgetting things? Not a good sign, *ma soeur.*"

Izzy twisted her lips in annoyance. The grimace quickly softened when Rose fished into her pocket and waggled the missing pack.

"I find this on the hall table." Rose passed the cigarettes to her sister.

"Ah, yes, now I remember putting it there last night when I picked up my bedtime reading." Izzy plucked a Lucifer from the can above the stove, scratched it on the stove pipe, and lit up. "Ahh, much better," she sighed after taking her first draught.

"And I just remember this dream I have. Make your tea and I tell you about it."

Izzy groaned, but after pouring a cup, settled into the chair opposite Rose. "So?"

"You, me, and Uncle Edward, we're all in the church for St. Anne. St. Anne de Beaupré. Up in Quebec. Except you're old, like today. I'm young, then old. Edward is just like he is when we're growing up in Quebec. And St. Anne's statue, she winks at me."

"Your storytelling powers leave something to be desired," Izzy said, taking another suck on her cigarette. "And why is this important?"

"I get the time mixed up. In the dream, I walk up those stairs, on my knees. But you don't. I know I really do go up those stairs on my knees.

But when? With Uncle Edward sometime when we're little ones?"

"Don't you remember? Visiting the basilica was his farewell treat before we left Quebec. But you certainly did not climb up the stairs, the Scala Santa. They weren't built until years later."

"Ah, I remember now! I climb those stairs that time Vincent drives me to Quebec."

"I don't remember you ever being pious. Why on earth would you do that? Or is that another fractured memory?"

Rose frowned. "Yes, I climb those stairs. I want to see if I can. Even as an old married woman of forty. And I can! What a beautiful church!"

"I don't recall your being all that impressed with it when Uncle Edward was giving us the tour. You seemed bored."

Rose tapped her lower lip as she recalled the actual visit with Uncle Edward and Izzy. "Not bored. Sad. All I can think of is leaving."

"Sounds bored to me if all you could think of was getting out of the basilica."

"No, leaving *Quebec*. Just a few days later, we're gone. You get to say goodbye to Edward. I never say goodbye to Mère Agathe. Never see Noir again, either."

Izzy rolled her eyes and shuddered. "I never understood what you saw in either of those creatures."

Rose's face colored. "And I never see what's so great about Edward. But you, you act like he's some storybook hero, him! You see what you want to in him."

"I saw an educated, generous man with refined manners, someone who was willing to take the time to let a little girl know there was a much bigger world out there than our wretched farm. And if that's not important, I don't know what is." Izzy folded her arms over her chest and stared a challenge at her sister.

"You see what you want to see. Like when you see him as Mama's boyfriend. Like when you wish Edward's your father, not Papa."

"You're being ridiculous, I never thought that!"

Rose leaned forward and pressed a forefinger to her head. "This brain forgets stuff. But not that. You tell me how Mama likes Edward better than Papa. How Papa gets jealous. How Mama maybe not gonna stay with Papa. And maybe Mama and you go live with Uncle Edward."

Izzy pressed her palms against the table edge. "I never!"

"Yeah, you do! And most of what you see? All *merde!* Mama and

Papa not so happy, but not because of Uncle Edward. Because their life, it's so hard. Mama and Edward? They never like each other the way you think, the crazy way you see."

Izzy sat back in her hair and pushed her glasses closer to her nose. "I see clearly enough, unlike some people I could mention."

"Me, yeah?"

"You, yeah. You never could see that Francis for what he was. An Irish thug!"

"Pah, whatever Francis is all about, he's mine. And we make a good life together, us. A life you try to spoil, just like you try to spoil Mama and Papa."

"Oh, here we go. I've been wondering how long it would take for ancient history to surface. Wasn't it my sisterly duty to tell you Francis was cheating on you? With that low-brow Driscoll barmaid?"

Rose slapped a palm on the table. "Francis never cheats! May Driscoll, she's a friend. Maybe more of a friend than me back then. I'm so busy with the boys, I don't see how sad he is when he loses his brother. Dinny is his last link to Ireland, the country he never wants to leave, just like I never want to leave Quebec. But he has to leave, just like I have to leave. I should understand all this. But I don't listen enough to his sadness. May, she listens.

"And you, you never come to Dinny's funeral. Francis feels so hurt, him. And then you make that big scene in May Driscoll's bar. Everyone there hears the lies you tell. They repeat those lies, over and over. Your lies hurt Francis's dreams. Suddenly he looks bad to people who want him to run for some big-shot job in Boston. He even has to give up that council job here in Quincy. He never forgives you. You know, he tells me he doesn't want to see you in our house again. And what do I do? I put my foot down. I tell him, 'Izzy, she's my sister. If I want Izzy here, Izzy gonna be here.'"

Izzy shook her head. "Except I wasn't here so much after that, was I? As for Dennis, why in heaven's name should I ask for time off work so I could attend the funeral of someone I never liked?"

"Dinny's family!"

"Dennis wasn't *my* family. Neither was Francis, for that matter, but I attended *his* funeral, didn't I? I did that for you. And it was for your sake that I told you about Francis and May Driscoll. It was for your sake that I confronted that woman in her wretched bar. I did all that for you! And look at the thanks I got!"

"Pah!" Rose shouted. "You do all that for you! You don't think I already know about all them talks Francis has with May? You don't think I worry? But you make a big fuss. You kill Francis's dreams."

"Oh please, the likes of Francis Dowd was never going to achieve political prominence. That much is perfectly obvious. What is *not* obvious to me is why you never did anything about that Driscoll woman yourself."

Rose shook her head sadly. "Izzy, you know plenty from books. You don't know marriage. Husbands and wives, they have good days. They have bad days. You gonna throw the marriage away for a bad day? For a bad year? You wait. You remember the good days. You wait some more. Francis and me, we wait maybe two years after Maryellen dies. And you know what? Life does get better. As long as you don't do nothing stupid. But you make it harder for me to wait when he starts having them talks with May. I hear you nag, nag about Francis this and Francis that. You make me feel worse. You make me feel stupid."

"I don't have to sit here and take this," Izzy harrumphed, rising from the table. She was halfway out the kitchen door when she pivoted back, snatched the pack of Lucky Strikes, and stomped off again.

Rose stood over the bread dough on her kitchen counter, the late afternoon sun making her eyes tear. "No, no crying," she said aloud, as she punched the floury mound. She worked the heel of her hand into it, folded it over, and began the soothing rhythm of kneading.

Rose Dowd, you're an old woman, you. But you not dead yet, eh? You just have less time. Less time for all them thoughts to think. Maybe you forget things. Things you want to remember, not just the bad stuff. You simpleminded, they say. Maybe so. Or maybe the mind, she's deep in conversation. And if time's getting short, you need to make time to chat with yourself.

Let them all jibber-jabber. Let them watch you and wait for you to say something wrong. Let them ask you what day it is. Let them get all worried when you say "Tuesday." Maybe you say Tuesday because Tuesday is where your mind is when they interrupt. A Tuesday in March, say. Or maybe a Tuesday in 1888.

222

Maybe when you get old enough, you get invisible. Maybe Izzy finally leaves you alone. Maybe everyone leaves you alone. No, not Vincent and Netty. You don't want them to leave you. But they worry when you forget. They don't understand. Don't understand when you say a bunch of words in French. "How come you forget to talk like an American?" asks little Netty.

Forget? How am I ever gonna forget trying to fit in, use all the right English words, in the right order? Trying so hard. So much effort. Too much effort now when the brain, she wants to think other stuff. Like, why you lose your home? Like, why you lose your parents? Like, why that farm in Manitoba's not big enough for you? Why you're not good enough?

A single tear rolled down Rose's cheek and landed on the dough. She slammed her fist into it, folded the dough in half then in half again, extinguishing any sign of the tear's existence.

"You gotta be tough, old woman. Gotta be tough."

THIRTY-THREE

Upside Down

The world was upside down, Vince thought as he drove the sleek English sports car down the wrong side of the tracks, *his* side of the tracks. Normally he would be enjoying the satisfaction of rescuing Nate's ancient MG from the junkyard and giving it a second life as a zippy roadster. Normally, he would savor the irony of the son of two immigrants mastering a car that, when new, was something only a rich man could have afforded (rich by West Quincy standards, at least). Normally, Vince harbored little envy for the rich. He was fully aware that, rich or poor, everyone faced heartache, tragedy, death. But this was an upside down kind of day, one when it was hard to be philosophical.

How could the world make sense when madmen ruled half of it? When pennies were steel, instead of copper, because copper was needed for the war effort? When there were death marches like the one in Bataan, where armed men beheaded starving, wounded, dehydrated, sick, unarmed men? When Nora Dowd had disappeared somewhere deep inside her mind, somewhere Vince couldn't reach? And what could he do about any of it?

He shifted gears and shrugged. "I guess I can help build warships that will kill some of the bastards that order death marches and strip innocent people of their livelihood before marching them off to prison."

He snorted with the realization that the bastards killed by his warships probably weren't all that different from himself. They were just ordinary Joes working for bastards who worked for even bigger bastards in Berlin and Tokyo. If enough of the ordinary Joes became shark bait in the bloody waters on both halves of the globe, would the world right itself and start spinning properly again? Normally, Vince's answer would be "yes." But these were not normal times.

He caught his reflection in the rearview mirror and snorted again when he noticed the sweat glistening on his forehead. It was late March and well over eighty degrees in the sun. It was New England, where abnormal weather was normal. He wondered if Old Man Flint would blow a snowstorm in tomorrow. He wondered where the hell he'd heard about Old Man Flint.

He ratcheted up the emergency brake as he pulled in front of Nate's two-story clapboard house.

The youngest Kagan lurched out the front door before Vince reached the curb. "Oh wow, oh wow! You're a magician, Vince! A miracle worker! What a throaty rumble the engine has now. I heard it from inside the house. You've got her absolutely purring!"

Vince twisted his mouth into a lopsided grin and waggled the car keys from forefinger and thumb. Nate snatched them, "Thank you so much. C'mon inside and have a beer to celebrate."

Vince cocked his head. "I only just dumped Netty off after Sunday school. Not even noon, yet. Your parents are gonna think I'm corrupting their only son."

"Oh," Nate said, dejected.

Vince slapped his friend's shoulder. "But you can make me a cup of coffee." He didn't want to disappoint the young man. And he didn't want to return too early to the troubles awaiting him on his side of the tracks.

Nate beamed. "Yeah, yeah. Better idea."

The elder Kagans greeted the guest in the front hall and exchanged a few bland comments about the lovely weather before returning to the living room where they had been poring over the war news. Passing by the living room en route to the kitchen, Vince spotted the dismembered

Sunday Globe and Advertiser sections littering the carpet like fallen soldiers. He wondered how many soldiers' deaths those newspapers were reporting this Sunday.

Nate motioned to his guest to sit at the kitchen table while he busied himself at the stove. "Real coffee," he said pointing proudly to the percolator basket. "With none of that awful chicory filler."

Vince grimaced. "Beats me why anyone thought it a good idea to add a roadside weed to the coffee pot. I'd rather drink hot water."

"Who knew chicory was patriotic? Ma made some coffee cake, too. Real sugar. Real butter. Want some?"

"Don't mind if I do." Vince smiled, realizing his mood was lifting ever so slightly. The young man's enthusiasm was infectious.

After placing two sweets-filled plates on the table, Nate raised an index finger, ducked into a hallway containing a coat rack, and fished inside the front pocket of a corduroy jacket. Re-entering the kitchen, he waved two envelopes and slapped them on the table. "I got news," he said, grinning. "Look at that one first."

Vince slid the appointed envelope across the table. "Harvard University Law School?" He removed the contents and scanned the first page. "Umm, they didn't accept you? I'm sorry?"

Nate fluttered his palm. "I'm not. Okay, now the second one."

Vince suppressed irritation, but complied. "Associated Press?" He zigged and zagged a fingertip across the first page. "You're in? London? June? Human interest stories? That's good, right? You gonna take it? Have you told your parents yet?"

Nate's sunny expression dimmed. "Soon. The timing couldn't be better. I never thought I'd hear this early on any law school application. Got both of these in yesterday's mail. So now I can tell my parents my plans. I'll lead with the Harvard letter. Then, just as they start worrying about what to do with me, I'll whip out the other letter. Genius!"

"Umm, didn't you apply to *two* law schools? What about the other one."

"Haven't heard from B.U. yet."

"Aren't your parents gonna want you to wait until you do?"

"First of all, they had their hearts set on their baby boy hitting the Ivy League. And they're practical enough to value the bird in the hand. They don't want to worry about pestering some relative into shoehorning me into some job just to avoid the stigma of unemployment. They'll understand that I can't afford to wait around, especially with a job offer waiting for a response."

"They gonna understand about you moving to London, where bombs fall from the sky?"

"Nowhere near as many bombs lately. Besides, now that you've finished the MG, I'll offer it to my parents, to soften them up. Something jazzy to take on Sunday drives."

"You really think your mother's gonna want a jazzy car?"

"Of course not. But my old man will. He's always been a car nut. That swell ride will take ten years off him. He'll realize he wouldn't have the use of the MG if I was driving it to and from law school every day."

"I guess." Vince shrugged. "You know your parents better than I do."

"And you know who I can thank for all this?"

"Have no idea."

"Your mother!"

Vince groaned. "What'd she do now?"

"She had an interesting life, that's what. I handed in the first half of my history thesis. My professor doesn't much like what I've done, because it isn't objective enough. So I've got lots of rewriting to do. And frankly, my editing is making it boring. Just like so many history texts. Somehow I've got to explain why Madame Rose and her parents don't fit the mold. My adviser actually had the nerve to accuse me of making stuff up. 'Why didn't your subjects move to one of the Francophone mill towns in New England, where they'd have a ready infrastructure for absorbing immigrants?' he asked. According to him, no French Canadian in his right mind would move to a place like Quincy for the privilege of 'laboring like dogs in the quarries.'" Nate crooked his fingers to indicate quotation marks.

"Professor Leibowitz questioned the truthfulness of my reporting since Quincy has very few Quebeckers and is a place where nobody speaks French. And get this, Vince. The jerk added, 'It's a place where people can barely speak English properly.' Swell guy, right? He has a big house in Wellesley Hills, so naturally we're beneath contempt living here in the armpit of the South Shore."

Vince chuckled. "So what'd you say?"

"I said real people are more complex than the ethnic stereotypes that often turn up in history books."

"Bet that got him all hot under the collar. How'd he react?"

Nate rolled his eyes. "He accused me of having no objectivity. Again."

Vince motioned toward the burbling coffee pot on the stove. "But what does any of this have to do with your new job?"

Nate raised a staying hand, poured the coffee, and returned grinning broadly. "It seems that some people actually appreciate subjective writing. I mailed the first version of my thesis to this wire service editor a buddy told me about. I wanted to give a sample of my writing style and figured, what the hell, writing about the Quentins isn't all that different from writing about the displaced people all over Europe these days. A risky move if he was looking for someone to just rattle off battlefield statistics. But I figured, with my limp, I wasn't likely to be assigned to any battle zone anyway. I guess I got lucky. Turns out the guy was looking for someone to write human interest features. You know, stories about the London kids who were evacuated to the English countryside during the Blitz. Or interviews with American airmen flying into German ack-ack over and over again. There's gotta be a million different features out there. Really interesting stuff, involving real people, not statistics or stereotypes."

Vince laughed appreciatively as Nate, splaying his palms enthusiastically, nearly overturned his coffee mug. "It's good to see you like this, kid. You've been so down at the mouth about the whole law school thing. I'm glad you've found a place where you think you'll fit. Where you can make a difference. Not all of us do."

Nate raised his eyebrows. "I thought you really liked the shipyard job?"

"I do. But ... but I don't think I'm making much of a difference in other ways." Vince broke off a piece of coffee cake and jammed it into his mouth, as if to muzzle himself.

"You're worried about your mother, huh?"

Rose was far from Vince's mind at this moment. His worries were focused much closer to home. But how do you tell a college kid who's never been married that you think your wife is going off her nut? That maybe you're the reason why, because you aren't smart enough or

228

don't make enough money or can't give her the life she deserves? That you have no idea how to make things better? That some days, when you come home from work and find Nora sitting in the dark with tears rolling down her face, when your little girl greets you with desperate cheer, you'd just like to turn on your heel and walk out that door and never come back? How do you tell anyone that you've thought about stashing your wife in some hospital, if only you could afford it? How do you tell anyone that you're actually afraid that, one day, when you're at work, your wife might do something bad to the daughter she loves?

You don't. You stuff your mouth with coffee cake and curse yourself for coming so close to blabbing your family's private business.

Vince realized the last thing he had heard was Nate's voice rising in a questioning tone. He shook his head, swallowed, and said, "What?"

"Have there been any new memory lapses? I thought Madame Rose was doing better."

"No, not that I know of. You really think she's better?"

Nate nodded. "She seemed pretty sharp when I was over there last week. She even crafted a metaphor about Isabelle. She said her sister was a hawk so tempted by a juicy morsel that it flies into a thorn bush, only to realize the juicy morsel is a leaf trembling in the breeze. I don't know what Isabelle did to prompt that observation. But the metaphor is fairly sophisticated. Something you wouldn't expect from someone who's supposedly simpleminded. So maybe her brain is starting to clear since she's stopped drinking contaminated water."

"Ma said, 'a leaf trembling in the breeze'?"

"Umm, not exactly. She said, 'a leaf, she jiggles in the wind.'"

"You know, that history teacher may not be all that wrong about you."

Nate pressed a hand to his heart. "You wound me, sir! So I embellish things a bit! It might make me a lousy historian, but I hope it will make me a good feature writer. And one day, a good novelist."

"All right. I get what you're saying. Sure hope you're right about Ma, trembling leaves and all. But now I'm wondering what's up with her and Izzy."

"Maybe just a sisterly spat?"

"Maybe. I guess I'll find out when I go over there this afternoon. I've gotta give Izzy another driving lesson." Vince gobbled down the last piece of cake and slurped from his mug. "But first you gotta drive me back home in your fancy almost-new wheels."

Nate glugged the last of his coffee, stood abruptly, and said. "Can't wait! But first I gotta get appropriately attired." He shuffled into the adjacent hall and returned wearing an English tweed racing cap.

Vince choked on his coffee. "You look ridiculous!"

Nate grinned. "Yeah, I know. I'm gonna play this role to the hilt. Let's go."

THIRTY-FOUR

Driving Relations

Vince braced for a lecture from his aunt. Izzy usually attended the ten o'clock Mass at St. Mary's, the same one the Dowds attended. She and Nora shared a reluctance to rise too early. But she would not have seen her youngest nephew there today. He had merely dropped off and picked up his wife and daughter. Although glad that Nora had not completely jettisoned a normal weekly routine, Vince just could not abide witnessing the desperate piety his wife was manifesting lately.

Nora had always been a regular church-goer, sharing her husband's take on religion. Neither saw Sunday Mass as a socializing opportunity or a source of inspiration. But it rooted them in their culture, both the French Canadian and Irish sides. It gave them some sense of belonging. And if their attendance counterbalanced their expressions of pettiness, selfishness, anger, and envy on some cosmic scoreboard, so much the better. Lately, however, Nora appeared to be seeking some kind of healing from church attendance, an all-purpose remedy, calming her down when she was frantic and enlivening her when she was blue. If only if had worked, Vince thought. Instead, Nora would return from Mass disappointed and sad or disappointed and contemptuous. So this Sunday, he pleaded a bad headache as justification for merely driving his family to St. Mary's. If he had to watch his wife solemnly fingering her rosary beads or enthusiastically nodding with every word from the pulpit, he really would have ended up with a colossal headache.

Izzy said nothing about his absence, even though she had indeed attended the same service as Nora and Netty, as Netty reported. Indeed, Izzy had very little to say all the way down to the usual parking lot where she would hone her driving skills. When a driver ran a stop sign and forced Vince to slam on the brakes, she didn't complain about the "miscreant" or cluck about the city's "irresponsible" failure to cut tree limbs obscuring traffic signs. She merely uttered a soft gasp and patted her chest.

"You okay, Izzy?" Vince asked, after arriving at their destination and just before he and his aunt switched sides, so she could take the wheel.

Izzy nodded. "I'd like to take the car on the road, someplace where there's not too much traffic, but where I can open her up a little."

Vince chuckled. "You're feeling like a speed demon today, huh?"

"Don't be silly," she snapped. "I'd just like the chance to clear my head. Driving does that, I think. Your mind can concentrate on nothing more pressing than keeping the car on the right side of the road."

"Sure," Vince said, impressed that his aunt had already absorbed that truth. After he guided her onto an appropriate route, he was also impressed by the improvement in her driving skills. So he let silence fill the space between them, while he wondered just why Izzy needed to clear her head.

After twenty minutes, he spoke up. "We're almost halfway to Plymouth, Izzy. Fine by me if you want to keep going, but we'd better find an open gas station."

"Oh, have we gone that far already? No, show me where I can turn around. I don't want to use up Rose's gas ration for the month. I can't afford her to get any angrier at me than she already is."

"Okay, take that next right, which will loop around so we can head back. So what's up? Ma isn't one to stay angry very long."

Izzy bit her lip. "That's what I always thought, too. But this time … this time is different. I'm afraid I may have made a mess of things,

Vincent."

She squinted hard at the road. For one terrifying moment Vince feared his aunt might cry. Had he ever seen her cry? With relief, he watched out of the corner of his eye as she squared her thin shoulders and exhaled sharply.

"You two had a spat, I guess?"

"You could say that. It was one of those spats where you both bring up ancient history. Grievances that should stay buried."

"Did this have something to do with the time when you stopped coming over the house? I never knew why. Ma never said. And I never really thought to ask. I was working pretty long hours and courting Nora back then. Had other things on my mind, I guess."

"Of course you did. Why would a young man bother himself with the petty bickering of two middle-aged women?"

"It had something to do with Pa, didn't it?"

Izzy risked turning her head away from the road, shock draining the color from her olive skin. "How did you know?"

Vince shrugged. "You'd have to be deaf, dumb, and blind to miss that you and Pa didn't like each other. I always figured it was just because you were so different. But it was something more than that, wasn't it?"

Izzy nodded and bit her lip again. "You know, I've heard other people say you should never interfere in someone else's marriage, no matter how good your intentions are. And my intentions really were good, Vincent. They really were." She turned briefly toward her passenger.

Vince nodded, but restrained himself from asking any questions. He figured his aunt needed to spin her story at her own pace. And he wasn't all that sure he wanted to hear the answers to any questions he might ask.

After a few minutes, Izzy continued, eyes riveted on the road ahead. "Francis did something, something that would hurt Rose. Would hurt my sister. Or maybe he didn't. Now I'm not so sure. But I thought she should know. She was my sister, after all. I owed her that, didn't I?"

Izzy rapped the steering wheel. "Oh, who am I kidding? I told her because I hoped she'd leave Francis, whether it was good for her or not. After all those years, I was still jealous and hurt." She shook her head.

"Jealous? You weren't ever interested in Pa, were you? I mean, before he and Ma got married?"

233

"Don't be ridiculous, Vincent! Surely you can't believe that your mother and I ever competed for Francis's attention!" She shook her head more vigorously before continuing. "No, I was jealous that Rose would leave me for him. I could see from the very start how besotted they were with each other. I was jealous that she had someone to care for, someone to care for her. Rose was all I had. And not just here in Quincy, after our parents abandoned us. We were all we had back on that wretched farm, too. Mama was too busy for us, always had some little one tugging at her skirt. And if Papa wasn't desperately trying to coax food out of the ground or cajoling the pigs not to die before slaughter, he was taking odd jobs at logging camps far from home. If he had an accident or bad weather kept him from returning, God only knows how we would have survived.

"Rose, more than Mama, kept us going. She rigged traps to catch rabbits. She even brought down a few doves with a slingshot. But mostly she kept my mind from focusing on the gnawing hunger pains or next month's rent. She'd tell me some stupid story about her stupid raven or about how the Northern Lights were the reflection of the big fire God lit after he finished making Earth, to let man know he hadn't forgotten him. And I'd get so wrapped up with explaining that the Northern Lights were caused by electrically charged solar particles that I'd forget my hunger pains."

"Jeez, you guys actually went hungry? I knew things were tight and you often didn't have much food in the house, but you were that close to the edge?"

"Pah! Didn't Rose ever tell you about our fiddle-leaf fern hunts? Of course, she probably described them as childhood excursions, exploring the wonders of Mother Nature. Hardly! You've heard of spring fever. You know what it really means? Scurvy! Even if we still had some dried meat or vegetables left over, we were starved for fresh vegetables and would scrounge the woods for the first fern shoots to eat. Now maybe if we had some butter to fry them up in, they might have been palatable. But basically it was like munching on grass. As bad as they were, the fern shoots were better than the nettles. Stinging nettles. Lots of nutrition in the young shoots, before they developed those damnable barbs. But there were times I thought scurvy would be better than the irritation of all those nasty little nettle hairs. Even though Rose and I would wear gloves and swaddle our sleeves in muslin, those hairs would work their way into everything and release this chemical to make you burn and itch all over."

"No wonder you never had any interest in revisiting Quebec. I wonder why Ma has always been so nostalgic for it."

"*Voyageur* blood. She should have been a man born two centuries earlier. She would have thrived. It's so ironic that Papa had such disregard for her, just because she was a girl. His first five children, all of us born in Quebec, were all girls, you know, and he needed boys to help with all the farm chores. Never mind all the heavy labor we girls did, especially Rose. It's ironic that he never realized how much like him she really was."

"I knew she was tough. I guess I never knew how tough. She's always been so cheerful."

"Well, she's not very cheerful now. At least not toward me. She's downright flinty."

"The quarreling didn't stop with that spat about ancient history? You guys are still at it?"

"I wish. She isn't talking at all, not to me anyway. Oh, just enough to cover the basics."

"What do you do at mealtimes?"

"Well, we've always eaten breakfast at different times, because I wait until the sun actually rises before I get up, and I'm rarely hungry for lunch. It's dinner time that I find so awful. Oddly, she still cooks for both of us, but she takes her plate into the living room and listens to the radio while she eats, while I'm alone in the kitchen. I actually miss her prattle. I feel abandoned all over again."

"Jeez, have you tried apologizing?"

Izzy swiveled her head to the right and arched a brow. "I think the harsh words were doled out in equal measure, Vincent."

Vince sighed. "Izzy, you can have your pride or you can have peace."

She harrumphed.

"Do you have any idea how many times I've apologized to Nora, often when I didn't even know what I'd done wrong?"

"And does that make you happy?" Izzy tightened her grip on the steering wheel.

Vince puffed his cheeks and exhaled audibly. "I dunno what to tell you. But I've got a feeling you're the only one who can fix this. And fixing things only gets harder the more time goes by."

Silently, he pointed to the right-hand turn that would lead them back to Willard Street. One mile later, he said, "Turn left onto that side street."

"Why here?"

"Because almost every household on this street has a car, and they all park at the curb. It's a good place for you to practice parallel parking. How about that spot up there?"

Izzy squinted in the direction her nephew pointed, took a deep breath, and flawlessly inserted the car into the space, with not one correction forward or reverse.

Vince smiled. "Terrific job! Now do a three-point turn."

Izzy complied. Once again, flawlessly. "Now what?" she said, smirking with pride.

"Now we go home. And you make an appointment with the Registry of Motor Vehicles. You're more than ready to get your license."

Izzy beamed. "Thank you, Vincent. Will you drive me to the appointment?"

"No can do. Not with all the extra shifts I'm working. Ask Ma to take you." He couldn't stifle a grin when he saw Izzy's erect posture crumple.

THIRTY-FIVE

Reflections of a Quarry Diver

It was the kind of early April day that could make the world's greatest cynic believe in happy endings. It was the kind of early April day that made Vince forget for a while about Nora's increasingly frequent detours to Crazy Town or Netty's latest trip to the doctor. The temperature was balmy. The air was clean. The sky was cloudless. And Vince had just done the impossible. He definitively fixed the engine of a crawler that had spent more time befuddling mechanics in the garage than hauling mobile cranes around the yard. To make life even better, he got to drive that monstrous tracked vehicle to its next work site. Vince felt like General George S. Patton, standing in the turret hatch of a tank speeding toward Tunis. He couldn't stop grinning.

"What you grinning at?" shouted Walter as Vince turned his resurrected vehicle over to its grateful operator.

Vince jerked a thumb toward the crawler. "Finally fixed that fucker."

"That's why they pay you all that wampum. You heading back to the garage or have you got time to do me a favor?"

"I don't have to go back right away. Whatcha need?"

"Doug went home sick and I need someone to spot for me as I double-check some couplings on that metal scaffolding." He pointed to a temporary platform attached to the far side of a ship undergoing repair. "My shit's already up there so all you have to do is sit and watch me and make the bosses happy. They'll fry my ass if I work up there alone. Shouldn't take more than half an hour."

Vince glanced at his watch, nodded, and said, "Sure. I won't be missed for a while."

Walter tossed him the extra hardhat tucked under his left armpit. The two men headed for the scaffolding.

"Did I mention we're climbing?"

"I didn't think we were flying up there," Vince said.

Walter wagged a finger. "It's the flying *down* you gotta worry about."

He shinnied up the forty-foot structure as if it were a marble staircase in some palatial Beacon Hill estate. Vince's ascent was considerably slower.

"You climb pretty good for a white boy."

"My mother used to say I had monkey blood."

Walter snorted. "More like hairy gorilla blood by the look of you. Park your butt there and I'll get started."

As the ironworker, toolbox in hand, walked confidently along the planks laid out on the metal pipes, Vince called out, "Just what am I supposed to watch for?"

"Seagulls. I can't stand seagulls. If they shit on me one more time…"

So, Vince watched, for what, he wasn't sure. It didn't seem like his confident, agile co-worker needed any assistance. So, Vince assumed his presence was a matter of form, not substance. Until the wind picked up. He felt the scaffolding sway and white-knuckled the pipe that served as a guard rail. He made the mistake of looking down and experienced a wave of nausea. So he looked at Walter and felt relief that the ironworker seemed unperturbed by the gusts. He looked beyond Walter at the load of steel pipes being lowered onto the deck by a crane. He looked beyond that operation toward the Fore River Bridge, to get his bearings and to focus on something other than the wind, the swaying scaffolding, and his jumpy stomach. To the left of the bridge

238

lay Quincy, he told himself; to the right was the town of Weymouth. He marveled, not for the first time, at the modern engineering that allowed such an enormous structure to open up so that even the tallest warships could glide into Hingham Bay and eventually the vast Atlantic. The nausea passed and Vince focused on Walter, crouched by one of the couplings, his body hiding whatever he was working on.

A righteous blast of salt air blew in from the east. The scaffolding shuddered again. This time both Walter and Vince grabbed onto the nearest pipe.

"Shit!" Walter yelled suddenly.

"You okay?"

"Yeah, but I dropped my damn spud wrench."

"Hope you didn't bean anyone."

"Nah," Walter said walking back toward Vince, more cautiously than he had walked away. "It fell into the water. But I need another one that size to finish up. Now I gotta climb down and get one. Fuck me!" The big Mohawk shook his head. "You stay here. No sense both of us making the climb twice just because I got a case of the dropsies. I'll be back in a jiffy."

Vince nodded and watched his friend climb down, cursing all the way. Vince chuckled at the creativity with which the expletives were strung together. He eased his grip on the pipe and tested the air with his free hand. He could sense no wind and hoped the calm would hold. Feeling more at ease, he savored the adventure of hanging forty feet over the water, the satisfaction of doing work that had purpose. Vince had never aspired to fame or glory but had always sought a useful life. Being useful gave him a reason to get up in the morning and allowed him to sleep soundly at night. He figured he could die without regret if he managed to be of use throughout his life. He celebrated that realization with a gentle, childlike swing of both lower legs over the edge of the scaffolding. He even ventured a look downward, at the water, then at the busy activity on deck. He felt no nausea this time. He felt happy, at peace, worry-free.

Until the earth shook. His first thought was to wrap both arms and legs around the scaffolding, because Old Man Flint was blowing in a nor'easter, a blast of fury headed straight for him. His next thought was that it was April, and not even New England had nor'easters in April.

His next thought was why the wind should sound so strange. It didn't howl. It boomed. And underneath the boom, underneath him, he could hear shouts of distress. He looked down and to his right and saw the last of a load of pipes sliding in slow motion off the crane hook and colliding with the base of the scaffolding. *His* scaffolding.

Suddenly he was on his feet, more or less, trying to scramble uphill, as far away from the collision as possible. The planks beneath his feet had another idea and skidded downward, toward that collision. With the same reluctance he felt as a five-year-old, diving off that quarry ledge, Vince pushed with all his strength to get away from the doomed scaffolding. He looked down at the water. He told himself he was an experienced quarry diver. He could do this. With relief, he noted that his feet were below his head. He wasn't exactly vertical, but his feet would hit the water first, and they could handle the impact a lot better than his skull. With gratitude, he remembered that Fore River was deep, deep enough to handle mighty warships. Even with the speed of his descent, that depth should protect him. He would not hit bottom, he figured, before he could pedal upward. He knew from all those quarry dives that he had the lung power to hold his breath for however long it took to plummet deep into the murky river and rise back up to the surface.

In the seconds that his descent lasted, Vince processed all those evaluations. He did not think of Nora or Netty or his mother. He did not see his past flash before him. He focused on the moment at hand, what he could do to make it better. His only job was to survive. And he was good at his job. He liked being good at his job. He risked a smile, even though the onslaught of salt air stung his gums.

Two days passed before divers retrieved Vince's body from the opaque depths of Fore River. Workers who witnessed the fall reported how Vince had managed somehow to right himself, how his arms and legs did not flail. He seemed halfway in control of his descent, they told the newspapermen flooding the shipyard. It looked like he might actually make it.

He might have made it, commented one witness, if a sudden gust hadn't conspired against survival. The wind pushed the falling man closer to the ship and into a dislodged scaffolding pipe that had caught on the hull on its journey to the bottom of Fore River. The back of Vince's skull collided with that pipe, just a few feet above the water. The coroner speculated that Vince was probably dead before his booted feet broke the surface. The coroner's report made no mention of any smile on the corpse's bloated face.

THIRTY-SIX

Clearing the Air

"I know there's a lot to do, Ma, but you've got to check on Netty. I'm so worried about her. I don't think Nora's up to mothering right now."

Brushing her hair in front of the mirror, Rose smiled sadly at the worried countenance of her youngest son. "Sometimes I think I bring you up too good, Vincent. You just can't stop taking care of everyone. Nora, she'll come around, her. Everything be *tiguidou*."

"No, Ma, it won't. Nora's mind isn't right. She needs help."

Rose continued brushing.

"Ma, you've got to do something! Please! Netty needs you! You and Aunt Izzy!"

"Izzy, pah!"

The image in the mirror groaned. "Are you and Aunt Izzy still feuding? You gotta get over it, Ma. You need her now, more than ever. And she needs you. She told me so. You know she's sorry. She just has trouble saying she's sorry. She has trouble being soft. She had to be tough for so long, being soft makes her feel shaky."

"*Izzy* had it tough? Living in that fancy brick house with all them pretty things? Looking down her long nose at all of us? At my Francis? Pah!" Rose yanked at her hair with the brush.

"I doubt Pa ever spent a second worrying about Aunt Izzy's opinion. Please, please, Ma, don't go back into the past. You're needed right here and right now. You seemed to be getting better since you stopped drinking the well water. I *need* you to get better. Now!"

"Go way, Vincent. I need to think."

The image in the mirror vanished. Rose instantly regretted snapping. Why had she shooed her son away? How many times had she been too busy for him? When she was cooking a million meals for a million people, and he would pester her to show her something he made or something he read, she would tell him, "Not now, *mon cher*. Later." And here it was, later, and she was still shooing him away. No, it wasn't later. It was too late.

Rose leaned into the mirror and growled, "You a foolish old woman, you!"

Outside the closed bathroom door, Izzy eavesdropped on the one-sided conversation. She stood ramrod-straight, one fist clutched to her breast as she wept softly.

From the kitchen table, Izzy grimly drew on a cigarette as she watched her sister bustling about, making cookies and brownies. Were the sweet treats for Vince's wake? Were they a distraction for a grieving mother? Rose's awareness of what had happened to her youngest son seemed to switch on and off. No one had yet seen her cry for him. Staying busy was not unusual for someone like her, of course. Or perhaps it was a sign her mind had shut down completely.

"I tried calling Nora. To see about the funeral arrangements. To help," Izzy said.

Rose continued dropping blobs of cookie dough onto a baking sheet.

"No one answered the phone," Izzy continued. "Don't you think that's odd?"

Rose popped the baking sheet into the oven.

"Rose? Did you hear me?"

Rose finally turned around, shrugged, and said, "I bring these cookies over to Nora and Netty. Everything be *tiguidou*." She turned back to the second baking sheet on the counter.

"No, Rose!" Izzy said slammed a palm on the table. "Everything won't be *tiguidou*. How on earth could cookies and brownies make anything better for a young woman who just lost her husband and a little girl whose father will never come home again?"

Rose dropped more balls of dough onto the second sheet. "Funny, Vincent, he says the same thing."

"What?" Izzy stood abruptly, walked toward her sister, grabbed her from behind by both shoulders, and spun her around. "Vincent is dead. He couldn't possibly have just said anything to you. And if you thought he did, well, you need to snap out of it." She dug more deeply into Rose's shoulders. "Netty needs you. And I ... I need you, too, *ma soeur.*"

Rose's face slowly transitioned from an opaque mask of contentment to an expression of skepticism. "You need me? Since when you need stupid, silly me? Or my stupid, silly husband?"

"Are you actually trying to pick a fight with me, Rose? Now?"

Rose shrugged out of her sister's grasp. "I don't know what you want, Izzy. I never know. You worry when I marry Francis. Maybe you won't have a roof over your head. But we want you to live with us. You say no. Like we're not good enough for you. You ruin Francis's reputation. You try and break up Francis and me. And I still act like your sister. I tell Francis to forgive you. I tell Francis I still want you to come over. And what do you do? You stop coming over. Sometimes a year goes by and I don't see my sister."

Stunned by the calm manner in which Rose was talking, Izzy stuttered, "But I, I never thought ... I thought you were so mad at me you didn't want to see me."

"Sure, I get mad. But you're family, you. You're supposed to come for birthdays and holidays. And when you don't, I figure you don't want to see me no more."

"But you never invited me."

"I never invite you before, either. Sisters, we don't need invitations. You always have a seat at the table. At this table." Rose reached forward and pounded a fist on the kitchen table. "I always set out a place for you, on all them holidays. It makes me so sad seeing that empty place."

244

"You mean this was all some stupid misunderstanding? All those years, when we barely spoke to each other? If I'd just shown up one of those Thanksgivings, if I'd just sat at this table, all the bad blood between us would have cleared?"

"We have a big fight, first." Rose said, hands on hips.

Izzy dropped into one of the kitchen chairs. "Well, fine. Here I am. Let me have it."

Rose remained standing. She wagged a wooden spoon. "You make me feel so bad. Always criticize me. What I wear. How I talk. Who I marry. Most times, I don't care. I say, 'That's just her way.' But when you think I'm so small, too small to love more than one person ... that really hurts. I'm better than that, me! I can love Francis and you. I can have you both in the same house. And if Francis don't like it, well, he comes around. For me. I can love you at the same time I love Vincent and Hank and Eddie and Dave and Maryellen."

"I never believed that," Izzy said solemnly.

"Why? Because of Mama and Papa?"

Izzy squared her shoulders and shot defiance at her sister. "Look, just because you..." Then she bit her lip and her shoulders sagged. "Oh, I don't know. Maybe. Maybe because they left me."

"They leave *us*. Not just you. There you go again. You gotta be the reason why things happen. Papa leaves us because he's unhappy here. Maybe he likes to leave all of us, to run away and be happy. But you and me, we're the only ones old enough. So we get left behind. That simple. Not because we do anything bad."

"But did you truly understand that, way back then? Weren't you just as hurt and shocked and angry and sad as I was?"

Rose shook her head sadly. "Sure. I feel all that. I don't understand why I'm not good enough. But I look back now and think, maybe Izzy and me better off. We make pretty good lives here, no?"

"Is 'pretty good' enough, Rose? Just once, I'd like to be first. The best at something. The first with someone. Just once. I thought I had that with you. But then came Francis. You at least know what it's like to rate first with someone. With Francis. At least for a while."

Rose sat down. She nodded. "I come first with every baby, too. They need me so bad, it hurts. Feels good. But hurts, too. Sometime you just wanna break free from all that need. And you know what hurts worse?

245

When they stop needing you. But I never stop needing my sister. Sometimes you come first, even over Francis. Sometimes you come seventh, after Francis and Maryellen and Hank and the rest. But the need for my sister, it's always here." She sketched a circle over her chest.

Izzy's throat made a low, strangled noise, throttling a sob. Rose reached across the table and patted her hand. Izzy's sobs erupted.

"Vincent, he tells me you feel sorry. He's a smart boy, him."

Izzy's head snapped up. "When?"

"Just now."

Mopping her eyes with a handkerchief, Izzy asked, "You do know Vincent is dead, don't you?"

"Sure, I know. But talking to Vincent makes me feel better. I feel him all around this old house. Just like I feel Francis when he dies. Just like I feel Maryellen. And when you die, old woman, I'll feel you, too."

Izzy scanned her sister's face. She thought she saw just a glimmer of irony in those placid blue eyes. "You're planning on outliving me? Even though you're older?"

"Sure. Mère Agathe, she tells me I live to be ninety. She's never wrong, her."

"Hmmph. So did that crone tell you when I would die, too?"

"No. But I figure anyone who's so angry, so often. She's not gonna make ninety."

"You're baiting me, Rose. You know that."

Rose folded her arms across her chest and grinned.

"And you know what else, Rose? It would do you good to get angry. I mean really angry. Even if it means you live to only eighty-nine. You've just lost your son! In a horrible accident. Why aren't you screaming and cursing God?"

"I cry a little that first night. In bed. After they find Vincent. I cry a little last night. But talking to Vincent, it feels better than crying. But I worry…"

"About what?"

"About when Vincent stops talking back. I hope that don't happen for a long time. Just like with Francis. But I worry."

"For heaven's sake, Rose, just tell me. What's got you worried?"

Rose sighed. "I think I make my Vincent mad. I tell him to go away, because he pesters me to see to Nora. I don't want to see Nora. I don't want to see her cry. I don't want to feel her hurt. It's too much. I just want to bake."

"But you can't afford to retreat into yourself right now. Vincent is right. As far as I can tell, Nora has done nothing about the funeral arrangements. And Lord knows how she's handling poor Netty. You've got to step in. No, *we've* got to step in. And once we do, I'll bet there'll be no end to those chats with Vincent. And next time you talk, say hello from me."

Izzy reached both hands across the table and beckoned with her fingers. Rose unfolded her arms and grabbed her sister's hands. Hard.

THIRTY-SEVEN

Stepping In

When no one responded to Rose's knocking or her calls of "*Allô,
Nora? Netty?*" Izzy turned the knob and pushed the front door
open. A dense, chest-constricting fog wafted toward them. Even Izzy,
seasoned smoker though she was, tried to wave the miasma away, while
Rose erupted in coughs. Cigarette butts filled ashtrays. The windows
were tightly closed despite the lovely spring weather. The shades were
pulled low. The nylon sheers were yellowed with nicotine.

Fanning her face, Izzy nodded toward the hallway leading to the
bedrooms, where a dim light glowed. As both women approached the
entrance to Nora's and Vincent's bedroom, they began wheezing. The
haze, they suddenly realized, was not from too many cigarettes smoked
too often in too small a space. The light they had spotted was coming
from a pillow, fallen on the floor beside the bed. Black smoke curled
from a hellish red glow deep inside.

Rose dashed into the room and grabbed at the pillow. "*Jésus, Marie,
Joseph!*" she yelped, as the tiny flame inside the pillow flared.

"Drop it, Rose, you'll only fan the flames. I'll get water from the bathroom."

"Wet towels. Bring them!" shouted Rose, coughing.

Izzy returned with two dribbling bath towels and tossed one over the pillow. The crematory reek of feathers briefly intensified then faded as she wrapped the now merely smoldering pillow in one towel, while Rose used her foot to press the second towel into a smoky patch in the carpet. Then she stomped on an adjacent cigarette butt, not quite burned through.

The two coughing women stepped back to survey the situation. "I think it's out, yeah?" said Rose.

"Looks like it is. But let me drag the pillow into the bathtub to make sure. I left the water running."

While Izzy executed her plan, Rose opened the windows and raised the shades in both bedrooms. It wasn't until the smoke cleared that she spotted the blanket-wrapped lump in the bed. "*Saccajé chien!*" She drew a cross on her chest and approached the bed. "Nora?" she said, prodding the lump.

It didn't move.

From the doorway, Izzy gasped. "Oh, Christ! Has she been here all along? I never saw her! Is she breathing?"

It took some effort to unwrap the blanket wedged between Nora's head and fist. Rose bent over her daughter-in-law, face close to Nora's nose and mouth. After a minute, Rose nodded, "I feel breath."

"Why isn't she waking?"

Rose shrugged before bending over Nora again. She nudged the younger woman's shoulder, but got no response. She grabbed her by both shoulders and rolled her onto her back. No response. She shook her, hard. She sighed and slapped Nora on the face. Nora groaned.

"*Ma cocotte*, you gotta wake up, you. You breathe okay? You need to cough? Where's Netty?"

"Oh my God! Netty!" gasped Izzy from the foot of the bed. "I'll look for her."

Rose grunted as she pulled Nora into a more-or-less sitting position, propped against the undamaged pillow still on the bed. Nora's eyes fluttered open then closed again. Rose sat on the bed and grasped the younger woman in an awkward embrace, curved over her shoulder. She began thumping Nora's back.

"Leave me alone. I just wanna sleep."

"You cough first. Clear the lungs. Then we get you out of this smoky room, yeah? Then you sleep."

Nora coughed a little, then tried to slump backward, but Rose restrained her.

"You think you can stand?"

"Don't wanna."

With difficulty, since her left shoulder was still propping up her charge's torso, she yanked with her right hand to free Nora's legs from the blanket. Then she pulled Nora's right arm over her neck and, with great effort, stood up. Grabbing the hand dangling over her shoulder while circling Nora's waist with her other hand, Rose slowly dragged the younger woman out of the bedroom and into the living room. She deposited the patient in an armchair then opened all the windows. "You sit. Don't go nowhere, eh?"

After shoving a wooden chair across the floor and positioning it beside the armchair, Rose allowed herself a minute to recover. She dropped into the wooden chair, mopped her eyebrows, dripping stinging sweat droplets into her eyes, and pondered her next move. "You want some water. Soothe your throat?" she asked.

"Nuh," Nora said sluggishly shaking her head.

"Where's Netty?"

Nora shrugged and closed her eyes.

"Izzy?" Rose called into the ceiling, with just a hint of panic. "You find Netty?"

After a moment, she heard a welcome message from the back door. "Everything's *tiguidou*, Rose! Netty was playing in the backyard with her dolls."

Rose blessed herself again. "Good. Maybe you keep her back there, yeah? While I fix things here."

Izzy released Netty's hand to crane around the corner. When she glimpsed the scene in the living room, she nodded sharply then shooed the little girl outside, before Netty could witness her mother's dishabille.

Walking briskly to the back yard with her grand-niece in tow, Izzy pointed at one of the playthings lying on the grass. "What's the name of this doll?"

Netty shrugged.

"Oh, surely you know her name. By the worn look of her, she's one

250

of your favorites." Izzy picked up the doll and settled on the wooden bench Vince had crafted from lumber left over from a home-repair project.

"Rachel. I don't want to play with her now." Netty nestled beside Izzy, hip against hip. Head down, she kicked her legs idly against the bench's cross-brace.

"I guess I don't feel like playing, either." Izzy curled her arm loosely around the child. "It's been a rough couple of days, eh?"

Netty sucked her lower lip and nodded, still looking down.

"But you'll be okay. Your nana and I will make sure of that. Looks like we'll be taking care of you for a while."

Netty looked up, stricken. "Something bad is wrong with Mummy, isn't it?"

"Well, she's been sick for a while and losing your father has made her worse. But just because someone's sick doesn't mean they won't get better. Your mother will get better."

"Is she gonna go away like Daddy did?"

"Oh, Netty, your mother isn't going to die. She may need to go to a hospital for a while to rest up. So the doctors can work their magic on her. And when she's fixed, she'll take good care of you."

The pace of bench-kicking accelerated. "I'd rather stay with Nana."

"Would you? Well, your nana and I would certainly like that. And so would Jolie. That beast needs a child to run around with. Maybe you could keep her out of trouble."

For the first time, the child looked up, scrutinizing her great-aunt's face. "Mummy's scary sometimes. Like today."

Izzy nodded. "That's the sickness."

"She's been scary a lot. I don't want to be scared anymore. If I live at Nana's, I don't think it will be as scary."

"Hmmph. I must be losing my touch. I'm told that I'm very scary."

Netty scanned Izzy's face again. "That's different. You're teacher-scary. Like Mrs. Rogers. She teaches six grade, and even the biggest, brattiest boys behave in her class."

"I think I'd like Mrs. Rogers."

Netty looked down again. "The only thing is..." The kicking kept up.

"The only thing is what?"

"Well, you and Nana, you're so old. So much older than Daddy. And he died. What if I live with you, and you die. Then what would I do?"

"It's true that we're old. It's true that we all die eventually. But your nana just told me recently that she plans on living another twenty years at least. When she was very young, a wise old woman told her that. And you know, I think will power has a lot to do with how long we live and how healthy we are. It also helps to come from good stock."

"Good stock?" Netty looked up.

"What you inherit from your ancestors. Rose and I come from some very strong ancestors. You see that tree there?" Izzy pointed to the giant beech that dominated the back yard. "People say that tree is at least two hundred years old. It was around before the American Revolution. And look at it! See how it's producing fresh young leaves. It's robustly healthy and will probably be around for another century yet. Beech trees have a very long, healthy life. Your nana told me that and she knows her trees.

"Our ancestors are a lot like that beech tree. Tough and resilient. *Doux et sauvage*, like so much of the Quebec landscape." Seeing the question furrowing Netty's brow, Izzy explained, "That's French for 'sweet and wild.' Why, when my great-grandfather was my age, he was still paddling his canoe, and sometimes carrying it, all over the North American wilderness. He traded with the Indians and trapped fur-bearing animals. And do you know how cold it gets in Canada? Well, I tell you, that didn't slow him down one bit. Not even when he was very old. His blood runs strongly in our veins, your nana's and mine. Especially Rose's. As hardy as my great-grandfather was, Rose is hardier. I've never known anyone tougher."

"Honest?"

"As God is my witness." Izzy placed a palm over her heart. "Our parents left us when we were quite young. And Rose made sure we had a house to keep us safe from the elements, a hearth fire to keep us warm, and food to fill our bellies. To be able to do all that when you're only seventeen is about as tough as one can get."

"Your parents died when you were young?"

"No. They just left us." Aware that her last comment dripped with bitterness, Izzy added, "But only because they knew we were so strong we'd be okay. And thanks to Rose, we were. You will be too. Thanks to Rose. And me." Izzy squeezed Netty's shoulder.

While Izzy occupied Netty, Rose followed through on her mission to "fix" things. She summoned an ambulance for Nora, then telephoned Dr. Kelley and Nora's parents. The medical professionals initially thought the traumatized widow had overdosed on barbiturates, until they noted only a few pills missing from her prescription bottle, purchased one week earlier. They then decided she was in some kind of grief-induced fugue state. Perhaps something worse, when Dr. Kelley filled them in on the patient's history of mood swings.

The doctor was responsible for bringing the elder Gavins into the drama. Nora, he advised, would need hospital assessment, which could take a while. He would need a close relative to authorize hospitalization. He didn't think a mother-in-law was close enough to satisfy legal requirements. Rose protested that Mrs. Gavin was already dealing with her own health problems. To which Kelley responded, "And you're dealing with the loss of a son, Rose. I think you have enough problems to handle, without taking on Nora's, as well."

Much, much later in that long day, after airing out the house and tidying up, Rose and Izzy stuffed some of Netty's belongings into an empty laundry bag they found in one closet. After shutting all the windows and locking the doors, all three wearily wedged themselves into the front bench seat of Rose's geriatric Ford.

THIRTY-EIGHT

Disruptive Events

Rose lied. She told Izzy she needed to sleep in this morning, maybe all the way until eight, because she had been up late preparing for the rituals of bidding farewell to Vincent. The daylight hours were consumed by calls to the funeral parlor, church, and whatever family members remained unaware of the collective tragedy. There was no time for all the cooking chores—to feed guests attending the wake and post-funeral gathering at Vince's childhood home—until the evening hours. So Izzy agreed to rise earlier than usual to oversee Netty's breakfast and generally entertain the little girl, who would not return to school until after the funeral.

Rose was constitutionally unable to sleep past six o'clock. But she needed quiet time in the early morning for something else. She needed to think hard about her youngest son. Why had she shooed him away? Just because of his perfectly reasonable requests? Losing his bloodless apparition was almost as bad as losing his flesh-and-blood reality. Perhaps if she thought about him really hard, she could break through the mists that separated this life and the next and find him again, persuade him that she was worthy of visitations.

For all of Mère Agathe's stories about old Indian myths, Rose was no mystic. She had a well-developed skepticism toward mediums who interpreted thumps as messages from deceased loved ones. Rose knew there was nothing mystical about loved ones checking in with relatives after death. Maryellen appeared occasionally. As did Mère Agathe. Francis visited her often. Those appearances never struck her as extraordinary. Initially, they seemed connected to the grieving process. Later, they just ... happened spontaneously, often triggered by a memory, happy or sad. Unfortunately, Rose had no idea how to *make* them happen.

But she did recall elders telling her how thoughts can sometimes become reality. The message was often couched in superstition: If you worry about catching the grippe, you'll catch the grippe; if you envision falling on the ice and breaking your leg, well, you just might need crutches for the next six weeks. In one of the rare overlaps of beliefs held by Mère Agathe and Uncle Edward, Rose had also absorbed a more enlightened version of this philosophy. You can't expect good things to come into your life until you envision that happy home or that full larder for *reveillon*.

So Rose decided to focus on all the happy times with Vincent. She resolved to begin at the very beginning, the moment of his conception.

She recalled how she and Francis agreed early on about a moderate number of children. She had seen her mother gaunted by giving birth five times and miscarrying once before even leaving Quebec, then enduring five more births in Quincy and bleeding to death from yet another miscarriage just two years after the move to Manitoba. So the Dowds aimed for a mid-sized family, with adequate spacing between pregnancies. That plan served them well. Rose bore four children without problem, at home. The Dowds' frugal habits and Francis's strong constitution for quarry work enabled them to feed, clothe, shelter, and doctor their four children reasonably well. After Rose reached the ancient age of thirty, Francis figured four would be the final figure. She had other ideas. She never told him Mère Agathe had "seen" her with five children. But she did tell him she was fit as a fiddle. She reminded him how good she was at mothering. She insisted children were more fun than work. She persuaded him that children were visual evidence of a man's virility. Her enthusiasm was infectious.

Finely attuned to her body rhythms, Rose knew precisely when she was most likely to conceive her fifth child. Her timing had worked efficiently four times before, after all, just as abstinence during key days in her monthly cycle had prevented unplanned pregnancies. She gave Francis twenty-four hours' notice, informing him they must have sex every day for the next five days. He complied, albeit less enthusiastically as the week wore on. After three days, the prospect of six solid hours of sleep before trudging off to a physically demanding job had far more appeal than orgasmic release.

Francis's waning enthusiasm bothered Rose not one bit. She knew, she absolutely knew, that her Vincent had started growing in her womb after that very first lovemaking session. And oh, what a session! Francis insisted she straddle him, so he could get the best possible view of her nakedness. He insisted they keep the gas lantern lit. It felt deliciously brazen. They were no longer an old married couple. They were as young as Francis decided they were. So when he told her she had the body of an eighteen-year-old virgin, she believed him, despite sagging breasts and hands as rough as a fifty-something washer-woman's. Husband and wife took their time in the wee hours of pre-dawn. Rose wondered how Francis managed to handle his workload with so little sleep.

How could any child, conceived in such a way, be anything but a joy?

Rose recalled how easy that last pregnancy had been. No nausea, no bloating. Her back didn't hurt until the very last month. Labor pains were no walk in the park, but they lasted just four hours. You can stand almost anything for four hours.

Between healthy baby and experienced mother, nursing was free of complications. There was no colic or fussing. By four months of age, the baby was sleeping through the night. That good start in life predisposed a robustness that enabled young Vincent to weather childhood ailments in record time. After reaching the age of five, had he ever thrown up?

"Ah yeah, that time he get a snoot on," Rose remembered, chuckling.

He was eighteen years old and trying to prove something to his buddies by drinking bootleg whiskey one Saturday night. She and Francis insisted, if he was old enough for such nonsense, he was old enough to handle the hangover. They forced him to go to Mass early the next morning. She doubted he ever drank to excess again.

He wasn't perfect, of course. He disappointed his father by refusing to follow his brothers into the police department. Rose told her husband it didn't matter. Was it better to have a son with a good job or a son who would cheerfully lend a helping hand when needed? Was it better to have a son with a successful career or one who was kind and resourceful and well regarded by peers and elders alike? Sure, Vincent's working career was spotty. The Great Depression closed down all too many of the places that hired him. And yes, he got fired twice, when he wouldn't take guff from a boss. Sure, Rose worried about Vincent making ends meet. She worried about him working one or two extra jobs to keep the wolf from the door. And then, finally, he landed a great job. One with security. One with wartime prestige. One with solid pay. One that made him feel good about himself. The kind of job even Francis would have endorsed. And look what happened! That great job killed Vincent.

The trip down memory lane was taking Rose to its inevitably grim end. She tried to remind herself that she was better for the thirty-eight years Vincent had blessed her life. But it was hard to focus on blessings when she felt such loss. Reminding herself how much fun Vincent could be, how helpful he could be, only made the loss hurt more.

None of those memories conjured him back into half-life.

Disgusted with herself, Rose sat up in bed. She might as well start the grim day that lay ahead. The day when everyone would publicly acknowledge that her youngest son no longer walked the planet. She could rage about how no mother should outlive her children. But two of her children would be no less dead. She could weep about how empty her life would be without Vincent. But weeping would fill that hole with nothing but salty tears. So the only thing she knew to do was to put one foot in front of the other, to take one breath and then the next.

In Nora's absence, Vincent's brothers and their wives helped with innumerable details regarding the two days of waking, the funeral at St. Mary's, and the interment in the family plot on church grounds. But Rose was most grateful for their support in the hour before the rituals began. The undertaker, apparently proud of the challenging work he had accomplished on a body that had spent two days at the bottom of Fore River, was insisting that the casket absolutely must be open. It was tradition and mourners often lived to regret casting tradition aside, he warned ominously. But when Vincent's three closest blood relatives viewed the contents of that casket, they barely recognized the deceased. The three policemen had developed thick hides after witnessing far too many grisly accident scenes but were nonetheless appalled. They quickly agreed with their mother that mourners, especially little Netty, should not suffer this grotesquely rouged and powdered chimera as their final view of Vince Dowd. All three brothers ordered the casket closed.

As the undertaker sputtered his objections, Hank had an inspired idea dating from his service as best man at Vince's wedding, He recalled one photograph a friend had taken of the groom, in his childhood home just before leaving for the church. The candid photograph captured an unusually well-groomed Vince wearing a huge, lopsided grin that radiated child-like delight. Hank always meant to get that photo framed and present it to his younger brother. But intention never met execution. He was, however, certain where the photo was stashed. A quick call home to Gert proved him correct. She would ferry the photo to the funeral home as soon as possible. She arrived with the picture in a cheap but serviceable frame that, just half an hour before, had held a vacation photo of her and her sisters at White Horse Beach.

Once the mourners started showing up, the day became more bearable for Rose. The preponderance of Irish mourners turned the ritual into a proper Irish wake, with more laughter than tears. As shocked as they all were by Vince's untimely death, they shared innumerable anecdotes about the deceased. Rose wondered if Francis was somehow inspiring this outpouring of fond and funny memories. During his brief political career, he had shown up at many wakes and enlivened them. He always knew just the right thing to say to put a small smile on the face of the grieving widow.

Francis, despite his oft professed aversion to deviant nationalities (occasionally including Quebeckers), would have particularly liked one of the mourners, Walter Tekanatoken. The big Mohawk's sheer bulk would have been enough to command Francis's respect. But he also shared Francis's knack for brightening a dark landscape.

Gripping his visor cap in both hands, Walter made his way through the crowded funeral home to address Rose. "I'm Walter, ma'am," he started. "Don't know if Vince mentioned me. But I'm the ironworker he sometimes worked with. And I may just be the reason why your son is dead." He placed his hat over his heart and added, "I can't say how sorry I am. And how much I miss that son-of-a ... that fella, already. One helluva good spinner of yarns, that one."

Rose noted the slightly sing-song intonation, so typical of Quebec, as well as the Indian facial features and complexion. "Sure, he talks about you. You the big Mohawk fella, yeah? So why are you the reason my Vincent's dead?"

"I asked him to do me a favor, spot for me when I was working on some high scaffolding. The bosses make us do that. So that's why he was up there, in the first place. The only reason why I wasn't up there when that crane load hit the scaffolding was because I went to get a tool I needed. I'm so sorry, ma'am." Walter slapped at his chest with his cap.

"If you up there with him, then two mothers feel sad. What good does that do? Are you the reason why that scaffold falls? I don't think so, me."

"No, ma'am. Thanks, ma'am," Walter mumbled as he fingered his cap.

"You from Quebec?"

"Some of my people lived there way back. I'm from near Platts-burgh, upstate New York. Not too far from Quebec, though."

"Close to Montreal, yeah? I never go there. Pretty, I bet."

"Real pretty. And a whole lot cooler than down here."

"Summers down here, too hot." Rose pulled at her blouse for emphasis. "I miss Quebec."

"Your home turf gets in the blood, no? Don't get me wrong, I get a kick out of traveling around. I like the Fore River job. Wish all of the fellas I work with were like Vince. He knew how to get things done. And there was no kissing up to bosses with him. Solid guy, who had your back. He was one damn ... one dang good climber, too. Guess he learned that in these here quarries, eh?"

"See that big guy over there? That's Vincent's brother. He's the reason why."

"Huh?"

"When Vincent's just five years old, Hank over there, he pushes his

259

little brother off the ledge into the quarry water. Deep water. Way far down."

"Did Vince know how to swim?"

"He learns pretty fast, after that shove. And Hank, he learns how to run real fast, after I find out. I chase him one block with a wooden spoon in my hand. I know how deep that water is. How cold. I swim there sometimes, too."

"Yeah? Ya gotta be tough to be a quarry diver. Must be your Indian blood, eh? I knew I liked you." He nudged an elbow into Rose's forearm.

"You a good boy. No wonder Vincent likes you. Go grab some food over there. Big Indian like you gotta eat a lot to stay strong." She pointed toward the homemade offerings on a side table in the next room.

"You're singing my song, Mrs. Dowd. Pleasure to meet you. Sorry it's under these circumstances." With a sad smile, Walter gave her a jaunty salute before lumbering toward the next room.

Rose focused on his broad back and imagined him and Vincent swapping tales and sharing coffee on some girder high above the shipyard. The image made her smile briefly.

"Madame Rose?"

Realizing Nate Kagan had suddenly materialized on her left, she returned the greeting. "Hi, you! You just get here? Skipping class again, eh?"

"I woulda skipped the whole semester to pay my respects. I heard the news on the radio yesterday. I'm just ... stunned. Well, jeez, I don't have to tell you about being stunned. I'm so, so sorry, Madame Rose. What a loss for you! Vince was such a great guy. The world won't be the same without him." Nate was horrified that his throat choked up with his last comment.

Rose patted him on the shoulder. "Vincent, he has such fun with you."

"Same here. Do you know that Vince is a big reason why I'm heading for London in another month or so, to work for a wire service? As a reporter?"

"You not gonna be a lawyer?"

"That's what my parents wanted. I never did. I talked about it a lot to Vince. He made me realize life is too short." Nate cleared his throat. "He made me realize we have to live the life we want. And I think he did that himself. He wasn't cut out to be a cop any more than I'm cut out to be a lawyer. He married the girl he fell in love with and had a daughter he fell in love with. A pretty good life."

Rose nodded, hoping Nate was right.

"Is Mrs. Dowd around? I mean, the other Mrs. Dowd? I'd like to pay my respects."

Rose shook her head. "Nora, she's in the hospital. Taking things hard, her."

"Oh no! Will she be okay?"

Rose shrugged. "Maybe she comes home next week. The doctors, they figure things out."

"What about Netty?"

"She stays a while with me and Izzy. Everything be *tiguidou*."

"Netty's lucky to have you. Where is Isabelle? I'd like to say hello."

"We figure Netty's too young to stay for the whole wake. So Izzy and her walk over later."

"Walk over? That's quite some walk! How about I go to your house and pick them up? The wake's over in another hour and a half, right? They could drive home with you. Think that would work out?"

"Sure. You drive that little green car my Vincent fixes up?"

"Yeah, but Netty can squeeze in between me and Isabelle on the front seat."

"You ride with the top down, yeah? Like an adventure. Netty needs some fun."

"Top down it is. Back in a flash." Nate limped toward the exit.

Rose waved goodbye. Her smile faded when she saw Dan Gavin blessing himself on the kneeler in front of the casket. As he rose, he caught her eye and nodded solemnly. After shaking a few hands of fellow mourners, he headed her way.

"Mrs. Dowd, I'm so very sorry for your loss."

"You call me Rose, yeah? We're family, me and you."

"I'd hoped to see Antoinette here."

"My sister brings her later. Netty misses her mama. How is Nora?"

Dan cleared his throat. "Of course, Netty misses her mother. But I'm afraid there's not much to be done about that. Nora will be in the hospital for at least another week, and the doctors…"

"So I tell Netty her mama comes back in one, two weeks? And then Netty can go home where she knows where everything is, all her toys,

261

her stuffed animals?"

"As I was saying, the doctors think Nora will need to be on medication for the rest of her life. Losing her husband may have precipitated this current ... episode, but Nora's problems apparently started long before Vince's death. Those problems may date back to when she got married. Louisa and I noticed something off way back then, and it's only gotten worse. Nora's just not right in the head, Mrs. Dowd. And the doctors doubt she'll be able to take care of a household by herself, let alone take care of a child."

"My poor *cocotte*! But you say Nora goes home in a week or so, no?"

"That's right. She won't need long-term hospitalization, if she stays on medication. But she'll need someone to look after her. I've already hired a day nurse a few days a week to help with Louisa's heart condition. The nurse can make sure Nora is keeping up with her medication, too. And since nothing is wrong with Nora physically, she can help with some of the simple chores with Louisa, like cooking meals. I'll start looking for a renter to stay in Nora's house here in West Quincy. Eventually, we'll probably sell it, but for now, renting makes the most sense, especially since wartime dislocation has caused a shortage of rental units."

Rose squinted in an effort to focus on the Gavins' plans. "So, Netty, she stays with Nora and you in Dorchester?"

"Oh, God, no! As fond as Louisa and I are of Antoinette, my wife's condition just could not tolerate the energy of a small child. Louisa gets around all right, as long as she has plenty of rest, which means she needs peace and quiet, not the disruption an eight-year-old can cause. So it would be best if you kept Antoinette, for the foreseeable future."

A quiver of anger pulsed the vein in Rose's forehead. "What about an eleven-year-old?"

"I'm sorry?"

"When Netty is eleven years old, then she's not too much, how you say, disruption?"

"Well, I don't think youthful energy fades that quickly. And goodness knows, adolescence brings other problems. Of course, we can arrange visits for Nora and Antoinette. In a structured setting."

"Sure, we keep Netty with us. Such a joy, her. Sorry you don't know that already." Rose folded her arms over her chest and looked Dan up

262

and down.

"Well, that's good to hear. I was hoping to clear up that little detail sooner rather than later. Now Nora can move on with her treatment, without concern for her daughter."

"I visit Nora in a few days and tell her myself."

Dan raised a staying palm. "I'm afraid that won't be possible. Not even I am allowed to visit until next week. The doctors are observing her behavior around the clock as they adjust her dosage. They don't want any disruptions during that process."

"Lotta disruptions, yeah? Too bad Vincent cause such a disruption when he dies." She glowered at Dan.

"His death certainly came at an unfortunate time," he said coolly, pulling a pocket watch from his vest. "Ah, well, *tempus fugit*. I'll be sure and give Nora your best. When next I see her. And once again, my condolences, Mrs. Dowd."

After favoring Rose with a stiff smile, Dan turned briskly and exited the funeral parlor.

"*Bâtarde!*" Rose grumbled under her breath. She clenched her teeth and spat onto the room's plush carpet.

THIRTY-NINE

Sisterly Solidarity

As soon as Nate, Izzy, and Netty arrived at the funeral home, Hank pulled his aunt aside. "Something weird just happened. Let's go into the foyer, so I can fill you in." He grabbed Izzy's elbow, while nodding toward Netty and rolling his eyes.

"Very well. Nate, can you look after Netty for a few minutes while I speak with Hank?"

Nate nodded. After watching Hank and Izzy leave the room, he turned to the little girl beside him and asked, "Okay, kid, wanna take a tour of the joint? I came in the wrong way and saw this really snazzy organ and a whole bunch of flowers."

"I guess."

Nate pointed toward the room containing the organ. Netty picked absentmindedly at a loose sleeve thread tickling her upper arm. Finally, she shuffled after him.

"Where do people go when they die?" she asked as they entered the organ room.

Nate sighed. "Don't you go to Sunday school?"

264

"Yeah, but all we ever do there is memorize stuff in the Baltimore Catechism. And repeat it for the nuns. Mostly about what we owe God."

"Oh. Well. The nuns would probably say you go to heaven after you die. You know, with angels and cherubs. And there are harps playing."

"Will Jolly be there?"

"Who's Jolly?"

"Nana Rose's dog. He died last year."

"Well, sure. Jolly must be in heaven. Look at this organ here. Have you ever seen a musical instrument this big before? It's the size of two baby grands, at least. I'll bet it rocks this whole building when it starts playing."

Netty ignored the organ. "With all the people that die all the time, heaven must be awfully big. And awfully crowded. How will Daddy find Jolly there?"

"Are you kidding me? Jolly will find *him*. You know how sensitive a dog's nose is? Something like a million times more sensitive than a human's. Remember when Jolie found that piece of cheese your nana dropped between the icebox and the kitchen counter? It was a week later, but that dog found it. If a dog can find a tiny piece of cheese, Jolly will have no problem finding something as big as your father."

Netty stopped obsessing about the loose thread and looked up at Nate. "You think?"

"Sure. Wanna see if I can get someone to play the organ?"

"I don't like organs. They sound loud and fuzzy."

"Okay. Wanna check out the room with all the flowers? So many. You wouldn't believe there could be that many flowers this time of year. It's only April, for Pete's sake. Where do you suppose they get them?"

"Greenhouses."

"Oh. Okay. Wanna take a walk outside? The weather is still nice and warm."

"I guess." Netty resumed fingering the annoying thread.

As the pair exited through a side door, Netty asked, "I'm worried about Daddy. Mummy, too."

"The doctors are taking good care of your mother. And I'll bet the angels are taking good care of your father."

"I know Mummy's in the hospital. But people don't always come out of hospitals."

Nate pointed to a low stone wall and sat down. Netty plopped down beside him, eyes scanning his face.

"Your mother's pretty young. Most people who are young get better from whatever's making them sick. She'll be okay." Nate stifled the childish instinct to cross his fingers.

"I dunno. She's been sick for a while. Sick in the head." Netty patted her right temple.

"There are lots of ways of being sick in the head. And these days, there are lots of pills to treat those illnesses. I bet the doctors are just deciding which pills your mother will need. They'll figure it out."

"They didn't figure out why I kept getting sick in the tummy."

"Maybe not, but here you are. And your tummy must be feeling okay since you were mooning over that soda fountain we drove past on the way here."

Netty favored Nate with a small giggle. Then her face clouded over again. "But what about Daddy? I don't think he'll be very happy in heaven."

"Why not?"

"'Cause one time, when I asked him about heaven, he said it sounded awfully boring. He didn't like the idea of just sitting around while angels played harps. I bet he'd rather fix the harps when they broke. He'd be good at that."

"So, is that why you hope he and Jolly get together? So your father wouldn't be bored."

"Yup. They could take care of each other."

"You know, Netty, I wonder if heaven isn't whatever we need it to be."

Netty craned her head to scan Nate's face again. "Whaddya mean?"

"I dunno. But it seems to me, if you've lived a good life, if you were a really good person like your father was, then God would want to reward you. And if Vince would be bored silly just sitting around on a cloud, then I imagine God could whip up something Vince would like. I mean, he's God, after all. He made the oceans and the mountains and the trees and dogs and lions and people. So why couldn't he make a heaven your father would like?"

"I think Daddy would like heaven to look like that shipyard."

"Really?" Nate gulped, thinking of the horrific accidents that take place in shipyards. Ones even worse than the scaffolding collapse that

266

sent Vince into the murky depths of Fore River.

"Daddy really, really liked working there. He was happy. Happier than he was before. He told me all about the warships he was making. How big they were. But they can still float. Isn't that something? Kinda like how bumblebees can fly. Daddy said bumblebees shouldn't be able to fly because they're so heavy and clumsy and have little, short wings. But they do. They fly good. And those giant warships float good."

"They do, don't they? So if we have all those miracles down here on earth, just think of all the miracles that must be going on in heaven. I don't think your father will be bored at all."

"Maybe God will put him to work in a shipyard, with Jolly following him around?"

"And that would make your father happy?"

"Yup."

"Then I'll bet he's showing Jolly a bunch of huge, heavenly warships right now. And Jolly is wagging his tail. And Vince is laughing."

"I'll bet he is, too." Netty nodded thoughtfully.

Izzy made a beeline for her sister, who was chatting with some neighbors. "A minute, Rose?" She took Rose by the arm and led her to a secluded corner.

"Where's Netty?"

"She's fine. Nate's with her. Look, I heard you had a little fit. You actually spat at Nora's father? Hank is worried you're having some spell of simplemindedness. I'm skeptical. The few times I met Dan Gavin, I thought he was a pompous jerk. If I'd been around him any longer, I might have wanted to spit at him, too. But in a funeral parlor, Rose? What happened?"

"I don't spit *at* him. I spit after he leaves."

It was impossible to determine whether Rose was being petulant or wry. "Tell me what he said to make you so mad."

Rose sighed and replayed the conversation. She offered no commentary, merely repeated the words exchanged, with excellent recall.

When the story was done, Izzy exhaled sharply. "So, Mr. Gavin thinks of his own granddaughter as a disruptive nuisance?" Izzy made a feint of spitting on the floor. "Bastard, indeed!"

Rose's eyes widened. Then she laughed.

Izzy rummaged in her purse and produced a pack of cigarettes. Shaking her head repeatedly, she extracted one Lucky Strike, lit it, took a deep draw, and continued her rant. "And poor Nora! He'll sell her house out from under her and recruit her as a caretaker for her mother. I guess we should be glad he isn't hiding her away in some medieval asylum. Ah well, we don't have much say over Nora. Old man Gavin is her closest adult relative. But we can certainly make sure Netty is all right."

"We gonna raise Netty together, you and me?"

"We gonna raise Netty together, *ma soeur*." Izzy took another puff. As smoke curled from her nostrils, she added "Just don't you go loony on me."

"We're awful old," Rose said doubtfully.

"And we were awfully young when we raised ourselves, all those years ago. Besides, I thought you were supposed to live until you're ninety. Hell, Netty will be married with children of her own by then."

"You think so?"

"I think you know how to be a strong, loving mother. Look at the job you did with Vincent! And I civilized two generations of Winthrop children. Not a one of them was as smart or sweet as Netty. With both of us on the job, this will be a piece of cake."

FORTY

Fais Do-Do

The waking was over. The funeral was over. The next step was to put Vincent into the ground and figure out how to navigate a world without his presence, real or only glimpsed from the corner of a tear-swollen eye. When the mourners entered St. Mary's, the world had turned flint-gray and cold. New England's brief flirtation with spring was over. When the mourners exited the church, the world was a dull white, with sleet pellets littering the ground. Rose wondered if the planet was in mourning, too. Or was Old Man Flint merely reminding her that he would never be done with her?

The mourners began an informal procession, on foot, to the graveyard, while the funeral director supervised the motorized transport for Vince's remains. One of the funeral-home staffers stopped the crowd from arriving at the gravesite in order to clear a path for the hearse. The mourners broke into small groups, greeting one another, swapping anecdotes about the deceased, and complaining about the weather. When Rose saw the monsignor arrive at the gravesite, she broke away from Izzy and Netty and bolted ahead, to make sure the final arrangements were in place. Hank caught up with her and opened the conversation with Father Murray. She admired the confidence with which he addressed the priest. She listened quietly while he discussed the final salute he had planned, involving all six pall bearers—Vincent's three brothers and three other members of the police force, all in dress blues.

She wasn't sure how meaningful that tribute would be for Vincent, who had rejected the camaraderie of blue. But was Vincent's spirit even aware of what was going on? She didn't know. She knew only that it was her living sons' way of honoring their brother and handling their own grief.

Then she admired how smoothly Hank's gloved hand passed the monsignor his honorarium, which disappeared inside the priestly vestments. She was grateful that task had not fallen to her. All she had to do was thank Father for his services and listen to his words of condolence.

His words of condolence amounted to "Okay, now. Okay. You'll be fine, dear. Know that Vincent is okay, too. He's with God, now, dear." He pumped her hand repeatedly.

While her hand was still imprisoned in both of Father Murray's beefy palms, she angled her head back toward where she had left Izzy and Netty and gave a quick nod. Izzy understood the signal. Leaving her grand-niece with neighbors, she strode ahead to join her sister. Her forceful advance apparently put Father on alert. Perhaps this was someone important? In a congregation as large as his, he certainly did not know every parishioner by sight. And even though Izzy rarely missed Sunday Mass, she had joined the parish relatively recently. So the monsignor abruptly dropped Rose's hand and flashed a smile at Izzy. She was the first to extend her hand, grasped his forcefully, and said, "Isabelle Quentin, Monsignor. Thank you for your services. I think we're ready to start now."

Father Murray blinked, unaccustomed to a female assuming an authority role, but recovered sufficiently to say, "Ah yes, Miss Quentin. It's good to have you in our little parish. Your nephew will be much missed, but as much as his loved ones grieve, our heavenly Father is glad to have Vincent with Him. Know that Vincent rests…"

"Indeed," replied Izzy, extracting her hand. She grabbed her sister's elbow and said, "We'd best fetch Netty now and get into position." She gave a departing nod to the monsignor and hustled Rose back toward the mourners, now following the hearse to the gravesite.

Netty shivered visibly, despite her brown woolen coat. Because of the cold weather, most of the mourners were wearing outerwear, in a range of colors. None of the mourners was affluent enough to have more than one dress coat, and black was not a common color for woolen coats. Rose was glad. Seeing black garment after black garment would have been too much to bear. Black just didn't fit her sunny child. And even though she and Izzy abided by tradition, with black dresses beneath their loden green and dull maroon coats, neither had any intention of dressing Netty in black. They chose a white blouse and gray plaid skirt. The only funereal touch was purely coincidental–the black patent leather of the little girl's Mary Janes.

As the priest spoke over the open grave, the sleet picked up, stinging Rose's face. As she wiped it from her cheeks, she wondered if her sons would worry she was crying. But she had no tears. She felt as dry as a long-fallen maple leaf in February. Dry and stiff. She also felt numb, unaware of the loved ones near her side. She wondered if she was losing touch with reality again. She wondered if simplemindedness wouldn't be welcome right now, but reminded herself that she couldn't afford to slip back into happier days, back to Quebec with Noir or back to the early days with Francis. Netty needed her to stay firmly grounded in the present.

She jumped a little as one of the police officers barked the pall-bearers to attention. In one synchronized, slow-motion arc, their white gloves touched their right temples. Rose heard sniffles from several mourners. Her eyes remained dry.

She became aware of Izzy craning her head toward someone standing perhaps fifty feet from the crowd. As snowflakes now swirled around the mourners, Rose had difficulty scanning this stranger, now raising his left hand in response to Izzy's nod. She could see, however, that he was neither muffled in a woolen coat, nor wearing a dark suit.

He was wearing some kind of dark, heavy shirt, perhaps of flannel, and baggy woolen trousers. When he turned slightly, she noticed something fluttering by his knees. Surely not, she thought. But as she squinted, she made out the bright colors of a *ceinture fléchée*, the handwoven sash that had marked male clothing in Quebec since the heyday of the *voyageurs*. The sash that farmers, including her own papa, had worn on holidays into the turn of the century. She had not laid eyes on such a sash since the eighteen-eighties. Her father had left his *ceinture* behind, with so many other vestiges of Quebecois culture. She wondered if she was merely imagining it.

She decided she was not hallucinating when the man opened a violin case lying at his feet and tucked the instrument between chin and left shoulder. No, it was not a violin, it was a fiddle. She recognized the cadence of the notes that rose from the instrument before she recognized the melody, the halting rhythm typical of Quebec folk music. Then she recognized the tune. Her eyes welled with tears. She let them roll down her cheeks. How often had she sung that same tune to Vincent, to all of her children when they were small, a lullaby reminding the little one of attentive parents and the sweet treats they were preparing for him. It was a gentle little tune, featuring the kind of repetition that delights children. But the repetitive refrains bracketed plaintive notes, suggesting the melancholy aspects of life from which those attentive parents struggled to protect their child.

Rose whispered the words of the refrain, but substituted her youngest son's name. "*Fais do-do, Vincent, mon doux fils.*" Go to sleep, Vincent, my sweet son.

She felt a squeeze on her left palm. When she looked to her left, there stood Vincent, all six feet of him, goofy smile on his face. "You done good, Ma," he said. "And you *will* do so much good. For Netty. For years to come. How did I get so lucky?"

Before she could respond, Rose felt pressure on her right hand. Turning right, she saw Mère Agathe. "*Doux et sauvage*, little one. That's what you gotta be. Both. Lots of bumps on the road ahead. Lots of good times, too. Lots of road. You remember where you come from, yeah? Where you come from, it gets you where you going."

The old Métis woman vanished into the swirling snowflakes. Rose whipped her head back to the left and released a small groan when she saw that Vincent had vanished, as well. In his place was Netty, wide blue eyes gazing up at her.

"You okay, Nana?"

"I'm *tiguidou*, little one. Sad, just like you. But we got each other, yeah? We gonna get through this okay."

"You bet we will, sister," said Izzy on her right. "Hope you liked that fiddler."

"You do that?"

"I do that," Izzy replied, with just a hint of a self-satisfied smirk. "I thought Vincent's sendoff was getting much too Irish. Everyone needed a little reminder of the other side of his family. Our side. I think he would have liked it. Of all your children, Vincent always seemed the most attuned with his French Canadian ancestry."

"How? Where you find this fiddler? You the one picks this tune?"

"I called L'Etoile in Lowell. It's a French-language newspaper that's been around forever. They knew of a local French Canadian folk music group and gave me the names of some of the musicians in it. I got lucky with my first call, to Guy Fontaine; that's our fiddler. Luckily, he knew the tune I was thinking of. I remember you singing this lullaby to the children. Had no idea what it was called. But I remembered that refrain. So there I was humming a few bars over the phone, like an idiot. Mr. Fontaine instantly recognized it."

"You remember all that? You do all that? For me?"

"Of course. We Quebeckers gotta stick together, no? And maybe you'll sing that same lullaby to Miss Netty, here." She squeezed Rose's hand.

A glare from the monsignor hushed the conversation. The two chastised sisters exchanged impish looks then bowed their heads and listened to the final prayers over the grave.

Hand in hand, Rose, Izzy, and Netty walked, three-abreast, to their car parked on a side street near the church. They spoke not a word. They could not yet relax. Many of the mourners would soon gather at their home. There were plates to set out, chairs to arrange, and napkins to fold. Work. Duty. Rose both longed for and feared the end of this long day. Her body craved rest. Her mind dreaded the inevitable hour when the world would move on from Vincent Dowd, when she would be expected to move on, too.

Netty interrupted her weary thoughts. "Look!" she shouted, pointing toward the sidewalk.

All three stopped and stared at a fragile yellow crocus, dusted with snow. Somehow, it had forced its way through a crack in the hard, cold concrete. And bloomed.

FORTY-ONE

New Chapters

Sitting in his green MG, with the top down, Nate was furiously scribbling in the small notebook he always carried when he heard a car approaching. Looking up, he recognized Rose's old Ford. He was surprised to see Izzy, not Rose, at the wheel. He smiled and waved as the car pulled into Rose's driveway.

"Oh, good, I didn't miss you after all," he said, getting out of the MG.

"Long time no see," Rose said, exiting the passenger door and waggling her fingers at him.

"I know. Not since Vince's wake. I've been so busy, what with graduation and getting ready to go to London. You ladies doing okay?

Rose ignored the question and asked, "You graduate already? Get a degree and everything?"

"Yup. So I see you've got a new driver in the family." He nodded toward Izzy, as she handed the car keys to her sister.

She favored him with a grin. "You've got a shiny new degree. And I've got a shiny new license. I think that's cause for celebration, don't you? Let's go inside and see what we can find to drink."

Nate looked at his watch. "A little early, but what the heck."

Jolie yodeled impatiently from inside as the humans headed for the side door. Rose jerked a thumb toward her sister and said, "She done good, her. That Registry guy, he's one mean fella. Puts her through all sorts of tests. Finds a real tight parking spot. Tells her to parallel-park. That's what they call it, right? She sticks that car into that little space just like that. Just like Vincent."

Izzy, idly scrabbling the tousled canine head by her hip, said, "I had good teachers. You and Vincent. So, what brings you here, young Master Kagan?" She motioned for him to sit at the kitchen table then sat down herself.

"I didn't want to leave the country without saying goodbye. When I didn't find you home, I thought I'd have to leave you a note." He fished the notebook out of his pocket and waved it. "But I was afraid I'd run out of paper. Had more to say than I thought."

Rose, standing at the open icebox while Jolie peered inside, tail thumping, interrupted. "You want beer, Nate? I still got some of that Narragansett Vincent likes so much."

"Sure, Madame Rose, that would be fine."

"I'll have some of that Canadian whiskey, Rose."

"And I'll have some brandy, me. Got a little bit left. And you, Mademoiselle Jolie, you go lie down over there."

The dog complied, and Nate continued. "Mainly, I wanted to thank you ladies, for all your time, for all the stories you shared with me about Quebec and about coming to this country."

Rose deposited a tray containing three bottles and three glasses. "Your teacher, that history professor, he likes what you write about us?"

Nate chuckled. "No, he did not. He was disappointed your family didn't end up working textile mill jobs in Lowell. You don't fit the mold, he said, like that was a bad thing. And then he told me I lacked sufficient objectivity. Said I got too close to the subjects I was writing about. He was right on that point, at least. I did. I had a lot of fun talking to you, and it was impossible to think of you as 'subjects.'"

"Hear that, Rose? We're not too old to be fun. We should tell that to that wretched young man who delivers the Patriot Ledger. He absolutely hates to talk with us. Even when he has to collect his paper money. He acts like old age is contagious."

276

"His loss, Isabelle."

Rose poured spirits into each of the glasses. "So you get a passing grade anyway?"

"Just barely. And only after a lot of rewriting. But my work didn't go wholly unappreciated. I may have told you that I used an excerpt of my interviews with you as a sample of my writing style. It helped me land the job with the AP. But it gets even better. I sent a query to a literary agent right here in Boston."

Rose distributed the glasses. "What's that?"

Izzy explained, "It's someone who represents aspiring authors. Helps them find publishers. You're hoping to publish an account of our family's story?"

"Not exactly. I wanted to talk with this agent about writing a novel inspired by your family's story. So it wouldn't exactly be about you. I'd create characters like you. And certainly like Vincent, too."

"My Vincent, eh? I like that."

"Well, remember, the characters would end up somewhat different from you. I'll probably make some changes in your life events, maybe some changes in how you talk and act. I may add characters or drop other members of your extended family. I won't know until I really get into the writing and see where it takes me. But the agent was interested. These days, with all the displaced persons wandering around Europe and the Americas, there's a lot of interest in immigrant stories. Ones that turn out well. To remind us all that there's light at the end of the tunnel. The agent made no commitment, of course. But he's promised to look at what I come up with. And he suggested some changes in where I thought I was going. Changes that will make for a better book. And a more marketable one."

"Make me smart," Rose said, winking.

"Make me pretty," Izzy added. Raising her whiskey glass, she said, "To the next Hemingway."

Nate laughed and raised his beer glass. "To the new Massachusetts driver."

As all three drank, Jolie's head snapped up from the floor. She barked just once, to alert everyone to the opening of the side door. Netty trudged inside, the embodiment of dejection, and headed silently for the living room.

Rose followed after her, with Jolie in tow. From the kitchen, Nate and Izzy heard the maternal admonishment. "No, no. You pick up that sweater you drop on the floor. And you say hello to your nana and your Aunt Izzy and our guest, Nate. You know better, you." The voice was gentle, but firm.

Izzy nodded approvingly. Nate smiled.

A minute later, Netty, braced against the big dog, appeared at the entrance to the kitchen. She raised a limp forearm and said, in one prolonged sigh, "Hi, Tante Izzy. Hi, Nate."

Standing behind the child, hands on hips, Rose nodded. "Now you sit over there. And tell your nana what's wrong, eh?"

Netty slumped into one of the chairs and made figure-eights on the tabletop with a forefinger. Head down, she finally grumbled, "I hate school."

Rose sat down beside her, thumped the child's back, and waited.

Everyone noticed the solitary teardrop that splattered onto the table. When Netty looked up, her eyes were filled with tears. "Why do all the other kids hate me?"

While Rose's palm polished Netty's back, Izzy asked, "All the other children hate you? I find that hard to believe."

"They do so!"

"I want names, missy."

Netty gulped. You're not gonna do anything to them, are you?"

"We'll decide that when we hear the whole story."

The adults waited.

"Well, it's that Tommy Copeland. He hates me. For sure. And when he makes fun of me, all the other kids laugh."

"What this Tommy say, *ma cocotte?*"

"He points at me and calls me 'Netty Spaghetti Legs,' because I'm so skinny," the child wailed, erupting in sobs.

Jolie emitted a soft whine and nuzzled the child's right shin, while Rose folded Netty's head into her bosom. "Yeah, that hurts plenty, I bet." She squeezed the tiny rib cage. "I'm sorry you have such a bad day."

Tears still flowing, Netty pulled away just a bit to gaze up at her grandmother. As she dramatically sniffled, she asked, "Can I skip school tomorrow?"

Rose smiled wearily. "I don't think so. That only makes it tougher to go back to school the day after tomorrow. You can't just stay home

278

with Izzy and me."

"Why not?" Netty challenged, rubbing her eyes with the heel of her hand.

"Well, maybe." Rose tapped on her chin. "Maybe you get that big mop and pail and scour this floor, yeah? I gonna do that tomorrow. And that toilet in the bathroom? It needs scrubbing bad. And then you fix that screen that's letting in flies. Maybe put up some fly strips, too. Oh yeah, we have lots for you to do, if you're not in school."

Netty regarded her grandmother with horror. Nate covered his mouth to hide the smile forming there.

Rose continued. "Bad stuff, it happens lots. And kids they can be mean sometimes. But we don't let them stop us. You think your Aunt Izzy let that arthritis stop her? You think Nate, here, he stops everything and stays home in bed because his foot don't work right?"

Netty looked from Izzy to Nate, now nodding solemnly.

"You shoulda heard what the kids used to call me, because of my limp. Yeah, it hurt. But it got better, it really did. The mean kids didn't get any better. But lots of the other kids became my friends. Sometimes they even told off the bullies calling me names. Sometimes I told off the bullies."

Netty eyed him skeptically.

"And you know what? I'm glad I stayed in school and toughed it out. Because now I have the chance to do what I always wanted to do–be a writer and travel all over the world. Couldn't have done that if I'd stayed home where the mean kids couldn't call me names."

Netty swallowed audibly. "You told them off?"

"Sometimes." Nate decided to keep his answer as brief as possible, as he remembered getting slammed on his butt by one of the bullies he challenged.

Rose thumped Netty's back. "I still got some of them cookies you like in the jar. Go get one and a glass of milk. You feel better with them in your tummy."

As Netty headed for the kitchen counter and strained to reach the cookie jar, Izzy weighed in. "This boy who thinks you're skinny. His name is Tommy?"

The cookie already jammed in her mouth prevented the child from an articulate response. She merely nodded.

"Tell me what this Tommy looks like."

279

Netty poured milk into a glass. "I dunno. He looks like a boy."

Izzy exhaled sharply. "Is he short, tall, big, small, fat, thin? What kind of hair does he have? What shape eyes."

Netty looked thoughtful as she brought her milk and another cookie to the table. "He is kinda fat, I guess. And his eyes are funny. Like he's always squinting, because there's lots of skin around his eyes. I don't know what color his eyes are. He never opens them wide enough to see, because of all the skin folds."

Izzy made a loud snuffling noise, just like the pigs she had tended as a child.

Netty gaped in wonder. Nate burst out laughing.

Rose said, "Izzy! You awful, you!" But she chuckled, too.

"So," Izzy continued. "Next time Tubby Tommy says something mean to you, you point at him, call him Tubby Tommy, and make the noise I just made. Like a grunting pig. I guarantee the other kids won't be laughing at you. They'll be laughing at him."

Netty giggled, then frowned with heroic concentration as she tried to replicate the noise. Her attempts fell well short of the mark.

"No, you make the noise while sucking air in through both nose and mouth. Like this." Izzy snorkeled air with impressive volume.

Netty tried again. On the third attempt she succeeded.

Izzy thumped the table with both palms, "*C'est ça!* Perfection!"

Nate clapped his hands. Jolie barked appreciatively.

Rose shook her head slowly. "You gonna choke, you! You finish your cookies and milk before you make like *le petit cochon* again. You practice later, not at the table, yeah?"

Netty wolfed down the second cookie, gulped the milk, brushed her mouth with the back of her hand, and asked, "Can I go now?"

Rose nodded smiling. Izzy intoned primly, "May I be excused?" and waited.

"May I be excused?" Netty repeated, smiling beatifically.

"You may."

Netty dashed toward the living room, with Jolie galumphing two paces behind her.

The adults craned their heads toward the other room, until they heard the expected snorts. They all laughed.

After taking a sip of brandy, Rose aimed her glass at her sister. "You gonna get her in trouble, you!"

"Maybe. But at least it will be trouble of her own making. How do you think Edgar Winthrop, that poor pantywaist boy, made it to adulthood? Because I taught him to stand up for himself. Girls need to learn that, too. Every bit as much as boys."

"Hey, where you learn to stand up for yourself?" Rose jabbed an index finger into her breastbone.

"All right. I learned it from you." Turning to Nate, she said, "I was the skinny, four-eyed girl with the funny accent. I heard lots of names. This one taught me how to fight back."

"Maybe she taught you too well." Nate grinned.

Izzy swatted his elbow.

"Miss Netty is lucky to have both of you. I see a whole new chapter in my book." He finished his beer, stood, and added, "I wish you nothing but joy in the new chapter you've just launched. And now I'd best be on my way. Got lots of packing left to do before I start my own new chapter, in London."

Rose stood and wrapped her arms around Nate. "You stay out of trouble." She patted his cheek for emphasis.

"I'm sure gonna try, Madame Rose."

Izzy stood and shook his hand. "It's been a pleasure getting to know you, Mr. Kagan. I expect to hear great things from you. In the New York Times Book Review, among other places."

"I'll send you both signed copies of my book. Might take a few years."

"You'd better." Izzy wagged a knobby forefinger.

Reluctant to part, the three adults slowly entered the hallway. As Nate opened the side door, a volley of stertorous snorts, followed by mad giggles, emanated from the living room. Laughter replaced the wistful expressions as Rose and Izzy watched the young man get back into his MG and motor off into his future.

www.ingramcontent.com/pod-product-compliance
Lightning Source LLC
Chambersburg PA
CBHW022003010726
47494CB00003B/861